A HORSEMAN RIDING BY, R. F. Delderfield's rich
and heartwarming saga of English country life,
stands as one of the most engrossing family chron-
icles of the last forty years.

In his latest novel, THE GREEN GAUNTLET, we
return to the seven families whose lives are rooted
in the green acres of the great farming valley of
Shallowford. The time is just at the outbreak of
the Second World War, when the valiant pilots of
the RAF are locked in combat with the Luftwaffe
in the skies above Devon and England stands
imperilled as never before by the dark shadow of
Nazi invasion. The hero again is Paul Craddock—
older, wiser, but still fiercely dedicated to his land,
to his children and grandchildren, to his tenants
and to the vanishing way of life they represent.

THE GREEN GAUNTLET distills the essence of three
decades of modern English life—bringing to a
magnificent close a vast and thrilling panorama
that has already won the hearts of so many
readers.

"Bathed in a love of land, love of tradition, a
sense of responsibility, 'Gauntlet's' Shallowford
estate and the Sorrel Valley become a kind of
modern Camelot, a never-never-land that still
exists for a happy few."

—*Des Moines Sunday Register*

By R. F. DELDERFIELD

History

NAPOLEON'S MARSHALS
RETREAT FROM MOSCOW
THE GOLDEN MILLSTONES
NAPOLEON IN LOVE
IMPERIAL SUNSET:THE FALL OF NAPOLEON, 1813-14

Novels

A Horseman Riding By

*I—LONG SUMMER DAY
*II—POST OF HONOR

*THE GREEN GAUNTLET

The Avenue

*I—THE DREAMING SUBURB
*II—THE AVENUE GOES TO WAR

DIANA

ALL OVER THE TOWN

THERE WAS A FAIR MAID DWELLING

ON THE FIDDLE

Juvenile

THE ADVENTURES OF BEN GUNN

*Published by Ballantine Books

The Green Gauntlet

R. F. DELDERFIELD

BALLANTINE BOOKS • NEW YORK
An Intext Publisher

This edition published by arrangement with
Simon & Schuster, Inc.

First printing: February 1970

Cover Painting: John Berkey

Printed in the United States of America

BALLANTINE BOOKS, INC.
101 Fifth Avenue, New York, N. Y. 10003

My dear Olive and Cyril,

In the brave old days of the three-decker novel authors wrote their dedication in the form of an amiable, rambling letter. This is old-fashioned but then so am I, so I make no apology for reverting to the practice.

Time and again you have been lured from that over-crowded, frenetic south-eastern corner of the island in which you live and work, to this less populous, more leisurely south-western corner, seeking rest and refreshment. I invite you here again, without leaving your fireside.

This book is an expression of my thanks to you both for all the years of encouragement you have contributed, not only to me personally, but to our way of life "downalong".

Affectionately,

R.F.D.

April, 1967

CONTENTS

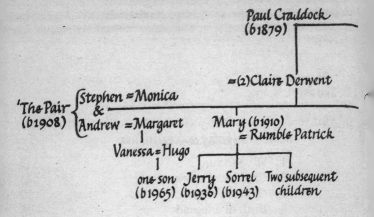

Paul Craddock
(b1879)

=(2) Claire Derwent

'The Pair
(b1908)
{ Stephen = Monica
&
Andrew = Margaret

Mary (b1910)
= Rumble Patrick

Vanessa = Hugo

one son   Jerry   Sorrel   Two subsequent
(b1965)   (b1938) (b1943)   children

Shallowford Farm

Home Farm
The Honeymans (until 1944)
Rumble Patrick and Mary (subsequently)

Four Winds
The Codsalls (until 1904)
The Eveleighs (subsequently)

Hermitage
The Pitts

Low Coombe
The Potters (until 1918)
Bellchamber & Brissot (until post-war fragmentation)
Jerry Palfrey (on restoration)

= (1) Grace Lovell

Simon = (1) Rachel (no issue)
 = (2) Evie

Mark (b 1945) &
Two other children

'Whiz' (b 1913) = Ian   Young Claire (b 1918)   John (b 1934) = Anne
                                (killed in aircrash 1934)

Elspeth

& Four subsequent
children

Tenants, 1902–1965

Deepdene
The Willoughbys (until 1954)
The Honeymans (subsequently)

High Coombe
The Derwents (until 1931)
Derelict until 1937
The Potters (until 1940)
The Archer-Forbes (during the war years)
The Potters (subsequently)

Periwinkle
The Codsalls (until 1932)
Derelict until 1935
Rumble and Mary (until 1942)

PART ONE
THE BELEAGUERED

CHAPTER ONE

HIT AND RUN

I

THE gull, canting uncertainly into the wind, rose from its ledge a hundred feet above the landslip and flew along the tideline before turning inland over the first cottages of Coombe Bay, searching for its first circling point, Smut Potter's tall brick chimney, near the foot of the steep village street.

From the elevation of the Bluff the Valley was seen as a great gauntlet, a green and russet gauntlet of the kind falconers used centuries ago. The glove was left-handed, with the knob of the Bluff, the highest point of the coast, as the thumb. The forefinger, pointing due north, was the wooded Coombe, with its three farms showing as blood or rust stains. The less-soiled middle and third fingers were the green inroads of Shallowford Woods and the more open coppices of French Wood and Hermitage Clump. The little finger, crooked at a wide angle, was Blackberry Moor, now almost obliterated by the Royal Marine Camp and showing slate-green on the far side of the silver streak that was the River Sorrel. The back of the gauntlet, a great flattish wedge extending between the Bluff and the western crest of the moor, was not as blotched as the fingers but seamed with age, here stubble fields showing as regular brown patches, there a pantiled roof or a sheet of corrugated iron suggesting older bloodstains, blood shed when the gauntlet was warm from the hand of a Tudor falconer.

The entire Valley was there, five miles across, six miles deep, and at two hundred feet it did not look over-populated, although the gull, foraging through its fifth winter, could detect many changes since the day it had made its first

3

circuit. The centre of Valley activity had shifted. Before the war, when men still fished off the sandbars, and families picnicked on the white sands between Coombe Bay and the landslip, it had been unnecessary to fly inland in search of food. Gutted fish were abundant near the stone quay and the flotsam of picnic parties was taken out by the tide and washed round the Bluff to Tamer's Cove, where the sodden paper soon shredded away and strips of ham-fat and shards of crust caused squabbles among the herring gulls. But now these larders no longer existed. Nobody fished off bars that were laced with barbed wire and iron poles and picnickers were forbidden a beach reserved for the military. The younger gulls had taken to foraging further out to sea round the shores of Nun's Island, leaving inland picking to the lazy and the handicapped.

The handicapped gull had learned to exist on these pickings ever since the blob of oil had hardened on its wing tip, causing it to fly in a curiously lopsided fashion, as though permanently battling against an offshore gale, and when it landed and spread its wings, it staggered slightly, not only because its braking power was limited, but also because its left leg had puckered and bent under the stresses of the years. For all that it had survived. Like the Valley folk below it had come to terms with its limitations and it had forced the war to show a profit, for the presence of the great camp on the western flank of the estate meant waste and waste kept the painted bins behind the cookhouse and N.A.A.F.I. filled and overflowing.

The moment it became aware of the chimney of the Potter bakery it dipped, coasting down on the edge of the wind and making a clumsy landing on the wall that separated Smut Potter's premises from the old brickyard at the bottom of his garden. Smut saw it land and grinned. Lame himself from two machine-gun bullets received in an ambush east of Valenciennes on the last day of the 1914-18 war (the "First War" as they now called it), he welcomed a fellow cripple. He called, cheerfully, "Youm scrounging again then?" and tossed it half a pork pie that he had been munching whilst stocktaking in the store. Unfortunately for him his frugal French wife Marie saw the fragment soar through the air and came out of the kitchen screaming protests in her guttural English. The pie was only one of four dozen, surreptitiously baked from portions of a pig delivered after the blackouts

4

were up by the genial Henry Pitts, of Hermitage, and a crate of eggs, delivered an hour later by Jumbo Bellchamber, joint master of Low Coombe, but they had cost her more than twice the price of pre-war raw materials. Even though the baking represented a net profit of something like six hundred per cent, she was not disposed to waste it on gulls, reasoning that if Smut did not want it now he could put it by until he did. For nearly a minute she stormed at him without effacing his grin and when she paused for breath he said, tolerantly, "Giddon with 'ee! The poor bugger's gammy-legged, like me! 'Er's got to veed on zummat, so get back to what youm at woman and stop your ole chatter!"

Marie obeyed, as she invariably did when Smut issued an order. Honour satisfied by her protest she retreated to the steamy kitchen, while Smut watched the gull dispose of the piece of pie and fly away in the general direction of the Coombe. It flew, he thought, like a damaged fighter-plane but not one of those seen nowadays skimming south from the Polish station ten miles inland. Its speed was more that of one of the banana-crate aircraft he remembered crossing the Somme trenches in 1916. The comparison brought him satisfaction for it led him, as he returned to his stocktaking, to weigh the hideous discomforts of the last war against the unimagined profits of its successor. He remained cheerful for the rest of the morning, whistling "Over the Rainbow" as he checked the strategic reserves of Marie's shelves.

The gull flew on up the deep Coombe to the nearest of the three farms built on the eastern side of the seam. Long ago, long before the gull was hatched, the old Potter homestead at Low Coombe had been a ready source of titbits for inland flying birds. The Potters of the previous generation had been a lazy, shiftless lot and their holding was habitually strewn with everything from drying washing to unscoured pigswill troughs. Nowadays it had order, for Brissot, the cork-footed French Canadian who had married one of the Potter harlots and shared the farm with his Cockney chum, Jumbo Bell-chamber, was a conscientious farmer. All the gull got here was a glowering look from the plump, plodding Violet Bell-chamber, née Violet Potter, who was feeding hens and paused defensively when she saw the gull hovering, so it flew on to the southern meadow of Deepdene where it saw old Francis Willoughby leaning on one of his gates and apparent-ly feeding himself with a short tube, attached to a bulb. It

5

seemed an odd way to take food and the gull made a sprawling landing on the handle of a plough close by in order to watch. It had no way of knowing that Francis suffered from asthma and was not eating but inhaling as he cast a lugubrious eye at his Red Devons grubbing among the kale. There was a stillness about Deepdene that was becoming more apparent as the winter passed. The gull could remember a time when this had been a noisy, bustling farm, with men calling to one another as they worked, but now there was only this silent man standing by the gate, feeding himself with a tube. No discarded scraps were visible so the gull gathered itself for flight again, took off into the wind, and circled slowly over High Coombe, the northernmost and largest farm of the cleft.

Here, by contrast, there was promise. The new man at High Coombe, a townsman with a large family, had none of the built-in prejudice of the traditional soil-grubbers against scavengers and ignored the gull when it settled on the angle of the farmhouse roof to make a brief survey. The blonde wife of the farmer was at her usual occupation, a strange one for a housewife with innumerable children. She was sitting on a canvas stool on the front patch sketching and two or three of the children were pottering about the yard, one of them clutching a jam sandwich. The farmer himself had just finished feeding the pigs so the gull watched where he dumped two buckets at the entrance to the barn and the moment he had turned his back flopped across the yard and spent a busy five minutes scooping swill from the rims. Then one of the children spotted it and shouted a welcome so that the gull, uttering one of its short, derisive laughs, took off again and drifted down the eastern sweep of the Valley and across the dense thickets of Shallowford Woods to the Mere, a long, oval lake with a smooth surface that looked forbidding in the absence of sunlight.

There were plenty of fish in the Mere but there was also competition so the gull did not descend in the vicinity of the forester's cottage as it sometimes did in summer, when Sam Potter, the woodsman, was at work hereabouts. Sam was tolerant with gulls not ranking them as vermin, and in its time this gull had been given scraps in and around the hen-house. Today neither Sam nor his wife Joannie was around, so the bird set course south-west, crossed the Mere and the steep escarpment of oaks, beeches, sycamores and limes and drifted down into the paddocks of the Big House where it lurched to a standstill on the iron fence and studied the landscape. In the Home Farm meadows, between house and sea, no one was ploughing so there was no hope of worms and up here, near the house, there was no livestock to be fed apart from the two horses, Squire Craddock's grey and one pony, and both were in the stableyard. There were, however, scraps sometimes to be found in the forecourt, for in previous seasons the gull remembered that the gravel turn-around had been a busy place, with any number of cars coming and going and sometimes large flakes of pasty dropped by talkative huntsmen when there was a meet in the forecourt. No hunters had gathered here for some time, however, and the old house sat on dreaming of the lively past, its red creeper hanging in tatters along the entire façade, sadly in keeping with the winter landscape.

It was puzzling and a little disturbing to guess at what had happened over here lately. No more than half-a-dozen people seemed to inhabit the great, rambling place, the Squire, his wife, a small boy who appeared and disappeared at intervals, and two or three servants. A kind of decline had set in over the past two winters. It seemed to be waiting for something to quicken it into life again and even the old Squire himself had lost something of the spring in his step when he came out of the garden door of his library and stood on the terrace looking south to the sea. Leaves fluttered down from the ranks of avenue chestnuts and the gull, sensing failure, took off again and flew due east as far as Hermitage Farm where the ground began to dip towards the Sorrel. Here, on a long, sloping field, David Pitts was breaking soil with a chain harrow and showed no interest at all when the gull plopped into a shallow furrow and picked up a worm or two.

It was not much for such a long, circular flight but there was luck awaiting it at Periwinkle, the next farm on, where the Squire's daughter and her husband lived in their neat little house. Their child, Jerry, who seemed to live in the open, had been collecting eggs. Stalking his progress the gull picked up half a cropful of grain before the exertions of the morning began to advertise themselves and it rose and flew low over the edge of the plateau, across French Wood, across the Sorrel to the sprawling buildings of Four Winds, then due west to the camp, the area where, of late, the main activities of the Valley seem concentrated.

Unhurriedly, for no one ever bothered it here, the gull patrolled the vast rectangle, giving vent to an occasional sardonic *cark* as though to echo the distant shouts of the drill-sergeant bellowing at recruits on the square. Smoke rose from the kitchens and as it watched the gull saw a white-overalled cook emerge from the big hut and empty slops into one of the bins. Using the angle of the cookhouse as cover, it dropped down and made its lopsided landing on an iron bracket, slithering madly until balance was restored. Then, wondering perhaps why it had not flown here direct, it began to gorge itself on offal, ignoring the staccato shouts flung into the wind by the sergeant fifty yards further west. Take-off, on a distended crop, was slow, difficult business but when the cook came out with more waste it managed it somehow, taking advantage of a slight shift in the wind to flap south to its private crevice above the landslip. Reconnaissance over for another twenty-four hours it made its clumsy landing and perched, staring bleakly out across the shallows to the unsightly criss-cross of rusting iron that garnished the sand-banks.

II

They came in at wave-top level, driving out of the sea-mist like three starving hawks; unlike hawks they did not hover over their target but skimmed up into the wind currents that slipped between the Bluff in the east and the slope of Black-berry Moor to the west. Then they parted company, all three disappearing into low cloud but reappearing again within seconds, this time heading separately out to sea, perhaps to their base at Le Mans, perhaps further east to Orleans. In the meantime, at about five hundred feet, they had dropped six 250-pounders that erupted like six small volcanoes, casual visiting cards of a race of grey toads currently squatting on every province between Biscay and the Caucasus.

Four of the bombs fell on stubble or in hillside thickets, two on Home Farm land, two more on the lower slopes of the moor. Each dug a fifteen-foot crater, blasting every blade of grass and every shred of bracken within fifty yards but all they killed was a rabbit that had run under the lip of a heather terrace as soon as it heard the roar of the engines, a sound it had mistaken for the juggernaut approach of Farmer Pitts' tractor. It was a different matter with the two other bombs. One scored a direct hit on Periwinkle Farm, half-way up the second fold of the moor, the other blew Harold Eveleigh to pieces seconds after he had left the ditch he was digging to relieve flooding in the yard of Four Winds and had crouched, staring skywards, against a stack half-way between his farm and the brown flood of the Sorrel.

It was odd that Harold Eveleigh should be the first civilian casualty of the Valley in World War II because, as a boy of seventeen, he had survived some of the most murderous fighting on the Western Front in World War I, emerging with no more than a flesh wound. After that he had gone to Palestine and fought Turks and had been decorated for gallantry before he was twenty. He was now forty-two, the father of a family of two boys and a girl, and one of the most dedicated farmers in the Valley, even though he did not return to the soil until he was a casualty of the 1931 Slump. A war had claimed his brother Gilbert as long ago as 1916, and now Harold had met an almost identical death, for Gilbert had died from the blast of an inexpertly-thrown grenade without even getting to France. Their mother, who dabbled in spiritualism, might have seen the finger of fate in this coincidence but she had died in the first winter of the Second War.

There was another coincidence about that hit-and-run raid of February 12th, 1942. The only other casualty in the Valley was another of the long family of Eveleighs, who was also killed outright over at Periwinkle. Rachel Craddock, née Eveleigh, had been there by chance, sharing the farm with her sister-in-law, Mary Palfrey, elder daughter of Squire Craddock. Rachel's husband, Simon, was an infantry sergeant, serving somewhere in Britain, and he had sent Rachel to the west for safety and also to give her something to do while the war lasted. Rachel was reputedly the brainiest of the Eveleigh tribe and had an economics degree, but Valley folk said she had not made much use of it having spent a rather cheerless life campaigning for Socialism in the drab citadels of the Industrial North and Midlands. Then, when these curious activities were seen to be as profitless as Valley folk had always considered them, she came home and helped Mary and Mary's husband Rumble Patrick, about the farm, not exactly digging for victory but at least poultry-rearing to the same end.

9

Now she lay under a pile of rubble a mile north of her brother's unrecognisable corpse and everyone came running, convinced that the bomb had also killed Mary, her only child Jerry, and possibly Rumble Patrick as well. They were relieved to learn that Rachel had died alone, washing eggs at the scullery sink. They discovered this as soon as they scrambled into the yard, calling to one another through a fine rain of cob-dust, for Mary, clutching her six-year-old son, crawled from the ruins of the small barn, her dark hair powdered with dust, her overalls in ribbons. Both she and the boy were unmarked but they were shuddering from the effects of the shock. David Pitts and his wife from Hermitage, on the further slope, shouted with joy when they saw mother and child stumbling towards them but Mary only pointed distractedly to the pyramid of cob and splintered timber that had been her home since her eccentric young husband had come home from Canada and rebuilt the old Codsall smallholding with his own hands.

People began to arrive in twos and threes, all breathless, all eager to talk about their own miraculous escapes until they saw the havoc in Periwinkle Yard. Then they stopped and poked about in an aimless way, not caring to look Mary Palfrey in the face. They did not start digging for Rachel until Squire Craddock himself arrived with old Henry Pitts, some of the elderly labourers and two Land Army girls from the Home Farm. By then Mary had collapsed and she and the child were driven away in the landrover, to be put to bed at the Big House.

Squire Craddock, at sixty-two, was still an active man and so was Henry Pitts, a year or two older. Together, with the minimum of talk, they set about clearing a way through to the kitchen. They were both trench veterans and houses demolished by high explosives were not as novel to them as to their helpers. Henry said: "Us'll have to come at it from the back, Maister. It'll take us all day to get through from this side. Is 'er dead would 'ee say?"

"She's dead all right," Paul Craddock said. "Some of these beams are nearly two feet across. We'll go in from the scullery yard as you suggest."

They had cleared as far as the scullery window when reinforcements arrived from the camp on the moor and half-an-hour later Rachel Eveleigh was lifted out and laid in the henhouse, the only outbuilding that remained standing.

10

Squire Craddock and Henry Pitts looked down at her. She was not much marked and must have died instantly. She looked, Paul Craddock thought, her severe, humourless self, a woman who had been in arms against the ordered life of industrial and rural communities ever since she took up with that studious son of Parson Horsey. That was half-a-lifetime ago—back about the time of the old King's coronation when she was a chit of about seventeen. And then Young Horsey had been killed stretcher-bearing in Flanders and she had gone on crusading for what she called social justice, and had ultimately married another Valley misfit, his own son, Simon. Well, here was an end to all her trapesings, and she didn't look as if she minded all that much. Her hair was as grey as his own and the eyes were old and tired. A corporal of the Marines touched his arm.

"There's been another incident at that big farm, sir, the one nearer the sea."

"Four Winds?"

"Yes, sir. They missed the farm but killed the Gaffer. Name of Eveleigh. They were after our lot I imagine. Pretty poor shooting. The nearest was nearly a mile off target."

Paul only heard the first part of his comment. He was thinking how persistent was the ill luck of Four Winds, the largest of the Shallowford Farms and, over three generations, the most prosperous.

When he had come here, a raw, city-bred lad seeking a purpose in life, Four Winds had been occupied by the Codsalls and within two years crazy old Martin Codsall had killed his wife Arabella with a hay knife and hanged himself. Then Codsall's foreman, Norman Eveleigh, moved in and for a spell everything prospered, but Eveleigh's eldest son had been killed in the war, and young Harold had run off and enlisted, and Rachel had married a conscientious objector against her father's wishes, so that the unity of the large family was lost in a swirl of discord and anxiety, and Norman Eveleigh solaced himself with a land girl who created more scandal. Then, when that was smoothed out, Eveleigh had had a stroke and his second son Harold had come limping out of the unemployment queues and returned to the land but the curse of Four Winds could not, it seemed, be exorcised, for here was the new master dead in one of his own ditches while Fate, sparing the Four Winds' tenants nothing, had also struck at Rachel a mile to the north.

Suddenly he felt tired and angry, his spirit at one with the lowering skies and the bleak, wintry look of the countryside. It was all so pointless this deadly game that everybody was playing all over the world, and the pattern of order and progressive change that he had been at such pains to establish twice in his lifetime was again broken up by the drift of events over which nobody, least of all himself, had the slightest control. He wanted to go back over Codsall Bridge and up to French Wood, where he had often found courage in the past among trees planted in remembrance of men killed in the 1914–18 war, but a luxury like that would have to wait. There was his son Simon to be told and brought home for the funeral, and there were Connie Eveleigh and her children to be comforted. Neither duty could be put upon anyone else for both, son and tenant, had watched him at work over the years and would look to him for reassurance. For possibly the ten-thousandth time since he had ridden into the Valley as a young man he cursed himself for having taken up such a packload of obligations.

He took a final gloomy look at the rubble, wondering how his daughter Mary would take the loss of her home, even though her life and her son's life had been spared. Henry Pitts, still at his elbow, said, "Where's The Boy, then?" He meant Rumble Patrick, Mary's husband, whom many of the Valley folk still called The Boy, although he was now twenty-eight and had been master here for seven years. Paul said he had gone into Whinmouth for seed and left word that he was to be contacted at once through Whinmouth police, and as he said this he remembered how Rumble Patrick's hands, and perhaps his love for Mary, had transformed this gimcrack little farm into a pretty little home. The thought comforted him a little. "Good old Rumble," he muttered, "I can leave Mary to him. He's got Potter blood in him and those Potters can survive anything." He turned and climbed into the station waggon, driving it back on to the old dust road and down as far as Codsall Bridge where he turned into the muddy lane leading to Four Winds.

He had expected outcry but there was none. The pitiful remains of Harold had been gathered up by some unlucky weight and covered with sacking to await the ambulance. Connie Eveleigh was alone in the parlour, sipping tea made by one of the land girls. Everybody had a frozen face and spoke in undertones but Connie wasn't weeping, or railing against the Luftwaffe. He remembered then that she had come from the North and would know how to conduct herself, a pretty, chubby woman, not easily daunted. It was to her, rather than to her husband, that he had given the farm when they came to him penniless, for she had spoken up honestly and fearlessly, asking a favour but holding on to her pride. Harold had been a bit of a show-off but she had kept him at work and contented and would have courage to spare for the weeks ahead. She looked up hard-eyed when he came stumping in, his boots leaving a trail of cob-dust across her patterned carpet.

"The other one got Rachel, didn't it?"

"Yes," he said, "but at least the blast killed her before the roof fell in."

"Two bombs, two Eveleighs," Connie said. "They don't have much luck, do they? Thank God Mary and Jerry escaped."

It was strange. He wasn't thinking of the Eveleighs, or even of his own daughter and grandson, but of the original tenants, the Codsalls. Arabella Codsall had clacked at him endlessly in this very room and he had ridden over here with Martin, drunk as a fiddler, shortly before the man went off his head and committed murder. He it had been who had come here on the wings of a south-westerly gale the night his own boy Simon was born, to find Martin hanged in the barn and his wife an even worse mess than Harold Eveleigh outside. A damned unlucky farm but one that continued to fight back, as Connie was fighting now. He said, "How did the children take it?"

"They don't know yet. Bob went off with Rumble. Hughie and the girl won't be home from school until the camp 'bus gets in at teatime. Shall I meet it and break the news on the way over?"

"Yes," he said, after a moment's thought, "and I'll send Claire over to go along with you. The Marines are getting in touch with Whinmouth police, so the elder lad will be back in an hour or so. You can rely on him, can't you?"

"He's a good boy and a first-class farmer. He takes after his grandfather more than Harold. The younger one is more like Harold, full of enthusiasms that don't last long."

Her calmness astonished him, neither did he miss the hint of defensiveness in her praise of the elder boy. She was wondering, no doubt, if the tenancy would now pass to him.

13

The disposal of Four Winds' tenancy had been discussed here twice before.

"Keep him at it, Connie," Paul said, "and don't let him do anything damned silly, like enlist. We can't afford to have anyone else go."

"The Government wouldn't let him enlist."

"They should have had that much sense in the last war. Then we shouldn't have had so many trees in French Wood, or such a hell of a struggle to get going again through the 'twenties when you were so-high."

"I was a bit higher than that," she said, with a twitch of a smile. "Harold and I danced the Charleston the first night we met. He was a wonderful dancer, did you know that?"

He saw now that a tear glittered under the eyelash and crossing over he laid his hand on her shoulder.

"It was all over in a flash. He couldn't have known a thing. He died worse deaths in France after any number of nearmisses. There's some comfort in that I suppose. He wasn't the kind of chap who could have faced a half-life if he had been maimed."

"You don't have to tell me that," Connie said. "I knew our Harold." And then, almost as a challenge, "It was a good marriage. We had a lot of fun, Squire!"

The word "Squire" did not come naturally to her as it still did to the old stagers, like Henry Pitts. "Our Harold", of course, was pure Lancashire. No one in the Valley would use a possessive pronoun in that way. Musing on this, and a little fortified by her dignity and courage, he was able to get the dire results of this lunatic hit-and-run raid into perspective. It might, he supposed, have been worse. Six bombs and two deaths. If one bomb had veered a little to the west fifty Marines might have been blown to pieces in the N.A.A.F.I. on the crown of the moor.

"There's one thing about this picnic," he said, "we're all in it, every last one of us, no matter where you hide!"

He did not think she needed his presence any longer and drove back along the lane, thinking better of going home to 'phone Simon. Leaving the station waggon at the foot of the approach road to Hermitage Farm he climbed the gorse track to his favourite spot on the estate, the sharp ridge crowned by the memorial copse they called French Wood, coming at it from behind, threading his way through the little

14

glade without glancing at the plaques and sitting on a fallen birch that gave him a veiw of the whole Valley.

It was a long time since he had been up here and the view, so familiar in every detail, had changed during the last eighteen months. Over Periwinkle a mushroom of dust lingered like the smoke of a huge autumn bonfire and he could see the buildings of Four Winds and the straw-coloured circle that marked the place where Harold Eveleigh had died under his stack.

To the west, however, there were more noticeable changes. Blackberry Moor had once been a vast rectangle of yellow gorse, heath, heather and green or gold bracken according to the season of the year but now it was a town, row after row of huts looking like an enormous chicken farm made up of uniform hovers and here and there, alongside smaller rectangles, large buildings camouflaged green and brown, the N.A.A.F.I., S.H.Q., the gymnasium, the guardhouse. Specks moved across the parade ground and a sliver of sunlight, travelling across the landscape like a fugitive, lit upon somebody's bayonet, or a drop of moisture on the wire mesh that ran the length of the road. There had been a camp of sorts here in the First War but it was nothing like this, just an untidy huddle of bell-tents and a sagging marquee or two, where Kitchener's volunteers drilled and shivered and swore. This camp looked permanent and he wondered, when it was all over, how the devil anyone would restore the heath to its natural state. It wouldn't do to hunt over it for a decade or so. The place must be a labyrinth of hidden drains, slit trenches and coils of barbed wire.

He was surprised to find himself thinking of the future. For so long now there hadn't been one, just a chequered past and a cheerless present, involving blackouts, rationing, blackmarket wrangles, Government forms sown with verbal mantraps, battledress, Home Guard manoeuvres, air-raid warnings and miles of dragons' teeth along the once deserted shore as far as the Bluff. The vast camp signified all these things, a permanent reminder that freewill had blown away with the piece of paper that well-meaning ass Chamberlain had flourished after the Munich debacle. That was how it had seemed for a long time now and even the reckless mood of 1940 had departed, leaving a vacuum filled with glumness, boredom and worry.

His family were scattered. Of his four sons and two daughters only young John, the postscript, and Mary, now home-less, remained in the Valley. Stevie and Andy, the boneyard twins who had always patronised him and had gone off to make their money in scrap iron more than a decade ago, were both in the R.A.F., one at a Bomber Command airfield in Yorkshire, the other somewhere in North Africa with a fighter squadron. Simon, his eldest boy, was in Scotland, learning how to kill men with his bare hands and him getting on for forty! His daughter Karen, whom everybody called "Whiz", was in India, thank God, and so was her husband, Ian. Ian had some kind of staff job and it would probably keep him alive. So much for the children, two home and four away. Some of his pre-war cronies were still around but the young ones had mostly gone. Only here and there was a son carrying on, like David, Henry's son, at Hermitage. The rest were as far away as Alberta and Queensland, or caught up in some confused battle in Burmese jungle or North African desert. There was no continuity any more and as he sat here, looking out over the grey landscape, he realised it was continuity he had striven for for forty years, often with little success. In a way it was a kind of suspension of all natural processes, like waiting for a spring that would never come. The land looked as lifeless as Rachel Eveleigh down there in that hen-house, and in the pattern of fields and copses under his eye, nothing moved except the odd speck or two on the camp parade ground.

A Hurricane came zooming out of the blur of the woods, one of the Paxtonbury-based Polish fighters in tardy pursuit of the raiders and he realised how deeply he resented all aircraft as representing a hateful challenge to all that was predictable, slow and safe. His first wife, Grace, had been killed by a Gotha on the pavé road behind Ypres; his youngest daughter, Claire, Dairy Queen of the West, had died in one off the Dutch coast, as long ago as 1934; and now they menaced the slopes and riverbottoms of remote streams like the Sorrel. God curse the fool who had first invented them, and as he thought this he remembered how he had set his face against all mechanical gadgets right through the early morning of the machine-age, when old King Teddy had been ruling an England of three-horse ploughs and leg-o'-mutton sleeves.

Then, as always, his obstinacy reasserted itself and he stood up, dusting his breeches. It didn't pay to brood about

16

it. There was plenty to be done, here and elsewhere, and he had looked down on this Valley too many times and in too many contrasting moods to be fooled by the desolation of winter, even a wartime winter. The Valley had looked deceivingly cheerful from here in the summer of Dunkirk but things were far more hopeless then, with everyone waiting for the first German parachutists and only a few shotguns and rook-rifles to oppose a landing of Panzers. There had been many setbacks and more to come he wouldn't wonder, at least that madman who raved and frothed and bit carpets had been held, and the chances of invasion now were remote, notwithstanding this morning's escape of the battleships *Gneisenau* and *Scharnhorst* that had probably touched off this piddling little air-raid. He descended to the road, driving along it until he came to the two stone pillars that marked the drive and accelerating over the loose gravel between leafless chestnuts.

His wife Claire was awaiting him on the step and he felt better for seeing her there. At least she hadn't changed, or not that much in all these years. She was fifty-nine but looked about forty-three and it cheered him to reflect that Claire had always had magic at her command to adapt to any fashion that found its way this far west. In what people now called the Edwardian Afternoon she had been a buxom, laughing girl, with a wasp waist and flowing hips and bosom and in the period now called The Gay 'Twenties she had changed herself into a flapper showing shapely legs half-way up the thigh and cropping her lovely, corn-coloured hair in order to be at one with her daughters. Then, during the 'thirties, she had compromised between these two extremes and it was only when she was undressing to go to bed that he realised she was steadily losing the battle against excess flesh. But now a fourth compromise had been achieved for the kind of things that put weight on her belly and buttocks were difficult to get, so that recently she had been able to make a virtue out of necessity and had begun to slim in all the right places. Through all these changes her features and characteristics had remained the same, her fresh, pink and white complexion as unblemished as a girl's, her slightly prominent eyes reminding him of inshore water off the Coombe Bay sandbanks on a summer's day—those two things, plus her optimism, steadfastness and strong sexual attraction for him, that persisted even now, so that there never was a time when

17

he was not in some way stirred by her presence. She said anxiously, "Where on earth have you been? I 'phoned poor Connie and she said you left an hour ago!"

He was tempted to lie but thought better of it. "I had to pull myself together, old girl. I went up to French Wood," and was a little touched to see her smile.

"I might have known it. Did it work?"

"More or less. How is Mary and the kid?"

"Both scrubbed and sound asleep. Doctor Maureen came over and gave them something to counteract the shock. The police 'phoned from Whinmouth. They're looking all over for Rumble and Connie's boy. I didn't know what to say to Connie, poor kid."

"You don't have to worry about her," Paul said, "she's got more guts than any woman about here! And don't run away with the idea that it's because she and poor old Harold weren't close. They were, in their own kind of way."

Her teeth came over her heavy lower lip in a way it usually did when she was about to admit a shortcoming.

"If it had been you or Mary someone would have had a hell of a job comforting me!"

She went into the hall and he noticed she had avoided mentioning Rachel's death, or the need to contact Simon. It wasn't fear of making a fool of herself in front of him, and it wasn't lack of affection for the woman who had married her stepson. It was something more fundamental and he acknowledged it to himself as they passed into the library and she poured him a tot of whisky. "She doesn't give a damn about anyone except me," he thought, "and she never has." He said, feeling better for the whisky, "I shall have to wire Simon. They'll almost certainly give him compassionate leave, no matter what he's doing," and he began to move into the hall where the old-fashioned telephone was still bracketted to the wall, occupying the same place as when it was first installed in the days before Shallowford House had been a wartime convalescent home.

"Leave it!" she said suddenly and when he looked shocked, "Rumble will attend to it, it'll give him something to occupy his mind. After all, he was closer to Rachel than any of us."

He had forgotten. The shock of the morning's events had made him overlook yet another coincidence about the two-minute swoop of those damned Fokker-Wulfes. Rachel Eveleigh had actually delivered the boy in the year before the

18

First War, stumbling upon his half-witted mother in labour in the cave she sometimes occupied over the badger slope in Shallowford Woods and ever since, not unnaturally he supposed there had been a strong bond between Rumble Patrick and the childless Rachel Eveleigh.

"You're right," he said, "I'll let Rumble handle it," and sat down again, stretching his legs and suddenly feeling his age.

"What was the point of it anyway?" she asked, irritably. "It doesn't make any kind of sense, does it? A woman washing eggs at a sink. A man digging a drain in his fields. Is *that* going to get anyone anywhere? It's not even as if there was a terror element about it, like blitzing London or one of the ports. Do *we* do this kind of thing to their farms and villages?"

He explained that the Luftwaffe was aiming at the camp and that, in all probability, the German airmen had been trainees on a practice run to gain experience. She seized on the last word as though it had been a blasphemy.

"*Experience!*" she mocked. "You men are all the same! There isn't one of you, English, French, German or Jap, who can think straight! Experience of what for God's sake? Reducing human beings to pulp, in order to see how your silly machines work? Rumble rebuilt that home with his two hands and Mary made it pretty and cosy and exciting. It was like ... like a doll's house! What kind of sense is there in blowing it to smithereens like that?"

Her indignation was so typical of her, and so true to the form of her grumpy old father, Edward Derwent, once master of High Coombe, who had never had a moment's patience with anything he could not touch, sniff, eat, or sell. "Derwent-common-sense" Paul had always called it and there were times when it had stood him in good stead. She had never seen any point in the First War and for a long time he had agreed with her, but they had had many arguments about this one, for whilst he was convinced that it was just, she blamed it on the vanities and inefficiences of male animals from Plymouth to Pekin. It need never have happened, she said, and whilst granting that it had to be won at all costs, she had no confidence that the world would be any the better for it when the rubble was cleared away. To her it was the ultimate negation of commonsense and demonstrative proof of the obsession of men with inessentials. All that mattered to a Derwent was good food, warm clothes, a roof that didn't

19

leak, regular harvests, and the pleasure of sharing a double bed with your partner in all these things. She had never once bothered herself about politics, having seen what they had done to her predecessor, who left a good husband and a good home to march about London breaking windows and waving banners. Her detachment sometimes irritated Paul but today it brought a gleam of humour to the sombreness of the day.

He said with a grin, "I might have known the violation of Mary's chintzy little bedroom would have outraged you far more than the fact that two German battleships have got clear."

"Damn the battleships and damn the war! I'm terribly upset for that nice girl Connie, and for Simon as well, but for me the entire stupidity of everything that's happening is pinpointed by some fool hundreds of miles away making a bomb to drop on a home two people built for themselves out of nothing. I daresay it's illogical but there it is. I remember Periwinkle in the days before even you came here. It was nothing but a ratty old shack, and Rumble and Mary created it, but now it'll never be the same for them. It'll always be the place where somebody they liked was killed."

"Have some whisky yourself, old girl," he said tolerantly, and was crossing to the decanter when Rumble Patrick came in, having dropped Young Eveleigh at Codsall Bridge. He had been given the gist of what had happened at Periwinkle and Paul was puzzled by his phlegmatic approach to the destruction of the farm and the narrow escape of his wife and child. When Paul told him how they had found Rachel in the ruins of the scullery he shrugged. "I'm more upset about Harold Eveleigh," he said. "At least he still thought life was worth living."

"Didn't Rachel?"

"No. She was fed up and has been ever since Simon brought her here."

"She missed him that much?"

Rumble looked at him shrewdly, drawing his brows together in a way Paul remembered his father Ikey Palfrey had done, on the few occasions Ikey had wanted to say anything serious.

"How much do you know about Simon and Rachel, Gov'nor?"

"Practically nothing," Paul admitted, "except that they seemed to get along."

"Get along is about right. Like a couple of elderly work-men digging a trench. They haven't been man and wife to one another for a long time. Rachel told me that herself, although I guessed it when Simon had his last leave."

"You mean they quarrelled?"

"Not quarrelled, just parted company. Spiritually you might say. She was a pacifist."

"I knew she was once. She never really got over her first husband's death in the First War but Simon was always very 'anti' himself."

"Not since he fought in Spain. He'd kill every bloody Fascist he met with a spanner, or anything handy! That was where they split. She believed in Gandhi's theory of peaceful absorption of invaders, even Nazi invaders, and Simon thought that was damn silly. Most men and women could agree to differ on an abstract issue of that kind but they were political animals. It was in their veins—pamphlets, speeches, attitudes, ideals, the lot. They've spent their whole lives at it, poor devils. I can understand Simon—it's inherited from his mother I imagine—but Rachel was a farmer's daughter, Valley born and bred. It's difficult to know why she was so intense."

Paul, remembering other times, thought he did know but he was too tired to argue the point. Instead he said, "You can get a licence to rebuild Periwinkle. It'll come under essential works."

"Let it wait," Rumble said, offhandedly and then, more thoughtfully, "Mary and the kid can stay here for the time being, can't they?"

"As long as you like," said Paul and then, a new worry suggesting itself, "You aren't thinking of leaving and . . ." but Rumble grinned and said, "Well, certainly not tonight, Gov'nor!" and was gone, and Paul, finishing his drink, heard him run up the stairs, along the passage and open the door of the room Mary had occupied all her life until she married. He found himself thinking about the mutual attraction of these two, his hot favourites among all his sons, daughters, and in-laws. It went right back to their earliest childhood and he had watched it grow from a tiny seed and flower into the wholly satisfactory thing it had become. They were the com-plement of one another, Rumble a boisterous, happy-go-lucky extrovert, Mary a gentle, affectionate introvert. Of the lives and marriages resulting from his own theirs alone had been safe and predictable. Neither one of them—and he would swear to this—had ever held another man or woman in their arms, and somehow, at this moment, he was able to see through ceilings and doors into that little room of hers and know, with a sense of relief, that Rumble was already comforting her and that soon their bodies would fuse, as though anxious to replace life obliterated by the bombs. It was strange and a little indecent, he thought, that a man should find such reassurance in the physical possession of one's own daughter but he did, relating it directly to the extreme pleasure he had always found in the body of the girl's mother.

He poured himself some more whisky and took it over to the fireplace, kicking a log there until a splutter of blue flame devoured the sullen spiral of smoke. Fancifully he saw the shooting flame as a symbol of Rumble Patrick's virility, and deep inside him there stirred the vague promise of a great tribe of grandchildren. He felt himself starved of grandchildren. Mary had one son but so far neither Simon nor The Pair had produced any and the baby daughter of Whiz, born in India, had been trapped there by the war. He sat on musing about his children collectively and individually, wondering why none of them save Mary seemed to belong to this great sprawling house, or professed loyalty to the fields and woods outside. He supposed everybody threw down their own roots and that those roots need not necessarily be based in soil. They might—as he suspected in the case of Simon—be anchored to ideas or, in the case of The Pair, to money and machines. He wondered whether he would ever see them congregate under this roof again and doubted it, for they seemed to have lost touch with his way of life and Claire's. Well, for the meantime, there was nothing to do but hold on and he was good at holding on. Anyone hereabouts would vouch for that.

Outside the light began to face over the leafless chestnuts and overhead, invisible above low cloud, one of the Paxton-bury-based Polish aircraft buzzed in from the sea.

CHAPTER TWO

CRADDOCKS AT WAR

I

SOMETIMES the musings of Valley-based people like Paul had the power to travel telepathic paths, spreading like sound waves half-way across the world where they were picked up in billet and bivouac and contemplated, sentimentally or unsentimentally, depending upon the strength of the pre-war ties of those who received them. Distance had no bearing upon their interpretation. Those preoccupied with their own pursuits and surroundings could disregard them but there were others who, in peacetime, had thought of Shallowford as a dead-and-alive backwater, but were now having second thoughts about it. News from home used them as a sounding board, producing pangs of homesickness and impatience with new scenes and new faces.

Paul Craddock's sons and his absent daughter Whiz were not of this latter group. To each of them the Valley had never been more than a jumping-off place where, years ago, they had eaten, slept, and exchanged sly jokes about their father's dedication to the land, or their mother's Victorian approach to their father.

Simon, the eldest, had disappeared into the murk of the Northcountry after a number of false starts in life. The Pair, Stevie and Andy, had followed him although, unlike Simon, they had made a success of their exodus. Whiz turned her back on the Valley the day she married and had rarely visited it since. Her home now was the Service and if she thought of the Valley at all it was as a rustic backwater where there had once been some good hunting. Now it was as dead to her as Atlantis. Like Stevie and Andrew she had always lived for the present.

With Simon it was different again. He did not see his father's patriachial pretensions as ridiculous, or his stepmother's devotion as naïve, but he could see neither one of them as having, in this day and age, a meaningful place in the structure of Western civilisation. They were pleasant anachronisms, clinging to a way of life that had crumbled as long ago as the summer of 1914. They had been unable to adapt to the demands of his own generation, currently facing the most dire threat since the westward surge of Attila. Possibly this was why he was able to read the wire informing him of his wife's death without much sense of shock. It did not surprise him overmuch that, here and there in the process of total war, a civilian living in a remote agricultural area could be blotted out. He had fought in Spain and he had fought in France and in each campaign he had seen dwellings reduced to rubble and women and children reduced to pulp. Such things no longer horrified him, they only fed his hatred of a system that had accepted a policy of drift through the 'thirties and braced itself when it was all but too late. He had been a professional hater of privilege since his youth and now he was a dedicated hater of Fascism who found himself temporarily allied to bankers, merchants and other former enemies. He had compassion, too much of it perhaps, but he could no longer waste it on an individual, not even when that individual was the tight-lipped woman who had been his wife and comrade in the long prelude to this cacophony. Thus he was able to ride out the shock of the news they brought him when he came in dripping from the grenade range on that winter's afternoon. Anyone watching him might have assumed him to be reading a posting signal. His reactions were limited to a blink or two and a swallow of saliva. Then, very abruptly, he left the mess and went out into the thin, pattering rain to the cookhouse where his chief crony, Sergeant Rawlinson, was serving tea to recruits.

He called through the hatch, "Rawley! You got a minute?" and Rawlinson's red face appeared at the opening.

Their friendship was stronger than most wartime friendships for both, having served in the International Brigade, had special entries against their names in the green, confidential files of the unit. They were not exactly suspect but were what a regular officer might describe as "*Men with strong, Leftist sympathies*". The rankers had a much simpler way of putting it: they called them "Bolshies" but now that Russia

24

had joined the Allies the term had lost some of its opprobrium.

It was strange that a man like Simon Craddock, whose mother had been killed driving an ambulance in 1917, whose father, veteran of two wars, owned thirteen hundred English acres, and who himself was a 1939 volunteer, should be regarded so warily but there it was. This was Britain and this was the British way of assessing loyalty to the crown.

Both Simon and Sergeant Rawlinson knew about the entry on their documents but neither resented it. In the six years that had passed between now and the day they had sailed for Spain so much had happened that political confusion could be forgiven. The war had made them tolerant towards every sect and party in Europe except the Nazi Party. They had even lost much of their resentment for Italian Fascists after the mass surrenders in North Africa.

Rawlinson emerged from the kitchen carrying two pint mugs of tea and set them down on an empty table near the pot-bellied stove. Simon's battledress began to steam. Without comment he handed the telegram to Rawlinson who read it, handed it back, and looked down at the stained table top.

"Bastards!" he said, and waited for endorsement.

Simon lifted his shoulders. He had inherited his mother's political fanaticism and his father's obstinacy but few of their physical characteristics. At thirty-eight he was spare and loose-jointed. He had narrow, thoughtful features and what his father would have called "an authentic Cassius look" produced by dark hair, deepset eyes and prominent cheekbones. He did not share his friend's blanket assessment of the German nation.

"It probably happens regularly over there, Rawley. If it hasn't already it will as soon as Bomber Command steps up its offensive."

"Fair enough," Rawlinson said, "but they began it. Bastards! Every bloody one of them! You'll be putting in for compassionate?"

"I don't know, I shall want to think about it."

Rawlinson, once a Lancashire shoeshop clerk, whistled through teeth, shocked because the rich panoply of death had been built into his personality from earliest childhood. In the back streets of Burnley, with a father and two brothers on the dole, a good funeral was about all one ever got in the way of ceremony or spectacle.

25

"You'll *have* to go! You can't let your wife be buried by strangers!"

"There won't be a stranger present," Simon told him. "The entire bloody Valley will be there. She was born on one of the farms and it will be the best-attended funeral in local history. My entry passes out on Friday and some of them need watching. It would take me all of three days to get there and back and I daresay the adj. would insist on me taking a week to sort things out. That's the usual drill. What sense is there to it when I'm up to my neck in work here? They got Rachel. Okay."

Rawlinson regarded him warily. He admired Simon Craddock but he had never understood him, and that despite sharing bivouacs in Spain with other volunteers from what he still regarded as The Upper Crust.

"I don't get it," he muttered. "You implied it was six of one and half-a-dozen of the other, didn't you?"

"No I didn't, Rawley. It's a question of time, don't you see? If we don't get this bloody war finished in a couple of years Europe will fall apart at the seams, win or lose. The dead can't help one way or the other."

Fanaticism of any kind impressed Rawlinson but he was still unconvinced. "If it was my missus I'd want to *be* there. Okay, so it's cant, all that cock they say over an open grave. But she's your missus and she was one of us! You owe her that much! Just to *be* there!" When Simon did not reply but quietly sipped his tea, he added, "How long you been married?"

"More than ten years."

"You hit it off, didn't you?"

"At first, and even when we split over this business we still respected one another. I saw her point of view but I don't think she ever saw mine, not after Spain anyhow. She thought we had all been marching up a wrong turning so she packed in. Just like that. She went right back to the Sermon on the Mount. Love conquers all! But she didn't know the first damn thing about love as most women understand it. We haven't even slept together since I got survivor's leave after Dunkirk. No Rawley, she wasn't one of us. It was a different kind of love she meant. Leper-colonies, the Untouchables, prison and hospital visiting."

Rawlinson pondered on whether or not this put a different complexion on things but decided that it didn't. "She was your missus." he repeated, obstinately, "and they'll all expect you to go." A note of irritation entered Rawlinson's voice. "Dammit, you don't *want* to go, do you? You just don't want to go! Now why not?"

It wasn't an easy question. He felt about Rachel the way he felt about Rawlinson. They were partners in an expanding business that had gone through some very bad times in the 'twenties and 'thirties but was now on the mend. They thought of that business as progress, social justice, self-determination for minorities and equality of opportunity, but now all the old battle-cries had been amalgamated into one and was on the lips of many former enemies, including Big Business, the Conservative Party, and that old whipping boy the Bourgeoisie. Rachel had dropped out and he was surprised, even a little ashamed, at his lack of reaction to news of her death. Just that one stab under the ribs and then nothing but a kind of nostalgia for the early years of their marriage when they had shared platforms at so many ill-attended meetings in so many hopeless campaigns, when they went calling on indifferent electors with their leaflets and torrents of words, and then home to bed to furnished rooms where the beds were lumpy, wardrobe drawers stuck half-way out, and the linoleum was cold to bare feet. Had there ever been any ecstasy? He couldn't be sure after all this time. All he remembered was the clip-clop of her sensible brogues on cobbles, rain streaming down her unpowdered cheeks and stray tendrils of hair hanging limply over the collar of a cheap, off-the-peg coat. In a way he was glad she was out of it. Her spirit, mortally injured by the assaults of the First War, had been too sickly to challenge its successor. She was worn out and used up, not physically perhaps but mentally. Too many doors had been slammed in her face. Too many of her leaflets had found their way to the lavatory and on September 3rd, 1939, she had turned her face to the wall.

He made his decision as he swallowed the rest of his tea. "I'm going to put a call through," he said briefly and Rawley watched him hunch his shoulders against the rain and recross the parade ground to the sergeant's mess. "Queer bugger, Crad!" he murmured aloud. "Queer, but Christ Almighty, tough! Tougher than anyone in this bloody outfit!"

The telephone rang in the hall an hour or so after they had returned to the Big House from the funeral. Claire Craddock, answering it, told herself that it was Simon ringing to ask who had been there, how many wreaths had been sent and from whom. She had been as shocked as Rawlinson by his refusal to ask for compassionate leave to attend but when she received his letter on the morning of the funeral, and had had time to think about it, she understood better than any of them. The relationship between them had always been easy and comfortable, perhaps because, in the days after his mother had abandoned him and Claire had taken her place at Shallowford, she had always made very certain that he wasn't left out in the cold. Simon, a sensitive child, had recognised and appreciated her good intentions, and as he grew from a lonely child into a lonely young man it was Claire who had more of his confidence than his father, or his noisy half-brothers. She had never taken his marriage to that Eveleigh girl very seriously, recognising it for what it was, an attempt on the part of a young war widow to find her way back into the mainstream of life, but she had always respected the woman they had just laid in the Eveleigh patch at Coombe Bay churchyard. If she had little capacity for love, as Claire had practised it all her life, she had plenty of loyalty and had helped Simon through some difficult times, particularly when he returned from Franco's prison weighing six stones.

The call, however, was not a conventional enquiry from Simon but a terse request from Stephen, technically the senior of the twins ("by ninety seconds", as Claire always put it) and Stevie was ringing from Yorkshire asking for his sister-in-law's last address. She knew at once he meant the address of his twin-brother's wife, Margaret, and that his call had nothing to do with the funeral of his other sister-in-law, Rachel, or the wreath that had somehow gone astray. Her twin sons and their wives had always operated as a foursome, ever since their marriages in the early 'thirties and long before that Stevie and Andy had seldom been seen apart, having gone to school together, skylarked through the 'twenties together, and finally, to their father's unspeakable disgust, gone back into the scrap business together. They had also prospered together and had made, she suspected, quite a pile of money before rushing into the R.A.F. at the outbreak of war. She had admired them for this, despite Paul's rumblings to the contrary. They were both young men obsessed with flashy sports cars, golf, old-boy talk, jars of wallop and polkadot scarves, so that they seemed to her tailor-made for the R.A.F. and would have moped behind desks for the duration, despite their mastery of modern business techniques and their innumerable shady contacts in the world of scrap metal. Now, at last, they were separated. Stevie was on a conversion course to heavy aircraft in Yorkshire, and Andy, if anything the more dashing of the two, was in Egypt with his fighter squadron, whence he wrote illegible letters reminding her of the letters she had once had from him at school.

There was, she thought, a curious urgency in Stevie's voice and also an unusual reluctance to enter into a chatty conversation. He was fit, he said, and unlikely to go on ops. for months. He was also missing Andy whom he referred to as "the old clot", but what he wanted right now was his sister-in-law Margaret's London address. He didn't say why and she didn't ask him because it would have seemed an unnecessary question. She gave the telephone number and then Stevie asked how everybody was and whether they were going to rebuild Rumble Patrick's farm "after old Jerry's flying visit". She had begun to tell him about the current family dispute concerning Rumble's proposed enlistment but she didn't get the chance to finish. The pips went and Stevie snapped, "No more change. Carry on regardless . . ." and the line went dead.

She came away slightly puzzled. He hadn't mentioned Rachel being killed but only the farm and although, taken all round, he had sounded his brash, breezy self, she had sensed a certain tension that disturbed her a little. She decided then that he had been lying about his prospects of going on operations and this comforted her, for somehow she never worried about the twins' chances of survival. They had already survived half-a-dozen car crashes, two light aeroplane crashes and one drowning when their home-made boat overturned in the bay. It would, she reminded herself, take more than Hitler to bring stillness to The Pair.

In one respect Claire was right. In another she was as wrong as she could be. Stevie had told her the truth regarding his prospects of going on operations. His conversion course would confine him to base area flights for some weeks but Claire's instinct had not been at fault. The tension, conveyed over the wire, had nothing to do with flying, or his enforced separation from Andy. It was the result of a profound shock administered by his wife who had just left him, threatening never to return.

The rift between them had been widening over a period of eighteen months. The first crack showed shortly after the twins had turned their backs on money-making and enlisted in a barrage balloon unit whence, by pulling a fistful of strings, they had transferred to a fighter-pilot course completed in time to enable them to harry the Luftwaffe through the final fortnight of the Battle of Britain. Their surrender of civilian status and the break-up of their small scrap-metal empire, had been no real sacrifice on their part. Money, as such, did not interest them and never had, not since their coming-of-age when old Franz Zorndorff, their cicerone, had lured them out of the Valley and trained them as his acolytes. What they found rewarding about life was its constant movement and the element of gambling inherent in the scrap market but when something even more boisterous presented itself they were happy to abandon scrap for the duration and whoop it up in the skies over south-eastern England.

Margaret, Andy's Welsh wife, accepted the situation, making the best of what could not be altered, but Monica, Stevie's partner, had never ceased to regard the war as an attempt on the part of all engaged in it to thwart her personal plans for the future. She had, in fact, argued strenuously against their enlistment and when she failed to carry her point she had sulked through the phoney war period and on into the Dunkirk summer and beyond. Now, after nearly two years of camp-following, she could contain her frustration no longer and the resultant flare-up promised to drive a wedge between man and wife that could never be withdrawn. It was the near-certainty of this that had put the note of urgency into Stevie's voice when, in a frantic attempt to find a mediator, he had remembered his brother's wife and asked for Margaret's address.

He did not have much hope that Margaret's intervention would cause his wife to change her mind. The two had never been close friends although, in the whirl of foreign business trips, shopping sprees, the buying and selling of homes, and the cut-and-thrust of business life, they had half-convinced both men that their relationship was cordial. The truth was, of course, neither Stephen, nor Andrew, nor even Margaret had ever been privy to Monica's long-term plans for herself, her husband and, if they had to come along, for the other pair.

The spoiled daughter of the most pontifical-looking cleric in Devon Monica Dearden had never, or not until now, repented her pursuit and capture of the harebrained son of a small country squire. She told herself, the first night they met at an Assembly Room dance, that, given the chance, she could make something of Stephen Craddock, and in a way she had, dragging Andy and his Welsh wife along in her wake. Under her tutelage they had ceased to roar about the countryside in sports cars that looked like angry red beetles and had bought more dignified forms of transport. She had also redressed all three of them, persuading the boys to discard their loud sports clothes and the yard of knitted scarf that trailed behind them wherever they went. As to their social life, she had made shift to sort that out to a degree, encouraging them to devote only business hours to men who could hardly read or write, who kept no banking accounts, but who, at a moment's notice, could produce half a battleship or ten miles of disused railway line. Together as a quartette they assembled round them a group of pseudo-sophisticated people and had begun to cultivate an acquaintance with what, in the middle 'thirties, passed for art. They attended a play or two by unarrived dramatists, discussed the work of a few fashionable novelists and patronised a succession of artists whose canvasses, usually covered with clocks, fishbones, detached limbs, assorted triangles and solitary eyes puzzled Stevie very much but were loudly acclaimed by Monica's friends.

It was not Stevie's philistinism, however, that enlarged his wife's exasperation with him into frantic resentment and neither was their quarrel connected with her refusal to encumber herself with children. Stevie conceded that she might well be right when she declared him unfitted to be anybody's father. The flaw in their marriage was exposed by the same pressures as those brought to bear on Simon and Rachel. Neither could view the present war from a common standpoint. Stevie saw it as a kind of nonstop rugby football match between a sporting team and opponents inclined to foul.

31

Monica saw it as the most unmitigated bore ever contrived to try the patience of the human family. It was bad enough, she thought, to have to break off her social contacts, pretend to be rationed as regards food, clothes and petrol, and stumble about small market towns where the street lighting had never been adequate and was now non-existent. What was worse, in her eyes, was an obligation to support the role of a twentieth-century vivandière in one dreary camp after another, in order to be on hand to embrace one of the beefiest threequarters in the British team. For Monica Craddock did not see her husband and his messmates as heroes but as a mob of hairy school-prefects. To her they were not the defenders of democracy but extroverts who had opted out of the serious business of life to enjoy an unlooked-for holiday. When introduced to the twins' group-captain on one of the Battle of Britain airfields she thought of him as a bemedalled Doctor Arnold of Rugby, impossibly stupid, impossibly priggish and self-deprecating into the bargain and as time passed she grew to hate everything about the R.A.F. She hated its silly slang and its obsession with gadgets. She hated its juvenile enthusiasms and its affected insouciance in matters of dress and deportment. Born and bred in the precincts of a Cathedral Close, her life regulated by the clamour of bells and the proprieties expected of an Archdeacon's daughter, she had once yearned for adventure, for the bizarre and the unpredictable. In the years between marriage and the outbreak of war she had found all three in the company of Stephen and his brother. Then, against all probability, they entered the Fellowship of the Dedicated and overnight had become more catholic than the Pope, reverting to schoolboys, crumpling their caps, leaving their top tunic button undone to prove that they were numbered among the élite, growing fair, droopy moustaches and, above all, prattling endlessly of "prangs" and "popsies" and "wizard shows". This was not the kind of adventure Monica had envisaged and the façade of these people did not deceive her for a moment. They claimed to despise those who, in their own idiom, "shot a line", but to Monica the lines shot by the men (and their women) of Bomber and Fighter Commands criss-crossed the entire country so that there was no way of escaping the tangle.

She stuck it out, month after month, hoping that something would happen to make life worth living again and then, in a chintzy hotel room in the small market town near

Stevie's Yorkshire station, she suddenly ran out of patience. Either Stephen accepted the opportunity she had made for him of escaping from this life and re-entering a world where one had access to civilized diversions, or she would call a truce to the marriage at least for the duration and possibly forever.

It was not a lighthearted decision. In her own deliberate way she had loved him ever since he had whisked her away from that dreary cathedral close and through the years of their rackety marriage she had been faithful to him, although she had her suspicions that the same could not be said of him. She thought of herself as modern and broadminded, however, and was not disposed to worry about an occasional peccadillo on the part of a lusty young man if, as she had rightly assumed, he was anchored by more important ties. He had always looked to her for stability and she did not fail him after arriving at the conclusion that he was under the spell of those glittering little machines and the mystique of the comradeship he found in the mess. He needed, she felt to be hauled outside of the magic circle and she knew, or thought she knew, exactly how this could be achieved. On the excuse of visiting her parents she made a tour of pre-war contacts, visiting two knights (both former scrap merchants), a Cabinet Minister, and a nameless millionaire allegedly responsible for the flow of aluminium into every aircraft factory in the country. The result was more encouraging than she had hoped. At the stroke of a pen and the rustle of a few papers Stephen could walk out of the R.A.F. camp in the time it took him to get his clearance chit, and become a civilian with prospects of not only making money but scooping up postwar honours. When she had things nicely arranged she went to him with her plan.

To her amazement and disgust he turned it down flat, and even laughed at her for making such a grotesque proposal.

He had never realised that the quietly-spoken Archdeacon's daughter he had married back in 1934 could bring herself to utter the words and phrases she used with such fluency when she had recovered from the shock of being brushed aside like a child offering a bankrupt father the contents of her piggy-bank.

He had just returned from what, in his ridiculous language, he described as "circuits-and-bumps", and had apparently acquitted himself well for he bawled naughty R.A.F. ditties as he soaped himself in the bath. She went in and sat on a cork-topped stool looking down at what, once again, struck her as a captain of football tubbing himself after a successful match. He did not look his age, or anywhere near his age, which she knew to be old for flying duties. He said, in the irritating fashion of his clodhopping father, "Hullo, old girl? Spruce yourself up. Big do tonight! Chaps from Four-One-Eleven coming over for a binge. Foregathering at The Mitre. The popsie behind the bar has laid on off-the-ration wallop!"

"You'll be far too busy for that," she said, and handed him a towel and two letters. One letter bore the House of Commons imprint. He glanced at them casually and then, half-leaping out of the water, with a squint of dismay.

It was clear from his expression that he only half understood the portent of the documents. He said at length, "What the blazes *is* this, old girl? Put me in the picture, will you?" and she said the letters, presented in the right quarters, would result in his immediate discharge to industry.

He looked at her as if she had said something obscene, saying "Come again?" and when she shrugged, "But where did you *get* them? How did they arrive?"

She said, still patiently, "They didn't arrive, Stevie. I did the rounds, saw the right people, and there they are!"

He was being, she thought, extraordinarily obtuse. He looked at the papers again, then at her and finally said, "But this is crazy! I couldn't go along with this! What gave you the idea that I might?"

He looked very foolish squatting there naked, half in and half out of the bath, his extravagant moustache bisecting his sunburned face, his mouth slightly open. She felt like a mother who had just informed a thirteen-year-old son of the consequence of some juvenile folly, raiding a neighbour's orchard perhaps, or breaking somebody's greenhouse with a cricket ball. She said, quietly, "Well it's done now, so you'll just have to make the best of it. In the end you'll thank me for it, for at least you'll stay alive. It's a pity some of the others haven't got wives to take the necessary steps!"

He put the letters aside and continued to gape at her. "But you're off your chump, old girl! You must be! Clean off your chump!"

It might have been the "old girl" that did it. Only since he had moved into this circle had he reverted to the patronising form of address, borrowed from his father. In the past he

34

had used slang phrases when addressing her but they had been more flattering. "Glam" was one, and "Kid" was another. She had never liked them but had put up with them for they signified nothing worse than delayed adolescence. Now she snapped, "For Jesus Christ's sake stop calling me 'old girl'! I've told you before and I'll not tell you again! Get your silly clothes on, go and see that hearty C.O. of yours and tell him what's happened."

"But it hasn't happened!" he protested, as pitifully as a boy falsely accused of cheating, "it hasn't happened, and it's bloody well not going to happen! Do you think I could crawl out by the back door while this show is still going full blast? God Almighty, I'd sooner ... sooner be *grounded!* You've got a damned nerve, old girl, going to these lengths behind my back and I'll tell you something you've overlooked. Those letters are only so much bumph until I apply for a discharge back to industry. Nobody can hook me back to Civvy Street without my signature on a lot more bumph, and I can't see me letting myself in for that!"

"Letting yourself in for what? For doing a real job of work and doing it in comfort? For living a civilised life among civilised people, instead of holing-up in places like this where you never meet anyone but a knock-kneed old waiter, a Brylcream Boy, or one of their synthetic little wives? There's nothing disgraceful in making armaments instead of using them, is there? God knows what might result from you being a civilian today and in your line of business! Sit and think about it a moment if you have to, but it shouldn't take you long to weigh the money and risks you're taking now against what those two letters represent."

Suddenly he remembered he was naked and at a disadvantage. He draped a towel round his middle and trailed after her into the bedroom. Outside, across the patch of sky seen between the oh-so-gay curtains, a trainer plane chugged slowly from east to west. His eye followed it and when it disappeared he sat down on a mock antique chair that was too low for him.

"Let's get this clear, Monica," he said, talking slowly and carefully, like a man anxious to give an impression of sobriety. "I'm in for the duration, and flying for as long as I can wangle it. At thirty-plus I had a hell of a job to get this far and I'm not putting on civvies again until it's all over. You can pull what strings you like, you won't get me budged! A

35

trained pilot is worth a damned sight more than a trained civvy, no matter what you hear from the civvies you've been touting!"

"You mean this kind of life is to go on indefinitely? For both of us?"

"What's wrong with it? What's happened to you all of a sudden?"

"You think it is all-of-a-sudden?"

He looked at her with a degree of patience, noting the set of her mouth, the hardness of her blue eyes, and deciding that they were a bit too blue, like the inner core of an oxy-acetylene flame. It struck him then that she was and always had been a woman who would go her own way regardless of ties and loyalties and at the same time he made another disconcerting discovery. She had hated every minute of the time she had spent following him round from camp to camp and he must have been blind not to have realised it months ago, when he and Andy and Andy's wife had been living it up in the local pubs and jaunting about on fiddled petrol between operations and courses. He said quietly, "Can't you *begin* to look at it from my point of view?"

"No," she said, "and I'm not trying any more. Either you take advantage of this opportunity or I'm off!"

He was astonished in spite of himself. He was also incredulous. "You mean we split up? Just like that! For good?"

"If necessary, yes. In your own silly language I've had it! Right up to here," and she raised a well-manicured forefinger level with her chin.

He said quietly, "Okay, Monica. Then that's how it'll have to be until you come to your senses."

He seemed to have succeeded in surprising her for she turned pale and clenched her fists as though she would have liked to beat reason into him. Then, bracing herself, she returned to the attack. *"Senses!"* she screamed. *"Senses!* Who's talking about sense? You're a grown man, or I once thought you were. Do you imagine the life we've been leading since 1939 makes any sense to me? Or to anyone else except those bloody fools in fancy dress out there, risking their lives every day for a gesture? They're phonies! The biggest phonies I've ever met, pretending they're making the most tremendous sacrifices when real sacrifices are being made by overworked little clerks doing a day's chores on a rasher of bloody spam and a tin of pilchards. Christ, you

36

make me vomit, the whole damned lot of you, with your squadron scoreboards, and all that mumbo-jumbo you use to convince one another you're a race apart. Talk about the Germans seeing themselves as Herrenvolk! You people are a damned sight worse than the Nazis. You're steeped in self-deception without even knowing it. I could understand it in kids about nineteen, with the candle marks still on their backsides, but you and Andy, and all those other married men in that mess over there, you're old enough to recognize it for what it is, for something people will feed to red-nosed comedians at the end of the pier after the war. If you don't understand this at your age you never will, so to hell with it all! I'll give you five minutes to get your clothes on and go over to that camp with these letters. If you don't then I'm going, and if you want to get in touch with me you can do it through my solicitors."

He was appalled at her vehemence and protested, "But good God, old girl, we can't just break up like that . . ." but she cut him short with a sweep of her arm that came close to overturning the bedside light.

"We can and damned well will," she said. "I packed a case thinking you would get a forty-eight hour pass to fix things up but if I go out of here alone I go for good, understand?"

He did not look foolish now so much as drunk and drained of the power of decision. He sat looking across at her as she dragged her night case and vanity case out of the wardrobe, flung them on the bed and then shrugged herself into her leopardskin coat. Overhead more aircraft zoomed towards the runway and downstairs a tiny gong was beaten for the evening meal. To Monica the sounds were the knell of their past and future. She said, cramming on her hat, "Well? You still think I'm bluffing?"

"I don't know what the hell to think unless you're tight." he answered. "You've been talking cock ever since you came in, flapping those damn silly papers under my nose. Dammit, I've never thought of myself as having much upstairs, but I've got far more than to do what you're asking me to do! Now for God's sake let's both have a drink and . . ."

He stopped because she had walked out and he sprang in pursuit, not realising he was naked until he reached the stairhead and saw her walk into the circle of light thrown on the first landing by the miserable 25-watt bulb. Then, feeling more deflated than he had ever felt in his life, he rushed

37

back to the bedroom and pulled on his trousers and greatcoat, but on recrossing the threshold he stopped, recollecting that there was no main line train to York until half-past-seven and that he would have plenty of time to dress and pursue her to the station. He rang down for a large whisky that was brought up by the hotel's sole waiter, a man who moved as if he had served drinks to officers home from the Crimea. Stevie called him "George". He called all waiters George and had done, long before the R.A.F. made so free with the name.

"When you go down hold the taxi, George," he said, "I want it to take me to the station," but George said, in the deferential voice he had used to address young hunting bucks who met at the pub before the airfield was built, "Madam took it, sir, and it can't make the return journey to York in less than an hour. Would you like me to find out if Mr. Armitage's hack is free?"

"No, scrub it," Stevie said, and finished his whiskey at a gulp.

When George had creaked away he sat on the bed a long time, racking his brains over what event or chain of events could have led to such an extraordinary scene and wondering if it had anything to do with his current flirtation with a W.A.A.F. parachute-packer called Gwen. He thought not or Gwen's name would certainly have been flung into the dispute at one point or another and besides, so far, he had not taken Gwen to bed and had not even intended to. He wondered then if Monica's outburst had its origin in nervous strain due to the possibility of him crashing, but again he ruled a line through the supposition. Monica had been sharing living-out billets with him when he had been on daily operations and had never shown a flicker of nervousness, so that occasionally he saw other men's wives looking at her in a curious, half-envious way. Margaret, on the other hand, had been a bag of nerves, and had once shamed Andy by bursting into tears in the middle of a flap, but now that he thought about it he had never seen Monica shed a tear on his behalf or anyone else's, so that it followed, to some extent, that she meant what she said about being browned off with the role of camp-follower. Even so, her furious tactics, indeed, her overall strategy, continued to astound him. She must have been planning this back-door exit for weeks and it obviously hadn't occurred to her that he would reject a discharge to industry out of hand, not from reasons of patriotism but simply because a life that kept a man at a desk whilst such things were happening was not to be thought of, not even objectively. "She doesn't understand," he told himself, aloud, "and she's *never* bloody well understood."

He sat there drinking a large gin (the whisky had run out and George murmured that he was privileged to get the gin), thinking back over various aspects of their association, but although he recalled many occasions when she had seemed out of it at a party, or homesick for a place of her own, he could recall nothing that might have warned him that he was sitting on a land-mine; and the devil of it was he still hadn't the least idea what to do about it now that it had exploded. He supposed she would write, or he would write, and she might even 'phone, although not in her present mood. Normally he would have carried his troubles to Andy but Andy was a thousand miles away, fiddling about over Sidi Barrani or Mersa Matruh. He had plenty of friends on the station but none who were more than casually acquainted with Monica, and then he remembered that Andy's wife had gone back to nursing somewhere in town after his twin had been posted overseas and that Margaret, whom he had always liked for her amiability and the Celtic lilt in her voice, had known Monica intimately and might, conceivably, come up with an answer. He was a man of quick decisions both on the ground and above it and within minutes of getting Margaret's address he was 'phoning her number. The bell seemed to ring a long time and he had almost given up hope when the burr ceased and Margaret's voice said, "Who's there, now?"

He was delighted, not only because he could now unload his troubles on someone but also because, in the sharply rising note of the last word, he could picture her, a small, kittenish woman, with a shade too much of this and that here and there, but a feminity that Monica lacked, despite her good figure and impeccable taste in clothes. He said, "Margy? It's Steve. Look, I've got to talk to you. Something's happened. No, not a damn thing to do with Andy, to do with me and Monica. She's just walked out. Blew her top. Made me feel like something the cat's brought in! No, not a row, at least, not one I started. She's gone loco! She's been hawking me all over the ruddy auction. She got Monteith-Parkinson and God knows who else, to fix an industrial discharge for me. And when I told her to get knotted she said it was Civvy Street or else, just like that!"

He waited, giving her time as he thought to absorb the shock, but when she spoke she seemed no more than mildly surprised and even a little amused. She said, "Well now, where's she gone? Home to mother?"

"How the hell do I know where she's gone? She took a taxi to York and that's all I know. She surely wouldn't be fool enough to go back to the Archdeacon. He's church-militant and would soon send her packing if she shot the line she shot to me! The point is, *why!* I mean, what have I done for Christ's sake? No, there's no other Judy, cross my heart. If there was I could make some kind of sense out of it. Well damn it, what a bloody silly question. Of course I want her back! It's bad enough being stuck on an F.T.U. up this ruddy desert without having to sleep at the mess. Besides, she talked as if it was for good unless I agree to go back to Civvy Street!"

"When are you due for leave, Stevie?"

"Not until the course is finished but I could get a crafty forty-eight if I played my cards right."

Margaret laughed and the ripple that reached him brought some kind of sanity back into the evening. She said, reasonably, "Then you'd better play them, come to town and have a long talk with Auntie Margaret. You could take me out to a dinner and show. I'd love that, I've had no male company for months, except the odd Yank at the Embassy, and they're so *bad* at it! Pawing, I mean, and working overtime at being masculine."

"I'll put in for a forty-eight tomorrow. Right now I'm going to get plastered. Before I do tho', did you ever have the idea she might fly off the handle like this?"

"Yes," Margaret said, "I think I did, Stevie, but it isn't the kind of thing I can discuss on the 'phone. Hold on— tomorrow's Wednesday—ring this number lunch-time Friday and I'll try and meet the train."

He scribbled the number on the back of his identity card and rang off, already feeling a great deal better. Quarrelling didn't come easily to him. Such disputes as had cropped up in the past had been adequately handled by Andy, the more aggressive of the two. Now that he had told somebody he could begin to relax and make some kind of attempt to come to terms with Monica's extraordinary conduct. Whistling

40

tunelessly he dressed, went downstairs and across the blacked-out town to The Mitre. He forgot that he hadn't eaten and when he was roused by George at seven the next morning he had no appetite for anything except a pick-me-up laced with Worcester sauce.

III

He did not see her in the crush at the barrier and had resigned himself to waiting in a telephone kiosk queue to ring the hospital when a knot of sailors, toting enormous kit bags, moved aside to reveal her standing alone outside the buffet, legs planted astride, hands clasped behind her back, her smile asking him to join her in a parody of the military turmoil of the platform with its aimless swirl of blue, navy-blue and khaki. To Stevie she looked like the last pre-war woman alive.

She gave him a couple of sisterly kisses but her gesture in holding on to his hand, and pressing it hard against her breast, told him at once how much she was missing Andy, and how genuinely pleased she was to see him. Stevie was not an intuitive man but there wasn't much you could teach him about affectionate women. He was flattered to note that she had gone to some pains to dress for him, for he had expected her to be wearing a coif and one of those dramatic cloaks nurses wear when they snatch an hour or two from the wards. She had never had Monica's taste but today he was glad of it. She was her old self, half jazzy, half svelte, with a hairstyle that was manifestly a copy of Veronica Lake's "peek-a-boo", one hazel eye almost masked by a shining husk of hair that swept across her cheek and ended defiantly under a small, dimpled chin. He said, "By God, Margy, it's a joy to look at you! Barring Monica every Judy I've seen in three months has been a compromise between a wardress and a musical-comedy bandsman. Where do we celebrate?"

"I'm off until six a.m. tomorrow," she said. "I swopped duties with a staff nurse. It cost me thirty bob. It took a world war to make me understand the real value of money!"

"What the hell made you go back to nursing?" he asked, chuckling. "You didn't have to. Andy told you to keep the Birmingham flat going. It couldn't have been the bombing or you wouldn't have come here."

41

"I was bored and I didn't fancy joining anything and being bawled at by one of those horse-faced daughters of the Empire. Besides, nursing was the only thing I knew. You remember how Andy abducted me from a hospital, don't you?"

He hadn't remembered but he did now. They had both been involved in a road crash in South Wales and Andy had been detained with a rib fracture. Later he had returned to the hospital and whisked her from under an outraged sister's nose, and Monica had thought it all rather silly and common, until she realised how completely Andy was bewitched by this droll little Welsh girl. She got used to her, however, for Andy had seen to that and so, in a less direct way, had Stephen himself, for he had never underestimated the value of her cheerfulness that offset, to a great extent, Monica's starchiness and Andy's occasional sulks. Until now he had never thought of her as anything more than a woman who was pretty and companionable, and he realised that this was because, without actually giving offence, Monica had always contrived to downgrade her into the shop-girl class. She said, as they hailed a taxi, "Don't unload now, Stevie, wait until we've got a meal inside us. I'll take you to a joint the Americans use in Soho. All the places you once knew are blitzed or closed up. It isn't easy to eat in town nowadays, you have to know the right people and pay the right price."

He was surprised by her newly-acquired sophistication and wondered where she had found it. Was it the company of civvies she hd taken up with since Andy had sailed away, and if so, did she do more than flirt with them? He decided that it wasn't his business and also that she was entitled to make the best of a bad job in this drab ruin of a city.

He had forgotten how heavily the Luftwaffe had plastered London in the winter of '40-'41, and the sight of rosebay willow herb growing in clumps on piles of rubble made him wonder if Bomber Command was doing the same to Hamburg, Dusseldorf and Cologne. He doubted it for, so far, the attacks were largely experimental and the night offensive had hardly got into its stride. He said, "You haven't had any bombing in a long time, have you?" and she told him not since the big fire-bomb attack of May last year and that Londoners were very pro-Russian on that account. Then she said, squeezing his hand, "Don't let's go on talking about the old war, Stevie! I can see Monica's point, you know, it is a fearful bore, although I don't see why she had to take it out on you." She leaned forward and called through the glass panel, "Turn right here, then first left! It's called '*Lune de Paris*'," she went on, "although God knows why! It's run by a crafty bunch of Cypriots!" and then she sat back rather heavily somehow contriving to half sit on his knee so that he thought again, with an inward laugh, "She's a sexy little bitch! I wonder if she'll tell me a pack of lies about what she does in her off-duty moments?" and they left the taxi and entered a café where the tables were already laid for dinner.

The food was good by wartime standards and Margaret told him that the owner had extensive black market contacts in Smithfield and who could blame him for using them? Everybody had to eat and could hardly be expected to survive on spam indefinitely. "You can bet they don't down among the cornfields," she added gaily, "I'll warrant Paul and Claire and the rest of them back in the Valley go to bed on something more substantial than powdered egg and mouse-trap cheese."

"Claire and others might," he said thoughtfully, "but I can't see the Old Man using the black market. He's too damned self-righteous for that!"

"I like him," Margaret said, unexpectedly, "I always have, from the moment Andy first took me there. Did you know that?"

"No," he said, pleased with the admission, "I don't think I did. I suppose I thought you took the Old Man for granted like the rest of us. What is it you like about him?"

She considered. "His honesty and singlemindedness. That place of his, that funny little Valley, it's the whole of him and always has been, and I can understand how a man would feel about land he owns. That's the Celt in me I suppose, even though I'm South-Walesian and that isn't the same any more. But my Granfer came from Merionethshire, and that's about as far Welsh as you can get. Not a soul speaks English up there and they still look on you ruffians as invaders." She paused a moment and looked down at her empty plate, so that he thought she was remembering Wales but she wasn't for when she looked up and smiled she said, "He knows exactly where he's going and so does Claire and that's rare these days, Stevie."

It was strange hearing her talk like this about his mother and father, for he rarely gave either one of them a thought, except as a couple of affectionate, sporting old stick-in-the-muds, nose-deep in the remote provinces and surrounded by a horde of chawbacons who used a lingo that was standard dialogue between a comedian and his bucolic feed posing as one of the audience. He said, suddenly, "Why don't you go back there, Margy? They'd be delighted to have you for the duration!" but she shook her head, saying, "Ah no! No, no! You and Andy and Monica spoiled me for that kind of thing. There's no going back, man!" and before he could question this curious pronouncement she asked if she could have a cognac and he watched her sip it, remembering that in pre-war days she had had to be coaxed to take a second gin and Italian. She said briskly, "How about that Coward Show? Gaspard could get tickets. Over the odds, of course. Are you flush?"

He asked her if they would take a cheque and she said this was easily arranged, Gaspard, the waiter, padding away like a Mediterranean pimp and returning ten minutes later with the promise of two rear stalls for *Blithe Spirit* that had been drawing London for months. "You've got the hang of things at last, Margy," he said, "and Andy would be proud of you." Then, realising that it was after seven o'clock and that he had yet to book in at an Officers' Club in Piccadilly, he said, "I haven't told you a damned thing about Monica's blitzkrieg!"

"It'll keep," she said, lightly, "we're here to relax and you don't have to trail around finding a bed. I've got a perfectly comfortable couch in the flat I share with Henrietta, who works at the Yank Embassy, and you can use it whenever you're in town. Now give me a minute to fix myself and ask Gaspard to find a taxi. There's no sense in walking when you can ride. One of Andy's dictums, remember?"

As he sat waiting for her to rejoin him he began to wonder about her again, pondering her sudden switches from brittle small talk to flashes of nostalgia in which Andy, his parents, and even the Shallowford Valley were involved, almost as though she was putting up a front to prevent her real mood showing through. There was not much doubt in his mind that she was on edge, or that prolonged separation from Andy was having its effect upon nerves already frayed by the Battle of Britain. When she reappeared, however, he thought she looked prettier and saucier than ever and her lively mood persisted right through the comedy and afterwards when they roamed the dark streets in search of a taxi to take them to

44

her flat on the second floor of a tall, Victorian building behind Smith Street. "It's handy to the hospital," she explained, as she fumbled for the key, "I can pop back here whenever I get an odd spell off duty. There used to be three of us but Vera got a commission in the A.T.S. and now there's only me and Henrietta. It costs us all getting on for a fiver a week. There's silliness for you. I only earn about half that, for ten hours a day on my flat feet!"

They groped their way up the broad staircase in the light of the bluish hall-bulb and she told him to wait on the landing while she fixed up the blackout. "We've got a Nazi air-raid warden round here," she said. "He calls up the riot squad every time he sees a sliver of light at a range of two feet! There, that's done. What'll you drink? I've got pretty well anything, Henrietta gets it from somewhere but I don't ask whether it's given, bought or earned!"

She brought him a large brandy and another for herself. The flat was comfortably furnished with large, heavy pieces of the kind one might expect to find in a town house owned by one of the Forsytes. It was still spacious in spite of being divided in two by a new-looking partition. In addition to a large living-room and an untidy kitchen there was a twin-bedded room cluttered with feminine odds and ends. "We don't do much housework as you can see," she told him. "We've got a Mrs. Mop who comes in once a week but its a terrible slut she is and tiddly most of the time."

"Won't Henrietta object to me parking myself in here?" he asked, when she brought out sheets and blankets and laid them on the leather couch in the bay window.

"Not her! She's not the conventional type. One or other of her boy friends is here every weekend but if she brings one back tonight he'll have to curl up on the hearth rug." She slumped down in the deep armchair after turning on the gas-fire. "I feel all cosy inside," she proclaimed. "It's the nicest evening I've had since Andy's embarkation leave. I'm jolly glad Monica ran out on you!"

She looked at him with speculative amusement, shooting her legs at the red glow of the gas-fire and cuddling her brandy glass as though it was a kitten. "Now tell me your troubles and see that you don't leave anything out."

He told her the truth as he saw it, describing the scene in the hotel bedroom in detail and his overall relationship with Monica in the last few months.

45

"It all sounds so casual," she said, frowning, "just a matter of using one another. It was never like that with Andy and me, not since the beginning," and before he could probe this unblushing announcement, she went on, "Do you think there *is* somebody else after all?"

He said, irritably, "Damn it, Margy, I told you over the blower ..." but she cut him short, saying, "I don't mean another woman, idiot. I mean another *man!*"

It was a possibility that had not even occured to him and now that it did it seemed almost an affront to contemplate the fastidious Monica climbing into bed with a stranger.

"No, that's way off target!" he said, "and if you think about her a minute you'll know it is! I haven't been one hundred per cent angelic but I'll bet the Bank of England she has. Not out of regard for me but because she's so damned hygienic."

"That's so," she admitted, with a kind of reluctance, "and for another thing she'd never have the nerve. She probably means exactly what she says about staying away until you change your mind. Will you? As time goes on and things get stickier?"

"How the hell can I? How would it look to the Top Brass? Just one more L.M.F. using the back door!"

"What's an L.M.F.?"

" 'Lack of Moral Fibre'. A crack-up. It happens now and again, particularly in Bomber Command."

He got up and began pacing up and down, "You're missing Andy, aren't you, Margy?"

"Like hell I am."

"Me too. I was thinking, this is the first time we've ever been parted. We've always done the same things and wanted to do them at the same moment. We had a hell of a lot of fun in the old days, the four of us." He stopped pacing and looked down at her. "Did you ever really like Monica?"

"No," she said, "and she didn't like me, but I put up with her for your sake." She looked at him speculatively for a moment. "Come to that, were *you* all that smitten? It always looked to me as if she married you and then woke up to the fact that she had married two men, not one."

It was, he thought, a very shrewd assessment but he was not prepared to admit it, or not yet. "That's cock," he grumbled, "Monica and I hit it off until she got these bloody silly ideas about Service life. She wasn't upstage when she was in bed!"

"No," Margaret said, "I can believe that. The snooty type usually aren't. But you don't live in bed, do you?"

She seemed to dismiss the subject and reached out to turn on the radio. Light music dribbled from the set, one of the current morale-boosters about the white cliffs of Dover. She said, kicking off her shoes, "I'm a bit tight, Stevie. I keep feeling giggly and then maudlin and anyway, I've got to be out of here by five-thirty tomorrow. I'd better turn in now. I'll brew you a cup of tea and kiss you good-bye in the morning!"

"Kiss me now," he said, for some reason feeling immensely grateful to her.

"Not likely! I've had half a bottle of Burgundy and three brandies and I can't hold liquor like you and Andy. If I felt your arms round me you'd have to put me to bed in a straight jacket!" She lifted her hand and walked, with deliberate steadiness, into the bedroom, continuing to talk to him through the open door as he made up his couch. "Don't open the windows no matter how stuffy it gets! You can't do it without taking the blackout down and that A.R.P. whipper-snapper will be hammering at the door in five seconds flat." He heard her yawn and stumble. "Are you all right, Margy?" She didn't answer so he finished making his shakedown and looked in at the open door. Her clothes were strewn about the floor and she was already asleep with the bedside light still burning. He crossed over to switch it off and looked down on her, noting her pleasing chubby face, fresh complexion, and that absurd peek-a-boo hair-do. He thought, glumly, "Old Andy always did know what he was doing, the lucky old sod!"

He awoke with a start, blinking into the blackness of the big room and seeing nothing but hearing, close at hand, a rhythmical sniffing, like someone tormented by a running cold. The couch, big as it was, did not accommodate him and he had cramp in one leg. It was cold and very still. No sound came from outside, only the long, regular sniffs from close at hand. He sat up, hitching the blankets about his shoulders. "Is that you, Margy?" and when he thought he heard a mumble between the sniffs, he said, "Hold on, I'll turn on the

47

light." but she said, urgently, "*No*, Stevie! Leave the light be," and he waited, puzzled and mildly apprehensive.

"What is it? Don't you feel so good?" and when the sniffs moderated and there was a short silence, "Is it Andy? Can't you cope, Margy?"

Then she was beside him and he felt her bare shoulders under his hand. She was wearing no dressing-gown, just a flimsy silk nightdress and suddenly he felt a terrible compassion for her as he might have felt for a child left out in the dark and the rain.

He dragged a blanket from the couch, threw it over her shoulders and held her close to him. "Don't mind me," he said, "if you want to snivel all night snivel and be done with it!" and he sat there feeling deeply moved by her helplessness and wondering, with part of his mind, where her flat-mate was and what conclusion she would be likely to draw from the pair of them huddling under a blanket at three o'clock on a winter's morning.

Presently the sniffs ceased but she did not move away. He could feel her hair against his face and the simple perfume she used reminded him, improbably, of summer in the Valley when he was a boy crossing Shallowford Woods on his cob. She was that kind of person he decided and had never been otherwise, despite their years of racketing about the fashionable resorts of the Continent and the cities of the North and Midlands. She didn't belong in cities but somewhere like that place in Wales she had mentioned. She was more akin to his mother than to Monica, someone who needed open spaces, country scents, plenty of good food and a big, hearty husband who threw her about and shared her primitive instincts. In a way she had always been the odd one out of the quartette, stringing along for Andy's sake and for his, sensing the strength of the link between two men emerging from the same womb within seconds of one another. She was worth, he thought, about ten Monicas, providing you had the sense to value her in real currency.

"I'll put the kettle on and brew some coffee," he said, but she reached out and held him, holding the blanket closely about them so that it would have needed a determined effort on his part to get up from the couch.

"You told me about you and Monica," she said presently, "but you don't know about me. I woke up and felt frightened, frightened about everything, Steve. You've got to help

48

me! I can't go on like this any longer and it's better you than just anybody, you understand?"

He didn't, or if he did he did not bring himself to believe the implications of her appeal. "You can talk," he said, "you can tell me any damn thing you like if it helps."

"It does," she said, "it helps more than you know! I can't face not having someone all that time. I knew I couldn't a few days after Andy left but I stuck it out as long as I could, longer than I could, you understand now? Then I went on the bottle and that helped for a time but later on it only made things worse. Last Christmas there was a man—Johnny, a medical student—and after him another, a Yank from the Embassy, someone Henrietta brought home. I felt awful about it afterwards and wanted to do myself in. Can you believe that? I wanted to plug the windows and doors and turn on that gas-fire. I felt like doing it again the other night just before you rang. It was either that or go out and find a man. *Any* man! All these other wives, I don't know how they cope! Maybe they aren't made like me, or maybe they weren't rolled once a night by someone as lusty as Andy. Anyway, that's the way it is, and if you write me off as a nympho I wouldn't blame you. That's what I am I suppose, only, like I say, it wouldn't have seemed so bad if there had been more to it than just using someone, the way I used Johnny and that Yank. What I mean is, if either of them had meant a damn thing apart from their sex." She was silent a moment. "Do you want to smash my face in, Stevie?"

She asked him to judge her but he had no useful comment to make. She had made it all too clear that she had been fighting a losing battle with herself from the moment Andy's troopship sailed into the blue. Men didn't get leave from the Middle East. It might be years before she could lie in his arms again and it might be never. She just wasn't the kind of person who could sit hoping and longing and remembering, or pouring her feelings on to sheets of paper. Then he had another thought and it disturbed him more deeply than her confession. Clearly something had been expected of him last night, and equally clearly the flat-mate, Henrietta, wasn't likely to show up. He remembered the casual way she had invited him here and the way she had relaxed half on to his knee in the taxi. He remembered also that impulsive gesture at the station, when she had seized his hand and pressed it hard against her breasts, and after that the way she had punished the wine and the brandy and then suddenly blundered off to bed before she gave herself away. And now here was a snivelling admission that she had already been to bed with two other men, and, although ravaged by guilt, she was still ready to admit to her terrible need of them. "It's better you than just anybody," she had said, and this seemed to clinch the point and, what was worse, leave the decision to him. It was almost as though she thought of him as part of Andy, someone to whom she could turn without disloyalty, not only because he was Andy's twin but because they have always lived on top of one another, had gone everywhere and done everything together, and he wondered if any kind of case could be made out for either of them in these terms and whether, in fact, it was more treacherous or less treacherous on her part and his. He said, gruffly, "Last night . . . when we came back here . . . what did you expect, Margy?" and she said, "I don't know, I knew Henrietta wouldn't be back and just hoped, I suppose. That way I could have told myself I was only half to blame for whatever happened and anyway, I'm not pretending when I say I've always thought of you as one person. You are, and you always have been. That's why, the minute I woke up and thought about you in here, I had to come in and blurt it out."

"Is that all?" he said soberly. "You feel better now that I know about it?"

"In one way I do. I should have gone mad if I had kept it bottled up any longer but just seeing you, and hearing your voice is hell. I couldn't have got through last evening without all that drink."

His instinct was to shy away from involvement. He said, breathlessly, "This is crazy, Margy! God knows, I like you a lot, and always have, but you and me—how would it help? You'd feel even worse when I'd gone, and me . . . I'd see myself as the all-time bastard every time I thought of either you or Andy."

She said nothing but under the blanket he felt her body contract slightly and her withdrawal seemed to reaffirm that the decision was his and that she had emptied herself of blame simply by telling him about the medical student and the man from the Embassy. He understood this and resented it but there seemed nothing to be done about it. He said, bitterly, "You would feel that way, wouldn't you?"

"No," she said, and he was shocked by the steadiness of

her voice, "I wouldn't feel any way, except glad. Glad because it was you and not someone who was out looking for a randy woman!"

He wanted then to escape from the folds of the blanket and reject her with a laugh or a conventional gesture of sympathy. A sound like a groan escaped him and, without in the least moderating his yearning for her, anger rose level with pity. She knew what he was going through but she didn't help him, and he knew that it was not from lack of sympathy on her part but because these last few months had robbed her of the power to make an emotional decision.

He had no idea how long they sat there, her head on his shoulder, her body inclined to him by the angle of the couch and the folds of the shared blanket, but presently she said, in the same emptied voice, "Anyway, Andy won't come back. I knew that the day we said good-bye at Chester Station, and he went off to that Personnel Despatch Centre. Maybe it was knowing it that made me act the way I did. I don't know, I don't know a damn thing any more, except that everything is going to pieces and only you being around keeps me from wanting to pack it in."

Her fatalistic acceptance of Andy's death, and the despair inherent in her voice frightened him as he had never been frightened by physical risks he faced almost every day of his life. He said, helplessly, "For Christ's sake, Margy—don't talk like that . . ." but suddenly she threw aside the blanket and moved away from the couch so that he thought she was crossing the room for the drink he so badly needed. He soon realised otherwise. She had returned to the bedroom leaving the door wide open and switched on her bedside light. He called, furiously, "Get something on and for God's sake let's both have a drink!"

"I don't want any more to drink," she said, quietly. "If you do, help yourself."

There was silence for a moment as he made a great effort of will to get up, pour himself a stiff brandy, drink it and get to hell out of the place before she would move within reach again but suddenly she reappeared in the doorway, the light behind her, so that she might as well have been naked. That way, he thought, she looked exactly as he had just imagined her without clothes, her limbs plump, rounded and nicely proportioned, so that he suddenly thought of his wife's figure as angular and without promise. She stood there perfectly

51

still, looking across at him without a flicker of embarrassment or apology. Then she said, very levelly, "In for a penny in for a pound! That was another of Andy's dictums, remember? Come in, man, and lock the damned door behind you!" and she shrugged herself out of her nightdress and climbed slowly into bed.

She had to shake him when she brought in the tea and he opened his eyes astonished to see her wearing that identical scarlet-lined cloak he had expected to see at the station. There was no hint in her manner or expression of the hysteria of less than three hours ago and when she addressed him by name she might have been hailing him on the beach at Deauville where he and Andy and Monica were sunbathing while she wandered off to fiddle with one of those idiotic little machines that accounted for her loose change wherever they went.

"I'm going now, Stevie. You take your time. You've nothing to get up for, have you now?"

"No," he said, "nothing" and then, as he took the cup a little of her tranquillity passed to him and he looked at her with a kind of awe that acknowledged her ability to solve her problems so swiftly and resolutely. He opened his mouth to say something but she lifted her hand and pushed a playful finger against his lips. "No inquest," she said. "When do you have to go back?"

"I'm due in camp at 0800 hours tomorrow and it'll mean catching the 1:30 a.m. from King's Cross. Will you be back in time?"

"I'll see that I am," she said, "and don't bother about Henrietta. She's off on a dirty weekend of her own. King's Lynn I think she said. She won't be here until tomorrow night. Goodbye now. There's cornflakes and a few rashers in the 'fridge. Milk too if you want to make yourself coffee." She bent and kissed him on the mouth and as she drew away she gave a little giggle. "You're plastered with lipstick," she said, "and you look like the broken-hearted clown! Don't worry! It's done and it'll stay done, so make the best of it before everything goes bang!"

It is just possible that Monica, married to Andrew instead of Stevie, might have become reconciled to the life of an R.A.F. camp-follower.

Most people, both in the Valley and out of it, thought of The Pair as interchangeable but Claire for one had always known they were not. There was a fanatical streak in Andy that reminded her of Paul and was entirely lacking in his twin. Both had been unspectacular scholars at school but once they were launched into the scrap world old Franz Zorndorff had soon recognised the complementary contributions each could make to his business concerns. Stevie had charm and an amiability capable of conjuring a profit from the crustiest dealer and the fields in which he operated, cozening, bribing, softening up prospects, were bars or clubs. Andy showed himself more adept at mastering the economics of the trade and later, when they became fliers, he was able to pay the same address to the scientific aspects of aerial warfare. With Stevie, at least up to the moment he flew a bomber on operations, the war in the air had been little more than a lark. Technicalities bored him, even though he never had much difficulty in absorbing enough of them to make him an average pilot, but Andy soon outgrew their initial approach to flying and became deeply interested in the slow build-up of tactical skills as opposed to the hit-and-miss approach of the dashing amateurs who filled the gaps made in professional cadres by the Battle of France and the Battle of Britain. With the development of this more objective attitude some of the natural exuberance left over from his youth departed, enabling him, to an extent, to regard the extravagances of the R.A.F. façade in much the same light as his down-to-earth sister-in-law. He did not crumple his cap. He did not use much slang. And he had no personal animosity against the enemy, thinking of him as he had once thought of schoolmasters and rival scrap dealers, people there to be outwitted, tragets for his ingenuity and daring.

When fighter aircraft became more sophisticated his appetite for concerted and preconceived action grew with every sortie. He operated less and less as a well-mounted buck in the hunting field and more and more like a seasoned boxer, fighting his way towards a world title. He was in line for promotion now and, as he himself would have put it, intended to keep his nose clean. As a squadron-leader he would have some sort of say in tactics and could progress from the dogsbody stage to ranks where he might be given a chance to put some of his theories to work.

Out here, in the Western Desert, the tempo of the aerial war was very different from the comparatively slapdash days of British-based operations in 1940 and early '41. Squadron scores and squadron casualties were more moderate and combats were by no means as frequent as over the Kentish Weald and the Channel. To an extent, despite the ceaseless sway of armies between the Qattara Depression and Bengha-zi, the contest had settled down. Andy, based in the region of the Ruweisat Ridge, east of Alexandria, was now flying every day, escorting coastal convoys or, once Rommel had launched his May offensive, the Blenheim bombers raiding enemy supply dumps and occasionally he tangled with a Stuka. In June of that year he got his first confirmed kill, a JU 88 lumbering into Tobruk after its surrender. Two days after that he shot out of the sun and killed a Stuka. He watched, impersonally, as the maimed aircraft hurtled down in wide circles to explode on the brown emptied landscape below and then made for base, unable to try his luck at straffing lorries crawling along the coastal road because his ammunition supply was exhausted.

All through the final eastward heave of the Afrika Korps towards Egypt he was happily engaged in this kind of ploy, peeling off and following his leader down to shoot up trans-port, tanks and self-propelled 80 mm guns. The overall prog-ress of the war, or even the campaign did not concern him. He concentrated on the immediate task and gave hardly a thought to his wife, to his brother Stevie, or to the future once this fascinating period of his life should end. He did not contemplate death either, despite the occasional failure of a messmate to return from a sweep across the great blue and white bowl of the sky enclosing this featureless desert. Some-times when he was alone up there he would give expression to the sheer exhilaration of flying by mouthing some dance tune of the past, when he, Stevie and their wives had zoomed about Britain and the Continent in one or other of their many fast cars and although he could not hear himself sing, the rhythm of a 'thirties tune would conjure up a fleeting picture of Margaret's chubby face puckered with laughter. The thing that sometimes puzzled him was that he no longer felt a physical need for women and he had once raised this subject with the unit M.O., who set about reassuring him with the paternal earnestness of the family G.P. In Andy's view the man talked nonsense. The fact was the highly complex business of handling aircraft, and evolving new techniques satisfied his creative urge if there was such a thing outside a book. When Margaret was available he had enjoyed her undemanding company and taken a great deal of pleasure in possessing her but the current demands made upon his energy far transcended the demands of these pleasant trivialities and he had never been much of a letter writer. It would, in fact, have surprised him a good deal to be reminded that there had once been a time when the sight of her, dressed for a night out, had enlivened him sufficiently to spoil her make-up and send her back to the dressing-table uttering counterfeit protests in her lilting Welsh accent. Because of this he did not think it strange that little or no word of her reached him when the squadron post-corporal shouted, "Mail up!" Home now belonged in the past, before this demanding and wholly satisfying occupation translated him into a sensitive machine. Home had to do with contracts and bargaining, with bluff and a kind of second-rate espionage waged from behind desks and over the telephone. Somehow he could not see himself returning to it, any more than he could picture himself a farmer like his father. He flew into the sun, automatically noting the few landmarks and searching the vast brown wasteland for targets. To Andy Craddock, who all his life had been seeking outlets for his explosive energy and technical know-how, the war in the Western Desert was a legacy that had come his way when he was still young enough to profit by it.

One morning he did get a letter from Margaret but it told him very little, for something she had written about Stevie's whereabouts had been blocked out by the censor. She was thinking of giving up nursing, she said (he had forgotten she had returned to it), and hoped he was well. She had seen something of Stevie but nothing of Monica. She sent her love and missed him. That was about all and a less preoccupied man might have read an effort of composition into the note—for it was little more. He stuffed the letter in his pocket and ambled across the hard sand to watch his ground crew warm up his Hurricane. Today they were all taking a closer look at Rommel's build-up in the Mersa Matru area.

V

Far away to the east, where the brassy Indian sun beat down on the trim white buildings of a Sports Club some two hundred miles west of the Burma battlefront, another member of the Craddock family basked in the warmth of her own content.

Karen McClean who, as "Whiz" Craddock, had once carried off all the gymkhana prizes within a twenty-mile radius of the Valley, sunbathed her honey-coloured body beside the staff pool, contemplating the present with a smugness that discouraged close attention to the letter from her mother that had come in with the last mail. Claire Craddock was a gossipy letter writer once launched upon Valley topics, but it had never occurred to her, poor dear, that her daughter Whiz did not place the same importance on good harvests, or the enlistment in the Armoured Corps of a Valley craftsman's son. Whiz had been interested but unmoved by news that the Luftwaffe had demolished Periwinkle, killing Rachel, her sister-in-law, and Rachel's brother Harold, but she was not deeply concerned about the prospect of her sister Mary's eccentric husband's intention to forsake the land for the sea. Rumble Patrick, like most of the other Valley characters, had always struck her as a hobbledehoy and she had never regretted rejecting offers of marriage pressed upon her by farmers' sons and marrying Ian who had now secured a staff appointment and seemed destined to move into the upper echelons of the Service. Some people, Mary for instance, would consider Ian very dull, with his Scots caution and infinite attention to detail but he suited Whiz because, alone among the Craddock tribe, her personality was undiluted by sentiment. All her life, and she was approaching thirty now, she had observed the conventions and, within those conventions, excelled. Singlemindedness, plus an uncompromising rejection of anything loosely described as romantic, had brought her precisely the kind of success she sought at any one time. She had been acknowledged the most expert equestrienne in the Valley and, later, its most expert dancer if one discounted fancy steps. At twenty she had married and had spent her life on foreign stations, getting to know people likely to contribute to Ian's advance and shamelessly flattering the leathery wives of station commanders. She could manage house-servants with the easy competence of someone who had never had to grapple with the perverse independence of the Anglo-Saxon working-class and, as far as anyone could remember, she had never been seen to laugh, not even at an air commodore's joke. Ian McClean had a very great respect for her and secretly acknowledged the part she had played in his promotion to the undreamed of status of group captain but, being a Scot, he would have found it too embarrassing to have told her as much, any more than he could have found words to express satisfaction or otherwise with her recent announcement (made under cover of darkness) that she was pregnant. He must, on the whole, have been pleased however, for his approach to her became even more ambassadorial as time passed. When she reached her fourth month of pregnancy they were treating one another like a couple of professional diplomats moving towards a common goal. The only moment of the day either of them unbent was when they discussed the forthcoming addition to the McClean family over the six o'clock drink that was now a ritual, for Ian saw comparatively little of his wife and child these days. He said, in a Perthshire accent magically released by a dram of Scots whisky, "It's a pity the bairn canna be born in Scotland but I see no prospect o' that." To which she replied, dutifully, that it was indeed a pity, for it would inflict upon his Aunt Jean, known to be very rich, a second disappointment, particularly if it was another girl. Ian said, after a thoughtful pause, "It'll no' be a girl," and she accepted this, supposing him to be on fairly intimate terms with God.

Their rectitude was like a wall of smooth Scots granite, isolating them from a war that had by now involved so many amateurs that professionals wondered whether it was worth winning at such a cost to tradition. Seen like this man and wife were extraordinarily alike. Simon, noticing this as long ago as their wedding day, had said, "They're not only made for one another, they were designed for mutal inflation!" a remark that still encouraged Claire, in her lighter moments, to make bawdy guesses at their bedroom conversation. Always inclined to tease her children Claire continued to begin her letters with "Dear Old Whiz . . ." and when Whiz's replies began "My Dearest Mother and Father . . ." she knew she had made her point.

Sitting beside the Club pool in the glaring sunlight Whiz turned the pages of her mother's latest letter, noting that

Periwinkle Farm would remain a ruin until the war was over, that the local black market was enriching certain Valley patriots, and that Stevie and his wife Monica had quarrelled over his refusal to accept a discharge to industry, but it was like listening to the prattle of Elspeth at present teaching a celluloid duck to swim in the shallow end. The only impact the letter made was to cause Whiz to wonder why her mother should bother to commit such trivia to paper and post it half-way across the world and soon she folded the sheets, returned them to her crocodile handbag and called for Club stationery to write a reply. She made no reference to her mother's gossip but demolished it for what it was worth in her opening paragraph that ran, *"Dearest Mother and Father, I received your letter by today's post and am happy to inform you that I expect our second child in the first week of December, almost certainly after the 4th but before the 7th . . ."* a perfectly logical prophecy that reduced Claire Craddock, reading it at the breakfast table six weeks later, to helpless laughter. Paul dried the tea-spluttered sheet of paper with a napkin and then joined in, so that the study rang with merriment. He said, when they had recovered somewhat, "Where on earth did she get it from? Do you suppose it was from me? Was I ever that pompous?"

"Oh yes, and sometimes still are, but God, in His infinite mercy, threw in a handful of self-doubt so that you deflate every now and again. Read the rest of it for I can't, it'll set me off again," and he relayed the news that Ian's staff appointment had been confirmed, that they had lunched with the Viceroy's aide-de-camp, that all three of them were in excellent health, and that Ian's batman had made little Elspeth a large rocking horse fitted with a howdah.

At this point he broke off to remark that he had always supposed howdahs were reserved for elephants, but Claire clearly could not have been listening for all she replied was: "I must be right, you know. I mean about Whiz and Ian. Those dates prove they've reduced sex to a ceremonial." And then, with one of her impulsively affectionate glances, "Oh God, Paul, I'm glad we were young a long time ago and not now. What's got into these youngsters since the 'thirties? They've so dreadfully earnest."

"They've plenty to be earnest about!" Paul said piously and returned to the *Western Morning News*.

CHAPTER THREE

GARRISON DUTY

I

IT was midsummer when Whiz's letter enlivened the breakfast table of the Big House. By then Paul had had plenty of time to absorb the shock and disappointment of Rumble Patrick's desertion from the Valley garrison.

About three months before, on an evening in early April, he had watched the battered family Austin grind over the loose gravel at the bend of the drive just as dusk stole across the paddock, a scurry of dry chestnut leaves preceding it like fussy outriders. He stood at the library window, his long face wearing what his family called "his Elizabethan expression", which meant that he was engaged in pondering a Valley problem that was complex but not necessarily insoluble.

The family joke—Paul's Elizabethan look—went a long way back in Valley history, dating from the day he had brought home an oval miniature, allegedly by Nicholas Hillyarde but almost certainly a mid-Victorian copy, and Claire, comparing the sombre features with those of her husband, exclaimed, "Why, it's *you*, Paul! When you're looking for a way around something," and since Paul rarely concerned himself with anything not linked to the thirteen hundred acres enclosed by the River Whin and Coombe Bay Bluff, the air of dignified gloom on the face of Hillyarde's model became "Paul Craddock's Elizabethan expression".

That particular day in 1942 the old joke had relevance. Paul had been bedevilled by a Valley problem ever since Rumble Patrick, son-in-law freeholder now without a farm, had talked of enlisting, and thus touched off a long, rumbling quarrel in the Big House. That morning Paul had seen him load an extra can of hoarded petrol into the boot of the

Austin and it occurred to him that Rumble could very well have got to and from his declared destination on the petrol in the tank. His uneasiness as to what Rumble was up to increased when the boy was gone all day and he had noticed his daughter Mary's air of abstraction at lunch. He told Claire, grumpily, "If he's gone off to join something I'll stop his gallop somehow, even if it means calling in the War Ag. Committee! It's plain bloody stupid and he knows it. Good God, we've already got three sons and a son-in-law in uniform, and most of the people round here are hugging their reserved occupations like lifebelts!"

This was not strictly true. There were only two young farmers, David Pitts of Hermitage and Bob Eveleigh of Four Winds left in the Valley, but Paul said it in an effort to justify himself. He really did think that Rumble Patrick's services were of far more value to the country here than in any fighting unit but that was not the real reason why he so strenuously opposed his son-in-law's enlistment. His opposition was at once more personal and more instinctive, for it was based on a belief that Rumble's involvement in the shooting war set the entire future at risk, not only the future of his daughter but that of the Valley itself. To a man who saw the Second World War as a winner-take-all contest between a mob of sadistic bullies and his particular corner of provincial England, it seemed to him absurd to stake so much for so little—the continuity of a way of life, in exchange for a single trained soldier in the field. It maddened him that nobody else, not even his own daughter who stood to lose her personal happiness, shared his viewpoint.

He turned away from the darkening window and lounged into his estate office that adjoined this favourite room of his. Here, above the elbow-height drawing-board desk hung the estate map, a huge, flapping affair, scored by the musical chairs of forty years. He studied it gloomily, doing the kind of sums he had done so often since he came here as a greenhorn of twenty-three and the answers, he decided, were suspiciously like those resulting from similar calculations in 1915 and 1916, when the Valley was hanging on to its community life by a shred of barbed wire.

To the west defences were still impressive. Bob Eveleigh was not only a sensible lad but a good son, unlikely to abandon his widowed mother to her own devices. That was one crumb of comfort to be gathered from that idiotic hit-and-run raid, for Harold Eveleigh had never been the farmer that his son promised to become. North-east of Four Winds the three hundred acres of Hermitage were also secure under the unimaginative hand of David Pitts, son of Paul's oldest friend in the Valley, and Henry himself was still capable of doing a good day's work when he was not compounding a felony by selling the odd pig and chuckling over the profits. Periwinkle, the farm without a farmhouse, was now joined to the Home Farm and the deep belt of woodland that ran behind Hermitage was safe for the time being. In 1916 he had had the devil's own job to save the timber from the grasping hands of Government pimps. So far this war had produced no demands in that direction for, to everyone's surprise, there had been no trench systems and therefore no need for millions of pit-props.

Further east, however, there was plenty to worry about. Here lay his father-in-law's old farm, High Coombe, Francis Willoughby's domain, Deepdene, and finally the old Potter holding, now farmed by the French Canadian Brissot and his partner Jumbo Bellchamber, and there was an inherent weakness in each bastion. High Coombe, healthy enough until Dick Potter had taken it into his silly head to enlist, was being fumbled by a fanciful amateur whom Paul had never trusted, notwithstanding his university degree and pseudo-scientific methods. He suspected that the new tenant, a townsman called Archer-Forbes, had turned farmer in 1940 partly to dodge military service and partly to fill the bellies of himself, his allegedly artistic wife, and their innumerable children, who were all called by pretentious names—Sebastian, Peregrine, Orela, Sonia and Rhoda. A man who could give his children names like that was surely unstable and Paul suspected that the Archer-Forbes tribe not only returned his distrust but considered him and his whole philosophy as anachronistic as feudalism.

Lower down the slope, at Deepdene, Francis Willoughby, son of a former tenant, farmed on, but the Willoughbys had never been a robust family and the asthmatic Francis, a confirmed bachelor, had no prospects of continuity. South again, at Low Coombe, sometimes known as The Dell, the two hundred acres once held by the Potter family were going through another of their periodical crises and the farmhouse, Paul believed, was a clearing house for the local black market, supervised by that old poacher and First World War

61

sniper, Smut Potter, and his avaricious French wife, Marie. He had no proof of this and Brissot, the French Canadian, was a sober enough fellow, but Brissot's partner Jumbo behaved as if he would have been more at home behind a barrow in Aldgate than cultivating land and raising stock in a remote corner of the Westcountry. Paul had seen Smut and Jumbo hobnobbing together in the private bar of The Raven and their presence there was proof that they were up to something for, until recently, both had used the public bar where private conversation was out of the question. Smut, he felt, could be trusted to keep the Valley out of the police courts, if only for his landlord's sake. The two men had a warm personal relationship that went right back to the Edwardian era but Jumbo Bellchamber was a relative newcomer to the Valley and his place there had been won by marrying one of the Potter girls, herself a reformed harlot.

It was in the attitude of these two men that Paul noticed the first signs of dry rot in the system of benevolent dispotism that had prevailed in the Sorrel Valley for so long. Neither had ever been subservient but he had always looked upon them as friends, owing him the kind of allegiance still paid by people like Henry Pitts and other tenants who consulted him on major changes of policy. Since the summer of Dunkirk, however, and the passing of the imminent danger of invasion, Smut and Jumbo had gone their own way with the air of freeholders and this was too clean a break with tradition to pass unnoticed by a diehard like Paul Craddock. He had said nothing, not even to Claire, but he had brooded on the possible effects this new attitude might have upon post-war trends. So much was changing and so quickly, far more rapidly than it had changed under the terrible stresses of the last war. For a time, back in 1940, the unity of the Valley families had seemed as indestructible as in the days when he had first settled there, but once the fear of national extinction had receded there had been a curious reaction evidenced in so many ways. He saw it in the cynical approach of men like Smut to the rationing regulations, and in the prices charged by Smut's wife to Royal Marines who patronised her shop. It was noticeable in the shallow, ultraleft chatter of Archer-Forbes' wife at High Coombe, and in a general atmosphere of lets-see-what-we-can-make-out-of-the-damned-war spirit that was like an epidemic that never ran its full course but was always breaking out in odd corners of the estate, like the pig-sties of the genial Henry Pitts, and could even be found in his own wife, Claire. It was nothing very much, he told himself, frankly admitting that his love for the Valley often made him a prig, but it was there, lurking in the casual superior smirk of that damned Archer-Forbes woman, or the casual "Giddon, Maister, us have to live, doan us?" of Smut Potter, when Paul warned him that he could be prosecuted for hoarding eggs that should have gone elsewhere. And now, as though the sickness had suddenly appeared on his own door-step, here was Rumble Patrick talking of abandoning his acres for the duration and opting for what was, despite all the claptrap they talked, the far less demanding life of the Forces.

He turned away from the estate map and, hands deep in breeches pockets, returned to the library, running his eye along a shelf of brown leather spines as though searching for a subject to take his mind off his immediate problem. He did not reach for a book however, for he was listening to sounds from the hall and presently they told him what he wanted to know, that Rumble Patrick had been upstairs to see Mary and was now standing in the passage leading to the library talking to Claire, apparently ascertaining whether or not this would be a propitious moment to explain where he had been all day and why he had needed that extra ration of petrol. He heard Claire say, "Yes, he's in there, Rumble . . ." and then, with a hint of uncertainty, "Well, that's up to you. I'm not taking sides, so don't count on me."

That was it, then. Another gap torn in Valley defences through which God alone knew what problems might advance. At best more work and more muddle; at worst a daughter left without a husband and condemned to a life of shadows, like so many Valley wives in the decade that followed the 1918 Armistice.

Rumble came in without knocking, cheerful, tousled and, Paul decided, a little too hearty in his approach. Glancing at him Paul's mind went back to an interview with the boy years and years ago, when Rumble, expelled from school for a series of extravagant practical jokes, had stood there by the window refusing Paul's offer to send him to the Agricultural College and announcing his intention to try his luck in Australia. Paul had loved him for that because he knew why the choice had been made. As an adopted son Rumble Patrick considered that the line of succession should remain with

Simon, Andy or Stevie, and nothing Paul or Claire could say had persuaded him to do otherwise. He had gone off, at sixteen, to make his own way in the world, and had not returned until the mid-thirties to claim Mary and Periwinkle Farm, but even then, with that independence that had been both his father's and mother's legacy, he had insisted on buying it and Paul could even remember what he had said: "If I farm I farm my own land, Gov'nor."

Well, here was the same obstinacy and for a moment Paul was able to study it objectively. He said, without looking at him, "You don't have to grope for the soft approach. I know where you've been and what you've been up to. All I'm interested in learning is *why*."

"I don't think I could say off my own bat, Gov'nor, but we might solve it together. Providing you were willing to try that is."

This time Paul did look at him, expecting to see the fleeting, half-quizzical smile that was something else the boy's urchin father had bestowed on him but Rumble was not smiling. He looked troubled so that Paul said, with a shrug, "I thought you had more sense than any of them but it seems you haven't. One bomb and you go overboard, looking for sharks with a knife between your teeth."

This growl did produce a smile and Rumble turned to the sideboard, his hand resting on the decanter. "How are you off for whisky, Gov'nor?" and Paul said grumpily, "Help yourself, and pour me a large one."

It must have been more than half a minute after the hiss of the siphon that Rumble said, "Look Gov'nor, you were in precisely the same situation as me in 1917, except that you were older and had a gammy leg. But *you* went. Suppose *you* try explaining?"

It was a treacherous blow, Paul thought, but without resenting it. Neither was it easy to give an honest answer, without supplying Rumble with more ammunition.

"It was a different kind of war," he said. "The entire attitude of people was different because it was fought exclusively by men between eighteen and fifty. No one else had a look in."

"Presumably people still had to eat and the U-boats were doing a pretty useful job, weren't they?"

"Yes, they were, and farming was just as vital to survival, but suppose I told you that, looking back, I see now that I

64

was a damned fool? I could have done a far better job here and saved myself a hole in the head into the bargain."

"Well I've gone one better already," Rumble said, "I'm not signing on for the Army, the R.A.F. or even the Navy. I'm going into the Merchant Service."

It occurred to Paul that there might be a clue here for Rumble, having knocked about during his adolescence, had acquired a taste for odd corners of the world and for the seas separating them. He wondered if there was not a selfish element in the boy's rejection of his offer to live out the rest of the war in the Big House, with his small farm tacked on to one or other of the larger units. He might even have become bored by the unremitting toil of the last two-and-a-half years, unrelieved as they had been by any of the pre-war recreations farmers traditionally enjoyed in and about the Valley. He felt he knew Rumble sufficiently well to ask a direct question.

"You wouldn't be looking forward to going? As a change, maybe?"

"That's part of it," Rumble admitted, "I enjoyed every moment of the time I spent at sea between '30 and '34, but there's a lot more to it than that, Gov."

Paul found his resentment ebbing more readily than he cared to admit. "All right, tell me if you can find the words. Is it to do with your father being killed in the Hindenberg Line?"

"Not in the least. My father was a professional and wars were his line of business. I'd say it was a lot more to do with my mother."

"You don't remember a damned thing about your mother. She was run over out there on the river road when you were four."

"I've got a pretty accurate picture of her none the less," Rumble said, "and I know what made her tick. She was reckoned half-witted, wasn't she?"

"Only by fools. She wasn't in the least half-witted. Sometimes I thought she was wiser than any of us. She liked living wild because freedom to go where she liked when she liked was the only life that made any sense to her!"

"We're getting warm." Rumble finished his drink at a gulp.

"What the hell are you trying to say?"

"Something I can't unless you come down from the seat of judgment. You learned a lot from my mother. I've heard you

65

admit it, and you learned as much again from Gypsy Meg, my grandmother. That's what I mean when I say we can only make sense of this together."

"What's the connection between you going and me learning my job from your mother and grandmother?"

"There is one. There were only four of us who ever made a cult out of this place and two of those are dead. That leaves you and me."

"Isn't that an argument for staying?"

"No, it isn't," Rumble said, with an emphasis Paul had never heard him use in the past, "because the Valley will tick over so long as you're alive and Claire and Mary are around to back you, but the *idea* of it—everything it has been, is, and will be—needs fighting for and by fighting I don't mean loading guns for other people to fire. I don't see this business as one war, I see it as three. One for stopping that bloody lunatic putting the clock back, one for preserving national independence, and the other—the one that's vital to you and me—a war to stop the local patterns changing so drastically that it won't be the same place any more, not even after we've beaten Jerry. Sure I could stay on as your lodger, and move back into Periwinkle the moment it had a new roof on it, but afterwards it wouldn't be the same, don't you see? It would belong to people like Simon and Andy and Stevie, and all those Marines up on the hill, people who risked their lives defending it. Me? I should have pawned it for the duration and had it handed back to me as a gesture. It wouldn't work, Gov'nor, not for me, and not really for you if you're honest."

He was beaten and he knew it. It was, after all, no more than an echo of the two previous discussions they had had in this room on the same topic, the first when this sun-burned, young man was a schoolboy, the other when he came rampaging into the house announcing that he intended marrying Mary and marrying her as a freeholder. The slight pang Paul experienced as he remembered this had nothing to do with Rumble's present decision and not much to do with the dread of being on hand if news came for Mary that he was dead. Its source was older and more deeply buried in his being, and the boy's logic, if you could call it that, was like the nag of a wound received half-a-lifetime ago, the bitterness of having sired four sons and seen three of them grow to manhood without giving a damn what happened to the stones and trees and red clay of this corner of the West where each of them had been born and raised. Alone among all the children who had lived in this house since Simon's birth, in January 1904, Rumble Patrick, son of a Thameside urchin, and the postscript of Gypsy Meg Potter, both understood and cherished his mystical love of the Valley, and here he was putting it into words that Paul himself could never have spoken. In one way it was proof of ultimate defeat but in another it was a kind of victory. Somehow he had been able to forge a link with Rumble that had never fused with those of his own blood. He held out his empty glass and Rumble, glad of an excuse to turn his back on him, refilled it as Paul said, "How does Mary feel about it? Have you discussed it or just sprung it on her?"

"I didn't have to discuss it," Rumble said. "I daresay she guessed what would happen the minute she saw the farm reduced to rubble and, in any case, it's the man who wears the pants in our family. That was another thing I learned from you, Gov'nor!"

He looked at the boy carefully, wondering how many facts he had guessed about his origins and how much nonsense had been fed to him by Valley gossip.

"I never told you much about how you arrived on the scene, Rumble," he said, "and maybe I should have. Claire and I always felt it might set you apart from the others."

"I asked around and filled in all the blank spaces. Rachel Eveleigh delivered me and she made no secret of it. Then there was Doctor Maureen, who seemed to know everything relevant to my mother. You never held back anything important about my father and finally there was my aunt, Joannie Potter."

"What did Joannie Potter tell you that we didn't?"

"She took me up to the badger slope in the woods and showed me the cave where I was born."

He grinned and somehow Paul was relieved by his gaiety. It all seemed so improbable and yet, here was the metal from which the link between had been forged all those years ago, the daughter of his most raggletailed tenant lying in a hillside and giving birth to a child sired by a raggamuffin he had rescued from a Bermondsey scrapyard. He said, "Did you ever hear that your father didn't know of your existence until you were two? Or that I had the one big row of my life with

Claire when she opposed your father's marriage to Hazel Potter?"

"No," said Rumble, "I never actually heard it, but you'd be surprised at the hints some of your chapel-going tenants dropped."

"You mean that I was your real father?"

"Well—in a way you were," Rumble said. "You not only hooked my father out of the slums and gave him everything you gave your own sons, you did precisely the same for me when my father and mother snuffed it."

"Snuffed it." It seemed an odd way to refer to the violent deaths of man and wife that had followed one another so swiftly in that pitiless period between 1917 and 1918, but then Rumble would have no clear recollection of his mother and none at all of his father, blown to pieces in a German dugout when the war was all but over.

"When are you going and what kind of job will you do?"

"I signed for a Canadian ship as gunner's mate. She sails from Plymouth next Friday in convoy. I always fancied myself popping off at Jerry aircraft. I might even get the silly sod who dropped an egg on Periwinkle!"

"Do you know where you'll be going?"

"Good God no. They wouldn't even give me a hint. But I've got my own ideas, based on the cargo they were taking aboard."

"Wherever it is it won't be a picnic, but I daresay you thought of that." For a moment he was preoccupied with the business of screening an unpleasant vision of Rumble struggling in Arctic waters, or cowering under a rain of cannon shells on the Malta run, and Rumble, with his usual prescience, must have known as much for he said, "I'll promise you something, Gov'nor. I'll come back in one piece."

Paul was tempted to say that he had heard this kind of talk from men now mouldering out on the veldt, or lying in one of those tidy cemeteries behind Ypres but he held his peace, reflecting that Mary would need all the reassurance either of them could give in the months ahead. Instead he said, "Will you want me to run you to Plymouth?"

"No, Gov'nor," Rumble replied, thoughtfully, "but there's something I'd like you to do instead. You can run Mary and me to Paxtonbury and I can catch the train there. Then, on the way home, I should like you to cut through the woods and show Mary the place."

"What place?"

"The cave. It sounds sentimental but I guarantee it would help. Gypsy medicine, maybe."

The odd request, and all that it implied, moved Paul so deeply that he turned away, looking out into the darkness that now enclosed the paddocks on each side of the drive.

"I'll do that," he said shortly, and then, "She's never been there?"

"No, but somehow it ties in with a pact we made a long time ago, when we were kids."

He was able to smile, recalling with sudden clarity this boy and his daughter climbing the long green slope behind the house bent on one of their childish forays about the countryside. He said, "You and Mary; you made up your minds about one another from the beginning, didn't you?"

"You could say that," Rumble said, and suddenly he was gone and Paul heard him calling as he went up the stairs two at a time.

Two or three stars showed through the branches of the avenue chestnuts, odd points of light exempted from the blackout. Something comforting was offered by their presence up there, something that had to do with the cycle of birth and death and rebirth that was the one unchanging feature of his forty years in this place. He pulled the curtain, switched on the light and went into the estate office. The map stirred in the draught from the library door Rumble had neglected to shut and somehow—he could not have explained why—the continuity of the Valley re-established itself as a pattern on the contours of the overscored canvas.

II

They talked generalities all the way home from Paxton-bury and Mary seemed to him very composed, so much so that it struck him she had matured a great deal since marriage. The last time Rumble Patrick had sailed away she had moped for weeks and had lived for his letters, and Paul found himself wondering if she had found fulfilment in motherhood and was now less dependent on the presence of the man they had just seen on to the Plymouth train. It was possible, he told himself, for she had always been the most maternal of his family and the least dependent on the diversions of noise and company. He had invited Claire to accompany them on this solemn, leave-taking trip but Claire had declined.

"The only props Mary ever needed were you and that scamp Rumble," she said. "I daresay she'll weep a bit but you'll have to put up with that. It's a long time since I sprinkled your shoulder."

"I can't remember an occasion since you discovered you were pregnant at fifty!" She had laughed at this, recollecting the unreasoning panic of the time she was carrying John, their youngest, and what a strain she had put upon his patience. Then she went cheerfully about her chores and he was reminded again of her heedless attitude towards the sprawling family they had raised, and how effortlessly she took each new crisis in her stride, as though a war was no worse than an occasional wet harvest and just about as inevitable.

When they reached the spot where Hermitage Lane joined the road down from the moor he stopped, saying, "Rumble asked me to show you something on the way home. Shall we leave it until after lunch and ride over there?" but Mary said no, she would like to be taken there now, and that Rumble, who could never keep a secret, had hinted so broadly at the diversion that she guessed it had to do with Hazel's cave in the woods.

"Then you know about it?" he asked, a little disconcerted. "I got the impression that it was something he had always kept to himself."

"We went looking for it several times," she admitted, "but he always pretended he couldn't find it. He was obviously saving it for a special occasion, like this."

"He got Joannie Potter to show him where it was and I must say I don't get the message. Do you think it's just another of his practical jokes?"

She looked shocked. "It's not a joke, Daddy," and for a moment he thought she was going to elaborate but she said no more until they had climbed the steep lane to the point where it narrowed between the orchard of the Big House and the edge of the escarpment and the southern stretch of Shallowford Woods marched down to the Mere. They left the car at the last point where it was possible to reverse and made their way down through the ranks of oaks and beeches to the oval sheet of water at the bottom of the dip. When they came to a moss-covered log lying opposite the ruin of the pagoda on the tiny island, a folly built by one of the Lovells who had owned the estate in the last century, she stopped and pointed. "I'll tell you something else you didn't know. Rumble proposed to me right there, a few hours before he went off to Australia," and she laughed at his astonishment.

"Good God. He couldn't have been more than sixteen. You mean, seriously?"

"Well, as seriously as he ever does anything," Mary said, "and he must have known what he was doing because as soon as he came back four years later, he took up the option. As a matter of fact he was seventeen and from that moment I stopped feeling three years older. There was never anyone else, but I imagine you always knew that."

"Yes," he said thankfully, "I always knew it. It bothered your mother a little but it never bothered me."

He had his own memories of the spot and they were more poignant than hers. In the early days of his first marriage, several centuries ago it now seemed, he had crossed over to the islet in a punt with Grace one blazing summer noontime and they had mended a long and bitter quarrel by making love in the bracken like a couple of precocious adolescents. He said nothing to her, however, remembering that she had never set eyes on Grace, and that no one, not even Grace's son Simon, mentioned her in the Valley nowadays. She and her suffragettes were as outmoded as the Lollards and Anabaptists, belonging to an age of voluminous, dust-raising skirts, picture hats and croquet parties on the lawn. Twice since then the world had torn itself to pieces and in between there had been the long, dismal haul from slump to agricultural convalescence.

They turned north-west along the path that ran beside the Mere, passed Sam Potter's cottage on the right, crossed a shallow stream and picked their way through tree stumps to a rabbit run that wound across the shoulder of the highest point of the woods to an open space crowned by a great slab of sandstone. It was not a good place to bring a horse and he seldom rode this way, but he had always known it was here that Hazel Potter had lived wild from April until late autumn.

He had forgotten how lonely it was, and how attractive too in a desolate way, the long slope studded with dwarf jack-pines and a sea of rhododendrons screening the margin of the Mere. Spring, it seemed to him, was late this year. The primroses were out and lower down there had been marsh marigolds and a few wild daffodils but no bluebells showed in the open patches below and if he remembered rightly there was always an April haze of bluebells on this south-facing slope. It was a grey, sunless day, with tattered clouds drifting slowly east and the breeze lacking its usual tang of the sea. He said, as though addressing himself, "Funny thing, wars always seem to shuffle the seasons. The rhythm changes when there's a war on but I'll promise you something more cheerful. The summer it finishes will be a scorcher. They had wet summers right through the Boer War and the Great War but in 1902, the year I came here and again in 1919, the heath caught fire and every stream went dry."

"How about the summer of Dunkirk?" she asked, smiling at his tendency to hark back over the years whenever they were alone, but he said this too conformed to pattern because it demonstrated Jerry's weather-luck. "They always have fine weather for their offensives," he said, "whereas whenever we launch one, everything is bogged down in mud."

They had reached the bend in the path opposite the jutting slab of sandstone and he suddenly recollected that the cave was somewhere close by and poked around in the stiff screen of gorse that ran along under the rock. Then, congratulating himself on his memory, he found a tiny tunnel that ran north straight into a short slide of stones and flints and called over his shoulder, "Here, Mary! I thought I hadn't forgotten. I haven't been up here in ten years but there it is," and he made room for her to brush past and then followed her into a shallow excavation under the spur, reflecting that he was now standing on the exact spot where Rachel Eveleigh delivered Hazel Potter of the child who was to sire his first grandson. It brought the past very close and for a moment he fancied he could see Ikey Palfrey's swift grin and the bloom on Hazel Potter's cheek, could even hear Ikey's laugh and soft, muffled burr of Hazel's brogue. "Now what the hell induced Rumble to send us on this goose chase?" he demanded, looking round the empty cave and sniffing the dank air of the place. Then he noticed that she was smiling and that her eyes, "spaniel's eyes" he always thought of them, were shining with excitement as she touched the dry earth walls where a root broke through the crust and curled into a question mark.

"It's just as I imagined," she said, "it's got a terrible privacy, as though it was the very heart of the Valley. Do *you* feel that?"

"No, I don't but I can imagine that was how Hazel Potter and Ikey thought of it. Nobody ever once saw them together until he married her early in the war, so they must have been intensely private people. But me, I like sun and a broad vista. My centrepiece is the edge of French Wood, looking south. What's this pact Rumble talked about? Do you mind telling me?"

"It's to do with his survival," she said, "and I don't care how ridiculous it sounds it makes sense to me. This is where he began and this is the hub of where he'll finish. It's the gypsy in him. He *knows,* don't you see? And he wants to convince me, so that I won't be jittery all the time he's away. He began in the Valley and he'll come back to the Valley in the end." She looked at him speculatively. "Sentimental tosh?"

"To anyone but you, me or Rumble," he said, and it occurred to him that, over the years, he had done her an injustice, imagining that even she, the most fanciful of the brood, had never shared his sense of communion with the Valley.

"You want to stay up here a bit?"

"Yes, a few minutes but first there's something I can tell you that I haven't told Rumble. You'll be having another grandchild before Christmas."

"You let him go? Without telling the boy? But that was crazy. He would have . . ."

"Backed down? Yes, I imagine he would. That was why I didn't tell him. Nobody hobbles Rumble, not even me. He'd made up his mind and I didn't want to be the one to bring more pressure on him. You brought all you could and I wasn't holding him to ransom. Do you imagine I don't know him by now?"

He stood just inside the entrance of the cave looking and feeling foolish, so much so that she laughed at his chap-fallen expression and said, "Run along, Dad, I'll find my own way back. And don't fuss! I've got seven months to go and I hope it's another boy. That'll give you that much more insurance, won't it?"

He took her hand, pressed it, and blundered back along the gorse tunnel into the open. The heaviness that had dragged at him all through the scurry of Rumble's departure was gone but it was not wholly as a result of the news she had passed to him so casually but rather her awareness of his desperate need for some kind of reassurance in the future. They must, he told himself, have often discussed his obsession with this tangle of woods, fields and streams that had been his being for so long, and it therefore followed that their estimate of him, and his involvement with the place, was not the rich joke it was to the rest of the family. It was comforting, he thought, to be tolerated to this extent, and his step as he descended to the clearing surrounding Sam Potter's cottage was almost jaunty.

"If I'm looking for continuity," he told himself smugly, "it's there I'm most likely to find it! I only hope to God that some damned U-boat doesn't make fools of us all."

Old Sam Potter came out of his back door carrying a bowl of chicken mash and Paul hailed him gratefully. Despite years of axe-swinging and constant plodding in clumsy boots about the bogs and coverts at this end of the estate, Sam had put on weight and Paul judged he would turn the scale at seventeen stone. "Hi, there!" he shouted, "Mary and I have just seen Rumble Patrick off. Any news of your boy?"

"Giddon no," said, "Dick doan put pen to paper any more than I ever did but 'er 'phoned his Uncle Smut a month or two back, asking for fags. They'm short of 'em out yonder it zeems."

"Out yonder," Paul reflected, might mean anywhere at all to Sam Potter, who still thought of Cornwall and Somerset as foreign countries. He declined Sam's invitation for "a dish o' tay" and leaned his elbows on the fence that surrounded the cottage. "Ah, they're a footloose lot, Sam," he commiserated, "but they'll grow tired of it I wouldn't wonder, and settle here like the rest of us," but Sam had no faith in the stability of Shallowfordians born after the death of Queen Victoria and said, scattering the mash among lean, long-legged hens, "Dornee believe it, Squire. They baint happy in one place more than an hour at a time, not none of 'em. And if they do come backalong they'll turn the bliddy plaace upzide down, you zee if they don't."

At any other time Paul would have confirmed Sam's prophecy but today, despite Rumble's departure, he felt op-

timistic and turning away passed down the long side of the
Mere to the point where he could find the shortest ascent to
the spot where they had left the car. As though to encourage
him the sun at last broke through the canopy of cloud and a
beam struck the underside of a giant beech, sprouting a
hundred thousand new leaves. The lesson of renewal could
not have been lost upon him for he thought, "We're a couple
of old cart-horses, Sam and I, and it's high time we were put
out to grass. It's just an accident that we're both still at it but
I'm damned if I do more than potter the moment the war's
over," and he tackled the last ten yards of the wooded slope
and began, thankfully, to descend to the level of the road.

III

Mary emerged from the cave and climbed the lip of
heather to the flat surface of the rock, asking herself whether
her serenity had been assumed for the benefit of her father,
admittedly the Valley's most persistent worrier, but deciding
that it had not and that she did indeed feel confidence in the
future. To that extent Rumble Patrick's notion of sending her
here had succeeded more than he could have hoped. It was
curious, she thought, but not more so than their association,
their long partnership as children, his solemn proposal at
seventeen, his sudden reappearance four years later and a
marriage that had resulted in the safe, unexacting life she had
always promised herself. He would almost certainly return as
he had promised, and within hours they would pick up the
threads of their life, exploiting his sense of purpose, rebuilding
Periwinkle to his design, and steadily adding to their family
and stock; another Paul and another Claire, caught up in the
rhythm of the Valley.

She sat there a long time looking down on the spread of
farms between the southern rim of the woods and the blue-
grey line of the heath and dunes where Four Winds and Home
Farm borders met the sea. Down there, she reflected, were
innumerable Pittses and Craddocks and Stokes and Eveleighs, and some of them had been there a very long time but
none as long as the Potters whose blood ran in her children,
born and unborn. It increased her sense of kinship with him
to reflect that when he had emerged, bawling and brick-red
from under this very slab of sandstone, she had been toddling

about the Big House yonder, almost as though she expected and awaited him. Now she could contemplate him as boy and man, as husband and lover, and think herself more fortunate than most. She wondered if seven years as Rumble Patrick's wife had not left her a little smug and decided, with the minimum of self reproach, that it had but why not? Their marriage had been modelled on that of her parents and this was her doing, not his. Her relationship with her mother was more that of a younger sister than a daughter and when all the others had gone their several ways, and she had stayed on awaiting Rumble's return, she had had a better opportunity to assess the Big House partnership than any of the others who dismissed man, wife and way of life as hopelessly old-fashioned. Perhaps they were and perhaps it was, but the point was it had worked, and so had her own marriage, a carbon copy of the original, so who cared a damn about sex-equality as proclaimed by poor old Rachel, or pursued by the sophisticated wives of The Pair?

It might have raised a blush on Claire's cheek to know how closely her eldest daughter had checked the simple arithmetic of her relationship with Paul, and how faithfully the answers had been applied at Periwinkle. For the first time in years Mary recalled her mother's blunt advice on the subject of marriage, offered only a week or two before Rumble had whisked her off to the little farm on the far side of the Valley. "The way to make it work is to be cheerfully available morning, noon and night, and go along with his major decisions, no matter how damn silly they seem at the time. If you do quarrel don't sulk but make it up in bed. In ten minutes you'll both be back to normal." That was about it, for Claire with thirty-four years' experience behind her, and for Mary with a mere seven. Looking back on those years she could remember no more than an occasional tiff, always resolved by mother's prescription.

In her new-found serenity she could ponder the family as a whole, sparing a thought for the marriages of her brothers, and it seemed to her that all three of them would have benefited by closer observance of the old couple—a partnership, with the man a short head out in front, and any little differences resolved horizontally. Well, there it was and there was nothing very complicated about it. For mother and daughter it had meant fulfilment and that, she supposed, was an end in itself.

Down on the nearest grey stub of a sawn pine a dog fox looked up at her and showed his teeth. Peace and certainty warmed her breasts and belly and she called, in the brogue of old Sam Potter, "Hullo there, you ole varmint!" The fox lifted a forepaw as though prepared to meet the challenge but suddenly changed his mind and padded unhurriedly down the long, sandy slope. In a moment, moving as jauntily as her father, she had slipped off the spur and followed him down to the Mere.

CHAPTER FOUR

BIRTH OF A LEGEND

I

BECAUSE he was rooted, because, apart from a two-year stint in Flanders he had lived his life here as community leader, Paul Craddock was as sensitive to the shifts and trends in local loyalties as the commander of a beleaguered garrison. As the war entered its third year he noted a steady diminution of what he had always thought of as the tribal impetus of the people around him.

In times past, both in peace and war, a Valley crisis had never failed to awaken that tribal instinct, promoting collective action and a dedicated pooling of skills and resources under his leadership. It was as though, in moments of stress, the people of the Valley were able to reach out and pluck the threads of initiative from the hedgerows and pastures and follow them wherever they might lead. Always they had led to achievement and sometimes to glory.

Such an occasion had been the rescue operation mounted for the survivors of the German merchantman wrecked off Tamer Potter's Cove in March, 1906. This (apart from the instance of a Craddock girl's election as Dairy Queen and her death in an air disaster) was the only occasion the Sorrel Valley made national headlines.

Now, well into the year 1942, Paul had lost his hold upon this ultimate handrail. The present war did not promote this kind of collectivism. Its alarms, sacrifices and manifestations were too regimented to sustain local individualism and too widespread to earn Shallowford more than a couple of paragraphs in the County Weekly. The hit-and-run raid, involving two civilian casualties, had passed almost unnoticed in the world outside, for what were two deaths matched against the hecatombs of Coventry and Merseyside? The bodies of Harold Eveleigh and his sister Rachel were two dead leaves on a flood that had now spread from the Coral Sea to the Newfoundland Banks, from the jungles of Malaysia to the Forest of Dean. Anonymity masked the exertions of Sorrel men and women in uniform. In the First War as people now called it, the Valley had been rich in heroes, men like Smut Potter, who hid out behind the German lines for almost a year, and Jem Pollock of Lower Coombe, who won a posthumous medal supporting the splintered timbers of a blown mineshaft. There were no local heroes in this war. No garlands were heaped upon men and women leaving the train at Sorrel Halt to begin their nine days' leave. Mostly they were greeted by indifferent civilians with "Hello. Home again?"

What was badly needed, Paul reflected, was a sharp boost to Valley morale and this, in the absence of heroes, could only be achieved by a collective endeavour of some sort that was not only revitalising but was seen to be so by the world north and east of the main road. He could not see where it was coming from. The tribal spirit was dead.

In this, of course, he was mistaken. It was not dead but dormant, awaiting the right set of circumstances to galvanise it into organised endeavour and, in so doing, eject an even more unlikely hero than Smut Potter or Jem Pollock. Such a set of circumstances lit a fuse in July and the resultant explosion not only boosted morale, and made national headlines, but added chapter and verse to Valley folklore. The chapter was the usual Sorrel compound of high drama and low comedy; the verse emerged as a piece of lewd doggerel to be chanted by Valley schoolboys long after the circumstances that had produced it had been swept away with the debris of the Third Reich. The hero this incident produced was Henry Pitts of Hermitage. The heroine was Claire Craddock herself. The villain, as sinister as any in Victorian melodrama, was Otto von Shratt, an ex-U-boat lieutenant, who capered across the Sorrel stage for one summer afternoon and evening before disappearing into obscurity. What made this incident memorable however, was not its circumstance but its shape. It had, in retrospect, an almost classic form in that its caste included not only a hero-clown, a heroine, and a cleanshaven Victorian villain, but a maltreated child plus any number of walk-on parts, most of them armed to the teeth. It was this that caught the Valley's fancy, for

Sorrel people liked their drama in black and white. They were confused by subtle shades and subtle interpretations; even in 1942 few of them had heard of Professor Freud.

Inspector Everett, of Paxtonbury, rang the Home Guard Command Post at ten a.m. that morning, warning the duty unit to look out for a desperate character who had jumped the train en route for Plymouth, his port of embarkation for a Canadian P.O.W. Camp. Paul, getting a garbled message during his morning round, at once rang back for more information and Everett was able to supply it. The prisoner, a dedicated Nazi who had given the authorities a great deal of trouble since his capture the previous year, was called Otto von Shratt. The "von" was deemed to be spurious but Otto's reputation was not. He was, according to the inspector's information, a very truculent character, and a man of considerable strength, agility and ingenuity. He had already escaped twice and on one occasion had been free for nearly a week. This, in fact was why he was being shipped overseas but his escort, bringing him south-west, had been foolish enough to sanction a visit to the lavatory whilst changing stations and he was now at large again and had last been seen heading for the coast. The military, he said, were not unduly alarmed for it was deemed impossible for Shratt to leave the country but they thought it not unlikely that he might attempt a little sabotage and were extremely anxious to lay hands on him without a moment's delay.

"He'll almost certainly make for cover and lie up for a spell," Everett told Paul. "My instructions are for your people to beat the woods, working north and joining up with the Paxtonbury Home Guard moving south-east. How many men can you get together in the next hour or so?"

Paul said no more than a dozen or so but that number, he felt, would suffice. "Someone is sure to see him and 'phone in," he added, "and once they do we can pinpoint the area and concentrate. He won't be likely to put up a fight, will he?"

"Not if he has any sense, but how many of those hairy apes have? This one is a real beauty. He might tackle a single individual unless he found himself looking down the barrel of a rifle. I'll send a detailed description and picture the minute I get one. It gives me blood pressure to think of those clots at the camp entrusting a man like that to a couple of recruits and a middle-aged corporal. They won't ask for our co-operation. They prefer to fight the entire bloody war on their own, like all the Services!"

Paul was rather elated by the assignment and so, when he rode over to the Command Post at Coombe Bay to organise the hunt, was the rump of Valley originals and their teenage troops. The local Home Guard had made appreciable strides towards military perfection since the days of Dunkirk when it had consisted of a scratch group of volunteers manning a coastal strip six miles long and three miles deep. Today every man had a uniform, a rifle and plenty of ammunition. Training was still sketchy and discipline often depended on mood and variations in weather, but every volunteer possessed the merit of enthusiasm and a thorough knowledge of the local terrain. The prospect of flushing a real live Nazi from Shallowford coverts was one that promised not only adventure but kudos. Even Henry Pitts, a courtesy sergeant again at sixty-plus, begged to be numbered in the posse, and that despite the fact that he was not on duty and had left his rifle and ammunition at home.

"Giddon, Maister," he protested when Paul relayed the Inspector's warning, "us worn have no trouble flushing the bugger out o' yer! I can borrow Smut's rook-rifle and follow on zoon as I pick up the car. 'Er's havin' carburettor trouble and I'm waitin' on 'er!"

Paul left it at that and assembled, by means of the telephone and boy-runner, some fifteen men, including Henry's son David, Harold Eveleigh's boy, three Coombe Bay servicemen home on leave, and the pot-bellied Francis Willoughby, of Deepdene. In three cars they drove to the point of departure, the head of the Coombe, and set off in a north-westerly direction, forming a long, ragged line and moving within hailing distance of one another. Latecomers had instructions to move forward on the same line of march about a mile behind the vanguard, if possible covering the gaps. The reserve was placed in nominal command of Henry and all were warned to work in pairs and rendezvous on the main road that formed the northern boundary of the woods.

Shallowford Woods were ideal cover for a fugitive at this time of year. Every beech, oak, ash and sycamore was in full leaf and the bracken between the trunks of the older trees was waist high. The going was comparatively easy up to the crest of the southern slope and down the far side to the margins of the Mere but from here on, inclining north, the way was very rough and Paul, passing Sam Potter's cottage, reflected ruefully that he would need at least a hundred men to search the vast rhododendron thickets and fir coppices at the northern end of the Mere. He checked the beaters in order to consult with Sam, whose knowledge of this part of the Valley was unsurpassed, even by his brother Smut, the ex-poacher. Sam was not very sanguine about their hopes of forcing the Nazi to break cover.

"Tiz a praper ole wilderness about yer," he grumbled. "Us have done little or no cuttin' back zince the start o' the war. You could hide an elephant upalong. If you'll taake my advice, Squire, you'll shorten your line an' go over the ground dree or fower times, leavin' markers to show where us've been. I got a stack o' flags in the shed us used for the sports, backalong. Lend me a couple o' men to hump 'em and us'll go about it methodical-like."

They went about it methodical-like, narrowing their field and planting markers every hundred yards or so as they pushed their way through bracken, gorse and blackberry bushes to the higher ground known, from time immemorial, as the Badgers' Slope, for badgers had occupied setts here for centuries.

Paul, handling some of the flags, remembered the last time they had been used in a collective exercise, the occasion of the sports promoted to celebrate King George V's Silver Jubilee in Big House paddocks, and he could recall the occasion before that, the local junketings that marked the signing of the Peace Treaty, in 1919. Many of the poles were old and rotten, with no more than a shred of rag adhering to the blunt ends but they served to narrow the field and enable the beaters to work with some kind of precision. Gradually, moving slowly and toilsomely in blazing sunshine, the Shallowford Home Guard worked its way up the sandy slope and over the crest into the last belt of woodland approaching the main road. An occasional rabbit scuttled ahead of them. A wide-eyed roebuck broke cover and dashed for the rhododendrons and at least a dozen pheasants flew squawking into the south, rising like heavy bombers and struggling madly to gain height. It was, for most of the beaters, a pleasant if tiring way of spending a summer afternoon and the general air of expectancy inclined them to keep in closer touch with one another than Paul had intended. Grunting along in their wake he said, "Tell them to spread out a bit, Sam. We're not covering nearly enough ground," and Sam, whose stride had not been shortened by age, hurried on ahead waving his arms and shouting directions to the younger men. In obedience to his directions they fanned out so that the couples were separated by more than a hundred yards. It was this dispersal that gave the fugitive the opportunity he had been awaiting since he first spied their approach shortly after noon.

II

He had holed up in a bramble-sown crevice at the very top of the Badger Slope, within fifty yards of the ridge where Hazel Potter had once kept her little house. It was a unique vantage point for he could remain unseen by anyone passing within yards and yet observe in detail the sweep of the woods as far as the Mere and the movements of at least half the men searching for him. It seemed to him that his best course at the moment was to wait for the last of them to pass the crest of the escarpment and move down into the heavy timber beyond. Then, he reasoned, he could break cover with reasonable safety, gain the security of the rhododendron forest below and from here work his way round the western side of the lake and find a secure place to await darkness.

He was not by any means clear about what he would do after that except to hunt for transport of some kind that would enable him to get clear away from the area. This, he felt, was essential for two reasons. They would not be looking for him with such enthusiasm if he could put distance between himself and his point of escape, already ten miles to the north-east, and the chances of stowing aboard a vessel for Eire would improve very considerably if he could enter the area of a port like Plymouth or Falmouth.

He knew the country better than some of the men searching for him. His ability to read maps had been built into his initial training as a member of the Hitler Youth movement ten years ago and his seagoing experience had enabled him to memorise topographical features at a glance. The only map he possessed now was inside his head but it was none the worse for that. During his fifteen months of captivity and again, in the course of his two escapes, he had had many opportunities to study maps either smuggled into the camp in

Cumberland, or displayed on railway stations he had passed through during his subsequent escapes. This ready availability of maps contributed to the unspeakable contempt he felt—and always had felt—for the British race. To his way of thinking their officials behaved with astonishing stupidity. They introduced an impenetrable blackout throughout the length and breadth of the country that made it very easy for escapers to move about at night, they removed the names of stations and carted away the signposts thereby causing themselves, and no one else, endless confusion and frustration. They did not, however, take the elementary precaution of covering pre-war tourist posters at some of their transport depots, or making certain that school atlases did not find their way into prisoner-of-war camps. Clearly photographed in the brain of Shratt was the general layout of the entire western peninsula and this photograph had been there ever since he learned that he was destined to travel to Plymouth by train in the custody of a trio of yokels in uniform. He could have given them the slip before but had waited until he was within easy walking distance of the coast. Once he had smelled the sea and seen a catch of fresh fish at the junction a few miles back, he had gone into the station lavatory, climbed out of the window into a siding, displayed himself running east between two lines of open trucks, doubled back, and concealed himself in a canvas water tank until it was dusk. Now, in this kind of weather, he was already dry and was not even tired or hungry for he had enjoyed six hours' sleep on reaching the Shallowford escarpment and had eaten his fill of fruit, vegetables and handfuls of corn gathered whilst crossing the open fields under the woods. For the first time since his last escape he felt confident of being the first German prisoner to escape from Britain. Von Werra had made it from Canada the previous year but Von Werra was dead, and Otto was confident that the Reich needed another hero to fête, cosset and promote, before sending him to make more inroads into Allied commerce. By now, he reasoned, he would have been among the most decorated of Admiral Doënitz's stalwarts, the men to whom the Reich would owe its ultimate triumph after the hopeless fumblings of the Wehrmacht in Russia and the pitiable display of Goering's Luftwaffe in the summer and autumn of 1940. For Shratt was not only a dedicated Nazi, fed and nurtured on the theory and practice of Teutonic supremacy. He was also a man who had come to

84

believe the only certain way of beating Britain was to starve her to death and the latest shipping losses quoted in the camp confirmed him in this belief. No country, whatever its resources, could hope to replace an annual shipping loss of upwards of three million tons. By this time next year, by late autumn if the U-boat men attended to their duty, Winston Churchill would be in the mood to agree to a truce in the West in order that Germany could eliminate Russia. There would be plenty of time to finish the war against Britain and America once Germany had the entire resources of the continent at her disposal. In the meantime the most important war aim in the mind of Otto von Shratt was to get home, have his picture in all the papers, and accept the command of one of Doënitz's most up-to-date U-boats.

The propaganda of ten years, seeping into the mind of an already aggressive personality, had simplified Shratt's political thinking to the point of absurdity, but it had not eroded his abundant stock of commonsense as regards how to survive or how to conduct himself as a professional fighting man. His instincts were sharp and keen. His powers of observation were considerable. Above all, his physical stamina and resolution were unimpared by the frustration of fifteen months behind barbed wire. In addition to all this he had something comparatively rare in the German soldier, an ability, indeed a preference, to act on his own initiative and make his own on-the-spot decisions and, if necessary adapt his plans to changing circumstances. Once having learned the rudiments of his craft at sea he had not found it necessary to go by the book. He had, in fact, thrown the book away for it was his experience that every separate decision was regulated by a specific set of circumstances and that circumstances were fluid and could flow in any direction. It was this basic characteristic that had enabled him to survive the sinking of his U-boat off Rosyth in the spring of 1941. Alone among the crew he had kept himself afloat in rough water for more than two hours, saved by a rubber flask of spirit and a lifebelt fitted with a luminous dial, gadgets he had thought out for himself when the superiors were too busy or too pigheaded to follow his advice. His initiative, plus his ability to convert his memory into a well-kept filing cabinet, had been the springboard of his two previous escapes and had he not been baulked by the sea barriers in all directions it is possible that he would have presented himself to the German Consul in

Dublin months ago. He had, against all probability, got as far as the Liverpool docks on the last occasion and might have found a ship had not hunger forced him to focus attention upon himself by an act of burglary. Hunger was no immediate problem today but transport was and as he watched the last of the beaters top the slope, he made ready to descend into the valley and search the area for an unwatched car or motor-cycle. He was in no particular hurry and could assess the situation calmly. One way and another Otto von Shratt was a rare bird.

When the cries of the beaters grew faint on the far side of the hill he slipped out of his cleft and made a fast, crouching descent to the edge of the Mere where he was able to disappear again inside a rhododendron clump but continue to observe the track that led to the woodman's cottage.

The woodman was not there. From his observation post high on the hill he had seen the man summoned into the open by the grey-haired old fellow who seemed to be in command of the detachment. But there was probably a woman around and there was nothing to be gained by inviting her outcry, so he moved very carefully along the fringe of the rhododendrons until he could look right across at the cottage and determine whether or not it was empty. He saw no woman, no movement of any kind within the area, but soon he saw something else on his immediate right that made him bob back into the leafy cave of the fronds. A ponderous man was plodding down the path beside the Mere, glancing left and right as he advanced. He did not look a formidable adversary. He was fat, old and short of wind. His mouth curved upwards in a permanent, rubbery grin. From his dense cover Shratt watched carefully, wondering if he was the laggard of the party over the hill. He was alone and carried a single-barrelled sporting gun of some kind held in the crook of his arm. Otto Shratt, a man destined for high rank in the German Navy, settled down to wait and watch.

III

Henry Pitts had never taken kindly to military discipline. His First World War record was impressive for he served three years in France and had been awarded the Military Medal for gallantry on the liquid slopes of Pilckhem Wood, in 1917. But his sergeant's stripes in that far-off war tended to come and go so rapidly that even Henry himself was sometimes not always sure of his rank. He was inclined to answer back. He was impassive in advance, imperturbable in retreat and his trench mates had thought of him as invulnerable but he was a man who, like Shratt, preferred to make his own decisions and dismiss directives as "bliddy lot o' rigmarole". Paul Craddock's instructions to await the assembly of the reserves had struck him as just this and when his car was returned to him, and no one else had arrived at the Command Post in Coombe Bay, he elected himself rearguard and told Smut Potter, who was lame, to tell anyone else who turned up to follow at their own convenience. Then, borrowing Smut's single shot rook-rifle and a box of cartridges, he drove to the point where the cars were parked under guard, climbed the slope, and picked his way down through the timber to the path beside the Mere.

It was quiet and cool down here. Pottering along the shore he almost forgot his purpose in entering the woods and watched a moorhen teaching her chicks to swim inshore of the islet. It was years, he reflected, since he had been down here, for his farm lay at the other end of the estate and the last visit he could recall to this section of the woods was during his courting days, when he had walked the buxom Gloria, long since laid in her Cornish grave, along this very path of a summer evening. The memory of youth suffused him. His rubbery grin expanded as he remembered her half-hearted squawks of protests when he had, as he himself would have put it, "rinned up an' down the scales a time or two". The filtered sunlight and the chorus of birdsong induced in him a sense of peace and fulfilment, particularly when he reflected that he had already outlived Gloria by a decade and had since married Ellie who had proved a great contrast to Gloria. Half-consciously he compared their merits and demerits, Gloria's inclination to nag and her capacity for hard work; Ellie's amiability, offset by her virtual uselessness as a farmer's wife when removed from bed or the cooking stove where she was adequate. Luxuriating in his memories he strolled along the path as far as Sam Potter's cottage and pausing there remembered that Sam kept a barrel of home-brewed cider under his kitchen-sink. The thought increased his sense of well-being, exorcising the final traces of Otto Shratt from his mind. He raised his head and bellowed "Sam!

Where be 'ee, Sam?" and getting no answer dropped his hand on the catch of the gate in the picket fence.

It was the gate-fastening that set in train everything else that happened in the Valley that afternoon. Had it lifted easily he could have opened the gate without setting aside his rifle. As it was he had to struggle with the rusted tongue of metal and to do this he was obliged to use both hands and a certain amount of force. Sam had not used that gate in years. Behind the cottage was a broken paling and he entered and left his garden via this section.

The gate opened at last and giving Sam another hail Henry went round to the wash-house and through into the scullery. His memory had been accurate. There was Sam's barrel and when he held a mug to the tap cider gushed out as though eager to be at Henry's service. It was very good cider indeed, Sam having got the recipe from his gypsy mother, Meg. It was, Henry decided, the best drink in the world on a hot summer afternoon after a walk over an incline of two hundred feet. He had no fears that Sam would resent him helping himself. The Potters were an open-handed lot and Henry's friendship with Sam went back to Victoria's reign. He smacked his lips, murmured "Here's to 'ee, Sam", and drank his second mug. By the time he had half-finished his third it would have taxed his powers of concentration to recall what circumstances had brought him here on a lazy summer's afternoon. He sat on Sam's kitchen chair, his weight thrown back, his gumbooted legs thrust forward, savouring and remembering, plucking incidents at random from a crowded past, and then his eye fell on a discarded newspaper and a headline that read, *"Russians Throw Back Kharkov Attack"*. With a mild jolt it brought him back to his duty. He washed the cider mug, put it on the draining-board, and waddled out into the sunshine and round to the front gate. Automatically he reached down for the Smut's rook-rifle. It was gone. There was nothing there but a tall clump of nettles, the topmost leaf dipping slightly under the weight of a cabbage white butterfly.

IV

Otto Shratt began to formulate a new plan before Henry had entered the cottage. In the next few minutes he had all but shaped it, dividing it into stages like a man planning a

88

long and complicated journey on a miserly budget. With a gun in his hand he did not have to comb the area for unguarded transport. He could ambush any car that came by and force the driver to take him north instead of west, for almost at once he isolated three advantages of an abrupt change of route. In the first place no one would expect him to double on his tracks and enter a more thickly populated area. In the second place he was familiar with the Liverpool dock area, having skulked in the district for several days during his second escape. Thirdly he was persuaded that his chances of stowing away on an Irish-bound vessel would be far more favourable in the north than in the west.

The key to the revised plan was the gun. In ten seconds flat he was out of his screen, across to the fence and back again. The weapon was not impressive, a .22 rifle with a single shot action but it was loaded and as a persuader it was as good as a Luger or a sub-machine gun. Contemplating it Shratt's dreams of fame and freedom expanded. He saw himself being driven the length of England by cowed civilians whom he could jettison in lonely stretches of country so that the forces of pursuit, catching up with them one by one, would be frustrated and confused. Petrol might prove a problem—he knew it was strictly rationed—but a gun could be made to produce petrol and food and money and anything else he might need on a sustained cross-country jaunt. With mounting confidence he moved along the margin of the little lake, crossed the main path, and climbed the long, timbered slope of the south-facing ridge where he could look down on a large sprawling house approached by a tree-lined drive and backed by an orchard and a yard. Like the woods the place seemed deserted and the prospects of finding transport there seemed to Shratt promising. He went on down, using the orchard hedgerows for cover.

He had reached the bottom of the orchard that gave on to a kitchen garden when he saw the two-seater turn off the river road and tackle the steep, curving drive. It was an old bull-nosed Morris, driven by a middle-aged woman, and beside the woman sat a boy aged about eight or nine. The car crawled up the incline to the forecourt and stopped. The woman and the boy got out and went into the house. In less than a minute Shratt had sidled round the wall enclosing the stableyard, crossed a laurel patch, and approached the Morris from its offside. A glance confirmed his suspicions. The car had been fitted with a detachable ignition key. This had been removed.

It crossed Otto's mind then that it might be wiser to move on across country and set up an ambush in a lonelier spot but then he reflected that privately-driven cars were not all that plentiful in wartime England and darkness might fall before a suitable one passed. During the interval all kinds of things might happen. The fat man would report the loss of his rook-rifle. The beaters might turn about and come down through the woods. And all the time his own progress, marked by raided vegetable patches, by footmarks, and the missing weapon, would be plotted on police maps. Viewed in the round it seemed to him that his chances of getting clear of the area in the car were more than even, providing he could get possession of the ignition key and, ideally, some reserve petrol. He decided to explore the petrol situation first. Returning the way he had come he regained the stableyard and poked about among the deserted sheds. It was clearly a day for bonuses. In the second shed was a tractor and beside it stood a two-gallon tin of petrol. He adjusted the rook-rifle under his right armpit keeping a finger on the trigger and carrying the petrol can in his free hand walked up the steps and into the big kitchen at the rear of the house.

Thirza Tremlett, the Craddocks' nanny for time out of mind and now general factotum in a house deprived of all other domestic staff, was working at the sink. When the latch of the door was lifted she did not even look up, assuming the entrant to be the Squire who always came in this way after parking the tractor or stabling his grey. When Thirza felt a gentle prod in the small of her back she hissed with indignation and half-turned, meeting the steady gaze of a young, thick-set man with short fair hair and a day's stubble on his suntanned face. She opened her mouth to scream but then closed it again. Something in the way the man looked at her warned her that it would be wiser not to scream. Instead she gobbled and turned her face away, gripping the edge of the sink to offset a sudden loss of power in her legs.

The young man said, in a foreign accent so strong that she could only just catch his meaning, "The lady of the house?" Nothing more, just those five words spoken as a query.

Thirza pushed herself away from the sink and tottered into the middle of the big room, her hands half-extended as though she had suddenly been deprived of vision. But the rifle barrel was still in close contact with her back and under its gentle pressure she moved through the swing door and into the dim passage beyond, the stranger keeping step with her.

She had heard nothing of escaped German prisoners and did not connect this young man's presence with the war, supposing him to be either a burglar or a madman. Burglars were exceedingly rare in the Valley but madmen were not. The Codsall family, over at Four Winds, had produced three madmen in three generations and she had known one of them personally, old Martin Codsall, who had killed his wife with a hay knife, fired his shotgun at the Shallowford stable-boy, and finally hanged himself in one of his own barns. There was nothing to be gained by arguing with a madman and she did not try. She responded, with faltering step, to the pressure of the gunbarrel. Her mouth opening and closing, and her false teeth performing a sympathetic undulatory movement, she led the way across the main hall and down another broader passage to a door that was ajar. She paused here for a moment but the man growled "Vorwarts!" and she went on, pushing the door open with her knee.

Claire Craddock and her youngest son John were at the table having their tea and Claire, facing the door, was the first to see them enter. A second or so later John, his mouth full of cake, turned his head and saw them too.

For a long moment mother and son stared and John's jaws ceased to champ. Nobody moved and nobody said anything. To an onlooker, glancing in from the terrace, the sunlit room might have contained four figures in a waxworks tableau. Then, grappling with amazement and indignation, Claire stood up and at that precise moment Thirza's knees buckled and she laid herself full-length on the floor. To Claire the movement had, or seemed to have, a certain grace, as though Thirza was simulating the climax of a ballerina and going through a parody of the dying swan. The young man remained standing on the threshold his glance moving casually about the room. She said, at last, "Who are you? What do you want?" and the young man, his face twitching momentarily, replied, "I want the keys of the car. The car outside of the house."

His English, apart from its accent, was near perfect but it was the accent that gave her her first clue. Each word was carefully enunciated, like a student trying to satisfy an oral examiner, and with part of her mind Claire pondered this perfection. It told her that this man was almost certainly a German and there was a logical reason for the guess. Away in a remote attic of her brain she heard again the guttural accents of old Professor Scholtzer who had lived in the Valley before the First War, and had all his windows smashed by a patriotic mob after the German excesses in Belgium in August, 1914. The young man's "w" and "s's" reminded her very sharply of the professor whom she had liked, and even more of his big, blond son, who used to ride out with the Sorrel Vale hunt and had been killed early in the war fighting against men like Will Codsall and Smut Potter. She had not heard about the hunt for the escaped prisoner, having driven over to Paxtonbury to collect young John at end of term but now she recalled having passed groups of Home Guardsmen on the main road and the man's clothes gave the impression that he was attached to some kind of institution. It did not occur to her that he was mad, only that he was some kind of enemy and, to a degree, both dangerous and desperate. She could not recall ever having looked into a pair of eyes that were harder, bluer, or less expressionless. Without another word she picked up her handbag, extracted a bunch of keys and selected one. Holding the bunch suspended by this key she reached across the table. Thirza lay quite still on the floor. John, his eyes blank with amazement, sat without moving a muscle, his jaws still parted by a mouthful of unmasticated cake.

The man took the keys with a curt nod and then seemed to reflect a moment. Finally, half-dismissing Claire, he turned to the boy and jerked his head towards the door. To Claire his meaning was quite clear. John was to accompany him, presumably as a hostage, and when she realized this she reacted violently, concern driving out shock and indignation.

"No!" she shouted, "leave the boy and take the car! You have petrol—enough petrol to get you sixty miles, and if you want money . . ."

With a kind of frenzy she whipped up her bag again and emptied it on the table. A lipstick clinked into a saucer and a spread of letters and papers cascaded to the floor. Their flutter roused Thirza somewhat and she half raised herself on her elbows but when the man gestured with his gun she subsided again. John, without fuss, got up, swallowed his cake and reached out a hand towards his mother, but then the man acted quickly and savagely. He stepped swiftly over the prostrate Thirza, spun the boy round by the shoulder and propelled him towards the open door with his knee. Then they were gone and the door was shut. Claire heard their steps in the passage and then a sharp, metallic sound followed by a loud crash.

The noise galvanised her into action. Shouting protests at the top of her voice she scrambled over Thirza and flung her weight against the door. It gave but only an inch or so. In the absence of a key Shratt had placed a hall chair under the outer handle. Still shrieking she wasted several seconds wrestling with it before turning and running through into the estate office with some idea of throwing open the garden door and reaching the forecourt via the terrace. She had her hand on the door when she remembered the man's eyes and paused.

From the library behind her she heard Thirza retching but the sound had no significance. Very rapidly she was coming to terms with the immediate situation in the forecourt, a car, a potential killer with the gun, and young John being carried away God knew where or for what purpose. With a tremendous effort she was able to concentrate on possibilities and her first thought was the telephone in the hall. Then she related the sounds she heard immediately after the door had been barred. On the way out the man must have ripped out the installation and the crash she had heard had been the wall-box striking the tiled floor.

The next sound she heard was more definitive. It was the growl of the self-starter and the asthmatic cough of the old engine. Something had to be done at once and clearly it would have to be done by her. Remedies began to pour through her mind like a shower of balls bouncing down a long flight of stairs but each of them escaped into an area of improbability. She stared through the glazed half of the garden door and saw the car in the act of turning. The young man was trying to make the turn in one but the narrowness of the drive and the steep camber of its surface made this difficult. John, sitting nearest Claire, still looked blank, almost as though he was sleep-walking, but his expression must have deceived both Claire and Shratt for when the car was reversing, and the German's head was turned, he suddenly jerked himself upright and half-projected himself over the edge of the nearside door. The German reacted very quickly. Lifting his left hand from the wheel he struck the boy's cheek with his open palm and the sound of the impact, and the cry that followed it, reached Claire where she stood with her nose pressed to the pane.

It might have been this action on Shratt's part that decided her next move in that it raised the level of her indignation high above that of her fear. Out of the tail of her eye she saw the means of combating the man's outrage, the sleek, brown stock of Paul's deer-rifle, the weapon she had given him for his sixty-first birthday present about the time of Dunkirk.

He no longer carried it on patrol, preferring to wear his Webley revolver and she was, as it happened, fairly familiar with the weapon. During the invasion scare, more from a sense of fun than with serious purpose in mind, Paul had taught her to use it, practising on marks in the orchard, and although by no means proficient she had at least learned to sight it correctly and to squeeze rather than jerk the trigger. She reached up and tore it from the peg, balancing it in her hands and experiencing a kind of demoniac pleasure in having the means to challenge a bully on his own terms. It was in fact, a far more formidable rifle than Shratt's having a magazine containing eight rounds operated by a bolt action. She knew that Paul did not keep it loaded but she also knew where he kept a full magazine, in an old tobacco tin beside his inkwell, and when she tore open the tin the magazine was there, half-buried in paper clips, screws and discarded fountain pens. She clipped it on and worked the bolt in the five seconds that it took Shratt to straighten out and point the car towards the topmost curve of the drive but even so she was almost too late. The car was still warm from the drive home from Paxtonbury and responded vigorously to the thrust of the accelerator, shooting off at what seemed to her a prodigious speed. Without waiting to wrestle with the catch of the garden door she jabbed the barrel through the glass and fired, aiming at the offside rear tyre.

She must have missed for the car shot round the laurel clump and continued its rapid descent of the drive but she was not beaten yet and when it reappeared on the far side of the laurels she fired twice in rapid succession before the first chestnut tree could mask the target. This time one of the shots must have struck home for there was a subdued explosion and the Morris lurched on to the grass verge, careering along within inches of the palings and then regaining the gravel with a long, grinding scrunch. After that, however, it continued on down the incline and Claire, thrusting wide the door and running on to the terrace, glimpsed its passage between the narrowly-spaced chestnuts of the drive. Seconds later there was a confused outcry from the direction of the gate and after that a prolonged uproar, culminating in a clatter like a pile of empty paint tins being tossed on to a stone floor. Silence followed as Claire, reloading as she ran, moved across the drive to a point beyond the laurels where she could survey the avenue as far as the twin stone pillars.

She could see little enough for the lower half of the drive was shrouded in a cloud of dust but what she did see filled her with a mixture of relief and dread. The car's offside wheel was clear of the ground and still spinning, and beyond it, clear of the dust, stood the solid figure of Henry Pitts, feet astride and arms outspread, as if in the act of coaxing an obstinate heifer into a pen.

V

In the many post-war Valley inquests held to determine who, in fact, played the major role in checking Otto Shratt's career as escaper extraordinary, no final decision was ever reached. The Morris was checked and rechecked (before being demolished for souvenirs), the participants questioned so frequently and at such length that they grew impatient with the subject. Various on-the-spot written accounts were scrutinised by Valley sages for flaws and discrepancies and, years later, by radio and television pundits, projecting "We Were There" programmes to audiences who were beginning to think of Hitler in terms of Napoleon and Kruger. The truth was, of course, no one person achieved the honour of restoring Shratt to his indignant escort but three—Claire Craddock, Henry Pitts and young John—each made independent contributions to what occurred at the foot of Shallowford House drive that July evening. The contribution of the two former could be described as deliberate; that of the latter involuntary.

When Henry Pitts reached for his rook-rifle outside Sam Potter's gate and found nothing more lethal than a bunch of stinging nettles he did not, at first, suspect theft but was inclined to attribute the absence of the gun to his own absent-mindedness and Sam's homebrewed scrumpy. The latter consideration did not engage him for more than a moment. He had been drinking cider all his life and had been known to down eleven pints at The Raven on national occasions, such as Mafeking Night and the collapse of the General Strike in May 1926. Sam's cider, of course, was powerful stuff but he had only swallowed three half-pint mugs and his head was clear and his gait steady.

After a moment's puzzled reflection he returned to Sam's kitchen and made a thorough search and when it failed to produce the missing weapon he went down on his hands and knees and crawled the length of the picket fence. Then, growing more puzzled every moment, he crossed the path where his countryman's eye noted a fresh tear in a rhododendron stalk exactly opposite the gate. Muttering "the bliddy young thief", and suspecting now that his gun had been borrowed by one of the youngsters following him as rearguard beaters, he pushed into the bushes where he found a far more sinister clue in the marshy ground adjoining the lake.

It consisted of four patterned depressions, two round and shallow and two, a calf's-length away, sharper and deeper. Henry had floundered in mud for nearly three years on the Western Front and he recognised the tracks for what they were without any difficulty at all. The shallow depressions were made by knees and the ones behind them by toecaps. They told him that whoever had taken his rifle had been crouching there when he put it aside to open the gate and from this fact he deduced that the theft had been furtive and deliberate and not a casual act of borrowing as he had at first supposed. Having decided this he made an identification in a single leap. Only a hunted man would crouch in the bushes and watch for a chance to steal a weapon and the realisation of what his carelessness had achieved made him break out in a cold sweat.

"By Christ!" he said aloud, "tiz that bliddy Nazi! He'll do mischief and I'll be to blaame vor it."

The certainty of being pilloried up and down the Valley as an accessory to nameless Nazi outrages acted as a spur to his powers of deduction. Having, albeit innocently, armed a truculent escaped prisoner, Henry took upon himself the full responsibility for recapturing the miscreant. On the assumption that Shratt would have turned away from the line of beaters he waddled along the margin of the lake looking for evidence of route and because the ground here was soft his search was rewarded by a whole series of footprints that recrossed the track about two hundred yards west of the cottage.

He was about to tackle the long timbered slope to the ridge when it occurred to him that he was weaponless so he hurried back along the path hoping to find one of the fire-brooms stacked close to the fence and thinking he could use the stave as a quarterstaff. On reaching the rack, however, it struck him that Sam might have a much handier weapon in his tool shed and so he had, a massive, six-foot pitchfork, with curved wooden prongs, the kind of agricultural implement that had been out of fashion in the Valley when Henry was a boy. He seized it gratefully and returned to the islet at a stumbling trot, plunging up the overgrown slope without the customary breather that he accepted as obligatory between all bursts of energy these days.

The ascent nearly killed him. At the point where the trees fell away his heart was pounding against his ribs and he was bathed in sweat but he saw something that made him redouble rather than slacken his pace on the easier slope down to the Big House. It was the stealthy retreat of Otto Shratt from the forecourt to the stableyard after his initial reconnaissance of the car.

Henry Pitts knew his limitations. He was sixteen stone and badly out of condition, even for a man nudging sixty-five, but he also knew his duty and was aware that, in the absence of visible allies, he must tackle this man alone, notwithstanding the disparity between a loaded rook-rifle and a wooden-pronged pitchfork. At the same time the lessons of the Somme and Passchendaele returned to him in his hour of need and he checked his pace somewhat, deciding on the indirect approach. Instead of setting up a view-halloo and rushing upon his quarry he took advantage of the eastern side of the hedgerow and worked his way down through the Shallowford rose-garden and across the edge of the eastern paddock to the double gates at the foot of the drive. There was no doubt in his mind that Shratt intended to steal Claire Craddock's runabout and that he was even now searching the stables for petrol. There was only one vehicular exit from Shallowford House and for this reason the big iron gates had never been closed in Henry's memory. He would shut them,

97

wait in ambush for Shratt to get out of the car, and then attack him before he could regain it, preferably whilst his back was turned.

Laying aside his pitchfork he grabbed hold of the rusted ironwork on his side of the drive but he had not bargained for the seals of the years. The heavy gate, sunk on one hinge and disconnected from the other did not yield an inch. Weeds anchored it to the ground and its sagging weight had dug a deep furrow in the gravel. Desperately he ran across the drive and put shoulder to the other gate reasoning that half a barrier was better than none but this was as rooted as its fellow. Lacking crowbar there seemed no hope at all of implementing his plan.

At that moment, when he was exerting his not inconsiderable strength on the lodge half of the gate, his attention was distracted by an outcry from the head of the drive. A woman was shouting and a second or so later there was a crash of glass and a single shot backed by the thin roar of a motor-engine. The sounds injected guilt into Henry with the thrust of a blunt hyperdermic needle. Someone—Claire Craddock most probably—was being shot down in her own house by a Nazi, and that Nazi had been equipped to kill by his—Henry Pitts'—carelessness. The realisation of this caused him so much dismay that he stopped heaving and stood forlornly in the centre of the gateway staring up the drive and at a loss what action to take.

Then the decision was made for him. Two more shots and a soft explosion prefaced the appearance of the bull-nosed Morris as it lurched round the first curve of the drive, mounted the grass verge and regained the roadway in a matter of yards. It approached him uncertainly but at a surprising speed and it is to his credit that he did not leap behind the gate pillar but stood his ground, as though he intended to use himself as a living barrier to the car's further progress.

Then another unexpected thing happened. The car began to lurch, first to its offside then to its nearside, and finally appeared to continue its descent almost broadside on to within about five yards of where Henry stood. Lacking even his pitchfork Henry resorted to the only means of aggression left to him. He began to make threatening gestures and hurl abuse at the approaching enemy, prancing up and down like an elderly witch-doctor in personal combat with a legion of devils. Improbably his incantations seemed to have some effect for the car, now seen to contain not only the German but also young John Craddock, sheered away to Henry's right, mounted the verge again and crashed broadside on into the gate pillar after which it bounced back and canted over at an angle of forty-five degrees.

To his immense relief Henry saw John scramble out, duck through the paddock railings that were now supporting the car, and run diagonally across the paddock at what Henry later described as "a bliddy hell of a lick". At the same time the German bobbed up from the shattered offside of the car and he too seemed to be unhurt for he glared at Henry and at once reached back into the debris for his rifle.

Henry himself was never specific on what occurred from that moment on. All that is certain is that Henry found his pitchfork and the German found his rifle so that they confronted one another at a range of about twelve feet. Something made the German hesitate. Either he was dazed by the impact or sufficiently clearheaded to reflect upon the dire penalties of shooting a civilian whilst on the run. Whatever the reason he turned aside, scrambled from the wreckage of the Morris and made a dash for the hedge abutting the lodge. Henry knew that pursuit on foot was out of the question. Even had he not been blown by his previous exertions he would have lost his man in a hundred yards. So he did what seemed to come naturally to him and used his pitchfork as a javelin, hurling it across the width of the drive with the full strength of his arm.

It was the luckiest toss imaginable. Its prongs enclosed Shratt's neck just as he was gathering himself for a leap down from the hedge and the terrible weight of the blow not only precipitated him head over heels into Maureen Rudd's delphiniums, but almost broke his neck into the bargain.

Henry, hardly able to believe his good luck, gaped at the hedge for half a minute before running across to the gate and entering the garden. When he saw his adversary flat on his face, and Smut's rook-rifle backsight-deep in the soft soil of the aster bed, he roared with triumph. He had every right to exult. Shratt was the first man brought down by a javelin hereabouts for more than a thousand years.

Claire, still holding the deer-rifle, was beside him in a moment and together they stared down at the prostrate foe. He noticed that her face, ordinarily a pleasing pink, was the colour of clotted cream and that her hands shook so violently that they had no business to be holding a loaded firearm. Taking the rifle he said quietly, "Did 'ee do any mischief upalong?"

"No," Claire said, "the boy is all right and Thirza just fainted. He *is* a German, isn't he?"

"Aar," Henry said, "'Er jumped a train backalong but I dorn reckon he'll try it again for a spell."

"Is he dead?"

"No, he baint dead but he's out cold. I'll watch un while you go an' ring the Command Post an' police."

"I can't. He ripped the 'phone out when he took John away."

"Did 'er now? Well then, us' better drag un inzide the lodge. Tak' his heels, will 'ee?"

But in the event there was no need to manhandle the prisoner for at that moment, horn blaring, a squad of Royal Marines raced up the river road, the sergeant explaining breathlessly that they had heard shots whilst beating the edge of the Moor.

"We'll take over, Ma'am," he said, jubilantly, as though he personally had made the capture. "Who knocked him out?"

"I did," said Henry, without pride.

"With your bare fists, gaffer?"

"No, with that bliddy pitchfork."

"Christ!" said the sergeant and left it at that.

Henry gathered up pitchfork and rook-rifle and stayed until they had lifted Shratt into the troop-carrier and driven him away. Then, with Claire, he walked up the drive to see how young John was faring. The boy did not seem much the worse for his adventure. In retrospect it seemed a splendid thing to have participated in such a dramatic incident and he was careful to remind them of his own contribution to the climax.

"I pulled the wheel round," he said. "Mother made it easy by pooping the tyre and he was having to use both hands to keep her on the road."

"That was right smart of you," said Henry, but sadly, for somehow he did not feel that his javelin throwing at the gate squared his idiocy in leaving a loaded gun about in the presence of a dangerous fugitive. It was several days before the deadly accuracy of his cast obliterated the magnitude of his folly but this line of reasoning was not general in the Valley. Nobody but Henry remembered how Otto "von"

100

Shratt had acquired the weapon but the manner of his capture passed into Valley legend within a month. Anyone passing the asphalt playgrounds of Coombe Bay or Whinmouth in the next year or so might have heard vulgar little boys chanting four lines of doggerel composed, within hours of the incident, by some unknown Shallowford jester with a sense of occasion and no particular regard for accuracy. Like "The Ram of Derbyshire", and other strictly localised folklore, it was an attempt on the part of provincials to ensure that their achievements were not entirely lost to posterity. It ran:

> "Jerry come to Shallowford
> Us woulden let un pass
> Us stuck a wooden pitchfork
> Right up his arse."

Henry never challenged the implied arrogance of the "us", or the regional accuracy of the impact but sometimes, in his declining years, he would pass the Shallowford entrance and pause awhile, glancing at the delphinium bed and murmuring, with intense pride, "Bliddy spot on, it was! Coulden've done better with a twelve-bore, I coulden."

CHAPTER FIVE

TOUR OF INSPECTION

I

ON the first Saturday of the holidays John Craddock, eight years old and probably the most self-contained person in the Sorrel Valley, packed his knapsack, slung his binoculars and box camera, and without telling his mother where he was going set off across the pasture land behind Home Farm in the direction of the Royal Marine camp on the moor.

Claire watched him go, restraining an impulse to call and ask his destination, for she had long ago come to terms with the inscrutability of her youngest child and had never, from the moment she had realised she was carrying another child at the almost indecent age of fifty, understood his place in the pattern of family life. Paul, she suspected, was equally baffled, although father and son got along well enough, and sometimes seemed to her like a couple of elderly relatives making polite conversation. He did not even look like any of the others, although there were moments when she thought she could see the stamp of a boyish Paul Craddock in the long face, serious eyes, and slightly mutinous set of the jaw. As for the Derwent half it was nowhere to be found, and Claire sometimes found herself looking at him with the same puzzled exasperation as she had experienced when Doctor Maureen assured her, with hoots of laughter, that the second honeymoon she and Paul had stolen just after their silver wedding anniversary had resulted in this unlooked-for bonus.

She said, as Paul came in and sat down to a late breakfast, "That boy is off again. Where do you suppose he goes with all that equipment he lugs about?"

"God knows," Paul said, "bird-watching probably. You're not worried about him losing himself, are you?"

"Of course I'm not," she replied, indignantly, "I should think any child of mine would have enough sense to find his way home by dark but there is something about him ... something I can't put a name to ... what I mean is, he never seems to *need* anyone!"

"Lucky chap!" Paul said, and returned to his toast and newspaper, but this morning she was not disposed to be shrugged off and said, "Oh, put that paper down, Paul! It's all rubbish anyway and you can hear far more up-to-date news on the wireless. What I'm trying to say is that it doesn't seem normal. I asked him if he'd like a friend to stay for a bit, or if he would like to go up to his aunt's in Gloucestershire where he could ride with some of her pupils, but he looked almost outraged at the idea. None of the others were the least bit like him at that age. The Pair had each other, and Whiz and Young Claire were always filling the house with young people, and even Mary tagged along behind Rumble wherever she went. But that boy lives in a world of his own."

"It's our world as well. There isn't a soul he doesn't know by Christian name between here and the main line, or a bush either, judging by those sketches of his."

"You mean you've been prying up in his room?"

"Not prying, just looking about a bit. He's got so many enthusiasms. Maybe that's why he doesn't need friends."

He had forgotten his newspaper and customary fourth cup of tea. "Have you got a minute? I'll show you what I mean." He filled his mouth with toast and lunged out of the room before she could protest but she trotted after him, saying, "I'm not sure I like rummaging among his things behind his back, Paul," but Paul only laughed and said, "Rubbish! We're entitled to know something about him and he'll not volunteer much. Besides, he knows I look at his books and drawings. I had quite a talk with him up there after we had that letter from his headmaster with last term's report."

She remembered the letter, a guardedly phrased communication, stressing the boy's preoccupation with what seemed to the Reverend Oliver Bowles, headmaster of the Paxtonbury Preparatory School, time-wasting and unorthodox subjects, among them free drawing, ornithology, photography, and even entomology. It had not been a critical letter but had contained tacit advice to them to bring the boy's mind to bear more directly upon subjects that would enable him to pass Common Entrance.

"Well, he's certainly got brains," Claire said reluctantly, "but what *kind* of brains exactly? Will he ever make a farmer, do you suppose?"

"Now how the devil can I tell you that at his age?"

She knew she was probing a tender spot and did not care to pursue this line of enquiry. With Simon spending his entire youth immersed in politics, and The Pair making a fortune out of scrap metal, she was aware that Paul put small faith in transmitting his enthusiasms to any of their children, and this, in itself, was odd for the Derwents had farmed High Coombe for generations and Paul himself hardly gave a thought to anything not rooted in red Devon soil. She followed him into the surprisingly tidy bedroom that had once been Simon's, and after that Rumble Patrick's, deciding that neither of the previous occupants had used it as anything but a sleeping place whereas John, whom she still thought of as hardly more than a toddler, had converted it into a cross between a library, a studio and a museum.

" 'I converse with myself alone and with my books'," Paul quoted and pointed to two rows of volumes devoted to British birds, woodcraft, fieldcraft, butterflies, fossils, amateur photography and other specifically outdoor subjects. There were two other books seldom found on the bedside shelf of an eight-year-old. One was White's *Natural History of Selborne,* the other some second-rate reproductions of the French Impressionists. Paul, who seemed to know his way around up here, showed her round like a professional guide. Under the window was a glass case containing more than fifty eggs, and on the dressing-table a collection of what seemed at first glance shapeless pieces of stone but on closer inspection were seen to be fossils. He had even rigged up a cupboard as a darkroom and some unsuccessful prints lay on the shelf among an assortment of jay's feathers. For some reason the wide range of interests advertised here comforted her and she said, "Well, of the whole lot of them he's obviously the most likely to take after you. Did you direct his attention to these kind of hobbies?"

"No, I didn't," he said emphatically, "and I didn't have to either. He already knows far more than I do about birds and insects and when did you see me grubbing for fossils? But this isn't what I wanted to show you."

He pulled out a drawer and took out a sketchbook, opening it at random and showing her a vigorous drawing of two men at work with a double-handed saw. It had nothing in common with the kind of pencil-sketches Claire remembered making as a child; there was truth and vitality in every line, and the back muscles of the sawyer turned away from the artist were seen as ripples under the taut skin. She knew nothing about drawing or painting but she did not have to be told that here was proof, not only of close observation, but of creativity. She said, once again confused, "It seems remarkable at his age. Oughtn't we to do something to encourage it? I mean, those school reports of his weren't anything to write home about, and perhaps he should go to a place where he could be taught this kind of thing properly? There are such places, aren't there?"

She had, he reflected, a rather naïve faith in his erudition and judgment in these matters and he knew its origin. She had seen him derive a good deal of pleasure from books left behind in the library by their predecessors, the Lovells, and had stood beside him at local auctions when he had put in a bid for a piece of porcelain, or a picture that took his fancy.

"Yes," he said, "there are such places but I wouldn't care to let him plough a furrow of that kind at eight. It seems to me that he hasn't yet made up his mind what dominates his interests and he'll have to make that discovery for himself. Most kids, growing up in a place like this, have passing obsessions with birds and eggs and insects and even cameras, but it's too early to head him in any one direction. I can only tell you one thing about him that's rare. He has a genius for organisation. Look at those hand-printed labels under the eggs, and the things he has written about the fossils. He got the idea from the local natural history museum of course, but the point is the pains he has taken to docket and arrange. Look at these sketches. Each of them is dated, and most of them are titled. That's far more unusual at his age than sketching and collecting, and I'm wondering if there is any relevance in what old Parson Horsey was telling me the other day after John had got him to show how brass rubbings were made. Horsey is quite taken with the kid and says it proves a theory."

"What theory is that?"

Paul said, with a broad grin, "The child of mature parents is always the brainiest. Something of the experience of life is supposed to be transmitted to a latecomer. It isn't just Horsey's notion, of course. I've heard it before but in our case it fits. He's certainly the most original of the litter! Do you remember how outraged you were when you realised you were having him?"

"I was thinking of it only this morning when I saw him mooching off with his little knapsack but I rather hoped you had forgotten!"

"Not me," he told her, "I don't forget things like that. It was just before we lost young Claire and I always thought John's arrival helped us ride that one out, but don't imagine I associate him with sadness. As a matter of fact I want to smile whenever I think of it. Do you remember that glorious romp we had up in Anglesey, the one that produced him? It was like being given a week of our youth back. We're not likely to have that experience again."

"You don't do so badly for sixty-plus," she said and as always when they were alone she felt a surge of affection for him and reaching out grabbed his shoulders and kissed him. "Let John find his own way around like we had to," she said, happy to dismiss the problem. "At least we can depend upon him being the final presentation! By God, you've had your moneysworth, haven't you? Six, and all nicely spaced over thirty-four years."

"It's often puzzled me that there weren't twenty-six," he said, catching her mood and they went down to finish a leisurely breakfast, glad of the privacy of the house and the sudden stillnesses that came to it these days.

II

Before the days of wireless and the regular delivery of London newspapers in the Valley, Paul had made a habit of riding the rounds like a leisurely despatch-rider charged with acquainting his tenants and their dependents with the substance of national events. Nowadays, of course, it would have been a pointless occupation. Every farm and cottage had its radio set and there were more than a score of telephones in the Valley, excluding those at the camp on the moor. Since Local Defence Volunteers had been upgraded to Home Guard urgent messages were passed through the camp exchange to the Observer Crops lookout post on the Bluff that had a line connecting it to the permanently manned Home Guard depot and the resident constable's house, in Coombe Bay. It was all very sophisticated compared with the old days. For every horseman you saw in the Valley there were at least three motor-cyclists. Paul took his turn of duty with the Home Guard and sometimes spent a night in the eastern outpost, half-way along the bay to Whinmouth, but whenever he rode nowadays he did it for exercise and went inland through the woods.

"Squire's Rounds", as they had once called them, were still made by a Craddock but in the person of young John, and during school holidays he covered a great deal of ground on his short, sturdy legs. Old timers like Henry Pitts and Smut Potter thought him rather comical, a parody of his over-conscientious father, but some of the womenfolk, and even some of the men training up at the camp, were concerned at the amount of gear he always carried and tried to reason with him, sometimes going so far as to employ goo-goo talk in the attempt, as though he had been three instead of eight and more familiar with the terrain than the best of them. He would never show impatience with their questions but would listen politely and then plod on his way, his head moving from side to side, as though to ensure that he missed nothing of interest.

Perhaps Paul knew him better than he supposed for he was close to the truth when he told Claire the boy had yet to find an overriding interest. He was interested in everything and in everybody, in colour patterns and sun patterns, in the sedge blades that guarded the shallows of the Sorrel like a forest of short, Roman swords, in the travelling "V" of a vole's progress downstream, in soldiers at drill and soldiers at ease, in the cackling sneer of the gull prospecting the camp dump, in the brilliant flash of the kingfisher and the monotonous call of the cuckoo. He knew both the common and local names of every wild flower that grew about here, and where and when it could be found. He knew the many eccentricities of the older inhabitants, the emphasis they put into their favourite swear words and the kind of thing that made them swear. He could have described the badges of rank on the sleeves and shoulders of every man up at the camp and he knew, from the speech idioms of new drafts, the county from which they had been recruited. Whatever he missed with his eye or neglected to memorise, he recorded with his camera or sketchbook that he usually carried along with his sandwiches and bottle of cold tea in his knapsack. He haunted the lanes and hedges and coppices of the area like an industrious but unhurried bee prospecting each foxglove bell for the nectar of knowledge, and when he returned home, tired but modestly triumphant, he would empty his box camera and his knapsack on the bed and arrange his day's haul into some kind of order.

He found pleasure in brief conversations with others, particularly adults who could tell him something new, or clarify some process that puzzled him, but on the whole he preferred his own company and could pass a pleasant afternoon watching and wondering and weighing one thing against another. He did not quarrel with the regimen of school, recognising it as a kind of obligatory penance imposed upon everyone once they reached the age of six. At school one could pay attention in certain lessons—history, English, geography, and basic science—and dream one's way through periods devoted to algebra, geometry and French. Schoolmasters as a whole, he decided, were well-meaning bores, and teaching was one profession that he had deleted from a long list of possibles, along with any other work that would confine him indoors. There were, however, a host of alternatives and time enough to make a deliberate choice. He could be an archeologist-explorer, a zoo-keeper, a painter in the style of anyone from, say, Renoir (whose pouting little girls fascinated him), to that Dutch chap with an unpronounceable name who specialised in crowd scenes of tiny figures beetling about vast, open landscapes. He could, he supposed, be a squire like his father, or a farmer like Rumble Patrick or old Francis Willoughby over at Deepdene, but these occupations lacked variety and every fresh holiday, when he could do as he pleased for as long as he pleased, promised more and more variety in an ever expanding field of possibility. It was an exciting prospect this growing-up, but lately he was approaching a stage where he found comfort in the knowledge that years must pass before he had to make a final decision. In the meantime, the thing to do was to explore and experiment, to circle the perimeter of every new experience and this, more or less consciously, was precisely what he was doing on this fine August morning, with something like four hours freedom in front of him and no questions asked on his return home.

He crossed the hedge dividing the last Home Farm meadow from the river road, stopped a moment to examine a tuft of cat's ear and wonder how it had acquired its name, studied a large yellow iris growing on the very edge of the Sorrel, and then wandered eastward beyond Codsall bridge, peering among the streamers of pond weed that old Martha Pitts called "Jinny-Green-Teeth", hoping to spot a trout or grayling. Seeing none he settled his equipment more comfortably on his shoulders and pottered up the hill to the crest of the moor where the huge camp came into view, the sun catching the bayonet of the guard patrolling the wide, clover-leaf approach that led to the guardhouse and gate through the wire.

He stood for a moment watching the scene below, wondering if the usual truckloads of khaki-clad figures would emerge and make for the assault course where he could follow on and watch men descend the death-slide like encumbered Tarzans but none did. Far away, across the parade ground, an N.C.O. Discip. could be heard warbling commands half an octave beyond his pre-war range. A sergeant in shirt-sleeves stood on the guardhouse porch polishing a boot. The sentry continued to pace ten steps left, ten steps back and it was only for want of something more entertaining that John gave him his full attention, noticing that there was something a little odd about his turnout. He continued to stare unblinkingly until he discovered what was amiss. The man's cap badge had dropped off his beret and a moment later John spotted it, shining like a silver star directly in the man's beat.

It was curious, he thought, that the sentry did not notice it for every twenty seconds his boots came crashing down within inches of it but then, John reasoned, it wasn't curious after all, for like all good sentries he marched with his eyes on the middle distance. Watching, John saw trouble approaching. A staff car came slowly up the main avenue of the camp and the sergeant, throwing aside his boot, moved towards the gate to let it through and John saw his chance while the attention of the officer in the car was on the sergeant. He moved forward, unslinging his camera and, at the same time, side-kicking the badge towards the sentry who had faced about and was in the act of slamming his butt in salute.

The man saw the badge and the officer saw John's camera in the same split second. The officer sprang out and doubled round the car, shouting, "Hi, there! *You*, there! You can't take pictures here, sonny!" and the sergeant, determined to get in on the act, roared, "You can't take pictures here!" but John understood that although both sounded fierce and emphatic they were also amused at this effrontery, and that this was a fortunate thing for it gave him an opportunity to occupy their attention long enough for the sentry to scoop up his cap badge, slip it on, and resume his rigid pose. This, in fact, was precisely what happened for the officer, a heavily-built middle-aged man suddenly became waggish and pointed to a security poster on the camp notice-board. "You're old enough to read, aren't you? What's that say up there?"

"Careless talk costs lives', sir," John said, equably, and then, as a polite qualification, "I wasn't talking, sir."

The officer looked baffled but then decided to laugh and at once the sergeant joined in, saying, "You live around here, don't you?" and John said, very politely, that he did, and that his father was Squire Craddock who owned the land as far as the River Whin, behind the camp.

At this the sergeant laughed first but straightened his face at once as the officer said, "Well, I'm sorry about that, but you still can't carry a camera around the camp. Nobody can! It's against regulations! Is that clear?"

"Yes, sir."

The sergeant, wishing perhaps to atone for his premature laugh, said, "Er—those binoculars, sir."

"Yes by George! It's a regular spy outfit, sergeant. Do you suppose we ought to clap him in the guardhouse?"

"No, sir," replied the sergeant, who was reckoned a bit of a humorist. "If we did his dad would give us notice to quit," and at this the balance of joviality was restored and they both laughed very heartily indeed.

John let them enjoy their joke. Out of the corner of his eye he saw that the sentry's cap badge was back in place so that when the officer said, "Run along then, and don't bring that kit round here again, there's a war on," he replied, "Yes, sir", and the officer climbed back into the car while the sergeant returned to his boot polishing.

When the car had disappeared John and the sentry exchanged grins but it was not until he was at the extreme end of his beat that the man said, "Thanks, chum. Nicely managed," in a stage whisper. It was a more than adequate acknowledgment John felt, enlarging both of them at nobody's expense, and he turned and plodded away over the lower crest of the moor having crossed yet another profession off his list, for who, in his senses, would want to be at the mercy of a little tin badge and superiors who indulged in Second Form jokes? It was not even worth the glory of dying on a bloodstained cloak like General Wolfe and whispering "Thank God!" when the aide-de-camp cried, "They run, sir! They run!" This was a future he had conjured with after seeing a colour-plate reproduction of "The Heights of Abraham" in his school history book.

III

Feeling that he had derived something worthwhile from the encounter he crossed the track at the point where it met Hermitage Lane and here, with a pant and a wriggle, Henry Pitts' aged Labrador, Nosey, ran up to him. John and Nosey were old friends and John foraged in his knapsack for a sandwich that the dog swallowed at a gulp. Anticipating more he trotted at John's heels when the boy tackled the steep slope up to French Wood and here, surprisingly, he encountered David Pitts, son of Henry and master of Hermitage contemplating a rusting tractor. John had a scale of intimates in the Valley and David was about half-way up the scale, several notches below Rumble Patrick, Mary and old Henry, a long way above the new people at High Coombe, who persisted in treating him as a five-year-old. David, a slow-thinking, serious man in his late thirties, said, "Wot be 'at then? Bird-watchin'?", and without waiting for an answer went on, "Bide a minnit, I seed a yellow-hammer yerabouts a minnit zince!"

They stood quite still by the bonnet of the tractor and John carefully unslung his binoculars and handed them to the broad-shouldered man at his side, who trained them on a section of hedge. Presently he said, "There 'er be. On thicky low branch, this zide o' the gap," and passed the binoculars back to John, who ranged the hedge for a minute before getting the bird in focus.

He studied it lovingly, for the yellow-hammer was one of his favourites and not often spotted. The nape, head and belly were like slivers of lemon peel but the duller wing feathers were the colour of the rubbed guinea that old

Francis Willoughby wore on his watch fob. "It's a male, David," he said, as the dog Nosey flopped and the bird, alerted, skimmed the hedge and dipped into the wood. "Is there a pair nesting up here?"

"Not as I know of," said David, "but I'll keep a look out. There was last year, with five eggs in but I didn't tell 'ee, I was afraid you'd raid 'un. I likes them yaller-boys. They eats a rare lot o' pests. Be 'ee going' backalong for a cup o' tay wi' Mother?"

"Tomorrow," John said, "I got to make the rounds today."

"Ah!" said David understandingly, "that's as it should be. Time was when Squire made 'em regular, once a week. Twice sometimes, depending on what was stirring, but he'll be busy so I reckon he's glad to have you backalong."

It did not strike him as odd that an eight-year-old should take himself seriously. He was a serious man himself, rooted in tradition, with very little of his father's sense of humour. He watched the boy climb through the gap and not until he had been swallowed up by the summer foliage of French Wood did he permit himself to exclaim.

"Gordamme!" he said aloud, "if he baint a chip off the old block! Tiz like old times just zeein' 'im." He made a mental note to describe the encounter to his wife and ensure that she did not miss the symbolism of it, but the past had no meaning for John so that he forgot about David by the time he had crossed the protective paling of the wood put there to keep out the deer. Then, on the far side of the coppice he saw two Red Admirals playing at falling leaves on a shaft of sunlight and waited for them to settle so that he could get a closer look at the chain of islands decorating the scalloped margins of the wings. They looked, he thought, like a map of the Hebrides and he had never before noticed that the spots were precisely balanced, as though put there by a painter with a passion for symmetry. It was the same, he reflected, with the four "eyes" on the wings of the Peacock butterfly, each pair being carefully matched, so that you could never mistake a hind wing "eye" for a fore wing "eye". The arrangement impressed him. God, he reflected, must be an extremely busy person, with a wonderful eye for detail. There was absolutely nothing, it seemed, he was likely to overlook once he had rolled up the sleeves of his nightshirt and got busy after his winter holiday. So far, try as he might, John had never been able to catch him out and find a piece of botched work, although he was disinclined to take things for granted and had hopes that one day he would chance upon a celestial error of one kind or another.

In the meantime, the butterflies having resumed their aimless saraband, he made his way down from the escarpment and into Shallowford Woods where he found a stump halfway down the wooded slope and ate his snack whilst contemplating a heron doing some leisurely fishing among the reeds at the eastern end of the Mere.

It was hot and still up here, with tree-talk reduced to the kind of whispers people exchanged in church. The only sounds that reached him, apart from the hushed tissing of the beeches, was the deliberate plop of a fish, or perhaps an otter, and the high undertone of bees searching the bells of foxgloves that grew in great straggling clumps beside the path. He did not worship trees, as his father obviously did, but he could understand his father's reluctance to cut one down, for they surely took many lifetimes to grow to this height and to fell one was to make a change. He was like his father in that respect, wanting everything to stay as he remembered it, and thinking this he wondered if he wished it was always summer and that he could stop growing up. There were certain advantages, he thought, in remaining a boy and obvious disadvantages in growing as old and sad-faced as his father, or as big around the rump as his mother, or, for that matter, as bristly as the officer at the camp, or as wheezy as old Francis Willoughby over at Deepdene. Ruthlessly, and with a certain relish, he considered the physical penalties of old age, among them the tiresome necessity of soaping one's face and scraping it with a razor like his father and his eldest brother Simon whose whiskers sprouted like tares. For a man as old as his father, however, he judged Paul pretty active, particularly on horseback, but the older women grew the more they seemed to spread and a tendency to acquire a fat belly was not confined to the impossibly old, like Martha Pitts. Even his sister Mary, whom he considered only middleaged, had recently put on a great deal of weight and was already walking clumsily and inclined to breathlessness.

He was considering this, and trying to equate Mary's present girth with his earliest memories of her at Periwinkle, when his eye was alerted by a flutter of white seen through the snarl of branches between his stump and the Mere, and

113

on looking more closely was surprised to see Mary sitting about a hundred yards below him on a mossy log, opposite the islet. He was not a person to contain curiosity and hitching his gear he drifted down the slope to ask her why she was there but he must have moved more silently than he intended, for when he emerged from the trees she gave a gasp and crammed the pages she was reading into her handbag. He was puzzled by the implied guilt of her action and wondered what it could be that she was reading, and then he remembered that a fat letter with an American stamp had been lying by her plate at breakfast and that she had made a poor pretence at ignoring it until everybody had finished eating and had then slipped away, taking the unopened letter with her. He noticed something else about her that puzzled him. Her eyes glittered as though she had been crying and it occurred to him that the letter must be from Rumble Patrick and contained bad news of one kind or another. He said, with the terrible candour of youth, "Who's dead? It isn't Rumble is it?"

She stared at him with her mouth slightly open, as though he had said something bad like the word "bugger" that had earned him a clout on the ear at Easter. Then, while he waited, she did her best to look ordinary again and he reminded himself that she was the quickest person he knew to turn pink and lose control of a situation. She said, with a laughable attempt at severity, "Of course he isn't dead! This letter's from him. What on earth makes you say a terrible thing like that?"

"You were blubbing," he said, calmly, "but I'm jolly glad Rumble is okay. It's funny him not being here this hols. It's not the same, somehow. I passed Periwinkle on the way down from the moor. It looks like a big bonfire. After it's out I mean."

He waited, hoping she would tell him about the letter but instead she did something that would have irritated him very much had she been anyone but Mary, who was born that way and couldn't help herself he supposed. She shot out her arms and embraced him, pressing him hard against her fat stomach, so that he suddenly remembered what had made him interrupt his rounds and approach her. He said as she released him, "What's up, then? Is it because you're getting fat?"

He was accustomed to adults reacting to perfectly reasonable questions with gusts of laughter or superior smiles but in her present mood her laughter surprised him. She said, struggling to contain it, "No, no, John. I wasn't crying about getting fat. I'm glad I'm getting fat. The fatter, the better," and then she stopped, wondering if she had gone too far. Their relationship, eased by Rumble, had always been an undemanding one but she shared her mother's uncertainty about him. Sometimes it seemed to her he had never been a baby at all but had come into the world as a precocious eight-year-old whom it was impossible to treat as a child. At first she was inclined to change the subject but suddenly, deciding that she badly needed a confidant, she said:

"I was crying because I miss Rumble even more than you do and this is to say he won't be home for longer than we thought. He's going through the Panama Canal and then right across the Pacific."

Digesting this news, and promising himself that he would look at a map as soon as he got home, John returned to the more pressing topic. "Why are you glad you're getting fat?"

She said, "Because I'm going to have a baby. That's what's making me fat and I like babies. It'll be someone for Jerry to play with and anyway, as soon as he arrives I'll be thin again." He said nothing so she went on. "You knew babies came from their mothers, didn't you? The same as cows and horses?"

One of the endearing things about John Craddock was his meticulous regard for the truth. He said, "No, not really. I knew of animals, of course. I saw one of Francis Willoughby's Red Devons calve—that time they had to kill the cow with the humane killer." His tone told her that he was concerned for her survival so she said gaily, "Well, they're not likely to use the humane killer on me so don't give it another thought."

"Why didn't you read the letter at breakfast?"

"Because I didn't want to cry in front of everybody."

"But how did you know you would if you hadn't read it?"

"Because I always do, I can't help it, it's just that I was born beside a waterworks—no, that's a joke—what I mean is, some people can control themselves and some can't. Just seeing Rumble's handwriting makes me start to snivel and I can't do a thing about it but you don't have to tell anyone up at the house you caught me at it."

"All right, I won't," he said, "but will you tell me something else about babies?"

She looked at him apprehensively and then smiled. More than ever he looked like a gnome, one of those wise, amiable gnomes who entertained Snow White in their house in the woods. "What do you want to know?"

"Can people who aren't married have them?"

She considered, reflecting that she might have anticipated this and said, at length, "Yes, they can, but it's silly of them because a baby has to have a father as well as a mother. Usually it's the father who earns the money that keeps all three and if a woman isn't married she's often in a fix." She wondered whether to leave it at that. He seemed satisfied but his honesty was infectious, so she went on, after a pause, "People fall in love and usually a baby arrives soon after that. Not always, of course, but as a rule. A baby isn't just something the mother produces. It's part of the father too and even with people who aren't married there has to be a father. It's like . . ."

"Like the bull?"

"Yes," she said gratefully, "like the bull."

"And Rumble Patrick is your bull?"

He paused, as always resenting adult laughter, although Mary's was moderate. "What's funny about that?"

"Nothing," she assured him, straightening her face, and for some reason feeling relieved at his innocence, "nothing at all. It was just an odd way of saying it. People are a bit different from animals and bulls don't love the cows, or not a particular cow. But men and women, Rumble and me for instance, happen to love one another, so it isn't in the least surprising that I'm having a baby and getting fat."

He intended asking her how this had been achieved in Rumble's absence but suddenly he understood that she had been making a considerable effort and decided that it would be unsporting to press her unduly, especially as she had been more patient with his line of questioning than his mother, the day he came home and sought further information concerning Francis Willoughby's cow. He said, rising from the log, "Do you want me to go now?"

He was, she told herself, a very penetrating person and suddenly she felt closer to him than to anyone since Rumble had left the Valley.

"No," she said, "it's nearly lunchtime. Let's go home to-

116

gether and you can show me where you found that spotted orchis you were talking about the other day."

Wild flowers was an interest they shared and in the climb through the open part of the wood he seemed to dismiss the subject of babies and their relation to her swelling figure, but when they had found the patch of orchis, and reached the gate that led through the long orchard to the stableyard, he said suddenly, "Will it be another boy?"

"I think so," she said, "but I can't be sure. It might be twins. Twins run in the family." And then, seizing him by the hand with an impulsive tug prompted by conspiratorial affection and genuine excitement, "Suppose it is? What shall we call them if they are a boy and a girl? Can you suggest something different?"

He said at once, "Yes. The boy could be Winston and the girl could be Sorrel."

"Why that's perfectly splendid," she said, meaning it. "We'll certainly bear that in mind at the christening," and as they clattered down the broad stone steps into the yard she told herself that meeting him out there had been very good for her morale, as good or better than the intended drag along the Mere to Rumble's cave, the sanctuary she usually sought on these occasions.

CHAPTER SIX

RATION PARTY

I

To some extent almost every living soul in the Valley was involved in the black market but the profits and privileges resulting for the majority were so insignificant that even a dedicated sleuth like Constable Voysey, resident officer at Coombe Bay, rarely bothered to investigate and check the steady traffic in pork, beef, poultry, illicitly produced clotted cream, butter and eggs. To do so would have involved a complex machinery of personnel and vehicles, a network of informers, the tapping of telephones, the establishment of lookout points and, probably, a huge gaol to accommodate the convicted. Up at the camp he suspected that there might be traffic in various commodities in short supply but this was the concern of the military police. All that the black-browed Voysey could do to control the flow of rationed food out of the Valley to Paxtonbury middlemen was to keep eyes and ears open and make an occasional pounce on careless minnows and this, being an extremely conscientious and patriotic officer, he did. Voysey did not have to be told, of course, that several much bigger fish swam freely round the pool without even approaching the net, or that, by this time, they had organised themselves into a syndicate capable, had they wished, of making nonsense of his endeavours as bailiff. Moreover, without any help from Squire Craddock (possibly Voysey's sole reliable ally in the entire Valley) he could identify those big fish and even classify them into weight categories.

The three Sorrel pike were Smut Potter, his French wife, Marie, and Jumbo Bellchamber, farming at The Dell halfway up the Coombe. They were at the hub of an organisation that reached out across the Valley, through farms and cottages, to the cold storage rooms of innumerable retailers extracting a steady profit from their regular peace-time customers, and Voysey, no matter how earnestly he tried, could only snatch the occasional customer and a local customer at that, for his superiors in Paxtonbury were clumsy at following up the leads he gave them after ducks and pigs and consignments of eggs had started on the first stage of their journey from his coastal patch.

It would be easy to see this widespread practice of selling rationed food as a war within a war, a vast and unsavoury conspiracy on the one hand and a determined preventive campaign on the other hand but it was not like that at all. There were no pitched battles, or even the odd skirmish of the kind Smut Potter had engaged in when he was king of the Valley poachers. There was no malice either, certainly not on the part of operators like Smut and Jumbo who, as survivors of one war, saw nothing unpatriotic in making a modest profit out of another. Smut, in fact, was prepared to defend himself when challenged by Squire Craddock, and his wife Marie, whose countrymen lay prostrate under the hated Boche, supported her husband's viewpoint. There was patriotism and there was profit, and far from seeing these virtues in conflict Marie had, with Gallic logicality, succeeded in marrying one to the other. As she pointed out to Squire when he argued that every fowl sold on the black market was a virtual betrayal of the Resistance, well-fed Englishmen were more likely to hound the Boche from her country than pallid, half-starved Englishmen, nourished on dried egg and spam. The occasional sustenance she put into the bellies of English families surely stiffened their determination and might even encourage them to launch a Second Front at the earliest opportunity. There was no answer to this kind of reasoning and when Paul, in desperation, appealed to Smut, he ran his head against another wall of unanswerable logic. Smut rolled up his trouser leg and displayed blue seams of flesh marking the leg wound he had received near Valenciennes, in 1918, and, to drive the lesson home, he pointed to the large portrait of his only son, locally known as "Bon-Bon", now serving in the Middle East.

"There's proof of what I got for a shillin' a day backalong," he said placidly, "and my boy tells me he's pickin' up vower-and zix a day in that bliddy ole desert where he's tu. If us can't make a bit extra when tiz there for the taakin' tiz a bliddy poor do, Maister. So dornee preach king-and-country to me. Us all does it one way or the other, an' you baint gonner tell me they Government chaps in London goes short of a fried egg or a leg o' chicken. Giddon, t'woulden surprise me if they didden zit down to oysters and champagne dree times a week!"

It was more or less the same when Paul pursued his investigations in the Coombe. Jumbo Bellchamber, and his wife Violet, stood shoulder to shoulder in defence of a black market that neither of them would admit existed to any great extent.

"You c'n tell that bloody nark Voysey he's welcome to look in here any day," Jumbo declared. "He won't see our larder overstocked, will he, Vi?"

"Damn it, I'm not talking abut the occasional fowl or the odd loin of pork you eat yourselves," protested Paul. "Everybody round here puts rationed food on their own table, and makes the occasional pound of butter on the side—you'd expect them to, seeing the opportunities they get. What Voysey suspects is that there's a regular run between here and Paxtonbury tradesmen and that the prime movers behind it are you and Smut. He isn't so sure about people like Francis Willoughby, the new people at High Coombe, and Henry Pitts, but he's got his eye on you two, so all I'm saying is watch out. If you're caught one of these days and end up in court don't expect bail or sympathy from me. I'm not at all sure that a conviction wouldn't amount to a breach of tenancy and give me the right to send you packing!"

The threat, if it was a threat, sobered Violet Bellchamber, in spite of the defensive grin it coaxed from her husband.

"Aw giddon Squire," she said, "you woulden do a thing like that to a Potter. We been here zince I don't know how long, and my Dad and Mother Meg thought a rare lot o' you from the very beginning. I'm not sayin' Jumbo and everyone else in the Valley is above makin' a shillin' or two zellin' butter an' crame to them as comes beggin' for it, but us baint losin' the war on that account, be us?"

Paul recognised the futility of arguing with them, of persuading them to involve themselves in the wider issues of the struggle. Nobody could call trench veterans like Smut Potter and Jumbo Bellchamber traitors, or even profiteers in the real sense of the word. Almost certainly, as in the last war, fortunes were being amassed by more sophisticated men who continued to think of themselves as patriots and by these standards the trickle of food that left the Valley by unauthorised routes was hardly worth a thought. All the same it would be degrading to see men and women he had always thought of as the real sinews of the country exposed in Paxtonbury police court as seedy rascals, cashing in on the U-boat campaign.

He reported the substance of his conversation to Voysey and left it at that, but the confrontations left a slightly sour taste in his mouth when he reflected that Valley men like Rumble Patrick were risking their lives to bring food and petrol across the Atlantic while this kind of hole-in-corner trading was common practice at home. He did not discuss the matter with Claire, suspecting, quite rightly, that she would laugh at his scruples. More than ever these days he was beginning to see himself as an ageing prig, deriving a glum satisfaction from the value he placed upon the old, cohesive loyalties of the Valley. "After all, who am I to preach?" he asked himself, hoisting his big frame into the saddle and riding through the open timber of Dell Wood to the sloping field that led down to the stableyard. "My own father made a packet out of the Boer War, and his partner, old Franz Zorndorff, made another out of the war after that, and both fortunes were used by me to keep this place in good heart over the last forty years. If I'm honest I suppose I don't give a damn what they do so long as they aren't caught redhanded and front-paged. That's something I wouldn't care to see at my time of life."

II

In point of fact he came within an inch of seeing it. Perhaps the fact that he did not was due less to Smut's dormant skill as a professional poacher than to the allegiance Paul had won during forty years of benevolent despotism in the area.

It was never established how the conscientious Constable Voysey got wind of Operation Christmas Stocking. He may have learned of Smut's plans to mount a seasonal delivery on an exceptionally big scale through an unguarded remark overheard at The Raven. Or he may have worked on assumption, keeping a close check on the goings and comings at Smut's bakery in Coombe Bay. At all events he went into action at dusk on December 23rd after peeping through the yard palings and watching Smut and Jumbo Bellchamber make a series of journeys to and from the bakery storehouse to a parked van. He knew Smut went to Paxtonbury for supplies once a week, and also that this was his usual day for going, and it must have seemed odd to him that his trip had been delayed until after blackout hours, when anyone driving about the Valley would have to do so on quarter-power headlights. In the event he kept the yard under close observation until he saw the van emerge with Smut at the wheel and Jumbo beside him. Having watched it climb the steep street and turn towards Codsall Bridge, he decided to stake everything on a hunch. Hurrying back to his quarters he 'phoned his inspector at Paxtonbury and suggested the setting up of a checkpoint at the site of the 1940 tank trap, where the Valley road, breasting the last swell of the moor, joined the main highway eight miles short of Paxtonbury. There were two alternative approaches to the city but Voysey, certain that he had not been spotted during his vigil, saw no reason why Smut should use them. Petrol was strictly rationed and each road meant a four-mile detour.

For once the inspector was alert and co-operative, promising to drive straight to the checkpoint and stop and search the van. Whatever it contained would have to be explained in detail and Voysey was confident that no explanations could account for a load that had necessitated at least a dozen encumbered journeys to and from the store. There was the time element, of course. The inspector would have to hurry to reach the road junction before the van turned into the main highway but Voysey calculated that Smut would make at least one stop en route, probably at Hermitage Farm, to pick up Henry Pitts' contribution to Cathedral Close Christmas dinners and in this surmise he was correct. The inspector reached the concrete buttresses at the junction without having seen the van pass in the opposite direction and here he waited, parking his Morris car across the single line approach of the moor road. It was just six o'clock, with little wind and a swirl of white mist shrouding the lower ground where the Sorrel wound its way past the Home Farm and Shallowford House to the sea.

In the meantime Voysey, leaving nothing to chance, got out

his own little car, an elderly Austin Seven, and drove after the van. Smut had had about fifteen minutes start but Voysey did not hurry. If, as would seem likely in the circumstances, Smut tried to double back into the Valley, he would find himself boxed between two police cars and panic was proof of guilt. Voysey, cruising along beside the swollen Sorrel, thought he had managed it all very nicely. Not only would he have struck a fatal blow at the Valley black market, there was also some likelihood of magisterial commendation when the case came to court.

It would surely have happened this way had it not been for Smut's poacher's instinct, a sixth sense inherent in all the Potters, whose ancestors had taken deer from Norman over-lords hereabouts as far back as the twelfth century. In Smut it was something stronger than an ancestral memory for its pulse had been adjusted by years of poaching over this very ground, and later by three years' practice as sniper and battalion scrounger on the Western Front. The moment he rose out of the Valley fog-blanket and tackled the last ascent of the moor, his eye registered an unnatural contour on the crest and when he ran his hand over the slightly misted windshield he saw a distant gleam about three feet long and two feet deep midway between the invisible concrete but-tresses of the tank trap. He said, shortly, "Someone's parked there, clean across the junction," and at once extinguished his lights and stopped the van. Jumbo Bellchamber, who was no poacher, showed impatience. "So what? It's only someone from the camp screwing a bint. Give 'em a toot to move over and let's get on. It's bloody parky up here in this perishing mist."

"I'm going to have a dekko," Smut said. "You wait here and if I whistle turn the van and we'll double back to Henry's."

Jumbo would have argued but in a matter of seconds, Smut had disappeared, moving with the utmost precision through the heather clumps on the steep side of the road until he was within twenty yards of the junction. Then he saw what, for all his vague uncertainties, he had not expected to see, the gleam of a row of silver-gilt buttons pinpointing a bulky shape left of the bonnet and it told him all he wanted to know. Turning, he zigzagged back across the moor and when within range of the van gave a low, penetrating whistle so that Jumbo, badly startled slid across the cushions, started up, slammed into reverse and pointed the van downhill just as Smut bobbed up on the nearside and jumped in.

"It's a bliddy copper!" he gasped, "Waitin' for us up there—jus' *waitin'* fer us! Get to hell out of here!"

Jumbo lacked Smut's nerve and fumbled with the gears so that Smut cried, "For Christ's sake . . ." as a powerful torch leaped out of the shadows above them and a distant voice called "Who's there? Stay where you are."

The challenge galvanised Jumbo into finding the right gear and the van shot off down the steep descent at forty miles an hour, driving straight into a baffling bank of mist so that Jumbo cried despairingly, "I can't see a bloody thing. I can't even see the bloody road."

"Just keep goin'," Smut said grimly, and reached out to steady the wheel as it juddered in a rut and the van bounced off the bank. "The minute Henry's gatepost shows up swing left, stop, and move over."

They saw the whitewashed gatepost when they were almost level with it and Jumbo wrenched the wheel hard over so that the van skidded and came into brief collision with the stones marking the entrance of Hermitage Lane. Then the engine stalled and Smut said, "Don't switch on and don't move neither," and was gone again, this time down the hill to a point where he could overlook the river road winding into the mist towards Codsall Bridge. One glance in that direction was enough. He saw, less than a quarter-mile to the east, two pinpricks of light moving uncertainly in his direction. Doubling back to the van he drove without lights down the narrow, squelching lane to Hermitage Yard.

"Call Henry. Bring his missus too," and he ran round to the rear of the van, flung open the doors and began hauling parcels wrapped in clean sacking out on to the cobbles. By the time Henry Pitts and his wife Ellie had emerged from the kitchen the van was half empty and Henry said, "In the barn. There's a feed bin just inside the door," and all four of them splashed across the slimy surface of the yard to dump their burdens in the half-empty bin. When the last was inside Henry slammed the lid and sealed it with a padlock.

"If it's the police, won't they look there?" Ellie said, breathlessly and Smut replied, "Not without a search warrant but they won't need one to look in the van. You got something I could be takin' in for repair, Henry? They might ask awkward questions."

"The wheelbarrow," Henry said and groped around until he laid hands on a half-dismembered wheelbarrow that had lain under the loft ladder since his father's time because nobody had ever bothered to move it. "You was takin' it over to Amos Smethick's for a new wheel," he said, and his wife added, with an excited giggle, "Make do an' mend. Just the job. I'll go and brew a dish o' tea."

They carried the ancient wheelbarrow into the yard, tossed it into the van and then trooped into the big kitchen where Jumbo, visibly shaken, spread his hands to the open hearth.

"Christ, that was a close shave," Smut said, looking as exhilarated as he felt. "That bliddy Voysey is a lot smarter'n I reckoned. He must have watched us load up, 'phoned Paxtonbury, and follered on. They'm probably up there now looking in all the rabbit holes but it won't take 'em long to figure out we doubled back yer. Us'd better plan the next move," and he sucked noisily at the mug of tea Ellie handed him.

Jumbo said bitterly, "Bastards. I got it all fixed where we was to drop off. Crawley, Symonds, and all the others will be waitin' for us. Maybe we better 'phone 'em and say we'll be late."

Henry said thoughtfully, "That stuff don't go out of here tonight, Jumbo."

"Why not? We could go round by the camp. It was on'y a spot check, wasn't it?"

"What do you say, Smut?"

In matters of strategy Henry was content to leave it to the professional, remembering a time when Smut Potter had successfully contended with Lord Gilroy's keepers until he clubbed one with a gun butt and served a stretch in gaol.

"We could try tomorrow night and go the long way round back o' the woods," he said, but to Jumbo his voice lacked conviction. He said, irritably, "Tomorrer night's too late! Crawley said they all want to deliver tomorrow for Christmas."

"I'm not going inside for a gang of bliddy butchers," said Henry and Ellie murmured agreement. "Come to that, I'd sooner dump it. Yes, dump the bliddy lot."

Jumbo was outraged. "*Dump* it! Getting on for two hundred's quid's worth! No you don't Henry. It can stay here until Boxing Day and we'll run it out one way or another. In

125

a cart, maybe, under bags o' manure if need be. After all, we ain't gonner eat it, are we?"

He waited, sensing something inscrutable in the thoughtful expression of the other men and presently Smut said slowly, "Be you thinking what I'm thinking, Henry?"

"Ah," said Henry, "I be. The fact o' the matter is we're rumbled and zooner or later us'll be nabbed. But it baint the fine nor the risk o' zeeing the New Year in behind bars as matters all that much."

"Then what the hell ...?" Jumbo demanded, but Henry went on, pacifically, "I doan reckon you'd understand, Jumbo. After all, you'm still half a bliddy vorriner. You baint been yer from the beginning, like me an' Smut."

"What's the time I been farming up the Dell got to do with it?" Jumbo demanded and Smut said, "Tiz the publicity. That's what youm driving at, baint it, Henry?"

"Arr," said Henry, "something on they lines. I don't give a tinker's curse wot folks say o' me but Squire's been on to us zame as he has you and Jumbo, and it doan zeem right somehow to mix him in with it. Takin' one thing with another I reckon we'd best cut our losses an' dump it. You doan have to bother, neither o' you. I'll do it meself, the minute the coast is clear."

"Now what the bloody hell 'as Squire Craddock got to do with it?" asked Jumbo. "It's not his pig and poultry, is it?"

"No," Henry said, still mildly, "but they was reared on his varms and he'd take it hard if we was nabbed and it got around generally. After all, we'm tenants, all three of us, and he's stood by us times enough. Ever zince he came here as a townee he's stood by us. Smut'll vouch for that, Jumbo, if you need tellin' that is."

Smut said nothing. His weatherbeaten features were puckered with the effort of concentration as he juggled loyalty and profit. He was no longer concerned with balancing risks but with weighing the cash value of those sacking-wrapped parcels in Henry's bin against memories of long ago, when Young Craddock, new to the Valley, had visited him in Paxtonbury gaol and assured him he would see that Tamer Potter, Mother Meg, and all the rest of the Potter tribe did not suffer on his account and would be confirmed in their tenure of the Dell. He remembered something else, too, the friendship and practical help given him by Craddock when he had emerged from prison and started a horticultural business on the slopes of the Bluff, and it seemed to him that he owed the man as much or more than Henry, whose line of reasoning he had no difficulty in following. He said at length, "Well, tiz money down the drain but youm right, Henry. From now on we'll play for smaller stakes and it's every man for himself. I'll drive on back presently and you dump the whole bliddy lot in the river. How much does your share stand you in at, Jumbo?"

"Round about seventy quid," replied Jumbo, looking helplessly from one to the other, "but if we took our time and fed it to the butchers . . ."

"We'll give you cost price. Thirty-five quid each," Smut said, "for like Henry says, you'm a vorriner, and it's no biziness o' yours, not really."

He looked carefully through a chink in the kitchen curtains and saw a torch-beam flickering at the rear of the van.

"They'm there," he told the others, "Voysey, the Inspector and another copper!"

"Will they knock?" Ellie asked anxiously but Smut shook his head. "No, they'll call it a day," he said. "They can't write out a summons on the strength of a bliddy wheelbarrow, can 'em? Do 'ee really want me to get it repaired for 'ee, Henry?"

"Giddon, no," said Henry glumly, "drive it home and use it for virewood."

They sat on sipping their tea but no knock came and presently they heard footsteps striking on the cobbles as the policemen returned up the lane to their car.

"Maybe they'll come back with a warrant and pull your place apart, Henry," suggested Jumbo but Henry pooh-poohed the idea and seemed unwilling to discuss the matter further. Between them he and Smut had been the losers by something like one hundred and seventy pounds but they were consoled by the reflection that there was no real alternative.

Voysey, still wondering why he had driven blindly up to the rendezvous instead of making a passing call at Hermitage drove slowly home with the Inspector's flea still buzzing in his ear. It had been impossible to persuade his superior to bluff Henry Pitts into making a search of his outbuildings. The inspector returned to Paxtonbury, deciding that Voysey had bungled the entire operation by not challenging Smut Potter in the bakery yard.

127

At three a.m. on Christmas Eve Henry Pitts drove his wife's two-seater to a spot about a mile above Codsall Bridge where, with a thoroughness that came close to masochism, he threw the better part of a pig and armfuls of trussed birds into eight feet of water. It was a kind of sacrifice on the altar of old times and it awoke in him a profound nostalgia for the splendours of his youth, "Before," as he might have put it, "the bliddy world went mazed."

Two days later, on Boxing morning, soggy bundles lay strung along the tideline west of the Sorrel outfall and the gulls gathred in streaming cohorts so that word was passed around that there had been a U-boat sinking far out to sea. Paul Craddock, hearing the rumour, asked around but nobody could give him accurate information, not even his oldest friend, Henry Pitts. All Henry would say, with one of his slow rubbery smiles, was, "Well, zeeing they'm geese an' chicken, Squire, tiz clear enough they come off a ship outalong but us didden 'ear no gunvire did us?" And Paul, knowing Henry's wry sense of humour, had no alternative but to keep his doubts to himself.

CHAPTER SEVEN

SURVIVAL

I

STEPHEN CRADDOCK's first tour of operations ended in spring and the morning he returned from a long haul from Cuxhaven he 'phoned Margaret suggesting they coincided a week's leave. He was based in Lincolnshire now and the green, flat vistas depressed him.

She said, when he admitted as much, "Suppose I packed everything in Stevie? Suppose I found a place somewhere you could come whenever you got a chance? You won't be flying again for six months, will you?"

He was surprised and touched. Since his capitulation in the Westminster flat they had met no more than a dozen times, widely spaced and rather frantic occasions when he could dash up to town on a thirty-six hour pass, and twice more when she had taken a room near one of his airfields, but despite the urgency and infrequency of their meetings they seemed to him to have had a profoundly calming effect upon her. After that first time, when she had crouched, trembling and weeping under his blanket, there had been no more hysteria, no more morbid talk of suicide. She seemed to accept the situation, bringing to him a warm, uncomplicated affection that was sometimes almost sisterly and even their climactic moments had a kind of deliberation, almost as though they were peaks to be scaled together before descending on to the plain of loneliness that followed separation. When they were together neither of them mentioned Andy or Monica, observing an unspoken pact to keep the madness of their association at bay a little longer, but sometimes, reliving these intervals during journeys back to camp, and the prospect of another eight-hour flight across the North Sea and

129

enemy-occupied Europe, Stevie thought of the last few hours as a murderer's last indulgence, the traditional hearty break-fast served in the condemned cell. He did not know how she thought of them. She never said but would lay quite still in his arms until it was time to go, so that sometimes he wondered if women could master the conscience in a way that a man found impossible.

He said, in response to her proposal, "How do you mean, Margy? Give up nursing and go back to the Valley?" and she said quickly, "God no, not the Valley! Anywhere but there, but certainly out of London. I'm sick to death of it anyway. I'm like your father, I never want to smell the place again. Could you meet me tomorrow at Chester?"

"Chester? Why Chester?" He remembered then that she had said good-bye to Andy at Chester in the autumn of '41 and somehow the coincidence was ominous.

"I'll explain later, but could you?"

"Yes I could, I've got nine days due and an aircrew's leave ration of petrol coupons."

"Fine. I'll see you in the bar of The Blossoms round about lunch-time. Can't say the exact hour, it depends on trains. They don't give nurses indulgence petrol."

Now she sounded gay and relieved and he had the impres-sion she had been planning something like this all the time he was clawing his way towards the final stages of the tour. He went back to the billet puzzled but excited, packed the minimum kit, had a final drink with his wireless operator and made out his "295" leave application.

By midday he was at the rendezvous and about an hour later she came in looking, he thought, like a mischievous kitten, with her absurd peek-a-boo hair-do crowned by a little blue hat that reminded him of a Foreign Legionaire's kepi. She said, gaily, "Foul journey. Five hours, packed like sardines. I'll have a gin and French. A double. Have you eaten?"

He told her he had and suggested seeing what he could get for her but she said, shrugging, "Don't bother, I've had sandwiches and we've some way to go. We don't want to arrive after dusk."

"Where are we going?"

"You'll see. It's a surprise. Don't nag or I might change my mind. Talk about something else until we get there."

He adjusted to her mood, partly because he was incurious

130

now that she was here, but more because she obviously wanted him to play and as they drove across the Cheshire plain and into the low hills of Flint towards the mountains, he felt more relaxed than he had felt since the night Monica had come into the bathroom and flung down her ultimatum. He was even able to convey to her, objectively, some of the changes the tension of thirty bombing missions had wrought in him and describe the tightly-knit comradeship of the crew that was their sole bonus. He described the "Brock's Benefit" of flak-patterns over heavily-defended German cities, and the steady attrition of his squadron—his crew was among the fifty-two per cent survivors of the tour—although, as he was quick to point out, many of those shot down had been made prisoners and two or three, who had pancaked into France, had ultimately turned up "shooting a terrific line about their adventures".

She asked a lot of direct questions. Was he frightened when he set out? Was he surprised to find himself alive and whole? Did he think he would ultimately qualify as one of those L.M.F. cases he had mentioned? He answered as best he could but they were not matters that could adequately be explained to a civilian who had never experienced the sweet-sour taste resulting from an "operation-scrubbed" announcement, or the gush of relief that was like a spurting tap when the words "Bombs gone!" came over the intercom and you were free to head for home. He said nothing of the blind panic of being caught in a searchlight beam, or the mad, half-exhilarating tumble about the sky that followed evasive action but he was astonished that he could talk as frankly as he did to anyone without reverting to the defensive banter the crews used among themselves to siphon off their dread.

Presently they came to the mountains, with the snow-capped shoulder of Snowdon on their right, and he said, "It's terrific. The air, the colours, the untamed look of the place. Why didn't we ever come here in the old days, Margy?"

"We had a silly set of values," she said and suddenly asked him to pull in beside a still tarn, fringed with reeds. The surface was blue-black in the shadow of a peak that rose almost vertically from the far bank.

"I've bought a cottage, Stevie," she announced. "No one knows about it, not even my gran who once lived in it. I shall stay there until it's over. That's where we're going right now."

131

He was a little startled. "If it was your grandmother's won't they know you?"

"No," she said, "for I've never been there since I was nine and when Gramp died Gran moved in with my parents, in South Wales. I got it through an agent and it's furnished."

He forced himself to ask, "Does Andy know?"

"No he doesn't. We don't write much, just notes you might say. It's funny, Andy's dried up on me. Perhaps it's the Desert. His letters don't mean a damn thing any more so now there's just you, Stevie. I'm only any good to *you* now and maybe that's why I've stopped worrying—about the future I mean. As long as you're on tap there's some point in life. What I mean is, I've got some kind of function." She paused a moment and gave him a shrewd glance. "You still worry, don't you."

"Yes," he admitted, "but there's not a bloody thing I can do about it. I'm very much in love with you and the experience is still fresh to me, fresh and very sweet. Just to see you and hear your voice is all I need. I can tell myself it's crazy and can only end one way but it doesn't make a damned bit of difference. You're the only reason for sticking it out."

"I'm glad," she said, laying her hand on his knee, "that's all I wanted to be sure about. I suppose I knew it after that first time but sometimes it seemed to me I was making all the running." Then, cheerfully, "To hell with the consequences. Let's go!"

They wound through a pass cunningly lit by an orange sun sinking over Cardigan Bay and dropped down to coastal level beyond a slate town that was called, she said, Ffestiniog. Then, within sight of the sea, they turned into a stoney track that twisted between two great belts of gnarled, incredibly old-looking woods, and here, in a clearing open on the sea side, was the cottage, a squat, single-storyed rectangle of white-washed stones, with a square of unkempt garden bounded by a sagging fence.

It had a name painted on a shingle, "*Ty-Bach*", and when he asked her what it meant she said "The Little House", and somehow this delighted him and he paused before getting out and threw his arms round her, kissing her hair and soft, plump cheeks and finally her mouth. There were no other houses in the clearing but away near the crown of the woods he could see a tall chimney and she said that was "*Ty-Mawr*", or "The Big House", and that her grandfather had been caretaker there for a wealthy family of Liverpool soap manufacturers who still owned it but never came there any more for it was in bad repair.

They entered the low-ceilinged living-room and he was surprised to find a fire burning and the floor and furniture polished. "The agent found me someone to give it a going-over," she told him, "the milkman's wife from the village, I believe. We'll see him in the morning and he's promised to bring eggs. I got everything else from the American PX through Henrietta. She can lay her hands on anything if she wants. Would you like something now?"

It was almost as if they had been married for years and were using this funny little house as a holiday base. He watched her hang her coat in the cupboard, unpack her case and his grip, make up the fire and reach down blue and white crockery from the black oak dresser but when, innocently, he asked her how much the place had cost, she said sharply, "Does it matter? It was my money, not Andy's." Then, relenting, she threw her arms round him and said, "I'm sorry, Stevie, but let's live for the next nine days! Let's blot out everything else, as if we were on an island and we are almost. This is a peninsula and at high tide it's surrounded when the creeks fill. It'll still be light after supper if we hurry and I'll show you."

They went down to the shore in fading light and crossed to one of the tongues of oak and ash that split the little estuary into sections. Seabirds Stevie did not recognise strutted in the shallows and the westering sun filled the bay with petal-pink light. The prospect moved him as a Valley sunset had never done so that he saw the marsh and the woods above "*Ty-Bach*" as a setting much older than its Sorrel counterpart in Devon. Down there the landscape was Georgian but up here it was Arthurian. The bay might have floated a barge full of lamenting queens, and the dwarf oaks might have concealed a dragon. It occurred to him that a landscape had never prompted these kind of fancies before and also that he knew so many of the wrong things and so few of the right ones. He did not know the name of that mottled, long-billed wader down there on the shore, and although the solitary blue flower growing on a patch of turf at the edge of the woods looked like a bluebell he knew that it was not but some other flower that did not flourish in the West. When he asked Margaret she said it was a harebell and he replied, "All the bloody silly things I've memorised. The thrust of an airscrew, the T.N.T. content of a bomb, the price of scrap aluminium—they don't seem worth remembering in a place like this, Margy," and she looked at him thoughtfully for a moment before saying, "No, they don't and they aren't. I realised that some time ago but it's nice to think you've come round to it on your own. Your father had it right from the beginning. Land and what grows on it, that's the only really important thing, that and people making do with what they've got and where they are."

He understood then that she must have changed her outlook even more drastically than he and, again like him, was currently recasting her philosophy in an entirely fresh mould, and he wondered what had begun this process and if, as in his case, it was brought about by the pressures of fear. He said, "You must be thinking a lot about the old folks and the Valley, Margy. They crop up every time we meet. In the old days we always thought of them as good for a laugh, remember?"

"I remember," she said, "but now the laugh is on us. They've had a wonderful marriage, better than most of our generation will ever have, and we can't blame the times either! They had their war, and it was even worse than this for the people caught up in it, people like Paul and Claire, and all those men he planted trees for in that funny little plantation of his."

"Where did we go wrong, then?"

"In telling ourselves that all that rushing around and money-making was fun. Happiness is stillness, that's what I've come to believe. Stillness, and putting down roots and taking stock." They stopped on the last spur of the wood and looked across at the low hills enclosing the estuary on the Carmarthen side. The rim of the sun was like the heart of a forge sending out regular pulse beats of crimson light that reached them as the wink of a distant heliograph. She said, without looking at him, "What you said back there—about loving me, Stevie. I'll tell you something. Andy never said that, not once in all the time we were together, if you don't count the marriage service, that is. It wasn't said on impulse, was it? You have thought about it?"

"I've not thought of much else since that first time in London," he admitted, and the answer must have given her the reassurance she needed for she caught up his hand and kissed it, saying, "Then that's that. I don't care any more. Let everything work itself out and there's something else I should tell you. I'm off the bottle. I haven't taken a real drink since I made up my mind about buying "*Ty-Bach*" and there's a reason as well as the obvious one. It'll keep, however. Let's go back now."

They went along the lip of seamed stone that divided woods and shore and when they reached the cottage she lit the lamp and made up the fire. Then, from the top shelf of the big cupboard, she took down a heavy mahogany box and threw open the lid. "There's no wireless here," she said, "so you'll have to make do with this," and he saw that it was a musical box of Swiss manufacture, with a repertoire of Welsh tunes. "My Gran owned it," she told him, "and it's one of the things I remember about this place when I was a child. Listen." She touched a spring and the box began to play a tinkling version of "The Ash Grove" and after that "Men of Harlech". He listened, amused but also impressed by the astounding change this place wrought in her. As long as they were here and together, he decided, time would stand still. It was a simple matter to shrug off the war and the fact that, out there behind the woods crowding down on "*Ty-Mawr*", there were so many bills to be paid. With the music still playing he tilted her face and studied it with the same objectivity as he had when she was asleep in her London flat. She looked, he thought, so much younger and more vulnerable, and yet there was peace in her eyes that had never been there before. He kissed her mouth very gently and the kiss set the pace of their lovemaking all the time they spent in that place. There was no urgency about it, and no more guilt.

II

Because he had not been able to give a leave-address when he left camp he had written the address of Wiley, his wireless-op. on the counterfoil of his pass and he did not remember this until the fourth morning of their stay in the cottage. Wiley, whom he had promised to ring, lived in Hampshire where he had once had a radio shop, and because there was always a possibility that he might be recalled it was not until the seventh day that he said, casually, "Where's the nearest 'phone box, darling? I'd better give Wiley a tinkle, just in case."

"You've finished your tour, so why should they expect you to 'phone in?"

"We're supposed to keep in touch and I haven't, all the time we've been here. I'm not due back for another forty-eight hours and even then it'll be a matter of stooging for upwards of six months." He had a comforting thought, "I'll wangle a posting reasonably close at hand," he said. "There's bound to be an O.T.U. or an F.T.S. fairly handy and then, with the kind of ground job I'm likely to land, I can pop over almost every weekend."

She directed him to a 'phone booth in the nearest village, a place with an unpronounceable name, and he asked trunks to connect him with Wiley. The moment the wireless-operator answered Stevie recognised urgency in is voice. "Skipper? Thank God you've rung! I've been hanging around this end for three days . . ." and when Stevie asked if they had been recalled by signal Wiley said, less eagerly, "No, Skipper, it's not that . . . it's about your brother. He's pranged. Missing they said, no confirmation either way. I got it from camp after your folks rang the adj. They're trying to locate his missus. Do you know where she's likely to be?"

Stevie stood quite still looking down at the pale gleam of his knuckles where his left hand was clenched round the receiver. He could think of nothing to say and after a moment Wiley called, with renewed urgency, "You still there, Skip?" and Stevie answered that he was, adding, "Is that all the gen. they gave you? Missing on ops.?" and Wiley said it was, adding, "He'll probably turn up. Bods often do out there, more often than in our bloody outfit."

Stevie said, slowly and carefully, "Look Wiley, will you do something for me? Ring home and tell my Old Man you've located me, that I can get in touch with Andy's wife and that I'll be ringing them the moment I do. Tell them what you just told me, that more often than not in the Desert Air Force "missing" means gone astray and that there is no reason to assume Andy has bought it. Will you do that?"

"Sure, Skip. Sorry to have to pass it on to you. Had a good leave?"

"Yes, until now."

He rang off and went out to the car, conjuring with crowding factors and spilling them one after another like blobs of

136

quicksilver. Irrelevancies invaded his brain, reinforcements hurried up to buttress him against the impact of Wiley's message, odd, fleeting memories of a schoolboy Andy in muddied football togs and yards of trailing scarf. Andy missing out there in the Blue! Fried almost certainly, in the tangled skein of a wrecked Hurricane, with nothing but sand and camel thorn for miles and miles and miles. And then his mind switched to Margaret and he wondered if anyone had ever had such a grotesque obligation thrust upon him, that of telling a twin-brother's wife who was also a mistress that she was now a widow. Driving over the winding, bumpy track needed attention that he could not spare. Every now and again the car lurched and pitched him forward, so that his head brushed the windscreen and the car slewed as his breastbone hit the wheel.

She was in the little kitchen making an omelette. Hearing him come in she called, "Lunch up! Won't be a minute," and he slumped down in the window recess looking out over the flooded estuary at the line of Carmarthen hills on the horizon. His body felt drained of moisture, as though it was an old stick that would crumble if prodded with a boot. Then she was standing there with two plates in her hands. "What is it? You've got to go back?"

He said, listening to his voice as though it belonged to someone a mile away, "It's Andy, they've been trying to contact you."

"He's dead?"

The word helped him to focus. "No, not dead. Missing. It probably happened more than a week ago. He must have given the Old Folks as his next-of-kin because he couldn't be sure where you were. They got the message and tried to 'phone me at the camp."

He was surprised that there was no outcry and that she carefully placed the plates on the table instead of dropping them. She looked serious enough but not overwhelmed and certainly not stricken. She lifted the hem of the little apron she was wearing and began twisting it, not agitatedly but idly. "Missing? What does that mean out there? The same as it would mean here?"

"No. Types can go missing for weeks out there. They run out of gas in the Blue, or make a forced landing for one reason or another. He might be in the bag, or he might even be back with his unit by now. They have air searches unless somebody saw him go down and nobody could have or the message would have been 'missing, believed prisoner'. They often say that to soften the blow."

"That's the truth?"

He hesitated, wondering if it was and finally deciding that it was not.

"No, Margy," he said at length, "it's ten to one he's bought it."

"That's what I thought."

There was silence in the sunlit room. Over by the fireplace the grandfather clock ticked, a sound you didn't hear unless you listened for it. She said, slowly, "Well, it's like I told you and I'm not all that surprised. I never believed he would make it, not from the minute I said good-bye to him. It was just a question of time. The thing I didn't bargain for was uncertainty and I imagine that will continue indefinitely, won't it?"

"It's impossible to say. I could write to his C.O. for details, and maybe form some kind of judgment from that. He'd probably tell me things he wouldn't tell you or the old folks."

"Perhaps you'd better do that, Stevie. Do it soon. We have to know as quickly as we can. I'm having your child in less than seven months."

It was an even heavier shock than Wiley's news and he must have reacted to it in a way that dismayed her for she ran across the room and threw her arms about him, pressing his face hard against her breasts. "I wasn't going to tell you until I had to. I had some vague idea of going away somewhere and then trying to get it adopted, but now everything's changed. I don't have to do that, do I? I could come back here with the child. I could do that, couldn't I?"

What puzzled him was the way Andy seemed to have slipped through the net of her consciousness, as though he had been someone they had known and liked but with whom they had no close relationship, and when he thought about it this did not make her callous, or even selfish but realistic, putting the unborn before the dead as a matter of prudence and common-sense. He said, putting his hands over hers, "I always thought you couldn't have children. I knew you wanted them, and that Andy didn't care either way, but you told us all after you went to that doctor that time that it was very unlikely and that was that. I remember Monica saying you were lucky because she sometimes had to say the same kind of thing to her mother and would have preferred not to be a liar. Were you lying as well?"

"No, I wasn't lying. Andy and me, we never tried not to have children, not after the first few months anyway, but nothing ever happened, so I got used to the idea of never having any. Andy didn't mind and ours didn't seem the kind of set-up where a child would have been welcome—but now everything's different. I want that baby badly and I was glad when I found out, even though I couldn't see a way of keeping it. Now it's silly to pretend any more. I'm sorry about Andy, but only in the way I was sorry about Simon's Rachel, or any of those twenty-year-olds who were shot down the summer before last. Does that shock you?"

It did shock him but it didn't make the smallest difference to how he felt about her and it didn't diminish her either, for he saw that anything less than complete honesty between them was unthinkable. "Whether Andy has bought it or not has very little to do with it any more, Margy, and if you're glad about the baby, so am I. I hope to God Andy turns up and if he does there'll have to be a showdown. Neither one of us—or Monica for that matter—could go on like this, pretending nothing had happened, and I was coming to that conclusion anyway. I'll do what I can to get the griff from his C.O. but in the meantime I've got to 'phone home and put them in touch with you. They'll almost certainly invite you down there. Could you bluff it out until we know, one way or the other?"

She considered and he waited, giving her time but not saying what he intended to do if and when confirmation of Andy's death reached him. He would, he supposed, have to contact Monica and ask for a divorce, perhaps citing some nameless person. There was no point in plaguing her with this now, but the thought did occur to him that if she went home she couldn't remain there long.

Her answer, when it came, astonished him. She said, "I'll go home but if I do I'll tell Claire. Not Paul, he'd never understand, but Claire would. She's made my way and she could make allowances, some kind of allowances. There's one thing I can fix my mind on. You won't be flying for a bit and that's some kind of comfort." she went back to the table and picked up the plates she had laid there. "We can eat later," she said, "if we've got any appetite. Go and 'phone home now. Say I've been visiting in Wales and that you've got in touch with me."

"Wouldn't it be better if you rang?"

She looked at him calmly. "No, it wouldn't. I could tell Claire everything but not over a telephone. Say I'll be down there the day after tomorrow. You're due back at 23.59 hours, aren't you? You could drop me off at Shrewsbury en route."

He went back to the car wondering if delicacy had prevented her from saying "Chester" instead of "Shrewsbury", or whether she had chosen it as being the more convenient town.

III

March 25th, 1943, proved a field day for Flight Lieutenant Andrew Craddock. It was the day the Eighth Army made its spectacular heave over the Mareth Line closing the jaws of the trap held open for so many weeks by the ingenuity of Rommel and the fighting qualities of the retreating Afrika Korps. There had never been so many tempting targets, from tanks and self-propelled guns, to beetling little scout cars speeding between embattled units. There was little opposition and to a fighter pilot who had flown against odds in the Battle of Britain it seemed a very one-sided contest up there in trailers of cloud.

All that morning, and again during an afternoon sortie, he cruised over the desert making carefully-timed swoops against ground targets and it was when he was heading back towards Tripoli, in the apparently lifeless area south of Gafsa, that he spotted the small concentration of vehicles around a tiny oasis and came down to have a closer look. It was probably a headquarters of some kind, an untidy spread of troop-carriers and scout cars grouped around a single tank and a battery of light flak guns mounted on half-tracks, vehicles almost certainly captured from the British during Rommel's advance the previous summer. He saw men scatter for their slit trenches when he came diving out of the west and concentrated his burst on the tank but then, a second or two later he saw the flak guns wink and a film of fine dust rose from the cockpit of his aircraft as a giant seized the tail of his machine in a casual, almost genial grasp, weaving it lightly left and right so that he had time to wonder whether his tailplane had been shot away. It could not have been however, for he was able to gain some height although overall control of the Hurricane was not possible and he continued to fly east in a series of dips and swoops that was an entirely new sensation, more like riding the big dipper at a fair than flying.

Then he noticed his left hand. The brown leather glove was stained a bright crimson and the fingers seemed to have splayed out of all angles. He tried to lift it to have a closer look but it did not respond to the impulse, resting inertly on his knee, a red, shapeless blob. Even then he did not realise he was hit and bleeding for he felt no pain, not even numbness of the kind he had felt when a tiny fragment of flak penetrated his boot and wounded him in the foot during the El Alamein skirmishing.

The aircraft was now bucketing about the sky like a fire-cracker and he reached for the rubber bulb to release the hood preparatory to baling out but before he could do this he was off on a long, swooping descent, losing height in staggered drifts like one of those paper darts he and Stevie had flung about in the second form at school. He had time to think, incredulously, "Christ! I've bought it! A pooping bloody flak gun, mounted on a captured half-track made in Coventry . . . !" and then the world exploded in a grinding, rending splutter but again he felt no pain and very little shock, just a sense of confusion and incredulity as what remained of the aircraft somersaulted into hillocks of soft, grey-brown sand.

The next thing he remembered was opening one eye and staring at the red ball of the sun just above the horizon and the temperature told him he was looking east. He was colder than he had ever been in his life, the cold sending feelers into his spine and under his ribs but he could see enough with one eye to realise that he was lying clear of the aircraft, now a ball of metal beflagged with ribbons of canvas and several yards nearer the sun. He wondered then at his presence here, marvelling that he could still think and reason for it occurred to him to wonder how violent had been the impact and also approximately where he was, behind or beyond the Mareth Line, or far south of it out in the Blue. He could remember very little of the incident over the oasis except that he had been knocked out of the sky by a flak gun mounted on British

141

half-tracks, and this seemed to him a curious irony. In the days before he had been a flier he had spent his days contracting for scrap metal that went to make this kind of product.

The penetrating dawn chill worried him far more than his chances for survival so that when, out of his one eye, he saw a group of Arabs standing over him he grimaced and said, "Parky! Bloody parky, chum . . .!" and one of the Arabs bent over him and he could smell the man's sour body odour and note the curiosity in his brown eyes. They were approximately the same colour as Margaret's eyes and a silly thought crossed his mind that the Welsh were a lost tribe of Israel and that this might account for the similarity. Then a spasm of pain gripped him, spreading upwards from his left side and spilling inwards from his shoulder so that the Arab was blotted out and the naked red ball of the sun was obliterated.

IV

It seemed to him seconds later when he opened his one eye again and this time he saw a man on a bed swathed in bandages looking exactly like a museum mummy. He studied the man a long time and slowly, very slowly, he came to equate his presence with a hospital and, by inference, could locate his own whereabouts inasmuch as he too was in bed and swathed in bandages. There were bandages all the way down his left arm and over most of his face and head. There was also a kind of frame enclosing the upper part of his body and the only movement he could make apart from opening and closing his right eye was to wiggle the toes of his feet. He thought, with tremendous relief, that he still had his feet, but he was by no means as certain that he had arms. Concentrating hard he thought he could sense a very faint tingling in other areas of his body but he could not be sure and the effort of concentration exhausted him so that he drifted away again, remembering no more until he found himself looking up into the sunburned face of an orderly who was trying to get him to drink something. He tried to co-operate for he was very thirsty indeed, the drops of lemonade or whatever it was striking his palate like spots of fat in a frying pan. He choked and the spasm set bells ringing in all areas of his body but after a moment or so their clamour subsided and he was able to ask the man where he was. The man, grinning in a faintly apologetic way, said "Tunis," and Andy knew by his accent that he was German. He thought, "Well blow me down, I'm in the bag!" and he asked the orderly how long he had been lying there. The man told him, in heavily accented English, that he had been brought into Tunis more than a week ago by Arabs and that the war, for him as well as his patient, was over, for the Afrika Korps was pulling out and all hospital staff were under orders to remain. The man in the next bed, he said, was a Dornier pilot fished out of the bay but he would not live. His spine was broken.

Days and nights passed without any real awareness of time. The Dornier pilot must have died for he was wheeled out and another man took his place, and then he died and a third man was lowered on to the bed, and he did not seem to be so badly injured for he sat up and ate food and grinned toothily at Andy, confirming that the orderly was right and that the war in North Africa was almost over. He was an Italian from near Naples and spoke comic-opera English. "Mussolini no bloody good!" he said, gaily, and drew his hand across his throat.

It was from this man that Andy learned something of his injuries, for the Italian watched his daily dressings. "Damn lucky," he said. "No hand, no more flying."

At first Andy did not absorb the fact that his left hand had been amputated above the wrist and when he did it was as though all his other injuries were scratches of the kind one was likely to get blackberrying in the Coombe. It took him about a fortnight to come to terms with the fact that, from now on, he would have to live out the rest of his life with one hand and probably one of those claw-like contrivances he had seen when visiting men of his squadron in hospital at home. The prospect did not frighten him so much as disgust him and he could only accept it by forcing himself to contemplate what it would have been like if he had lost a leg or legs instead of half an arm. At that time he did not know much about the burns down the left side of his face and when the British took Tunis, and he could talk freely with the American medics, secondary shock enfolded him in a lassitude that was like a long trance. He ate and slept and exchanged a few words with the Italian in the next bed, but there was no continuity in his existence, the focal points of which were the hospital smell and the pain of having his wounds dressed.

He came out of this trance when he began his saline baths and it was then, looking into a hand mirror, that he saw his reflection and found it unrecognisable. The left side of his face was the colour of a Victoria plum, and his left eye had a permanent droop. He was so shocked that he asked the orderly to bring the surgeon to his bedside and was only partially reassured when the man said, with a mid-Western drawl, that his face would not stay the colour of a plum but would respond to plastic surgery so that the only disfigurement—if you could call it that—would be a waxiness of the flesh under his eye and round as far as his jaw. It would be stiff, the man said, and unresponsive to jokes, but it would not frighten kids in the street.

One day a blonde nurse came and asked him if he would like to dictate a letter to his wife. When he asked how she knew he was married she gave a humour-the-invalid smile and said they had his papers in the office and that in a day or so someone from his own unit would be calling. The mention of his squadron was his first real handhold back to the everyday world and he said he would get one of his friends to write a letter home. The girl seemed disappointed.

"She'll want to know how you're going on," she protested. "Mail goes out of here for London twice a week. Just a note, maybe?"

What did one say in these circumstances? "Dear Margaret: I was shovelled up by a bunch of Arabs and am okay except that I'm short of a hand and my face is a fistful of plum jam! Look out for the one with the lobster claw when you meet the boat!" Suddenly he turned sulky and the fixed smile of the blonde nurse irritated him so much that he could have wiped it off with a smack. He growled, "Scrub it, sister. I'll wait for the lads to look me up."

They looked him up a day or two later, Johnny Boxall and "Twitch" Bannister, both of his squadron, the one with flaming red hair, the other with a slight tic resulting from a training crash in a Lockheed Hudson a long time ago. They seemed far more surprised to see him than he was to see them and Twitch said, "We'd written you, off, Crad. Christ, you're dead lucky. You not only pranged behind the Mareth Line but fifty miles south of Jerry's right flank. It's a bloody miracle! You must have got here by camel."

144

They made light of his injuries and said the same things he would have said himself in the circumstances. "Thank God it wasn't your leg ... anyone can get around with one paw ... plastic surgery on your mug will be an improvement ..." It was like conducting a conversation in nursery language. He found it only slightly less irritating than talking to the blonde nurse. They promised to write home on his behalf and he could imagine the cheery reassurance they would put into the letter and tried to forestall it by instructing them to contact his brother Stephen in Bomber Command, and describe exactly what had happened, leaving him to relay details to his wife and parents. Then they left, promising to return with gifts, and for the first time he realised that he was done with them and their kind for all time and that soon a new phase would begin for him, probably at Roehampton or some such place, learning how to operate a claw. Suddenly he rejected present and future in favour of the past, searching out moments of his life that he could pin down and contemplate like dead butterflies. Such moments, he discovered, were elusive. For so long now, ever since the balloon went up in 1939, he had been living in a world of machines and schoolboy prattle and his injuries not only prohibited re-entry into that world but definitely disqualified him for the life he had lived before the war with Stevie, Stevie's hard-faced wife, and roly-poly Margaret with whom he identified most of his pleasanter memories.

He remembered another hospital, a long time ago, where he had lain after a car crash and Margaret, liveliest of the probationers, had come rustling into his ward with her sing-song repartee and half-hearted protests, sharing a cigarette with him by taking alternate puffs and fanning the air in anticipation of night sister's rounds. Good days they had been, with laughter always near the surface, and Stevie, the old clot, making certain that that bloody Archdeacon's daughter he had married had her corners rubbed off in their joint company. But now that era was as dead as squadron life on the airstrips, for outside the hospital time rolled on and there was already talk of leapfrogging the Med. and chasing Jerry up the boot of Italy.

Even when they came to measure him for his artificial hand he remained listless and moody, living mainly in the past and seeing no way of filling the vacuum of his immediate future. There was no pivot for his thoughts and this was how he came to listen to the chatter of patients around him, mainly Shawcrosse's chatter, for Shawcrosse was the ward braggart, a tubby, sandy-haired gunner, who boasted that he would find a way of making his artificial leg show a profit in Civvy Street and skim the cream from the post-war property boom as soon as he got back to his North London estate agency.

Shawcrosse, Andy discovered, had spent some time in Canada and had absorbed some of the North American speech-idioms that he used rather self-consciously, like someone acting the role of a toughie in a second feature film. If you could overlook this Shawcrosse was original, lacking self-pity, without a trace of bitterness, getting by on a line of bluff that would have served him well in the pre-war scrap market. Andy discovered that he could admire him without liking him. He found his pseudo-frankness as impudent and engaging as the patter of an auctioneer selling tea-sets and five-pound-notes from a seaside stand. But the trained merchant in Andy saw a good deal more than bluff in Shawcrosse, recognising in him a ruthlessness and ingenuity and singlemindedness that would make him a hard man to beat in a battle of wits.

It was Shawcrosse's boast that he would make his artificial leg show a profit that gave him access to Shawcrosse as an individual rather than a clown. "I'm going to do more than learn to walk on the bloody thing," he announced, the day they fitted him. "You're going to show little Kenny Shawcrosse a thumping profit, aren't you my beauty" and he patted it.

"As a professional beggar?" Andy asked, and Shawcrosse looked at him seriously.

"In a manner of speaking, yes," he said, in a Cockney accent that had survived a temporary commission. "It's a free advert everywhere I go."

"Don't bank on it. After the war tin legs will be ten a penny."

"Yes they will," Shawcrosse answered, thoughtfully, "but there's a right and a wrong way of exploiting them."

"And your way?"

"I'm a house agent," Shawcrosse said, "and there's going to be a God-Almighty scramble in my business when this lot's over. But I'm the handicapped one. Handicapped but game, you follow? Half-a-dozen after the same building-plot but

146

only one with a tin leg. It pongs. 'That chap with one leg—we ought to give him a chance didn't we, Giles? You notice the way he ploughed through that mud, struggling to keep up with us on the survey?' That's my line from here on! I had a Rover before the war, a Rover and a bed-sit in Muswell Hill, old boy. Once I've got my ticket it's a Mercedes, a country house and a suite at the Savoy when I'm not in the Carlton, Cannes. First I get backing—somehow, somewhere, even if I have to marry it. And then—whoosh. Into battle!"

Perhaps because he had always been amused by professional braggarts of whom there had been so many in the scrap trade, Andy egged him on so that soon he had a very clear picture of Shawcrosse riding the crosstides of post-war property development, where speculators who knew how to operate like bootleggers in the 'twenties would come into their inheritance within weeks of the blackout bonfire. The smartest of them, Shawcrosse said, were already moving in on a seller's market, gambling against there being no more blitzes in and around London, but this was to stick one's neck out. Hitler might still have an ace up his sleeve. The thing to do, providing one could lay one's hand on capital of course, was to concentrate on land where post-war expansion was a certainty and where existing bricks and mortar were already scheduled for demolition. The market, he declared, would be virtually inexhaustible. Shawcrosse could wax almost lyrical on the population explosion that would be touched off by a million wartime marriages, prophecying that every single one of them, plus the results of another million fond reunions between couples separated by the war, meant a new semi-detached, a flatlet, or a three-bedroomed bungalow with all mod cons. He described successive rashes of new building in city, town and village with a kind of poetic frenzy that made Andy think how much his father would have detested Shawcrosse and is vulgar visions. He said, in an unguarded moment, "Suppose you had capital, twenty to thirty thousand of it? How and where would you begin?"

Shawcrosse drew a deep, satisfying breath. "With that much in the kitty? In coastal belts along the south coast within easy driving distance of a city. Not too large a city—too many old-established firms with tame county councillors on the payroll, but the kind of place Dad used to take the missus and kids for the fortnight in August before the war. That's where I'd invest because the fixes have yet to be made and no new building has gone up there since the slump of '31. You can keep London and Brum and Manchester. They've all been blitzed, and beady eyes are already trained on the gaps. I'd go for virgin territory and with that much woo in my wallet any virgin I ran across would soon be in the family way!" He brooded a moment and then added, "It's too much anyway. Make a man lazy that would. Ten thousand would be about right. Plenty to operate with but not enough to waste."

One day Andy said, "Shawcrosse, you've got yourself ten thousand," and as he said it the cloud of indecision that had clogged his brain since they had pumped him full of dope in the weeks following his crash cleared, so that he felt almost jocund, as though he was back in the days when he and Stevie were apprentices in the scrap empire of old Franz Zorndorff, the man who had made Paul Craddock two fortunes against his will.

For a long time Shawcrosse, suspicious of miracles, did not take his proposal seriously, but the longer they spent together the more he came to respect this half-fried R.A.F. type who was one of the few men he had met out here who could take his measure and look beyond the blowhard at a man with unlimited ambition based upon sound ideas. Taking nothing on trust, however, he pursued certain lines of private enquiry regarding Craddock and what he discovered not only increased his respect but his confidence in the future. There were two aspects of the man, however, that he never did understand, then or later. One was why a person who could have made a mint out of the war had volunteered for active service; the other was what impulse had guided Craddock, already comfortably off, to invest ten thousand pounds in a talkative stranger on the strength of a hunch. To understand the second of these things he would have had to have known Andy's original mentor, Zorndorff. To understand the first he would have had to have grown up in the Valley and observed the various interpretations the Craddocks brought to the word patriotism.

The day before they parted, Shawcrosse to be shipped home for his discharge, Andy to another hospital in Algiers, they exchanged addresses and Shawcrosse, serious for the first time, said, "You're not kidding, Craddock? You really would back me if I could come up with the right proposition?" and Andy said, "Yes, if I liked the look of it. I think you're on to something. Property will be a damned sight more lucrative than scrap after the war and what else is there left for crocks like you and me but to clean up?"

It was a chance encounter that was to set the course of Andrew Craddock's post-war career but not exclusively along the trade routes.

CHAPTER EIGHT

LONG RANGE SALVO

I

PAUL was well aware why the letter from Simon, announcing that he was coming on nine days' post-O.C.T.U. leave, pleased him so much. It was not only the prospect of seeing his eldest son after so long an interval but also Simon's request to be met with a horse at Sorrel Halt, proving that he knew his father better than any of them.

He set out about seven a.m. on what promised to be a warm July day, riding his well-mannered grey, Snowdrop II, and leading the cob that Mary sometimes used and was now the only hack in the Valley apart from an old hunter or two out to grass. He was feeling more at peace with himself than for some considerable time. The news that Andy had re-emerged from the fog of war, albeit minus half an arm, had cheered him, although he was still puzzled by the blankness with which the news had been received by Claire. But then, he reflected, she had never clucked much over any of them except her youngest daughter, killed in that air crash long before the war, and had always been happy to let Simon, The Pair, and Whiz go their own ways, leaving Mary in his special charge.

Stevie, he had heard with relief, was grounded for a spell, and Simon as a highly-trained instructor, was unlikely to see active service again, for he was now in his thirty-ninth year and wars were a young man's business. His daughter Whiz had never bothered him since the day she had married her dour Scotsman and Mary, despite the prolonged absence of Rumble Patrick, seemed contented enough, absorbed as she was in the care of her son Jerry and her new baby daughter whom she had christened Sorrel, after the river that ran past their door.

The valley, he told himself, was in good shape and producing more than it had ever yielded in the past, even during the final year of the 1914-18 war. Four Winds, on his left as he rode along under the park wall, was responding to the hand of Connie Eveleigh's boy. Fields of wheat rippled eastward as far as the edge of the moor, then south to the dunes. The fields of Hermitage, farmed by old hands like Henry Pitts and his son David, promised an equally good harvest if the weather held. In the great bowl between the moor and the Bluff grew acres of wheat, barley, beans, peas, kale, potatoes, mangold and many other crops, and somewhere on the pastures of the seven farms lived five herds of Friesians and Red Devons, as well as hundreds of pigs and ten thousand chickens. They were all using manufactured fertilisers now and doing it as a matter of course, but he could remember a time when he had had to bully every one of them to adopt modern methods and bring all kinds of pressures to bear on people like Henry to exchange plough-horse for tractor. Now there were no plough-horses to be seen from the western boundary of Four Winds to the cliff fields of High Coombe. They all had tractors, and most of them had many other contrivances of one sort or another, although they could never learn to keep them in good repair and he was always having to get mechanics down from Paxtonbury to replace broken parts or do a bit of welding.

He thought of them collectively and he thought of them individually and it seemed to him that they had adjusted, more or less, to the tremendous demands of the last three years. The black market, he suspected, was still active, despite that mysterious incident concerning packaged poultry along the tideline, a phenomenon that Constable Voysey had never referred to and Henry Pitts hugged to himself as a private joke, but it was limited to a hole-in-corner business and he had stopped prying. There was no point in knowing too much about tenants' business these days. The time had gone when he could threaten them with a feudal stick if they looked like disgracing him and themselves. He was still a landlord of sorts but they expected and received far more independence than in the past and each of them could have been mistaken for a pre-war freeholder and probably thought of themselves as such. He didn't really mind, for he was glad to be relieved of the responsibility. After the war, he supposed, most of them would want to buy their farms with profits put by during these boom years, and although he couldn't pretend that he liked the idea of Shallowford shrinking to a single farm and the Big House, he would probably sell if they were insistent. They all thought of him as old-fashioned and a generation behind the times, but he knew that he wasn't and that if the full truth were known it was he and old John Rudd, his agent for so long, who had dragged every man Jack of them into the twentieth century. He still missed the solace of John Rudd's companionship but a man couldn't live for ever and he supposed another ten years or so would see him laid in the crowded churchyard, alongside so many of the originals. The prospect did not depress him. Taken all round he had enjoyed his life and there was nowhere else he wanted to lie or would feel at home after all these years of striving, disappointment and guarded satisfaction.

He turned off the river road beyond Codsall Bridge and tackled the long slope of the moor, glancing, as always when he rode this way, at the feathered crown of French Wood. Those trees were coming on. Every one of them was in its twenty-fourth year and the spur over Hermitage would have looked odd without them, as odd, no doubt, as the meadowland between the river and the sea on his left if he had planted it with timber as Eveleigh Senior had once proposed. There were no other significant changes in the landscape since the day he had first ridden along this road in the company of old John Rudd and the momory of that sunny afternoon, getting on for half-a-century ago, made him smile, for he remembered they had talked about the Zulu war, now as remote as Waterloo. And here he was doing John Rudd's job for him, taking a led horse to the station to meet a passenger on the London train. It was, he reflected, untypical of Simon to propose such transport, and thinking of Simon's decision to take a commission after all he wondered if the boy's outlook had changed and whether he still thought of anyone who owned more than his own house in a suburb as a legitimate target for a cannonade of leaflets, fiery speeches and comparative statistics.

When he had crested the moor and could look over his shoulder at the great camp marching up the western slope to the Heronslea border, his thoughts turned to the war in general and here again he found cause for moderate satisfaction. It had been touch-and-go in the summer of 1940, and depressing enough in 1941 with new disasters coming one on top of the other but they had begun to see daylight in 1942, despite the local swoop of the Fokker-Wulfes, the surge of the Nazis into Southern Russia and the fall of Singapore. The tide had really begun to turn, he imagined, at El Alamein, and now the fighting was over in North Africa, for everyone as well as poor old Andy. Soon, he supposed, they would invade what that fire-eater Churchill was already calling "the soft underbelly of Europe", and with more and more Americans arriving eventual victory was certain, particularly as the Russians were now moving over to the offensive. He wondered, vaguely, what madness could have got into the Germans after their terrible lesson of 1918. He had never been a German-hater until they started slamming poor devils into concentration camps and shooting God knows how many wretched civilians in places like Poland and Czechoslovakia. The Germans of the trenches hadn't seemed such bad chaps when you got to know them, and he had always prided himself on being one of the very few hereabouts who had never subscribed to the hysteria that resulted from all those 1914 stories of bayoneted babies. But it seemed that the Valley patriots had been nearer the truth after all, for how else could one explain unspeakable crimes like Lidice? Well, it would all sort itself out he imagined, like the other war and like the slump period when he had had to subsidise every farm in the Valley. Mostly it was a matter of holding on and minding one's own business and he deliberately turned his back on global problems as he crossed the main road, trotted across the short stretch of moor to the railway cutting and rode into the station yard just as a distant puff of smoke over his right shoulder advertised the approach of the London train.

Simon looked fitter than Paul remembered him looking in years. With his combat experience, Paul thought, they ought to have given him a commission long ago, but his involvement with the militant left had probably held him back. Now that Russia was putting up such a fight everyone was inclining left and the irony of this had obviously not escaped Simon, for when Paul commented on the horses he said, with a grin, "Got to climb back in the saddle now, Gov'nor. I'm an officer and gentleman again!"

"How was the O.C.T.U. course?" Paul asked, "didn't you find it tough going at your age?"

"Piece of cake," Simon said, "probably because I'm in training after playing soldiers up in the Highlands so long! I had to watch the finer points, however. It still doesn't do to be caught whistling 'The Red Flag' or eating peas with your knife."

Paul liked the boy's sense of humour, seeing behind it a growth of tolerance, and he thought again of Simon's mother, and how unerringly her championship of the underdog had reproduced itself in the boy. He noticed too that Simon looked about him eagerly and asked intelligent questions about the Valley's contribution to the war. How cynical were the farmers in their approach to Government appeals to grow more and offset the U-boat campaign? What kind of prices were they getting for produce? How much of it was subsidy? How was High Coombe shaping under the new arty-crafty people Paul had written about? What had happened to Rumble Patrick's acres after the young idiot had gone to sea? Paul answered his questions in detail, reflecting that this was the first time any of his sons had shown even a passing interest in his life's work and presently Simon, reining in above the Sorrel, further enlarged himself by saying, with a chuckle, "Well Gov'nor, we all used to snigger at you and your mediaeval villeins down here, but the laugh was on us after all. I'm taking you more seriously from now on."

"Ah yes," Paul said, unable to resist a sly backhander. "I daresay you are, but you'll want all land nationalised after the war and chaps like me booted off to make room for civil servants!"

"No I won't," Simon said, unexpectedly, "I'm mellowing. We all wasted time and energy slanging one another through the 'twenties and 'thirties. In the end what happened? We had to form a Coalition and it worked a lot better than I hoped. The fact is, I suppose we ought to be grateful to that little bastard and his gang of psychopaths. At least he succeeded in uniting Left, Right and Centre."

"Down here it's easy to lose one's way among all the directives we get fired at us. What'll happen afterwards?"

"Well, we can't do a damned thing until we've got that bunch behind bars. After that some kind of world federation, with more teeth than the poor old League of Nations. Everyone will have to surrender some sovereignty. The Empire will be the first casualty, I imagine."

"I won't lose much sleep over that," Paul said grimly. "I daresay you and your brothers sometimes think of me as a flag-flapper but it's never been much more than a local flag." He had always envied his eldest son's comfortable grasp of the wider issues, however, so he went on, knitting his brows; "I was thinking of the Kaiser's Germans on the way over here. They were idiots, of course, with their brass bands and worship of uniforms but they weren't murderers, or not the ones I ran into. What do you suppose happened to them all of a sudden?"

"They were in a mess and took a short cut that landed them in an abattoir. It's happened before, and not only to them."

"Could it happen to us?"

"No. It might begin to but then a jack-in-office would have an old lady's pet poodle put down for imaginary rabies in Melton Mowbray and the entire bloody electorate would shout 'shame!' and throw the Government in the Thames!"

Paul laughed, the first really hearty laugh he had enjoyed in a long time. "You used to be partial to short cuts yourself," he said and Simon replied, "That's so, but a man likes familiar ground as he gets older. Don't forget I'm nudging forty!"

"It's not just a matter of age," Paul said, "it's a dampening-down process, of the kind that I noticed in your mother when I met her in France after the Somme. The last time you were home, just before Rachel was killed, your hatred of what was going on was oozing out of your pores. I didn't quarrel with that, mind you. You'd seen what Fascists were capable of in France and Spain, but now—well, you seem to me to be off the boil. More professional, perhaps? Is that it?"

Simon took his time answering and Paul gathered from his reaction to the question that he had lost a good deal of the intense privacy he had cultivated as a boy. He said, "Have you read a chap called Orwell?"

"*The Road to Wigan Pier?* Yes, I have and I liked him. He seemed to me to have more compassion than most of the authors you introduced into the house."

"I've met him and talked to him. He's not too optimistic about what could emerge from this showdown. It could be a

155

Robot State, with science taking over from the sociologists. Wells had the same notion, remember?"

"And what banner would you enlist under then?" Paul asked, with a smile, for he had a countryman's contempt for theorists of all kinds.

"Well, right alongside well-meaning reactionaries like you, Gov'nor! After all, looking around me I have to admit you've done a better job than any of those bloody politicians in Westminster. And I mean politicians with red ties as well as blue."

Paul was so unused to compliments of this kind from a member of his family that he felt vaguely embarrassed and said, clapping his heels into the grey and leading the way down the path, "I've done what I wanted to do, lived and worked in the open and raised a family on fresh air and good food! As to any wider complication, I've played it by instinct and I've never been that far out. I don't really give a damn what happens over there when they've cooked Hitler's goose but I think I know my own people and they won't let anyone push them around indefinitely. They never have and they never will, and if that sounds like something out of a Boer War music-hall ditty I can't help it. It's the way I'm made and what life has taught me over the last forty years."

He had not meant to amuse Simon but he did and Paul laughed too, for in the ring of Simon's laugh he heard another echo of his mother and it made him feel absurdly young for the moment.

After that they talked easily of one thing and another and it pleased Paul to see the eager way Simon looked about him as they dropped down to the river road and walked the fly-pestered horses along the bank to the lodge gates. Simon said suddenly, "It's got magic, I'll grant you that," and when Paul said it was losing it, like everywhere else, he said seriously, "It'll keep so long as you're around, Dad, and that's what's important to me." It was not the sentiment so much as the form of address that interested Paul. It must, he thought, be getting on for thirty years since Simon had addressed him as anything, but "Gov'nor", a semi-ironic term every one of them but Mary used. "Something *has* happened to him," he mused as they clattered into the yard and Claire and Mary ran out shouting their greetings, "but it'll take a woman to ferret out what!"

156

On the fourth day of his leave Simon saddled Paul's grey and rode across the ford and down to Coombe Bay, hoping to take a swim in the calm water between the sandbar and the landslide west of the village. It was a hot, shimmering day, and later he intended visiting Rachel's grave in the new acre beyond the churchyard wall, where lay most Shallowfordians who had died since the early 'thirties. First, however, he took advantage of his battledress to enter the prohibited beach, noting that the sea was doing its best to make the ugly crisscross of defences look part of the landscape. It was from this beach, he remembered, that Claire had taught him to swim and but for that he would have spent the last three years as a prisoner-of-war after the unit's surrender near Calais. The reflection increased his enjoyment of the occasion as he swam across the two hundred yards separating the beach from the nearest obstructions inside the bar. It was here, in a rectangle of rusting iron and trailing weed that he saw, or thought he saw, a mermaid.

She bobbed up from behind a thick, rusty crosspiece, her dark hair floating in a wide swirl, her expression as startled as one might expect of a mermaid surprised an eighth of a mile offshore. He was so astonished that he opened his mouth, swallowed half a gill of seawater and fell to coughing. When he was recovered and looked again she was gone.

He called, "Hi, there! Am I seeing things?" and she bobbed out again, smiling, a good-looking girl in her early 'twenties, with a smooth oval face and eyes that seemed, in the strong sunlight, only a shade less green than the weed clinging to the crossbar. Then he looked closer and saw that they were not green but hazel and that she had a laughing mouth with traces of lipstick on the underlip. He said, with moderate enthusiasm, "Oughtn't we to introduce ourselves? At first glance I could have sworn you had a tail!"

"I knew you hadn't," she said, "I saw you kicking on the way out but I thought you might have a warrant and a pair of handcuffs! It's verboten to swim here but I suppose you're privileged."

"More or less," he said, "because I arrived in uniform. All the same, I was stopped and asked for my identity card at the old gun emplacement. Why weren't you?"

"Because I came by boat," she said and waved her arm

towards the seaward side of the sandbank where a dinghy was moored under the overhang of the iron scaffolding. "That's even more verboten, of course, but they don't keep much of a lookout, do they? I might be a Hitler maiden, cruising inshore for a spot of sabotage!"

"You don't talk like one, or you've managed to acquire a first-rate East Anglian accent."

"That's clever of you," she said. "I come from Norwich but I've always thought it wasn't noticeable, except on a tape recorder."

"I'm very interested in regional accents," he said, "an amateur Professor Higgins. Are you on holiday?"

"No, I'm here for the duration. We were blitzed and I manage for Mr. Horsey, the Rector. Before we go any further, however, I ought to admit I know who you are. You're one of Squire Craddock's sons, aren't you? The one who is in the Army?"

"The oldest one," he said, "and getting on for superannuation. I'm on leave and this is the first time I've been back for more than two years."

She looked serious for a moment. "I remember—'Simon' isn't it?" and when he nodded, "My uncle talks about you as a tribe! He's a Craddock fan, did you know that? He has a terrific respect for your father and mother. He's really quite a dear."

He liked her voice and friendliness. He liked too the way water glistened on her smooth, pale face, like raindrops on the unblemished skin of an apple hanging in sunlight. "Let's take a look at your boat," he said. "We can keep the obstructions between us and the gun-post, otherwise the entire crew will come out to investigate."

They waded ashore and ran crouching across the narrow strip of sand to the boat. She was taller than he would have guessed and slimly built but out of the water she looked younger than he had judged. She had small, high breasts, long, sloping shoulders, a narrow waist and long legs that would carry her over the ground quickly. Poised on the edge of the boat she reminded him vaguely of a figure in a fifteenth century painting by someone like Baldung or Memling. There was something slightly mediaeval about her breasts and shoulders, suggesting a Virgin in a stained glass window. Her best feature, he decided, was her hair, black and very plentiful, darker and much curlier than his sister

Mary's. It was not her face or figure that attracted him, however, so much as her complete lack of artifice. She made no kind of effort to impress so that he had an odd impression they had already known one another a long time and had met again casually after a brief interval. He said, joining her on the gunwale, "Old Horsey must be over eighty. He can't be your real uncle, can he?"

"He could at that," she said, smiling, "for I'm twenty-eight, but he's not really an uncle at all, he's a cousin twice removed. My father is a parson like him. Parsons run in our family. The Horseys have had about a dozen in three generations. Did you know Uncle Horace's son, the one who was killed in the First War?"

"Yes," he said, "as a matter of fact I married his widow," and he smiled as her hand shot to her mouth like someone trying to mask a gaffe.

"Of course! What a stupid remark. She was killed in that hit-and-run raid, wasn't she? Uncle wrote about it at the time. I say—I'm sorry, I'm not very bright about that kind of thing."

"There's nothing to be sorry about," he said, making a circle in the sand with his great toe. "It happened, and that's that. If you were blitzed in Norwich I daresay you lost people the same way."

"Friends," she said, "about half a dozen of them. We were lucky but the Vicarage was burned down when a couple of incendiaries went through the roof. You're a Commando, aren't you?"

"I was, a sergeant instructor, but I was commissioned a week ago and now I don't know how they'll use me. Gliding, maybe, that's the latest fashion."

"I wanted to go in the A.T.S." she said, "but Mummy talked me out of it. I think she had an idea they share huts and blankets with the men. I wish I had joined. In Norwich I ran a canteen for a school and now I'm going to serve in the N.A.A.F.I. up at the camp."

"You'll be in great demand over there," he said, "the intake is about a thousand men every six weeks and there are only about a dozen women allowed inside the wire!"

"Yes," she said, "that's what I hoped!" and laughed, shaking out her dark curls and rubbing them gently with a towel she took from the thwarts.

"Still fancy free?"

"Still fancy free. I was engaged once but he fell for a W.A.A.F. and after a decent interval he brought her to the Vicarage for my approval. She was much more his type than me, very fair and fluffy, and well up with all the latest hot numbers. She played boogie-woogie on the church organ. Father never quite got over it but I did."

He said, surprised at his own initiative, "Look, when you've dressed, and sneaked back round the breakwater, will you wait for me up at the lych-gate? I've got my father's grey hobbled on the beach and I'll ride back along the dunes in about half an hour. Unless you want to stay out here that is."

"I've got to cope with Uncle's lunch," she said, "but he never knows what time it is. Yes, I'll meet you there, but why the lych-gate?"

He hesitated but then, meeting her frank, interested gaze, "I wanted to see where Rachel was buried," he said. "I've never been there and I'd prefer to go in company. Your kind of company anyway."

She said, calmly, "I can understand that. In about half an hour then, and if I'm caught landing back me up when I say I'm a refugee from Sark!"

He gave her a casual wave and went back across the sandspit, swimming to the landslip where he had left his clothes and the hobbled grey. He felt elated and even more relaxed than he had felt riding back over the moor with the Old Man. The girl's gaiety was infectious. It took him back to the times he used to come here with Claire for his swimming lessons, and the weather itself was co-operating for, in those days, it seemed to him that the sun was always hanging over Nun's Island like a pawnbroker's ball and the sand above highwater line was hot to the feet. He realised then why he had put off his duty visit to Rachel's grave, but in the company of a stranger like the girl it seemed no more than polite gesture calculated to satisfy the conventional side of Claire, who had asked him if he had been only that morning. He hurried into his battledress and rode up the slope of the dunes and from here he could see what the men on the jetty could not see, her little black dinghy, creeping along under cover of the breakwater. As he watched he saw it nose in among three or four other boats moored under the Bluff.

She was waiting when he got there and haltered the grey to the church railings, following her across the angled slope of the old churchyard crowded with headstones engraved with names that were a kind of alphabet to anyone who had grown up in the Valley; Willoughbys, Codsalls, Potters and Derwents, Stokeses, Morgans and Tozers. He had known most of them as a boy and could call to mind the faces of some of their children and grandchildren. He said suddenly, "Do you like it here? Does it seem dead-and-alive after a city like Norwich?" and she said it did not and that she liked it very much because it was "George-Ellioty".

"That's a rum adjective," he said, "but I know what you mean. I must tell the Gov'nor what you said. He's always quoting Tom, Maggie, and Silas Marner at us. He thinks a great many things have altered here but it seems much the same to me. I left here as long ago as 1929 just before I married, and I only returned on rare family occasions, apart from a spell of convalescence after they winkled me out of Franco's stinking gaol."

She didn't question him about Spain and he was grateful, but said, "You didn't have any children, did you?"

"No, we were too priggish. We used to tell each other it wasn't the kind of world to dump children in but I see now we were fooling ourselves and each other."

"How?"

"Who can pontificate on anything as basic as that? All these people—I knew most of them—had flocks of children, and God knows, they had their problems! Every generation has its problems and how the hell can you solve them by cutting down on population? We should look pretty sick right now if we hadn't got plenty of keen types to open a Second Front and were obliged to stay on the defensive indefinitely."

"It's a point," she said, and at that he laughed, saying, "Why am I talking to you like this? I don't even know your name. Is it Horsey?"

"It's Horsey," she said, equably, "Evelyn Horsey, but everyone except my mother calls me Evie. Mother is just the tiniest bit prissy. It probably comes from presiding over thousands of sewing circles and Save-the-Belfry bazaars! Have you any idea where the grave is because I know. It's over near the yew in the Intake. That's where all the Eveleighs are. I cut the grass there only last week."

She led the way across Church Lane into the new churchyard, already containing a score of graves. He remembered the Eveleigh patch then and stood beside the slate headstone, reading the weathered names of Norman and his son Gilbert, and the later inscriptions cut on behalf of Marian, his mother-in-law, Harold, his brother-in-law and, last of all, "*Rachel Craddock*", with the bald "1896-1942—*Killed by Enemy Action*" underneath. There was no Craddock patch as yet for they had never found his sister Claire's body after the Dutch air disaster in 1934 and that, he supposed, was the reason why his father had had Rachel laid here with the rest of her family. He said to the girl standing behind him, "I didn't come home for the funeral."

"You couldn't come?"

"I wouldn't. I was in the middle of a course up in the Highlands and it seemed to me more important to finish what I was doing than come five hundred miles to see Rachel buried. Some of my pals were shocked and so, I think, were my father and stepmother. What do you think?"

Extraordinary, he thought, asking her a question like that on the strength of an hour's acquaintance but he waited eagerly for her answer, knowing it would be an honest one.

"It's something no one has any right to comment on one way or the other," she said. "It was a matter for you. No one else, not even your people."

"She was a very intense person," he said. "She never got over Keith Horsey being sacrificed to the armchair patriots in World War I. She felt she owed it to him to spend the rest of her life crusading against injustice of that sort. All kinds of injustice, from bad housing to victimisation by Trade Unions. She wasn't really a Socialist at all, except in the nineteenth-century sense. It used her up by the time she was forty and damn near used me up too! It wasn't until I came to grips with reality that I realised theory isn't much good against Stukas and Panzers. You've got to strike some kind of bargain with the Top Hats, if only in order to stop the Steel Helmets taking over. You can always go back to pelting toppers when you've nothing better to do."

"Uncle Horace warned me you were the odd one out," she said, but when he looked up sharply and saw that she was smiling he smiled too, saying, "Yes I am, so thanks for coming. Let's go in and say hello to the Rector. Then I must go home. It's gone lunchtime now."

"Stay and lunch with us," she suggested. "You can put the horse in the loose-box and 'phone the Big House. Uncle Horace would like to meet someone actually taking part in the war. The only soldiers he ever sees are the local Home Guard and that elderly naval gun-crew down at the harbour. There isn't much to tempt you, I'm afraid, but at least it isn't one of those awful dishes the radio keeps telling you are much better for you than real food! As a matter of fact it's one of Farmer Bellchamber's ducks—cold. It's rather like the relationship that used to exist between professional smugglers and the local parson. Instead of leaving a cask of brandy on the doorstep they now leave eggs and poultry. I don't know what he's expected to do in return, probably intercede for them in the Quiet Moment before the sermon!"

She took him by the hand and he found her grasp cool and firm, exactly the kind of grasp he would have expected from someone as self-assured and sane and yet, in another way, as irresponsible as one of The Pair when they were seventeen. They led the grey round the churchyard and into the Rectory yard where there was an unused loose-box and Simon unsaddled while Evie went clattering into the big old-fashioned kitchen, calling to her uncle that she had a guest. Simon stood for a moment with his hand on Snowdrop's shoulder, warming himself in the mood that had been growing on him ever since he had looked out of the carriage window at Sorrel Halt and seen his father standing there with the reins of the two horses looped over his arm. "It's curious," he thought, "how tranquil everything has become since then, almost as though one was beginning again with the benefit of hindsight. But that isn't really anything to do with her, or the Gov'nor, it's the sameness of this place."

The frail old man greeted him with a cordiality he bestowed on all the children of Paul Craddock. Simon, alone among his brothers and sisters, could recall Horsey's early years in the Valley, when he had appeared as a diffident man from a London dockside parish, a freakish replacement in Shallowford eyes of the bustling, bullying Parson Bull, last of a long line of local hunting parsons.

Listening to the old man's knowledgeable observations on Valley flora and fauna (he did not, it appeared, have much interest in the war after all), Simon found himself assessing Horsey's unlikely success since he had settled among them, recalling his faltering sermons and self-effacing manner in the years leading up to the First World War, and his sudden access of spiritual strength after his only son had been killed in France. Today the old fellow did not look strong enough to climb a pulpit stair but Simon knew that there was steadfastness there for he had often heard Paul describe how, against all probability, Horsey had united the religious sects of the Valley and reconciled the mutual suspicions of the Anglicans, the tight little Nonconformist groups among tradesmen and fishermen, and the few Roman Catholics in the Valley. Somehow his essential faith and love of nature had compounded a kind of local patriotism and his courage and integrity was unquestioned by all.

With half his mind Simon listened to the old fellow's tale of tracking down a rare moth, identified by a long Latin name, and with the other half he contemplated the smiling, leggy girl who dispensed cold duck and green salad with the easy jocularity of a mother feeding her son and one of his friends who had strayed in for a meal after a day's romp. The peace of the old rectory was like balm. He found himself thinking, "This is what it is all about—this is the essence of what we're fighting for—peace, the well-stocked English countryside, predictability, and cold duck." He noticed too the casual grace of her long, white hands and once, when their eyes met and she smiled, the cheerlessness of his own life up to this point presented itself as a long tramp across the empty streets of an industrial city in January sleet. He thought, a little apprehensively, "She's late spring and there's an element of renewal about her," and the insecurity of his present life pricked him like a spur so that he thought, fleetingly, "If I want to change direction there's no time to be lost, not a day, not an hour . . .!"

III

Looking back on that period it seemed to Simon that the seed of their relationship sprouted overnight like Jack's Bean-stalk. He only had nine days, and three of them had passed before they met, but they made the very best of the remaining six. The day after lunching at the Rectory he took her home, and the day after that they walked across the cliffs to Whinmouth and had tea at a little cafe he knew on the Quay. On the fourth day he borrowed Bon-Bon Potter's abandoned motor-cycle and drove her pillion to Paxtonbury, where they saw *One Of Our Aircraft Is Missing* and he amused her throughout tea relating the pre-war antics of The Pair. That evening they had dinner at the Big House where anything but high tea was a rarity. Claire, watching them, reflected on the seesaw element of family life and fervently wished him well. He deserved, she thought, a real break this time and it was strange that he should look like getting one at the moment The Pair's nonstop hayride was on collision course.

Ever since Margaret had stayed a few days after Andy had been reported missing Claire had lived with their unsavoury problem, recoiling from it in a way she had never done when marginally involved in so many of their pranks. This, she realised, was not a prank at all but a desperately serious business, especially now that Andy had turned up again, and whenever she pondered his miraculous reappearance she felt bereft of common decency for she was unable to dismiss the uncomfortable thought that it might have been better for everybody if Andy had stayed missing.

And yet, knowing that Margaret must be thinking the same, she still felt desperately sorry for her and for that idiot Stevie as well. She did not know her sons very well. They had always lived at such a frightful pace, mostly away from home, and had seemed so well able to take care of themselves but now she was beginning to understand that this was a fiction and that both had been engaged in a game of bluff of which the end-product was a scandal that could age Paul twenty years.

Only one thing recommended itself, to keep it from him as long as possible, please God for ever, but how could this be achieved after Andy got home and found a wife six months gone with his brother's child? It would be better, she imagined, if Andy was led to think of the child as a stranger's. He was the kind of person who might in time overlook that, after an absence abroad of more than two years, but what would be his reaction when he learned that Margaret's feelings towards him were indifferent and that Stevie, under the stress of war, had become as vulnerable as Simon, now chattering away to this likeable girl he had fished out of the bay? Margaret had been appallingly frank but her identification of Stevie with Andy did not seem a piece of special pleading to Claire, herself a sensual woman who had lived for a man's embraces since she was a girl of nineteen. She had, in fact, seen a similarity between her own marriage and the marriage of Andy and Margaret, a partnership with a strong physical basis but not much else. Now, it seemed, the girl had found something else and found it where and when she least expected it.

Inability to confide in anyone, or even discuss the impasse with the parties concerned, made Claire distrait, so that even Paul, usually insensitive to her moods, was beginning to notice, attributing her moodiness to anxiety over Andy's injuries and Stevie's determination to fly again as soon as his rest period had ended. There was also Simon to worry about, and because he was a stepson she had always given him more attention than any of the others. She would have gladly confided in Simon if she had not been caught off balance by his newly-acquired peace of mind. As it was it seemed to her a shabby trick to knock him over the head just as he was standing upright after so long, so she said nothing, drawing what comfort she could from his unexpectedly high spirits and the pleasure they obviously gave his father.

Paul Craddock, unencumbered by such dismal forebodings, could sit back and enjoy what he thought the lady Victorian novelists might have called "a whirlwind courtship". For him one of the by-products of family life had been an opportunity to watch his children choosing mates and it was a pleasure that grew with the years, for he was now of an age when he didn't give a damn whether they made fools of themselves or otherwise. It was not always so. He had been embarrassed by the dourness of the Scotsman Whiz had brought home and rebuffed by the coolness of the Archdeacon's daughter and the Archdeacon's wife. Margaret, who had the kind of promise he always looked for in women, he had liked from the start and he had always felt sympathetic towards Rachel Eveleigh who had gone through such a bad time in the First War. His ewe lamb among his in-laws, of course was Rumble Patrick, who had always seemed so right for Mary, but now he found himself warming to this dark, leggy girl Simon had brought home so unexpectedly and he wondered whether the boy was as taken with her as he appeared to be, or was only going through a kind of thawing-out process after the drabness of his first marriage. He didn't know and he wouldn't bet on it but, like Claire, he wished Simon all the luck in the world and privately hoped the girl would forget she was a parson's daughter and remember there was a war on.

On the last day of his leave, when he and Evie Horsey had set off to visit the headwaters of the Sorrel where its source welled into the deep sandstone cleft running diagonally across the moor, Simon Craddock made up his mind in the way he had impressed upon so many recruits when they were introduced to the death-slide, or the hop, skip and jump across a twenty-foot wall on the assault course. He said, looking down at her as she dabbled her hands in the first yard of the Sorrel, "I don't ever recall enjoying a week like this, Evie, not in my entire life! It began even before you bobbed up from behind that bollard. What I do know is that it would have been temporary if I hadn't run into you." He paused a moment, as though gathering himself for the leap. "I'm due out of here at first light tomorrow. I'll write of course but why say the only important thing I have to say on paper? Will you marry me?"

It was, he thought, a rather casual, amateurish proposal but he saw that it was not entirely unexpected. Only the timing astonished her, for she thought of him as a man approaching middle age, who would pause to weigh factors that would not occur to a younger man. When she did not answer immediately but remained kneeling beside the stream letting the current run through her fingers, he said, quietly, "All right, think about it, and that isn't a conventional qualification. I'm eleven years older than you and I still haven't a clue what I'm going to do with my life when the war's over. I've always made most of my decisions on impulse and that's what I'm doing now."

When she still did not answer his nerve faltered a little and he said, breathlessly, "Well say *something*! Tell me I've got a nerve, or to stop making a damn fool of myself, or be my age, or something!" Then she stood upright, took his face between her hands and said, with a now familiar compromise between gaiety and sincerity, "Of course I'll marry you, providing you haven't thought better of it by the time you're home again and I do hope you haven't! I'd back my instinct about you. Any girl who had a ha'porth of sense would do that," and she kissed him, very gently, on the mouth.

It was as simple as that, the simplest and most satisfactory thing that had ever happened to him and he wondered at its simplicity for a very long time, remembering not only the spontaneity of her acceptance but also the setting, with its great hartstongue ferns and tinkling stream, birds in the thickets above and sunbeams probing the bank on which they stood, and something of this must have communicated itself to him at the time for he said thankfully, "I'm damned glad I was able to say it instead of writing it. Somehow I didn't think I would, and would have cursed myself for having to put it all on paper the minute I got back to camp. I'm out of practice, Evie, but you'll have noticed that by now."

"I've noticed," she said, "and it's a point in your favour." Then, unexpectedly, "Afterwards? Will you want to come back here? To settle I mean?"

"God knows! I'm no farmer and what else would I do?"

She took his hand and spread it out, regarding it intently for a moment and saying, "You could do anything very well so long as you believed enough in it, but you won't bother much with personal problems until there's hope for everybody's future. You're that kind of person and if you weren't you'd be just another widower looking for a fresh start. How long do you give it, Simon?"

He had thought about it many times, sometimes optimistically but more often gloomily, when it had looked like a siege that would endure for the rest of their lives. Today, understandably, he took a more cheerful view. "Two to three years at worst, eighteen months at best! But you aren't proposing to keep me waiting that long, are you? I'll be due for leave again in three months and even if I get posted overseas I'll get a few days' embarkation. It's July now. August, September, October . . ." but he broke off because he saw that she was laughing.

"You're right," she said, "you really are out of practice," and she threw her arms round him and kissed him in a way Rachel had never kissed him.

IV

The night after he had gone, perhaps because she had felt so cheered by his news, Claire slept more soundly than she had for weeks. Simon's announcement that he and Evie were to marry almost at once had pushed her consuming worry into the background for a few hours and the steady throb of aircraft hammering across the sky a mile or so to the west did not wake her as it awakened Paul, jerking him upright by its solid thrust. By now he could distinguish most enemy aircraft by the sound of their engines, and he realised at once that these were heavy bombers, crossing the coast near the mouth of the Whin, and in far larger numbers than at any time since the 1940 attack upon Plymouth.

He switched on the bedside light, automatically glancing towards the window to ensure that the blackout curtains were drawn. Then, with the roar of a volcano, the first salvo of bombs came down and the old house shuddered, plaster cascading from the ceiling round the central light fixture. He said, as Claire cried out in alarm, "It's Paxtonbury. Another Baedekker. My God, I thought we were through all that," and then the second shower of bombs exploded and all hell burst loose to the north

He shouted, "I'll get John, Mary, the kids ...!" but she clung to him with a dreadful intensity and even allowing for the fact that she had been literally bombed out of a deep sleep he was surprised at her panic. Before he could escape from her grasp the door crashed open and the others were there, John holding little Jerry by the hand, Mary cradling the baby, Sorrel. Mary's mouth was wide open, as though she was screaming, but he understood that she was only urging him to take shelter under the staircase where they had sheltered in 1940. He tore a blanket from the bed, threw it across Claire's shoulders and made a grab at his own dressing-gown. A glance at his watch showed him it was twenty minutes past two and then Claire pulled herself together and half rolled off the bed so that they ran along the vibrating passage and down the broad staircase in a group, John and Jerry just ahead.

Inland the inferno of noise continued, breaking into a regular pattern of sounds so that it was possible to distinguish the intermittent thud of high-explosive, the steady drone of night-fighters and the barking cough of anti-aircraft guns firing from the perimeter of the Polish airfield east of the city. Each of the heavier booms brought down more of the ceiling and they heard it pattering as they huddled together in a compact group in the broom recess that opened onto the kitchen passage. The kitchen was not blacked out in summer and through the panels of the outside door they could see the white flashes in the sky and presently a pinkish glow that seemed to be spreading over the sea but was, Paul realised, a reflection of fires over Paxtonbury. For twenty minutes the uproar continued and then faded to a rumble that lasted another five. In the comparative silence the anti-aircraft fire could be heard more distinctly and a few moments later the scattered throb of bombers recrossing the coast.

Claire said in his ear, "Is it over? Are they going?" but before he could answer there was a sound that came rushing down on them from much nearer at hand, a long, whistling howl that made each of them shrink and press themselves against the timbered wall of the cupboard. He thought he heard Claire scream but it might have been part of the sound itself and before he could enfold Mary and the baby a tremendous explosion seemed to lift them and blast them into the deepest recess of the cupboard. Then, as though a thousand bells had stopped ringing, there was silence, except for the baby's whimpers, the dry whistle of Claire's breath, and the distant throb of aero-engines away out to sea.

Minutes ticked by without any of them saying anything and at last Paul, switching on his torch, emerged from the recess and plucked up the receiver of the telephone, replacing it as soon as he realised the line was dead. They stayed there saying little until the distant blare of the "All Clear" sounded and was presently taken up by another, presumably in Whinmouth and then a third in Coombe Bay. Paul said, struck by the reediness of his own voice, "That was a terrific packet but the Poles were very quick off the mark. It wouldn't surprise me if they hadn't got some of them!"

John spoke unexpectedly and just as Paul had been ashamed of the tremor in his own voice so he was proud of the steadiness of the boy's. "That was a bomber down in the woods, Dad," and when Paul said this was nonsense he insisted, "It *was!* I *know* it was! There was a long crackling sound that went on and on, after the bang and it was quite near our side of the Mere."

Paul joggled the 'phone desperately and Claire, edging out of the cupboard, seemed to have recovered a little of her nerve.

"Take the baby back to bed, Mary. I'll keep Jerry in the kitchen and make tea," and without another word she threw the blanket over the child and led him away by the hand, switching on the hall lights as she went. Paul and John went across to the front door and flung it open. To the south it was still dark but behind the house the sky was like a summer sunset, a great pink and crimson glow over Paxtonbury, fifteen miles to the south-west. Fighters still droned overhead and John said, with his customary politeness, "Will they have hit the Cathedral, Dad? They didn't last time, remember?"

"Last time was a couple of strays," Paul said, "this time it was deliberate. Are you quite sure about that ripping sound?"

"Yes Dad, quite sure."

"As though something was crashing through the trees on the slope down to the Mere?"

"Yes. Oughtn't we to go and look?"

"We will, the moment it's light."

"You mean I can come?"

"Yes, you can come, and I'll tell you something else, son. You've got a hell of a lot of nerve. More than me, more than your mother and as much as any of your brothers!"

The boy said nothing, sensing humility in the big, grey-haired man. He followed him into the kitchen, where his mother, deathly pale, was retching into the sink.

"I'm sorry," she said helplessly, addressing all of them, including Jerry who had stopped snivelling and was staring at her bowed back, "I'm sorry, I can't stand much more of this," and she turned on both taps. John said, quietly, "Sit down, I'll make the tea," and gently edged her aside, lifting the big iron kettle and holding it under the cold jet. Paul said, "Don't apologise, it was enough to scare the living daylights out of anyone in their right mind. Would you like a dram?"

"No," she said, her eyes on John as he hauled the kettle on to the stove, "just tea. Hot and strong!"

"Coming up!" John said, and Paul thought "Great God! Is he only nine? He behaves more like one of those old sweats left over from First Ypres!" And then, turning to comfort Jerry, "It's all over now and that's the second time they've had a crack at you, isn't it? None of us will get hurt if you stay around," and he caught Claire's feeble attempt at a smile as he said it.

By the time the teapot was empty it was almost day. Jerry was yawning and Mary took him back to bed. John slipped away and came back fully dressed in mackintosh and gum-boots, and Claire said, "Where do you think you're going?"

"To see if that was a bomber down in the woods! Dad said I could, didn't you?"

"Yes I did," Paul conceded, adding, "there's no danger and

171

I might need him to run a message. You'll be all right for half an hour, won't you?"

"Yes, I'll be all right but come back right away. Someone is sure to call and maybe they hit the camp this time."

She dragged herself up feeling old and defeated. It had been bad enough getting through the last war, with Paul in France and half the Valley dead, but at least the children weren't under fire. Silently cursing the men who had been so confoundedly clever as to invent aeroplanes she went upstairs and along the passage to Mary's room.

Paul buckled on his revolver, more from habit than design, and they went out the back door and up across the dew-soaked orchard to the sunken lane that ran behind the house. If you could forget the lurid colour of the sky it was a soft, pleasant morning but in the presence of two separate dawns, one in the east and another in the west, it was not easy to appreciate hedgerow scents. They went up the lane as far as the gate leading to the long, upsloping meadow and then, turning left, climbed through the scrub towards the first of the tall trees. They were only a third of the way up when John shouted, "Look! Over there!" and Paul, glancing over his right shoulder, saw the billowing parachute, its folds lifting lightly in the breeze where it had come to rest under the hedge.

"I hadn't thought of that," he said, loosening the flap of his holster. "Get behind me, John, and keep your eyes open and if I tell you to go back go and don't argue. We don't want another Otto Shratt situation."

"Yes, sir," said John, dutifully, and Paul could tell how much he was enjoying himself.

The parachute told them little. There was nothing to identify it as German or British but its presence made them cautious and they breasted the slope in Indian file, moving carefully among the summer foliage.

They were beginning to descend the long, wooded slope when Paul saw that John's instinct had served him well. Down towards the Mere, looking utterly incongruous among stripped oaks and rakishly tilted smaller trees, was a sprawling tangle of twisted metal and canvas, with a single wing pointing skyward at an angle of about ninety degrees. They stared down at the wreck incredulously. Thin wisps of smoke still rose from it and a wide circle of brown under-growth showed that there had been a considerable blaze,

172

although possibly a short-lived one, for the timber was thick and heavy and there was very little breeze. Paul said, softly, "My God! Now I've seen everything!" and broke into a stumbling run with John beside him but then, recollecting the parachute back in the meadow, he drew his revolver, shouting, "Wait! If any others jumped they're hung up in the trees somewhere."

They went down more slowly, glancing from left to right but there was no one to be seen and Paul, reflecting that there might be roasting bodies scattered around, called, "Don't go too near, John. We'll just have a look then get in touch with the camp and Observer Corps."

It was at that moment he saw the German airman, a forlorn and by no means frightening figure, who raised himself from a clump of dwarf beeches about fifty yards north of the wreck.

He was, Paul would judge, no more than nineteen or twenty, and was still shaking with shock or fright, for the hands lifted above his head fluttered and from where he stood, on higher ground looking down, Paul could see his throat muscles working and his tongue moving slowly round his lips. His fur-lined flying-jacket hung open and he had removed his helmet, showing fair stubby hair, almost white it looked in the early morning sunshine. He heard John hiss but kept his eyes on the man, marking him with the pistol.

"*Hand hoche!*" he called, remembering his First War German, but it was a silly command for the man already had his hands raised in surrender and came stumbling out of the scrub, moving awkwardly in his clumsy flying boots.

It was clear from the way the German approached that he was no Otto Shratt and expected to be shot. Paul was surprised at himself for feeling no anger. The airman was so young, and so obviously at the end of his tether. He thought, grimly, "It's all mad! A few hours ago he was doing his damnedest to blow us all to hell and here he is cowering in my woods and wondering if I'm going to put a bullet through his head!" He beckoned, lowering the gun but keeping it pointed. The man seemed dazed and his eye flickered over the wreck so that Paul, remembering that most Germans spoke some English, said, slowly and carefully, "How many?" and pointed to the spiral of smoke below the scorched branches.

The airman accepted this as a reprieve and fear fell from

his face like a mask. Paul saw then that he was a good-looking boy with regular features and light blue eyes.

"Four," he said, holding up four fingers. "All dead. I came in the field," and he pointed up the slope towards the place where they had seen the parachute.

"And by God you were lucky to 'come in the field'," Paul thought, looking down at the debris, "you landed about twenty yards short of the timber. Another puff of wind and you would have dropped in the bay." Then he recollected John and saw that he had approached the debris. He called, "Come back up here. You hear me?"

John turned and came gingerly up the slope. "He's right," he said offhandedly, "the others are in there, at least, three are and another is a bit lower down." The boy's nerve again succeeded in astonishing him but he said sharply, "Run on ahead and warn the others. If there's no one at the house saddle the pony and ride across to Home Farm. Maybe their telephone is working. If it is get Honeyman to send word to Constable Voysey and the camp. Tell them to send a party over to the house to collect a prisoner and check up on this."

The boy looked at him with comical uncertainty. "Will you be all right on your own?"

"Of course I'll be all right. I've got a gun haven't I? And anyway, there's no fight left in this one. Hurry along. Do as I say."

Reluctantly the boy set himself at the slope and Paul saw him disappear among the close-set timber that grew up to the ridge. "Right," he said. "Walk ahead of me and no monkey tricks, Master Race," but as he followed the airman up the slope he thought, "What the hell am I talking about? My boys have been doing the same job over there ever since it started. We're all mad, the whole damned lot of us," and the reflection pricked the bubble of his arrogance so that he called, when they reached the open field where the parachute still lifted in the wind, "Would you like a cigarette?" and putting his revolver away he fumbled in his jacket pocket and brought out a half-empty packet of Players.

The German lit one from a curiously-shaped brass lighter and then Paul lit one too and they stared down at the parachute.

"Yours?" he asked, and the young man nodded and smiled, at the same time making a curiously English gesture, closing the fingers of both hands and elevating his two thumbs.

"I should say you're lucky," Paul grunted, "you made it by a few feet. What's your name?"

"Weber," the man said, and then, politely, "You are a soldier?"

"No, but that's my house down there. I was a soldier, I probably fought your father in France."

"Ach so," the young man said, like a stock character in a Continental play, "but it was a different kind of war."

"Very different," Paul said, grumpily. "We didn't kill women and kids, neither one of us."

The young man looked thoughtful. Then he said, unsentimentally, "My Mother and my aunt were killed by bombs in Stuttgart. In this year."

The last of Paul's resentment ebbed and with it went the exhilaration of the capture. He felt an absurd impulse to unclip his holster and toss the contents into the wood beside which they stood. Close by was the tree where there were once grey squirrels beloved of Hazel Potter, the mother of Rumble Patrick and he thought fleetingly of Rumble, and of Stevie and Andy and Simon, comparing them with this tall, good-looking boy miraculously saved from that holocaust back there in the woods. He said aloud, but not addressing the man, "We're sick, the whole damned lot of us. We must be," and the German said, "Please?" to which Paul gave no answer.

They went down the long meadow into an erupting household. John, a child once again, pranced out screaming that a jeep had arrived with an officer and two men from the camp. They had orders to search the woods after a report from the Polish Squadron that a bomber had crashed before crossing the coast. "Paxtonbury is still burning," he said, as though it was something to exhult over, "but nobody round here was hit."

They went into the kitchen, the German making a great effort to look dignified and the Royal Marine sergeant there said, "Christ! The boy was right, sir. We didn't really believe him."

"This is the only survivor," Paul said, "the others are back there this side of the Mere, done to a turn."

"How did Sonny Boy escape?"

"Parachute. The 'chute is back there too. None of your people hit?"

175

"No, sir, it was a Baedekker on Paxtonbury. There were casualties there I think but it was mostly incendiaries."

"They didn't sound like incendiaries," Paul said, "you'd better fetch your officer. This chap won't give any trouble," and he automatically put the kettle on the stove.

"They'll come for you soon," he told the prisoner. "Tea?"

The man nodded eagerly and Paul saw his eyes range round the big room. He said, as Paul busied himself with cups, "You are the Graf?"

"The Graf'?" Paul searched his memory for an approximate and said, "Well, I don't know, the people here think of me as 'Squire'."

"Ah yes," the young man said, "that is the word—'Squire'. I am very glad your property was not damaged last night."

"And so am I," thought Paul, "but it's no thanks to you that my wife, two of my children, and two of my grandchildren aren't smeared on the wall of the broom cupboard." And then he remembered the Stuttgart raid, and when Claire came in, tight-lipped, unsmiling and no more than curious, he said, "Go easy on him. He's got troubles of his own."

CHAPTER NINE

A VARIETY OF SALLIES

I

CHRISTMAS, 1943, the fifth Christmas of the war.

It had already lasted longer than the war that nobody in the Valley thought would ever end, and although there was no question of losing it now Paul felt that it had somehow bogged itself down in Italy, in Russia, and behind the much-advertised defences of what even the Valley people now called, in the jargon of the times, *Festung-Europa.*

It was surprising, he thought, that so many of the Valley youngsters were still alive, and also that they bobbed up so frequently. The blight he had anticipated back in 1939 had so far been averted. Bon-Bon, son of Smut and Marie Potter, came home sporting a medal, and so did Dick Potter, now a sergeant in a famous infantry regiment. So far, miraculously it seemed, none of his tenants had lost a son and fatal casualties were still numbered at two, Harold Eveleigh and Rachel Craddock, both civilians. His own family, apart from Andy, were still closely engaged: Stevie flying a Lancaster in the ever-mounting air attacks over Germany; Simon, training for some distant offensive, stationed in the Midlands; and Whiz's husband, Ian, living, as far as he could judge from her letters, a sybaritic life in India. Rumble Patrick had come home in September, sunburned and as cheerful as ever, ranging into the Valley like a sailor in a Victorian print with a bulging kitbag full of bizarre gifts and a repertoire of travellers' tales from the other side of the world. Paul was surprised that he had not appeared with a parrot and when he mentioned this Rumble said it had, in fact, occurred to him to buy one in Buenos Aires but all the parrots he interviewed talked Spanish so he hadn't bothered. He told

Paul he had had one or two near shaves, and that his ship had been holed by a torpedo off Halifax, Nova Scotia, but they had managed to float her into port. "Don't mention that to Mary," he said, "let her go on thinking I'm immortal. Claire had the same idea about you last time, I believe."

"Yes, that's so," Paul said, remembering how, alone in the Valley, Claire had persisted in thinking of him as alive when he had been lying in a coma in a German hospital at Soissons, and then he asked Rumble if the neutral countries he had visited considered the eventual collapse of the Third Reich inevitable.

"Everywhere but in the Argentine," he said, "Jerry has a special line in propaganda over there. We seem to be getting on top of the U-boats lately and the only crack I had at Jerry was at a Condor, off San Sebastian. Looking round it strikes me that you people see a damned sight more action than us. Paxtonbury is a right mess, I saw that while I was waiting for the 'bus. Is it true that about a hundred people were killed?"

"A hundred and eleven, and twice as many injured," Paul said, and because the subject depressed him he went on to give Rumble the family news, saying that Andy, who was to have returned home in August, had now been transferred to Cairo for further skin-grafting. He understood there were first-class facilities out there now that the Germans had been driven out of Africa.

"How is Andy's wife?" Rumble asked. "Does she ever look back here?" and Paul said no, and that Claire told him she was nursing in a hospital in Wales and sometimes met Stevie who had spent some time on a course at a Shropshire airfield and was within driving distance. Then he added, "I suppose Mary told you Stevie and Monica have split up? I can't say I'm devastated. I never liked that girl. I always thought her damned patronising, not only to us but to that little Welsh wife of Andy's. I believe there will be a divorce eventually and it'll be the first in my family, but the way people are carrying on lately it doesn't shock me as it might have twenty years ago. Claire seems to take it more seriously but she's not herself these days."

"I'd noticed that," Rumble said, "Mary thinks that raid upset her badly."

"She was off her oats before that," Paul said. "I think maternal anxiety about all of you has finally caught up with her, or perhaps it's just age. After all, she'll be sixty in a month or two and at last she's beginning to look it—fifty anyway. Will you be home for any length of time?"

"I've got a ship sailing mid-October," he said, "and I made sure it wasn't travelling a Northern route. In spite of what you think I don't stick my neck out more than I can help."

"There was no damned point in you sticking it out at all," Paul grumbled, "but maybe it's like you say, you're nearly as safe in the Atlantic as within a half-mile of that camp on the moor! I'll tell you something else. That last baby was a Godsend to Mary. It stopped her brooding and gave her something to think about. I'm glad it was a girl. Are you?"

Rumble said he was but was disappointed it was a blonde. "I was expecting it to be a brunette Craddock, like Mary," he said, "and it turns out to be a Derwent-Potter Anglo-Saxon!"

He lunged off in search of Mary and later Paul saw them both saddling his grey and the pony. They were going, Mary said, to take a look at the remains of the German bomber but privately, seeing that the September sunshine was warm and inviting, Paul thought this unlikely and that they were taking the opportunity offered to get away from the family and pretend they were ten years younger. "That's one aspect of being married to a sailor," he told himself, "every time he comes ashore it's another honeymoon," but went on to reflect that Rumble and Mary always had seemed newlyweds to him and probably always would, even if he survived their Silver Wedding. He wished heartily that some of his other children had mated by instinct, in the way he invariably thought of Mary's marriage to Rumble, but he was more philosophical nowadays concerning the troubles of others, particularly those of the generation that had grown up between the wars. He drove off to attend a War Agricultural Committee meeting in Whinmouth.

About two months after Rumble had departed Simon came home on leave to marry what Paul called his "Coombe Bay mermaid", niece of old Parson Horsey, who had been a regular visitor at the Big House since Simon and she had become engaged. He liked her immensely, finding her a sympathetic, uncomplicated person, more like one of the youngsters growing up hereabouts in Edward VII's reign than the brittle young people of the 'forties. They had a quiet church wedding and this in itself, thought Paul, was unusual nowadays when youngsters dragged one another off to the nearest Register Office and signed on, like couples qualifying for pensions or free coal. He enjoyed the wedding that took place under a light fall of snow, the first snow of the winter, and afterwards they all gathered at Parson Horsey's rectory for a frugal wedding breakfast. The old man himself had insisted on officiating, despite increasing feebleness. Looking at him during the ceremony Paul told himself that the old chap wouldn't last much longer and his mind went back to Horsey's predecessor, the rampaging Parson Bull, who had spent most of his time foxhunting and died as a result of an injury in the field. "It's like remembering someone who fought at Naseby," he thought, and wondered whom he would get to replace Horsey when he died. He was one of the last of Paul's intimates around here and they shared many memories, sad and joyful. He was glad Simon had lengthened the chain of association by marrying into the family but it was odd that both his eldest son's wives should have the same surname.

Claire welcomed the wedding. It took her mind off the nagging problem of the Stevie-Andy-Margaret triangle. She was still at her wits end what to do about it, for Margaret's child was due in a week or two but no word came from her or Stevie. She was not even certain that Stevie admitted paternity, although Margaret assured her that they intended to marry. That, however, was before Andy had returned from the dead and Margaret's reaction to this had been baffling. She seemed to withdraw from the situation, as though the mere act of transferring her affections from one brother to another meant that Andy would bow himself out of her life and this seemed to Claire (and would, she assumed, seem to any sane person) an outrageous supposition. She was not as appalled by the switch as she might have been, however, for she was a woman who had always found it easy to adjust to the mood of successive generations. In her own youth infidelity within the family would have been unthinkable but now, she realised, it was more likely to be regarded as a tiresome muddle than a disaster. She tried, over and over again, to think it out logically and arrive at some kind of compromise with herself, but the ramifications of the problem were beyond her and in the end she always came back to what seemed to her the best of a very bad job, a frank admission on Margaret's part that she had gone off the rails and been unlucky enough to conceive a child during Andy's absence abroad. This, she reasoned, would at least keep the scandal impersonal and Andy would have a straight choice of overlooking her adultery or divorcing her.

Divorce, in the old days, had been a terrible thing for all concerned, parents and in-laws as well as the parties themselves, but this was no longer so. People seemed to get married and divorced like getting on and off omnibuses and no one thought much less of them. Paul, of course, wouldn't see it this way at all although he had taken the prospect of Stevie's divorce quietly enough because he had never cared for Monica Dearden. She could imagine, however, how violently he would erupt if he discovered that Margaret's child was Stevie's and that only the unexpected delay in Andy's homecoming had prevented a confrontation before the child was born. It was the kind of situation you read about in the Sunday papers but her mind boggled at the impact it would have upon him.

Having considered but rejected Simon as a confidant and also, for roughly the same reasons, Rumble Patrick when he came home in late summer, she continued to keep her own counsel, extracting what satisfaction she could from the rehabilitation of Simon who at last, thank God, had found a nice, sensible girl to look after him. She was very generous when Evie came to her for advice about fixing up part of the Old Rectory as a temporary home. Sheets, blankets and curtains were almost impossible to buy on the miserly issue of coupons they gave to couples intending to marry, so Smut Porter drove over in his baker's van and returned to the Rectory with a load of furnishings that were no longer needed at the Big House.

"Look on it as my wedding present," she told Evie, when she called to protest at the prodigality of her mother-in-law. "You didn't know the boy in his gloomy days and therefore you can't possibly appreciate what you've done for him. His first marriage was a so-called intellectual-alliance and just about as frosty as it sounds. I'm not saying that Rachel wasn't a good wife. She was, or she tried to be, but he went through a terrible time in Spain and later in France and she wasn't much help to a normal healthy male. He was obviously crying out for somebody like you and I'm sure you'll make him very happy. I daresay he's told you the situation he found himself in after his mother walked out all those years ago and I married Paul and raised a tribe of my own? Well, I did my best to spoil him on that account, so you'll find he'll spoil easily, but one word of warning—for Heaven's sake don't take his politics seriously."

"I don't think he's got many now," Evie said. "He's very sold on the war against Hitler but then, so am I, and so is everyone else, aren't they?"

"You can count me out," Claire said. "I worked all the patriotism out of my system in 1918. What amazes me is that everybody else didn't. Oh, I know we had to fight this one when it happened but what guarantee have we it will be the last? If men didn't learn their lesson in those awful trenches they aren't likely to learn it gaping at the ruins of Paxtonbury." She looked at Evie's rather shocked expression and then laughed. "Don't mind me," she said, "I've had a basinful lately and the only thing I really care about is this Valley. I'm a local patriot you might say and to me, like Paul, foreigners begin on the far side of the railway line." She wondered, briefly, whether to ask the girl if she intended having any children but thought better of it. Simon was thirty-nine and Evie, she gathered, twenty-eight. If they needed encouragement in this direction they could look for it elsewhere.

Simon's marriage did solve part of her problem by supplying her desperate need for impartial advice inasmuch as it brought Doctor Maureen back into the Valley.

Maureen Rudd, the first lady doctor the Valley had ever heard of, much less attended, had married, late in life, the Shallowford agent, John Rudd, and stayed on after his death in the early 'thirties living in the lodge at the bottom of the drive. Early in the war, however, Maureen had pulled up stumps and gone off to Edinburgh to live with her only son and his wife and since then had not returned for she was getting on nowadays and did not care to face a long, wartime railway journey. The medical needs of the Valley, such as they were, were met by a young doctor called Truscott who had opened a practice in the greatly enlarged village of Coombe Bay. The newer families in the district got along with him well enough but Doctor Maureen, or "The Lady Doctor" as the older generation still thought of her, had been an intimate friend of the family and had supervised the birth of all the Craddock children except Simon.

As soon as Claire received Maureen's acceptance to the

182

invitation she wrote begging her to stay on for a spell and when she arrived, surprisingly vigorous considering her bulk and seventy-odd years, Claire installed her in the big bedroom in the east wing that had once been occupied by Paul's old friend, Jimmy Grenfell, the Valley M.P., who had spent his declining years with them. The old lodge, that Maureen and John had occupied for so long, was now uninhabitable and likely to remain so until after the war.

Looking into the big round face of Maureen, and hearing again her incurable but slightly suspect Irish brogue, Claire Craddock's spirits lifted for the first time in months. She said, impulsively, "Why don't you stay on for the duration, Maureen? Paul and I would love to have you. We've got this great barn of a place and only Mary and three children to share it with. It's so empty sometimes that it gives me the jim-jams. There's no hunting now and half the people in the Valley are strangers. Life isn't in the least like it used to be and that isn't because we're no longer young and spry. We recaptured a lot of the old spirit between the wars but it began to wilt in that first dreary winter of this latest nonsense and after Dunkirk it seemed to lie down and die. Paul and I live in a kind of vacuum, waiting for something worse to happen. What I mean is, it seems impossible that the old rhythm will ever re-establish itself after the war."

"Well, you wouldn't expect it to," Maureen said, with an encouraging fellow-glumness. "I'm sorry I let my boy persuade me to retire and go north. His wife is a nice enough girl, but it never pays to move in with your family and I should have known a damned sight better than to do it. Ought to have stuck to my round until I dropped, like my John and most of the other old-stagers round here. And like Paul, your man. He knows a thing or two. There's a man who'll die with his boots on, I promise you."

It was refreshing to hear someone talk like this again and the night after the wedding, with Maureen still in two minds whether to go or stay, Claire broke her silence and was astonished by the forthrightness of Maureen's opinion. She said, after a pause that was not ransom to shock but considered evaluation, "Well girl, there's only one role you can play in a farce like that and I'm surprised you haven't been rehearsing it ever since she told you. You've got a clear obligation to all three of them to get 'em straightened out before it's too late."

"And how do I begin to do that? That girl is deeply in love with Stevie. If she hadn't been she wouldn't have dared come to me with such a story. And she isn't bluffing either, I'll swear to that. She's found something in Stevie that doesn't exist in his brother and she's determined to have that baby. I wrote hinting that she had best pretend she wasn't even sure whose it was—that she was blind drunk at a party and passed out, or something of that sort. I know it sounds horrible but not to them, not to people who have led such crazy, disorganised lives. They've always set such store on sophistication—well, here's some kind of use for it. Let's see how broadminded they really are when it comes to the crunch. All I know is that nothing matters so long as Paul and Andy never know the truth. Surely you can see that, can't you?"

"You can't wriggle out of it as easily as that, girl, and anyway, it's obvious that Margaret won't take our damn silly advice. I'm just as relieved she didn't rush off to one of those damned abortionists as soon as she discovered she was pregnant. They're all crooks and most of them are charlatans. Did she reply to your letter?"

"No, she didn't, but later on—when the news was confirmed about Andy—I wrote again asking her to 'phone. She did and said she was looking forward to having the baby, that she had always wanted a baby but had come to believe she could never have one."

"And where does that leave us?"

"I'm asking you, Maureen. I'm half out of my mind with the worry of it. I don't know when Andy will come home but it must be soon. His wounds are practically healed and he's being fitted with one of those gadgets to replace his hand. You surely don't think she's right to brazen it out, do you? You can't think that, knowing how close those boys have been all their lives."

"I didn't say I did think it."

"Then what? For God's sake, *what?*"

"I think she's right to want to tell the truth but that's less important than what happens afterwards."

"Afterwards? I told you—she's going to ask Andy for a divorce, and then marry Stevie who is already getting one. He and Monica split up eighteen months ago. That was how it all began."

"It doesn't matter a damn how it began," Maureen said

obstinately, "it's how it ends. She's got to tell Andy the full truth and leave it to him."

"But won't that amount to the same thing?"

"Not if Stevie backs out. It's him you'll have to work on. You were quite right to keep it from Paul and if you take my advice you'll always keep it from him. But I wish you had had the sense to confide in me before. As it is you're pretty well on deadline, although there might still be time if you put your skates on."

"What do you mean? What more can I do at this stage?"

"Where is Stevie right now?"

"Serving on a station outside York."

"Then go and talk to him. Go tomorrow. Make some excuse, any excuse, but go there, and don't come back until you're sure in your own mind that he won't marry Margaret, no matter what kind of pressure she puts on him. That's the least you can do, girl."

"What about the child itself?"

"The child will have to take its chance like the rest of us," Maureen said, savagely. "Right now, with half an arm and half a face missing, she's got to give Andy a straight choice. She's got to take everything coming to her, until he adjusts to his handicap. That's not an old-fashioned notion, its common humanity. You'd owe that much compassion to a dog, never mind a husband. You see that, don't you?"

Claire saw it clearly enough. Perhaps she had seen it when Margaret, wooden and matter-of-fact, had told her what had happened after Stevie went to her for help and found she needed help far more desperately than he did, but given the essential rightness and urgency of what was expected of her Claire saw little prospect of achieving it, or not without Paul finding out.

She had reckoned, however, without Maureen's long experience in the art of hoodwinking males. When she came down to breakfast next morning, and found Paul and Maureen gossiping over their second cup of coffee, she only just avoided giving herself away when Paul said casually, "Maureen has been telling me about you envying her trip to town. If you'd really like a change then why not go along with her, as she suggests. Do you good, old girl. You haven't been out of the Valley in more than a year and you always were more taken with that Bedlam than me. Not that you'll recognise much of it from all I hear, or find any brighter lights up there than you will in Coombe Bay. They have a blackout there the same as anywhere else."

"They've a better organised black market too," said Maureen.

"I doubt it," Paul said, "in nylons and fancy goods maybe, but certainly not in food. However, if your son's friends really can put you in the way of doing a bit of under-the-counter shopping, good luck to the pair of you. There's never any bombing they tell me. We get it hotter than they do nowadays."

It was easy as that, and when they were settled in the crowded London train, recovering their breath after un-chivalrous competition with bumping kit bags, rifles and respirators, Maureen said, "He always was the easiest hus-band to diddle in all England. I suppose it's because he's so certain that you've never looked at another man in forty years." Claire admitted that this was almost true but not quite and was so relieved by her escape that she told Maureen of a wartime flirtation with an officer at the camp, something she had never admitted to a soul. It amused Maureen, who knew them both so well, and she chuckled all the way to Yeovil.

II

Maureen saw her as far as Euston, giving her an address to call at on her return. "I can stall for about three days," she said, "but it shouldn't take you that long and don't look to me for a briefing! From now on you're on your own. After all, you gave birth to the boy and it's time you took your duties as mother seriously. The only two of the seven you ever bothered your head about was Young Claire, and that poor, demented Grace Lovell's boy, Simon."

And this, thought Claire, as an even more crowded train clanked out of Euston, was about the truth and she was now, she supposed, paying the price for having expended nine-tenths of her nervous energy on Paul in preference to the family. "All the same," she told herself, "I don't regret it, and if I had my time over again I'd do just the same. God knows, one man is one woman's work. She can't be expected to do a good job on half-a-dozen."

It was the first time the war had appeared to her as a

186

global rather than a local event. Two things impressed her at once, the skeletal ruins of the suburbs that looked more like a series of rubbish-tips than the approaches to a capital city, and the presence of so many hardbitten youngsters in uniform. Evidence of large-scale bombing was depressing enough but what was more, in Claire's eyes, was the fatalistic glumness of the passengers. In the crowded corridor outside stood Dutchmen, Rhodesians and West Indians, forlorn strays identified by their shoulder flashes and all montrously encumbered by the ugly accoutrements of war. Youth and gaiety seemed to have emigrated to another planet. The air in the compartment reeked of cheap tobacco and damp cloth, imperfectly dyed. The luggage racks sagged under the kit these youngsters seemed condemned to drag from one end of the country to the other and in the faces of even the British she fancied she could read strain and unutterable boredom, so that she forgot her own troubles and found herself thinking back to that other war when you would never have witnessed a uniformed young woman inhaling a cigarette like a man in a billiards saloon. Some of the girls, she thought, still looked pretty, even with their hair bundled under those awful caps, and all of them used make-up. In her young days only street-walkers carmined their lips and war had been almost exclusively a man's concern. Now, it seemed, every living person was sucked into the vortex, participating in its dangers and shortages, its slang and its stale, unprofitable atmosphere. She listened, half-heartedly, to a desultory conversation between a bombardier and a sallow little W.A.A.F. but could make very little of it. So many of the words and sentiments were strange to her. The bombardier, it seemed, was returning to an outpost in the Hebrides, the W.A.A.F. to a bomber station like the one she herself was visiting. Both, it appeared, resented their lot but accepted it as a kind of purgatory separating their youth and whatever the future had in store for them. They talked laconically, like a couple of mercenaries reminiscing after a spell of sacking cities on the Continent. The bombardier had been in the Desert and said he was already regretting his home posting. "Too much bullshit back here," he complained, "even on a ruddy little rock doing Sweet F.A. most of the time!" The girl had troubles of her own. "Our section officer is a bitch—give me men officers all the time! Girl in my billet was engaged to an R.G. who bought it. Went on parade the day after hearing with hair showing under her cap. Had a strip torn off her—don't know where they find cows like that. Who did they chase from A to B before the war? Their skivvies I daresay, at five bob a week and keep!"

The bombardier murmured his sympathy but added, with a grin, "Well, you know what they say. Shouldn't have joined!" to which the girl replied promptly, "What do you take me for? I was pushed. Not quick enough off the mark, that's my trouble. Got a kid sister making eight-ten a week in a Wimpey factory . . . !" and so on, all the way to a stop that Claire could not identify for all the place names had been removed from the platforms as a precaution against an invasion threat now three years old.

As the long journey wore on she tried to rehearse what she would say to Stevie when she got there but nothing plausible suggested itself and she decided that she would have to play it by ear. The countryside grew more pastoral but the train became more and more crowded so that the acrid atmosphere of the compartment made her eyes smart. It was impossible to move along the corridor to the lavatory and someone who had managed it earlier told her there was no water in the taps. At another stop the bombardier unexpectedly produced a cup of tea for the W.A.A.F. and another for her and she sipped it gratefully, although it had the flavour of boiled swedes laced with soap. After that she was able, to some extent, to join in the conversation and asked the W.A.A.F. if she knew Stevie's station.

"Bomber Command dump? There's lashings of them up there. Is he operational?" and when Claire said he flew Lancasters the girl's approach softened to a mixture of interest and sympathy.

"How far is he on with his tour of ops.?" she asked, and Claire said she had no idea, for he wasn't much of a one for writing.

"He wouldn't say, anyway," the girl said, making Claire feel that their ages were reversed and that she was being gently patronised by her grandmother, "they live it up between trips and forget it when they're not flying," and when Claire mentioned that, earlier in the war he had been with Fighter Command, the girl volunteered more information, saying, "He'll have changed, I daresay. You can spot the difference right away. Bomber pilots are mostly—well, more serious if you know what I mean, and usually nicer. I've been

188

in both Commands, as well as T.T.—Technical Training—but I'd sooner serve on a bombing station." Then, with a frankness that made Claire smile, "Is he married?"

Claire settled for saying he was not and the girl seemed surprised. "They mostly are," she said, "or they soon get married to one of us, or one of the ack-ack A.T.S. or a WREN maybe. Friend of mine has been married twice and is now a widow again at twenty-two. That takes some beating ..." and then, suddenly recollecting herself, she actually blushed and mumbled, "Sorry. I was a clot to say that to someone with a son still on ops. Think I'll have another shot at fighting my way down the corridor," and she left very abruptly.

The bombardier said, grinning, "That's what they call a clanger, ma'am," and for the next hour Claire pondered the girl's gaffe and wished she could reassure her. Nothing much would happen to Stevie. Like Andy he was indestructible—his sort always were. It was the Simons of this world who "bought it" as they said, in their quaint, callous slang.

The interminable journey continued and presently, mercifully, she dropped off and snored gently, her head resting on the shoulder of the tolerant bombardier.

III

Berlin, Cuxhaven, Bremerhaven, Hamburg, on overnight 'bus stop to Turin, Leipzig, Dresden: Stevie had ploughed his way to and from them all but the one they feared and hated most was Essen, where the flak was vicious and the nightfighters had X-ray eyes. Once, a month or so back, he had been caught in a searchlight beam over Essen and had floundered about the sky like a singed moth, convinced that this was it, but it wasn't, for here he was with bombs gone circling over Essen once more, the cockpit lit by intermittent flashes winking from all quarters of the compass, and his tongue as dry as a dead stick. Over in the east pencils of searchlight beams wavered, sometimes striking the underside of clouds so that they suddenly turned into the over-filled icecream cornets he had once bought for a penny a cone at High Wood tuckshop. Then, far to the north and below him, he saw the soft orange ball of a burning kite that went skittering down the sky and was lost in the great belt of darkness beyond the winking landscape of the tormented city. He said over the intercom, "Who's for home then?" and Wiley, the only member of his original crew, said, "Me for one, Skip, and don't stop for hitchhikers."

Wiley, he reflected, was another Andy, someone who would glide in and out of trouble all his life and emerge, jostled and bruised perhaps but emotionally intact, not because he was hearty and unimaginative but because he had learned how to discard the apparatus of successive phases or professions and focus the whole of his attention on something new. Right now he was a radio operator in a Lancaster, and a very good one at that, but before transferring to the R.A.F. he had been a gunner in a territorial unit, and before that a garage operative, a salesman of leather goods, a gas-fitter, and a grocer's assistant in a country town in the North Riding. He was twenty-eight and had somehow got through his life without a serious attachment to anyone, and would probably stay single until he was in his mid-thirties when he would start looking for someone with a fat stocking. After that, Stevie supposed, he would settle down and grow a paunch at the local, and forget all about moments like these hauls into the south-east, and longer hauls back to a cheerless airfield where the dawn wind cut you in two.

He got a fix from Gibbins, his navigator and began to climb, settling down to make another attempt to isolate himself and fly by a complicated assortment of reflexes. He had made rare progress in this respect, telling himself that it was high time he did, for this was the seventeenth operation of his second tour.

Lately, ever since the autumn, he saw himself as a kind of steel filing orbiting a central point that was Margaret, and Margaret's improbable little cottage, "*Ty-Bach*", and it seemed to him that he circled on three separate planes that remained permanently equidistant from one another.

The outer circuit was his flying, regular sweeps that carried him into the endless vistas of space and were not, looking back, very exciting in themselves. The inner circuit was a very tight one, as tight as a pre-war fighter's turn, and its core was the thickening woman who waddled out to greet him whenever he drove along under the old woods to the sagging fence, announcing his arrival by a toot of the horn. It was more than a fortnight since he had withdrawn into this inner circuit and it seemed much longer, for the child she was expecting was overdue according to her and there was no means of contacting her other than by letter. She had told him over and over again not to worry, that she was booked in at a nursing home in Criccieth and had made arrangements to go there in advance and stay in a hotel until the doctor told her it was time to go. He had, in fact, checked these arrangements himself and was satisfied that they were adequate, but somehow he could not see her voluntarily turning her back on *"Ty-Bach"* and locking the door on the place that had been their lair and refuge, not only from everyone else in their lives but from their own thoughts.

Here, through the late spring and summer, they had been unbelievably safe and happy. From his airfield in Shropshire he had been able to get over almost every weekend and once or twice for odd days, but their meetings became less frequent when he moved back to Yorkshire and began his second tour. He had tried, without success, to get a telephone installed at *"Ty-Bach"* and had been obliged to be satisfied with jotting down the number of Jones the Milk on his identity card, Jones the Milk being their nearest neighbour who thought of them as man and wife.

Tonight, now that they were on their home run, he settled for his outer circuit, thinking of the trip and how near their cookie had dropped to the target, of other Lancasters throbbing through the darkness above and below him, and what the men who flew them thought about, and whether their lives on the ground were as complicated as his own. From time to time he exchanged a word or two with his crew and when their voices reached him over the intercom he visualised them individually, as a man wrecked on a desert island might itemise his few possessions. The Lancaster was rather like an island, with seven castaways thrown up by the breakers of the offensive. There was Wiley, the extrovert, who sometimes talked cock on the way home, and there was Gibbins, the worrier, who gave information grudgingly, as though it was small change and he was living on a fixed pension. There were the three sergeants, Gooding, Kitson and Awkwright, all married, two of them with kids. Gooding and Kitson had flown with him on every trip of the tour but Awkwright was a survivor from another crew and Stevie had a suspicion that his nerve was almost used up. Remembering this he called him up, making a facetious remark and getting a facetious answer.

191

So far so good. They were well on their way now. To starboard he saw a long strip of light and veered off to port. If it was the German night-fighter flarepath at Gilze-Rijen he was going to give it as wide a berth as possible, and the possibility of night-fighters made him remember Young Pidgeon in the rear-turret, whose nineteenth birthday they had celebrated by getting uproarously drunk—all but the sober Gibbins that is—in the Turk's Head. Pidgeon had had to be given a fireman's lift back to camp and had come to outside the guard-hut and started singing "Roll me over, in the clover." Then, gravely, and with a certain dignity, he had been sick.

He called the rear-turret: "How's tricks back there, kid-do?" and Pidgeon said, "Cold as a frog on an ice-bound pond, colder than charity—that's bloody chilly..." Stevie knew the ditty. It used up every low-temperature smile in the book and finished, "Colder than all is poor little Willie". It was the sort of chestnut any nineteen-year-old would use to an older man to assert devil-may-care masculinity and help to bridge the gap.

They flew on, endlessly it seemed, Stevie's thoughts switching to a central circuit that took him back to places like the Valley, and Old Franz Zorndorff's festering scrapyard south of the Thames. He remembered little things about Franz, his white, Habsburg-type whiskers tinged brown by the nicotine of his cigars, his wheezing laugh, and the amiable contempt he had for Paul as a man with a horror of cities, all cities ... "As if a man could get rich anywhere else!" Franz would say, when his father tried over and over again to launch The Pair on agricultural careers.

Then the circle of his thoughts contracted and he found himself on the inner circuit, usually closed when he was flying and he could contemplate Margaret, not as he had last seen her, with swollen belly and legs that carried her clumsily from dresser to fireplace, but as she had been the second time they met at the Smith Street flat, a woman who could be kissed into a frenzy. She had frightened him on that occasion and must have realised it because, later on, their love-making had adjusted to the rhythm of an affectionate married couple, particularly after they had moved into "*Ty-Bach*", where the seasons never hurried and seemed reluctant to give way to one another. He found he could contemplate "*Ty-Bach*" in a way he had never learned to contemplate inanimate things, its stones, its low ceilings, its pokey little kitchen-scullery that smelled of bran, soap and ancient woodwork, a smell he would always associate with Wales.

Gibbins said, carefully, "Dutch coast coming up. Vlieland to port ..." and a few minutes later it happened, a long, rattling thud that might have been caused by anything at all, by the sudden seizing up of one or more engines, by a blind discharge of heavy flak pouring up at nothing and searching them out, or the raking burst of a fighter that had followed them all the way from the Ruhr. He didn't know and he never had a chance to find out for, although voices clamoured over the intercom, he ignored them, concentrating the whole of his attention on the heavy starboard drag. He saw the coastline and realised he must have lost a great deal of height and was still losing it, for the altimeter read eleven thousand feet and when he had last looked at it it was over fifteen thousand. The Lancaster was acting like a young stallion turned loose in a field full of mares, bucketing and half-stalling, lurching and frisking as though determined to spill them out into the sky. He fought it madly, knowing it would defeat him but buying time while he made his decisions and the field of choice was not wide. Their words came to him like drops of rain, dashed in the face. "Flak ... for Christ's sake ... !" Going to ditch ... this far out ... ?" "Where are we? Can we make it?" This last from Wiley, surprisingly cool, so that it helped to steady him and ask Gibbins their position. Gibbins said, glumly, "Wait ... can't be absolutely sure ... West-north-west of Vlieland—that's about it—watch it—there's another bloody flak-ship ..." and a series of flashes exploded almost immediately below, a stream of little red balls trundling into their wake.

A few miles off the Dutch coast at ten thousand, and losing height all the time. They could ditch, he supposed, but what were their chances out there, in December? Then, Wiley spoke again, weighing his words one by one. "The kid ... rear-turret ... he's hit ... ! Kitson's seeing to him ..." and finally Kitson's voice, "Got it in the leg. Not too badly I think! Stopped the bleeding. Bloody shambles!"

That decided him. With Pidgeon injured there could be no question of ditching. Neither was there any question of returning to base. They would have to fly as long as possible and then a bit longer, and when the nearest piece of coastline showed he could order the able-bodied to bale out. From then it would be every man for himself and for him and Pidgeon a miserable attempt to pancake. That, in fact, was Pidgeon's only chance and it wasn't much of one, no better than his own.

Miraculously the Lancaster remained airborne. Minutes ticked by and every part of a minute increased the chances of each of them except rear-gunner and pilot. Seven thousand feet, six thousand five hundred, and the drag becoming heavier with every flick of the needle. He gave his orders crisply and nobody questioned them. He could imagine them clipping on their parachutes, swearing continously under their breath. Then Wiley said, "How about the kid? He can't make it, Skip," and Stevie snarled, "For Christ's sake, I *know* that. Do as you're told and bale out! I'll stick with it."

The coast, when it showed up, was like a thin, curving blade laid along the end of the moonpath and Stevie wondered fleetingly where it was, but before Gibbons could tell him the altimeter needle flickered its ultimate warning and the aircraft, that seemed now to be flying on its side, began to slip so that he called "Everybody out!" and Wiley's voice said "Good luck, Skip, good . . . !" and left the sentence unfinished.

He saw nothing of their going, if indeed they went, for a pattern of subdued light showed directly ahead and it looked as though it might be a flarepath although he could hardly believe it was. A man flying a disintegrating bomber with an injured tail-gunner aboard could hardly expect luck of that kind.

In the moonlight, at almost zero height, the countryside looked as neat and patterned as the Valley at harvest time. Frost rime sparkled down there and there seemed to be very few trees, just rectangular fields divided by hedges. Pushing with all his strength on the rudder bar he felt little or no response and called into the intercom, "We're coming down kid, brace yourself . . . !" but there was no answer and he wondered if he was crash-landing a dead man. Then he saw that it was a runway, some kind of runway, although it looked hopelessly short and the few buildings close by seemed to be no more than sheds. He struck the surface, bounced, struck it again, bounced again, and tried to think of something to fortify him against the impact but on the third touchdown the aircraft slewed violently and hurled him sideways so that landscape, instrument panel and moon merged into a confused, whirling catherine wheel and there was a roaring in his ears, the roaring of breakers and falling chimney stacks in brickyards that he and Andy had prospected for scrap when they were Zorndorff's apprentices.

CHAPTER TEN

A KIND OF CONFRONTATION

I

THE village near the airfield had a pub, The Prince Rupert, named, she supposed, in honour of the battle near here in the Civil War. Paul would be interested in this but then, she remembered, Paul must never learn she had been within two hundred miles of the place. Now that she was here and it was dusk she was uncertain of her next move. She had a telephone number Margaret had given her but did not know whether it was permitted to ring an operational airfield. She booked a room, washed and went down to the visitors' 'phone booth, a little glass box at the foot of the stairs. No one questioned her call and a girl's voice said, "Who is it? Who do you want?"

Her wits cleared suddenly and she said, "I'm the mother of one of your pilots. I was in the district and wondered if it would be possible to see him. He's called Craddock, Flight-Lieutenant S. Craddock," and she gave his Service number. The telephonist said, "Wait, I'll put you through to the officers' mess," and after a series of clicks a male voice said, "Officers' Mess. Someone asking for Flight-Lieutenant Craddock?" There was, she thought, a note of surprise in the voice but that was understandable. It was not often that a fond mamma called at the camp as if it was a prep. school. She said, "I hope I'm not bothering anyone, I'm Mrs. Craddock, his mother. I was in the district ..." The mess steward said, carefully, "Hold on a moment, Ma'am, I'll find somebody who can help you!"

"They're all very polite and pleasant," thought Claire, and waited patiently until another, rather grating voice spoke. It said, incredulously, "*Mrs.* Craddock? Crad's *mother?*" and she said yes and was he off duty or likely to be? She added that she was spending a night at The Prince Rupert in the village and it would be nice if he could come over for a meal.

The voice said, hesitantly, "He's ... er ... he's not around right now, Mrs. Craddock. This is P/O Wiley speaking, his radio-op—a member of his crew. I wonder if *I* could pop over right away? I could be there in about ten minutes ..."

He sounded, she thought, bashful and apologetic for being unable to produce Stevie out of a hat. She said, "By all means ... perhaps you could leave a message for him and he could join us. I'd like to meet you, Mr. Wiley."

It was, she decided, the least she could do. He sounded as if he very much wanted to come and she supposed it was rather like a school after all, where it was nice to be taken out once in a while by the parents of a chum. She was disappointed, however, that Stevie was not available and supposed she would have to hang around until he was. Perhaps Mr. Wiley might talk freely and help to build up some kind of background for her. At all events she had almost run him down and that, after such a journey, was an achievement.

He came hurrying into the foyer in less than ten minutes. Apparently the camp was very close and none of them had to walk anywhere. He was a spare, good-looking young man, with a sharp nose and pointed chin and there was a long strip of pink adhesive plaster on his cheek. He greeted her very diffidently and then asked her if she would join him in a drink. She said she would have a sherry if they had any and he said, "They've got everything, here, we see to that!" and disappeared with surprising alacrity. She took off her gloves and waited, opening her bag and peeping into her mirror. The feeling that she was paying a visit to a school grew upon her. She wouldn't have been surprised if a group of elderly men had appeared in the lounge in shredded gowns and honked at her in that assertive manner schoolmasters usually employ when addressing parents. Wiley came back, carrying a tankard of beer and a tall sherry. He said, rather helplessly, "About Crad ... er ... have you been travelling, Mrs. Craddock? What I mean is ... did you leave home today?"

"No, as a matter of fact I didn't," she said, wondering at his rather distracted manner, "I left yesterday and spent last night in London. Stevie had no idea I was coming." Then, seeing him look away quickly, "He's all right, isn't he? I mean, not sick or ... posted?" She had been going to say "Hurt", the word prompted by the sticking plaster on Wiley's cheek, but she changed her mind because it occurred to her that she might sound like a fussy old mum and downgrade Stevie in his eyes. It was rather absurd, she thought, to behave like this about a son who had been married nine years and was now in the process of being divorced and acknowledging the child of his brother's wife, but there it was. He startled her then with a kind of groan, as though the beer in his tankard was particularly unpleasant medicine. He said, bracing himself, "I'm sorry, Mrs. Craddock ... two nights ago ... down south ... we were belted from a flakship crossing the coast. Five of us made it ... baled out a couple of miles inland. But Crad stayed with the kite ... the aircraft; he had to, because the rear-gunner was wounded. He got down all right at a satellite, a ropey one it was, and they got the rear-gunner out. He's in dock now, and in pretty good shape all things considered, but Crad ..."

He dried up, looking away and through the curtain of shock she could see the silhouette of his embarrassment and misery and this, surprisingly, gave her something to hold on to for a moment so that she was able to push her hand across the little round table and enclose his, finding it cold and moist.

They sat there for a moment without moving and then his free hand came up and settled on top of hers and she found it wonderfully comforting. She said at length, making a tremendous effort to sound natural, "You knew him well, you've flown with him a long time?" and he said, eagerly and gratefully, "Two tours. We were pretty close, Mrs. Craddock. He was a terrific guy. None of us would have got back if he hadn't nursed the kite the way he did, and held on until we all had a sporting chance of getting down in one piece! Young Pidgeon, the rear-gunner, wouldn't have had a hope in hell. Like I said, that's why Crad stuck with it and pancaked. He almost made it. It was a bloody miracle really. I only got back today."

"You hurt your face."

His hand left hers and went to his cheek. He seemed surprised to find the plaster there. "It's only a cut. I just missed landing on a bit of fencing. The other four were shaken up a bit but nothing serious. The R.G.—rear-gunner —is the only one in dock". Then, cautiously, "I think the C.O. would like to know you're here, Mrs. Craddock. They sent off a wire earlier yesterday, as soon as the gen. came through on the blower, so I daresay someone at home is trying to get in touch with you now. Would you like me to find the C.O.? He's stooging around somewhere."

"No," she said, "I'd sooner just talk to you if you don't mind. It's odd, I've got three sons and two sons-in-law on active service but Stevie is the only one I never worried about. He always seemed to come out of it at the last moment."

"He almost did this time," Wiley said and after a pause, "Won't you finish your sherry? Would you like something a bit stronger?"

"No thank you. You've been very kind, Mr. Wiley. I'm so glad for my sake you were the one who had to tell me, although it must be dreadful for you." Then, as she felt her eyes filling with tears, "Excuse me . . . please don't go . . . not for a minute," and she turned aside and opened her bag while he waited, no longer embarrassed but patient and resigned.

"You knew he was getting a divorce?"

"Yes," Wiley said, "he did tell me that. But there was someone else, wasn't there? A girl living in Wales? He left a letter. We do that, most of us that is, just in case. I brought it with me. Just the one letter. It seems to be addressed to his wife, not the girl in Wales."

He groped in his pocket and handed her a clean, stamped envelope. It was addressed to *"Mrs. Margaret Craddock, 'Ty-Bach', Llanstynwdd, Merionethshire, Wales,"* and below, in brackets, *"If not received, please forward to St. Just Nursing Home, Criccieth, N. Wales"*. "I was going to post it tonight," he said, "but maybe you'd like to take it."

"Yes," she said, "I'll deliver it personally. It would be better that way."

The sight of the letter, with its two addresses, gave her a surprising access of strength. She no longer felt worn out by the journey. She said, "I think I will have that something stronger Mr. Wiley. A large brandy, but let me pay for it."

"No," he said, "certainly not! I'd much rather, Mrs. Craddock. I'd be very happy to," and she let him. When he returned with the drinks she said, "I'd like to make a start tonight. There's no sense in hanging around up here and I don't want her find out from anyone else. Could I hire a car somewhere? I don't mean to the station. Could I hire one that would take me all the way to Criccieth?"

He seemed doubtful. "It would cost a packet," he said, "even if it could be arranged. Probably a tenner or even more. Wouldn't it be better to stay on overnight and get a train from York in the morning?"

"No," she said, "it wouldn't, because I'm not likely to sleep, am I? I'd sooner do something. Something useful."

He nodded understandingly and went away again. Five minutes later he was back. "The gaffer says a hire car firm in Flaxton will do it. God knows where they get the gas these days. Maybe it's because they're undertakers as well. It'll cost fifteen pounds. I daresay they'd cash a cheque here. I could vouch for you, Mrs. Craddock."

"That won't be necessary. I have enough money and if I need more I can cash a cheque when I get there. Did you order it for me?"

"Be here in twenty minutes or so."

They sat on, saying little, until the landlord came and said the car was waiting. He looked at her gently and she thought Wiley must have told him who she was. "I'll get your bag down, ma'am," he said, and padded away. Wiley said, "Do you mind if I say something else, Mrs. Craddock?" and when she shook her head he went on, with a vehemence that brought a flush to his narrow face, "I think you're terrific! I never thought anyone could be so terrific, but knowing old Crad I'm not all that surprised, not really! You know something else? I wish to God you were my mother!"

"So do I," she said, and leaning forward she kissed him on the cheek that wasn't sealed by plaster. Unlike his hand, that had been so cold, his face was very warm.

II

The sea-front of the little town at that season was bleak and uninviting. Everything about it was slate grey, the sea, the stone Victorian houses, the sky, even the distances. She had slept after all, under a rug tucked around her by the elderly driver who must, she thought, be a hearse-driver, for his gestures were excessively dignified and he seemd to her to drive the entire distance at a steady thirty. She had decided to take a chance on Criccieth first and dismiss him if she located Margaret. Once that was done she could find a room at a hotel if one was open at this time of year, and brace herself to do what had to be done.

The nursing home was at the end of the long street, a tall, narrow building built of stone blocks and she asked the driver to wait while she made enquiries. It was a few minutes to eight o'clock and a maid was polishing the hall floor behind the locked, glass-panelled door. She signalled to her to open it. The girl looked surprised but she pulled the bolts and when Claire asked if she would make enquiries about a patient she said, in the strongest Welsh accent Claire had ever heard, that she would have to fetch Sister Pritchard who was having breakfast in her room.

Sister Pritchard came bustling up looking even more surprised and vaguely indignant. She held a napkin in her long, bony hand and dabbed her mouth with it as she descended the stairs. "It's far too early to visit," she said, "visiting is not until after lunch. Who is it you want to see?"

"I'm not even sure she's here yet," Claire said, "but she's booked. It's Mrs. Craddock, Margaret Craddock," and was relieved to see the look of irritation vanish from the Sister's face as she said, almost genially, "Ah yes . . . yes! She had her baby last Thursday and we've all been wondering why nobody called!" She opened a register that was lying on the reception table. "Thursday, that was it. She came in on Tuesday. False alarm. But they're both bonny. It all happened rather quickly. However . . ." her face went stiff again, "I'm afraid you can't see her yet. She won't have had breakfast and then Doctor has to see her. I could tell her you're here of course. I expect she'll be pleased; she hasn't had any messages. Not even a telephone call or letter," she added, rather reproachfully.

Claire said, "It was difficult to get here and anyway, I wasn't sure when it was due. Do you mind telling me what the baby is?"

"Why, it's a girl," and the woman looked at her a little oddly, as though astonished she didn't even know this much. "Will her husband be coming, or is he serving abroad? Mrs. Craddock didn't say. It was all rather tiresome. We wouldn't have known who to tell if there had been difficulties."

Claire, who had a lifelong prejudice against the medical profession (with the single exception of Maureen, who shared her antipathy to the "shall-we-brush-our-teeth" approach), decided to give nothing away. She said, "Don't tell her I'm here. I want it to be a surprise. I'll buy some flowers if I can and come back after lunch." Then, turning at the door, "A girl, you said? What weight?"

The question caught the Sister by surprise so that she relented a fraction. "Six pounds, twelve ounces. You could see her . . . just a quick peep."

"Thank you, I can wait," Claire said, with a small jet of sourness. "I've had six myself and I've been travelling all night!"

She left the woman feeling that she had had the better of the contest but it brought her no satisfaction. Her tiredness and flatness was at one with the grey stone buildings and the slate-coloured sea. She found a small, drab-looking hotel open and dismissed the driver, giving him a thirty-shilling tip because his eyes looked as exhausted as she felt, and went into the little lobby to be greeted by a slovenly, balding man whose accent, surprisingly, placed him hundreds of miles to the southeast. He mumbled something about "winter terms" and led her up to a vast, over-furnished bedroom overlooking the sea. There was an empty grate screened by a fan of shelf paper, a hideous patterned carpet and heavy lace curtains. The enormous wardrobe had one door fitted as a mirror and the bed had brass knobs, tarnished the colour of sand. The man shuffled off, promising to bring a pot of tea.

It was then, as she took off her hat, that she saw herself in the wardrobe mirror and the shock was salutory.

Claire had spent a long time in front of mirrors. Between the ages of eight and twenty-eight she had studied her reflection with satisfaction amounting to downright smugness, and for the next twenty odd years, having the flair of keeping pace with fashions, she had thought of herself as a woman who was putting up a bonny fight against time. Even lately, with the slow spread of flesh arrested by rationing, she had held her own, but the reflection she recoiled from in the oval mirror was that of a hollowed-eyed old hag and made her want to shriek with dismay. She sat on the bed fighting despair, running her gloved hands along her smooth, slightly pendulous cheeks, and the hopelessness of the situation sneered at her from the eye sockets and the compressed line of what she had once thought of as a ripe, country mouth.

She said, softly, "My God! What's the use of it all then?"

and her voice seemed to come from somewhere outside the room, from the stairs, or the recesses of the dark landing with its smell of carbolic and damp fibres. She saw, as it were, her life in the round. She had loved a man and borne him six children. Two of those children were already dead, mashed to a pulp in disintegrating aircraft, and another was disfigured and minus a hand. Of the rest, one was a remote child absorbed in his own interests, another wrote patronisingly from thousands of miles away, and the third was married to a man who, for all she knew, might be drifting about in the ocean in the track of heedless ships.

She did not think of the by-products. Grandchildren were not her business, not even the six pound, twelve ounce child down the street. All that she could think of was the source—herself—alone in the cheerless room looking out over a slate sea, cut off, exhausted by the demands made upon her, physically, spiritually, every way. Slowly and soundlessly she began to cry so that when the man slouched in with the tea she jerked herself upright and crossed to the window, blinking and making some kind of show at blowing her nose. The man said, in his unlikely Essex accent, "Could manage breakfast. Nothing much mind you, we don't get coupons for visitors after October. Not officially open, see?"

Perhaps it was his manner, his general churlishness, or, even more likely, that deadful word "coupons" that he pronounced as "koo-pongs". Somehow it threw into relief the frightful muddle of the last few years, and the supineness of people like herself who meekly accepted these idiotic interruptions in their lives and this warping of all natural functions, such as eating, loving, working at something worthwhile, and watching children you had carried in your womb develop and take on responsibilities of their own. Whatever it was it rallied her so that what Paul would have called a sharp injection of Derwent commonsense gushed through her and she whipped round on the creature and snapped, "I want a bath and I want a hot meal. And while I am bathing light a fire in here and don't give me that stuff about "there being a war on" either! I daresay you've got good Welsh coal stacked away somewhere below and bacon and eggs too, I wouldn't wonder! If I'm fed and rested and thawed out I'll pay you summer rates and something over the odds as well. It depends on you, understand?" and she grabbed her bag, plucked out a five-pound note and crammed it into his podgy hand.

The man couldn't have looked more startled if she had jammed a revolver into his belly. His mouth opened and closed not so much like a fish in a bowl but like a big mongrel dog being teased by a withheld ball. Then, unbelievably, he smiled, showing several broken teeth, and said, "You're from Devon. Recognise the ole burr! Served with the Devons in the last show. Look there!" and he bent forward, pointing to a bluish furrow that ran diagonally across his naked pate. "I got that at a place called Bois des Buttes. Devon battle honours. Had some good pals in that outfit. Most of 'em went west o' course."

Suddenly he was human and not only human but a kind of comrade. Claire said, sensing the surge of courage in her body, "You're right, I am from Devon, and I had friends in that battle. They still celebrate it every year down there. We got four V.C.'s, didn't we?"

"Five," the man said, and then seemed to pull himself together, almost as though he was gathering himself for a leap.

"I'll run the bath and tell the missus to fry something special and make more tea. I'll soon get a fire going. Sometimes she smokes but not today, not enough wind!" and he went out, massaging his scar as though to remind himself that it was still there.

III

The harsh rustle of coals awakened her and she saw that it was coming up to one-thirty. She washed herself in cold water and finding the room almost cosy she stood in her suspender-belt and bra in front of the mirror again.

This time it had a more encouraging message. She neither looked nor felt sixty. Just approaching the fifty mark maybe, about the time of that crazy second honeymoon she had spent with Paul a few miles up this same coast. Streaks of grey showed in her hair but her flesh, taken all round, was firm and smooth and her belly a good deal flatter than the bellies of her Valley contemporaries. Her legs, she noted, were still as shapely as they had been thirty years ago, and the broad swell of her hips and buttocks had never bothered

204

her, for Paul had so often assured her he preferred a woman with "something to catch hold of" and jeered at the straight lines of the 'twenties. She thought, as she continued to study herself critically, "I don't really look so different, not if I make the effort, only right now I don't have to make it on his behalf. He's got his precious Valley, and that sense of duty that is really male vanity, but my job is to see what can be done to straighten out this nasty little mess! Well, I'm glad I'm here to give it a go. It'll do me a damned sight more good than sitting around waiting for the balloon to go up."

She dressed carefully, gave herself a touch of lipstick and marched down to lunch, served with a double gin. Then, donning coat and hat, she sailed out into the long grey street ready, if necessary, to do battle with the Devil.

It was very far from being easy, but easier than she had bargained for. She had always thought of her daughter-in-law as a heedless little thing who, like her husband in pre-war days, had lived from hour to hour, and never had much capacity for wondering where her non-stop frolic would lead, if anywhere. She had forgotten the Welsh sense of doom that could exist side by side with fecklessness and a sensuality akin to her own, so that when it was over, and the shock-wave of the news had receded, she watched Margaret take refuge in the Celtic awareness of losing every fight in the end, the fight against Anglo-Saxons beyond Offa's Dyke, against the mountains, the weather, the rock-sown soil of the hill farms, and the unremitting greed of industrialists.

She said presently, "You must have lived with this possibility a long time now?" and Margaret said, slowly, "I pushed it away. Everyone does, don't they? We had plenty of happy times, happier than I ever had before."

The conviction of the statement puzzled Claire. It had always seemed to her that Margaret's marriage had been relatively successful, more rewarding, she would have thought, than Stevie's and Monica's. She said, "You and Andy hit it off once. You could try again, couldn't you? He's going to need someone with patience and you've got a lot more than I imagined."

"There's Vanessa," Margaret said.

"Vanessa?"

"Stevie's baby. That was the name we decided on. We found it in a book and liked it. It's a pretty name, both of us thought so."

"You've finally decided to keep the baby, then?"

Margaret looked at her steadily for the first time since she had been shown in by the cooing Sister Pritchard.

"That's something I won't even talk about, except to tell you again what I told you on the 'phone. I've always wanted a baby. It seemed daft being married and getting past thirty and not having one. But even after Andy went along with the idea nothing happened, not even a near-miss. I don't know why. There was nothing wrong with me. Vanessa came easily enough, in spite of all the twaddle they talk!"

"The twaddle they talk." Claire felt herself warming to the girl minute by minute. She had, it seemed, immense reserves of courage and far more commonsense than she had advertised in the past. She said, "Supposing Andy accepted the baby? have you thought of that possibility?"

"I never had to, did I?"

The answer, Claire thought, was a kind of rebuke. It made her wonder what decision, if any, had formed in the mind of Stevie, aside from his assurances to her that he would join Margaret in brazening it out, no matter what it cost in terms of family exile.

"No," she said, "but now everything's changed. You've got to look at it from a general instead of a personal standpoint. Andy's very much involved, and so, for that matter, am I and Paul, who doesn't even know I'm up here."

Margaret said, quickly, "You think I was so wrong? You think I did this deliberately, because I needed a man? Well I did now—at the beginning, but it soon changed and I was glad. If Vanessa hadn't been Stevie's she would have been just anyone's and that is worse, although I don't suppose you can see it like that being mother to both of them."

"Then set your mind at rest," Claire said, "because that's something I can understand. And when I heard Stevie was dead I was glad about the baby. Don't ask me why— something to do with continuity maybe, but I was glad. It was that that decided me to come here and it wasn't a light decision either. Paul is the only important person in my life and he's back there alone 'phoning London and wondering about me, and why I don't 'phone him back."

"He'll find out then?" Margaret said, "about us and Vanessa? He's bound to, isn't he?"

"Not until I think he can take it. I didn't come here

without some kind of plan but it involves all of us, not just you and Andy and that baby of yours."

To the girl in bed she had an obstinate strength that was difficult to oppose for there was kindness in her eyes, and deep concern. She waited and Claire said, "I gave you silly advice before. I don't think it would be a good idea to try and pretend Vanessa belonged to a stranger, but I think it would be even sillier to go off somewhere on your own and let the marriage go to pot the way Stevie's did. Monica belonged in their world but you never did, not really. In a way Andy is as much to blame as you for this awful muddle. It just isn't possible to throw discipline and responsibility out of the window, the way those two did all their lives and it seems to me Stevie realised this towards the end. There couldn't have been much wrong with him to finish the way he did, crashlanding on the off-chance of saving a man's life!"

"What does it all amount to in the end?" Margaret asked, dully. "Maybe Monica was right about this hero stuff. Now I've got to face up to it alone."

"You haven't! I'm here, and I'll do everything I can to help. I'm not blameless myself. All the time they were growing up in the Valley I pretended to myself their selfishness was just high spirits and let it go at that. How do you feel about Andy and how will he react to Vanessa?"

"I don't feel anything special about Andy," she said, deliberately. "I've forgotten him somehow and I can't even remember his voice. You still couple them in your mind but you didn't know Stevie once he began to grow up."

"Don't forget Andy will have changed too. He's probably not the same person at all."

"Maybe he isn't but how would any man react? You don't expect him to shed tears over Vanessa, do you? Would your husband, after the last war?"

She couldn't answer this because Paul and Andy, or Paul and Stevie for that matter, had very little in common unless it was virility. Paul had dragged himself away from the Valley to fight whereas The Pair, obsessed as they had always been in noise and gadgets, had gone whooping off to war like a couple of overgrown schoolboys. It was unlikely that either one of them had given a thought to their wives back in '39, and what had Andy ever done to keep his memory green in the heart of this pretty, sensitive girl, who must have ached for him, as she herself ached for Paul through the last war? Did he really deserve anything better than a cuckolding?

Then she thought of Paul and his overriding need for shape, pattern and stability, and it occurred to her that she was not pleading her son's cause at all but Paul's. If something—anything—could be done to put the pieces together the passages of time might impose some kind of solidarity on the family and prevent his withdrawal into a wilderness of frustration and loneliness that she alone could not prevent. She said, "I've thought about this very deeply, Margaret. Lately I've not thought about much else. It seems to me the only hope any of us have is to tell the truth as you told it to me. Andy isn't a puritan and I'll wager he's never lived like one. I remember a time when he was seeing a lot of that stupid little actress everyone was talking about, a couple of years after you were married. Can you be certain he was never unfaithful to you?"

"It didn't seem to matter in those days," Margaret said, absently. "Stevie had an affair or two and so, for that matter, did Andy but they didn't amount to much in our set and we managed to laugh them off. I didn't fancy anyone but Andy but if I had I daresay I should have gone right ahead. There wasn't the same depth if you follow me. Everything was on the surface and life was a kind of joke. None of us ever stayed in one place long enough to think about being married in the sense that you and Paul are, or my Dad and Mam are. In their case it was to do with having very little spare cash I suppose, and in yours it was being rooted in one place and belonging. Our Valleys in the Rhonddha aren't so very different. Only uglier, with the tip and the grime. It seemed a very wonderful thing then to be whisked out of it and given a cheque book, but there's a bill just the same, isn't there, now?"

"There's always a bill. The point is, are you prepared to meet it if I back you from start to finish?"

"Go back to Andy? Provided he's interested?"

"I mean just that."

She considered a long time. Sleet slashed against the darkening window-pane and a sense of impatience gripped Claire. The south-west usually shared the weather of Wales and for a moment she had a clear picture of Paul standing in the draught of the big front door, wondering at Maureen Rudd's evasions concerning her whereabouts, and also how he was likely to receive news of Stevie's death. She said, abruptly, "I can't stay around. I'll have to 'phone London, talk to Maureen, and see what she's told Paul. Then I'll have to go home. What I've got to know is will you follow on? You'll be very welcome to stay, both of you, as long as you like and no matter what happens when Andy comes home."

She said at last, "I'll try, but more for your sake and Paul's than mine. Like you say, we made a go of it one time, and if Andy accepts Vanessa it could work. There's one thing, though. I don't want you writing my part for me. You've done your share coming all this way. I couldn't have got through it on my own. I'm not so tough, in spite of all the training they put me through."

Claire kissed her then and went out, leaving her staring at the ceiling, her small, plump hands clasped behind her mop of brown hair and when she went in to take another quick look at the baby on the way out, with the fussy Sister Pritchard at her elbow, she said. "You were right. She is pretty, prettier than any of mine at that stage!" to which Sister Pritchard replied, with a heartiness that reminded Claire of women in the Valley who devoted themselves to Guides and V.A.D. work. "A real surprise packet for Mr. Craddock when he shows up! And a little dividend for Grandpa, eh?"

Claire went out into the street thanking God for her sense of humour, a legacy of her mother's, for her father, crusty old Edward Derwent, had never seen a joke in his life.

IV

It would have been very difficult, she assumed, to have bluffed many men as easily as she had bluffed him on her return home. He had accepted at face value Maureen's absurd story about Claire's sudden resolve to run down to Sevenoaks to see her cousins with whom, years before she was married, she had run a bunshop. Maureen told him, and he had believed her, that the relatives had been bombed and she had taken upon herself the duty of breaking the news about Stevie. Paul himself, Maureen had told her, seemed stoical about it, as though he had been expecting news of this kind every day now that Bomber Command's non-stop offensive was mentioned in every six o'clock bulletin, but when she got home she found that it wasn't fatalism or courage that sustained him but a kind of pride that had enabled him, by some tortuous path of reasoning, to see Stevie's sacrifice as the epitome of all he felt about this struggle for survival. He said, as though apologising for this, "I don't expect you to understand that. You've never been able to see this war as anything but a continuation of the last, but it helped me more than I can say. What I mean is, there's no kind of connection in my mind between the two wars. That last one was murder, badly managed, and quite unnecessary. But this is something very different. It's the only war I've ever heard about worth fighting. I've always seen it as a straight choice between civilisation and barbarism. I'll tell you something you must have sensed over the years. I never had a great deal of time for The Pair. They had far better chances than most of their generation growing up in a place like this, with a solid family background, a good education if they had cared to acquire one, and no shortage of money, but they didn't value any one of those things. They seemed to me to live shallow, silly lives and carry those wives of theirs along with them. They never had any children or did anything constructive, except to make the kind of money my father and old Franz Zorndorff made when there was more excuse for a man looking after Number One! But I was wrong about them just the same. They came up to scratch in the end and if they hadn't we wouldn't be here right now, with the prospect of starting all over again."

He glanced at her then as though expecting her to reject this line of reasoning outright but when she said, "Go on, Paul," he said, "I talked to the C.O. up there and he had a pretty high opinion of Stevie. Those chaps don't talk slosh and he wasn't just being kind. Afterwards I went up to French Wood and thought about it all, about Stevie and Andy, about Simon swimming for it at the time of Dunkirk, and Rumble Patrick sailing off because he felt he had to, and it seemed to me they weren't any different from the chaps who went west in that bloody slime at Passchendaele. They hung on long enough to give everyone else a breather and put those bastards where they belong, at the end of a rope. You don't have to see it this way but you have to know what got me over the hump."

It was the kind of reaction she might have expected from him, if only because he had always seen his own family as no more than a segment of the Valley and everyone else about here as part of a tribe he honestly believed to be superior to any other. It was an old-fashioned notion she supposed, at least thirty years out of date, but he was not a patriot in the sense that almost everybody had been when Kaiser Bill went berserk and all the men were hypnotised by Kitchener's manic start on the hoardings. His patriotism, as she saw it, was once more localised and more broadly based, drawing its strength from the books he read and the thoughts he thought. It had to do with Valley crafts and Valley loyalties, with the food they grew and the dialects they used. It reached back into the history of history books that, for most people, herself included, had no more reality than the stories of the Old Testament but for him had a message that had regulated the whole of his life since she had known him. If it brought him comfort now who was she to question it? It could do nothing at all for her but that was another matter.

As the days passed she saw that he had been able to absorb the beating he had taken and when, three weeks after her return they were told about the bar to Stevie's D.F.C., it meant a lot to him, even if she thought of it as one more manifestation of the male animal's curious ability to make a mystique of organised slaughter. The Craddocks, she reflected, were collectors of medals. Paul had won the M.C. and Croix de Guerre in 1918, Simon a D.C.M. at Calais, and both Stevie and Andy already had the D.F.C., but only Paul seemed to set much store on decorations and had always worn his at the annual Armistice Service, like his cronies Henry Pitts and Smut Potter.

It was about a week after this that she judged him ready to withstand another kind of shock, indeed, the decision was forced upon her by a 'phone call from Margaret saying she would arrive on the Saturday train. It was only a week or so before Andy was expected home for a final course of treatment at Roehampton Hospital.

She waited until the conventional hour for family topics, when she was already in bed and he was fiddling about over by the window, laying out his keys and small change on the dressing-table.

All their married life they had used this moment for clearing-house gossip, a time when they were alone and he had turned his back on the Valley, stealing quietly back to her or his books, or both. In the old days the timing was deliberate

211

for they had formed the habit of resolving the occasional difficulty or tiff on the spot. She had always had the power to distract him from all manner of worries, big and small, by the simple process of availing him of her impulsively generous body, after which his abstractions were somehow removed to a contemplative distance. Now, at sixty-four, his demands were no more than occasional and her own needs had become integrated into the quiet rhythm of their lives.

She said, watching him peel off his shirt and reach for his pyjama jacket, "You're not in bad condition for an over-sixty. Have I told you that before?"

"Not lately," he said, "unless there was an ulterior motive."

"There's one now."

He had never really learned about her. He was surely, she thought, the most guileless man created since Adam. He had not noticed, for instance, as he so rarely did, that she had fortified herself against crisis-point by going into Whinmouth for a shampoo and set, or that she had used a dab or two of a small bottle of perfume Rumble had brought her from abroad that she had been hoarding over the months. All he had learned, it seemed, was to read some kind of invitation in her bedroom chatter when it fitted his own mood and this originated more from male vanity than from an instinctive awareness that she had something important to discuss. It was no good rehearsing this kind of thing. One had to seize a timely moment like this, when he was relaxed and more his younger self. She said bluntly, "Come over here and sit down a minute. I've got something important to tell you. It'll give you a jolt but you'll get over it, providing you let yourself."

He looked startled but suddenly he grinned. "Don't tell me you're pregnant again," he said. "You usually are when you talk that way."

Suddenly she changed her mind about tactics, taking this unexpected chance of administering the medicine in a gulp instead of feeding it to him in small, bitter sips. She said, calmly, "Not me. Your daughter-in-law Margaret."

"Margaret!"

He had been on the point of sitting on the edge of the bed but he jerked upright so quickly that his head almost struck the beam in the ceiling. "But that's nonsense! Andy's been gone . . ." and then he stopped, staring down at her, so that she had to clutch at her courage and take a deep breath to keep the tremor out of her voice.

"She's had the baby," she said, and seeing a way to sidetrack his sense of outrage for a moment, "that's where I was when you couldn't get me in London. I was in North Wales and before that I was at Stevie's camp. I went there with the idea of talking it over with him but when I got there . . . well . . . you know what I found."

He seemed stupefied but his expression did not daunt her as it might have done, for somehow she understood that concern for her was involved in his astonishment and she could only suppose that the vision of her arrival at the camp, to be told the substance of the wire he had received, had temporarily effaced any thoughts about Margaret.

He said, slowly, "You did *that!* You trailed up there, just to talk about Margaret's baby to Stevie? All that rubbish Maureen fed me over the 'phone . . . you *didn't* hear about Stevie from her? . . . You got the news on the camp?"

"Yes, but that was something I didn't bargain for. I walked right into it and learned about it from one of his friends."

"Great God," he said, running his hand over the day's bristles on his long jaw. Then, "But *why!* Why talk to Stevie? Why not me?"

She reached out and took his hand, holding it tightly so that the pressure of her thumb momentarily erased the brown spots on his knuckles. "There was a particular reason," she said, "they have been seeing a great deal of one another all this time. It isn't just anyone's baby, Paul. It's Stevie's."

She gave him time to absorb this but not time enough to say the words that were on the point of tumbling from his mouth. "*Wait*, Paul. You've got to hear it all. You've got to trust me to know what I'm doing, what in fact I already have done. You've got to listen and *think*. Temper and disgust aren't going to help any of us. It's very important to let me explain."

Their relationship was strong enough to take the strain and when she was convinced of this confidence returned to her. She said. "*Will* you listen? Will you trust me to tell you what I've already done before you jump to all kinds of wrong conclusions?" and he said, bitterly, "Go ahead, say all you've got to say, but don't forget Stevie's dead and Andy's due back in just over a week."

"You think I'm likely to forget either of those things?"

"No." His head came up. "I'm sorry I said that but I'm entitled to know all there is to know before Andy arrives and finds her staying with us, and also that Stevie and she confided in you at the time!"

"Stevie didn't," she said, "but if Stevie hadn't been killed Margaret was going to ask Andy to divorce her. Then she and Stevie would have married, providing his own divorce came through."

It was too much for him. "They're like a lot of barnyard animals!" he burst out but she got hold of his hand again and said, "You promised to listen, Paul. I did what I did because somebody had to try and it was way beyond your capacity. That's why I acted on my own and I'm not sorry I did. There's still a chance my way."

"What way is that for God's sake?"

"Margaret's going to tell Andy it's Stevie's child. It wasn't difficult to persuade her to do that. It was far harder to prevent her backing out of the situation altogether. Now it all depends on Andy but my point in going there was to ensure she gave him the chance, if he wanted it. She owes him that. We all owe it him. I was going to make very sure Stevie stayed out of the way until he could make up his mind and that was the whole point of my going there. When things were taken out of my hands I did what seemed the next best thing."

"What was that?"

"I hired a car that same night and travelled half-way across England to find Margaret and say to her what I had intended saying to him."

He was beginning to understand and with understanding came the ability to assess her courage and coolheadedness. It had the effect of obscuring the harsh outlines of the dilemma, a heroic caper within a desperately squalid farce. He knew that this was how it must have appeared to her at the outset, that it had probably disgusted her as it disgusted him now, and yet she had managed to live with it for a long time and then, with nothing but instinct to guide her, had made some kind of attempt to sort things out. But even that was not all, not by a long chalk. Somehow she had found the nerve and resolution to hold on to her purpose in circumstances that would have sent most women reeling to the nearest source of comfort, and this seemed to him something one might witness once in a lifetime but not twice. Realisation of what the ordeal must have cost her humbled him, making him ashamed of his own recoil. He said, exchanging her grip on his hand for one of his own, "I'll listen. And I won't do Andy's work for him by bullying you. I've always said you had a damned sight more sense than most people but I didn't realise you had ten times as much guts. Go ahead, tell me how it looks from your viewpoint and I hope to God I can find the same focus."

She told him, then, everything she knew and much of what she had guessed. She didn't spare either one of them, for although it seemed to her fatally easy to use the handbook of words applicable to this kind of situation there were none of them, including Monica, who had not contributed in some way to what had happened. Andy, it seemed, had found fulfilment in aerobatics and Monica had shrugged off her obligations as carelessly as all of them had done in the past. It did not seem improbable that Stevie and Margaret should seek and find solace in one another and she supposed, times being what they were, one thing would very easily lead to another. She did not expect him to follow her this far and he did not, but at least he was able to contemplate it in a way that would have been impossible half an hour ago.

He said, when she told him that Stevie and Margaret had found a precarious happiness over the last few months, "I daresay they did once they were committed. What I can't begin to understand is how either of them got to the point of going to bed with one another. With a couple of strangers yes, but not with each other."

She owed him the whole truth. "Margaret tried strangers. I don't know about Stevie. She told me that it only made things worse because there was no love in it."

"What the hell do they know about love?"

"As much as us," she said, and his head came up sharply again. "Look, I was in France twenty months and you didn't go screaming round the Valley for someone to take my place of a night."

"There were two good reasons why I didn't. One, I had this entire place on my hands and plenty of old friends around me. Two, you took the trouble to write me a lot of affectionate letters, letters I still keep, and even re-read when I need a pick-me-up! Margaret showed me Andy's last letter.

215

It was like a note left at the back door for the baker or milkman."

He thought about this and it moderated his contempt to some extent. It also made him even more wary of doing battle with her, for it was clear that she had studied her brief.

"What is it?" he asked suddenly, "a boy or a girl?"

"A girl. Very dark. She looks like you must have looked at that age."

It struck no chord in him. He heaved himself up and mooched over to the window. The wind was rising and soughing across the Valley from the direction of the Bluff, an easterly wind, with plenty of sleet in it.

"What have you got in mind now?"

"Nothing beyond giving her a base for the time being. Andy won't be independent of the hospital for weeks. I told her she could bring the baby here and go and see Andy as soon as possible. The rest is up to her."

"What will he do? Have you any notion of that?"

"I've got my private thoughts."

"Well?"

"I think he'll take more kindly to Stevie's baby than to anyone else's. It's just a feeling I've had, since I heard about Stevie's death in those circumstances. Anyway, rightly or wrongly, it seemed to me the best we could hope for."

He finished undressing and came back to the bed. He was thinking hard but not getting very far. To an extent her own independent actions continued to obscure the main issue. He said, unexpectedly, "I've always accepted the convention that men were endowed with far more sexual energy than women."

"I've given you that impression?"

He considered her this time with a curious objectivity. "No," he said, with the faintest trace of a smile, "I can't honestly say that, but then I've always regarded you as eccentric in that respect. I meant women generally. Is that notion a Victorian hangover on my part?"

"Not entirely," she said, "it's just that women on the whole put a little more into it than men. Just a man, any man, isn't much good to the average woman. It has to be a particular man. In that sense there is a sound basis for the convention, no matter how 'liberated' the women of this generation fancy themselves. That was something Margaret discovered."

"She didn't act by it."

"In a way she did."

He put out his hand and ran it lightly across her hair.

"By God!" he said, suddenly, "we've been lucky with each other, Claire! I don't think of it often but when I do it hits me like a falling tree." He slipped his hand over her breast, stroking it absently and presently he leaned on his elbows, took her face between his hands and kissed her on the mouth. "It's odd. For a long, long time I thought of you as someone who was always a lot of fun horizontally but only adequate when you were vertical. Did you know that?"

"I knew it," she said equably, "and I didn't give a hoot. At my age, however, one has to start scratching around for fresh capital. That, I imagine, is what I've been doing lately."

"You needn't have bothered on my account," he said. "Right now, for instance, I'm as erotic as Old Honeyman's prize ram!"

It was an old joke between them. She could not remember how many years had passed since she had first made the comparison but it must have been more than thirty, when the children they had been discussing were toddlers, and their own world was still young. Tonight it told her that he had made up his mind to accept a situation that could not be altered except, perhaps, for the better, and also that, deep down, nothing counted for much in his heart and mind except their relationship rooted in this house and the Valley beyond it.

"What am I doing out here in the cold?" he asked and turned out the bedside light, heaving himself over her to his own side of the bed. His arms went around her with the vigour of a much younger man and in the same moment she told herself, laughing silently, that his reference to Old Honeyman's ram had not been an ageing man's boast.

CHAPTER ELEVEN

SALLIES BY ALL CONCERNED

I

JUNE, 1944.

The listing gull was still based on the landslip, still made its long, lazy circuits of the Valley. It was surprising that it was able to get airborne for its port wing had contracted to less than half a normal spread and the foot that had to take most of the strain of uncertain landings was like a shredded twig. For all that it fed well enough, its limitations teaching it things about the Valley based on certainties and not on casual observation. It took off that morning in a long, drooping curve, fighting to get enough height to clear the line of the dunes, then turning west along the coast until it reached the first of the camp huts where it noted the unusual stillness of the place. Smoke rose from the cookhouse and here and there an odd figure pottered among the huts but there was no stamping and shouting on the parade ground, no vehicles scuttling up and down the broad avenue from the guardhouse. It dipped, found some bacon rinds on the edge of a waste barrel and took off again, the rinds trailing from its beak.

Over four Winds it saw acres of green wheat and a herd of drowsing cattle but Farmer Eveleigh and two of his Land Army girls were at work down there and nothing presented itself as worth a stop. It flew on over the silent ruin of Periwinkle and across the high plateau of French Wood to Hermitage, where David Pitts was feeding pigs in the large sty behind the farmhouse. David was tolerant of gulls and the bird hovered, hoping he would slop swill from the pail Occasionally he did, particularly when the wind made him stagger but today he held his course, setting both buckets down very carefully outside the sty door. Unlike his father Davie was a frugal man, who thought of every pint of swill as money in the bank.

Henry, discussing David with his jolly wife Ellie, sometimes dismissed his son as "a bliddy ole skinflint", but secretly he admired him for making such a success of the three hundred acres casually farmed by Henry, and before that, by Henry's father, Arthur. A curious relationship had grown up between father and son since David had moved lower down the slope into a cottage built for him and his grandmother after Henry had remarried late in life. Henry, semi-retired, was content to take his orders from the boy and was very wary of his mother, old Martha, now entering her nineties. The farm was still in Henry's name but all the decisions were David's. Watching him sometimes Henry would shake his head, declaring that youngsters took themselves too seriously nowadays and had forgotten how to enjoy themselves. There had been no hunting in the Valley since the war but even had there been David would never have taken the field in the way that Henry and his father would turn their backs on toil and pound gaily across country with the Sorrel Vale pack.

The gull left Hermitage and beat eastward to circle the Home Farm, concentrating on the strawyard behind the house where David's sister Prudence, long married to Nelson Honeyman, the young master, dallied with one of the last of the American Rangers left in the area. The gull had profited by the brief American occupation of the coastal strip between Whinmouth and the Bluff, for the Rangers were not only well fed but wasteful. Sometimes they would discard a half-emptied tin of food during a break in their training out on the sandbars, but this morning there was only one of them to be seen and he stood behind the angle of the farm, enjoying a joke with Prudence. The gull knew Prudence as one of the few women in the Valley prodigal with titbits, and its curiosity was aroused now by a small, opened crate of brightly coloured packages and tins resting on a trestle closeby. It wondered if they would leave it unguarded so that it could flop down and investigate but they did not, standing there a long time talking and laughing, so that Prudence's brassy head, shining in the sun, periodically jerked back and her laughter reached the gull as it continued to circle hopefully. Then, lifting the carton, she took it into the barn and the Ranger followed, so the gull flew on over the Home

Farm paddocks and the big stone house that was silent, offering nothing until the ground rose steeply behind it and there was promise in the jam-buttie a little boy was nibbling at the top of the orchard.

The gull recognised the child as it had recognised Prudence, the source of an occasional meal, but today Mary Palfrey was there with her new baby who was tottering between mother and brother. Fearing nothing in this quarter the gull dropped down on a gatepost at the end of the orchard, not because it was interested in watching Sorrel Palfrey learn to walk but because, intent upon his sister's attempts, Jerry Palfrey had turned his back on his jam-smeared crust and was calling, in his high, piping voice, "Come on Sorrel, I'll catch you." It was an opportunity the listing gull had learned to watch for over the seasons. With a flurry of wings it was down, up and away, the crust in its beak. The boy Jerry did not resent the naked theft but shouted with laughter. The staggering child fell flat on her face with surprise.

The gull skirted the woods and looked down on the family at High Coombe where the farmer's wife, as usual, was sitting at her easel in an untidy front garden. It ignored the bright colours in the box beside the woman, knowing from past experience that they were inedible. Turning south it drifted down the wind funnel between the timber of Coombe Brake and the Bluff. There was nothing to be found here except an odd pig-nut outside Willoughby's farm, Deepdene, and soon it was coasting over the three detached houses that crowned the northern edge of Coombe Bay village.

Its ancestors had often found easy pickings here for one of those tall, greystone houses had once sheltered an old German who encouraged gulls to feed from his hand but that was long ago. The people living here now usually ignored visitors flying in from the Coombe. The gull knew two or three of them, however, the man who lived in the end house and walked with a bobbing roll as if his leg was injured like the gull's own, and the three people who lived next door, a man with a rigid hand, a woman and baby, who seemed to live in a pram on the lawn. The man was there now, leaning on the fence and looking directly up at the gull, as though comparing its clumsy aerobatics with the flight of the bright little machines that sometimes skimmed south over the woods, or inland from the sea.

The gull hovered long enough to study the upturned face that was unlike the face of any other man in the Valley. One side of it was dead like his hand, while the other could register expressions that the gull had learned, over the years, to recognise as like, dislike, interest, indifference or impatience. Today this side of the man's face was animated and he called softly to his wife who was bending over the baby's pram. The woman glanced up and presently went to the kitchen window, got something and gave it to the man, who placed it on his rigid hand and slowly extended his arm, a gesture the gull recognised as an invitation. It hovered a moment in order to make quite sure, then dipped to the fence where it alighted, staggered a full two feet, and steadied itself by half-opening its sound wing. The man stood quite still, the piece of bread resting on his gloved hand, and the woman watched too, so that for a moment there was absolute stillness in the garden.

The man said, "It's him all right, Margy. It must be oil. That port wing is U.S. and he's got a gammy leg as well, poor bastard!" Then, to the gull, "Here, boy! Take it! We bloody cripples ought to stick together," and the gull, reassured by the tone, heaved itself from the fence and took the crust, wheeling in an uncertain half circle and heading for the quay.

The man watched it go and the woman watched the man.

"Well, at least the poor old bugger is still airborne," he said, and lounged off into the house to turn on the radio. Sounds of a news-bulletin reached Margaret as she stood by the pram, rocking it gently, but the words carried on the breeze were only intermittently heard and therefore made little sense. ". . . making good their landing . . . considerable opposition at scattered points . . . advancing on two sectors . . ." And then, one complete sentence: "So far only one vessel reported lost." She called, "How is it going, Andy? Is there anything fresh?" and Andy, appearing at the French window with a cigarette in his mouth, said, "They've all got ashore and seem to be in business."

He stood there a minute and Margaret wondered uncertainly, if she should try and console him again. She knew the source and depth of his bitterness—an armada of aircraft, ships and men committed to the biggest enterprise of the war, and himself pottering about a garden with a woman, a child and an artificial hand. His depression had increased, she noticed, when the papers had begun to talk of the Second Front and all the American Rangers down on the shore had packed up and gone, taking their landing craft with them. Then Andy came lounging out of the house, calling, "I'm going to have a yarn with Ken Shawcrosse. Give me a shout when lunch is up." She thought, unhappily, "I'll probably have to give three shouts, and then Ken Shawcrosse will come lumbering back with you and expect me to feed him on our rations. And after that you'll both swill gin and French, and tonight you'll be sour-tempered until it's time for bed and might want to use me, as if I was something from the far end of a Sultan's harem." Then, as the baby gurgled, she drew her finger along the child's cheek. "We'll stick it out, Vanessa," she said, "we'll stick it out until it improves. And everyone except me seems to think it will."

II

The gull, being no fisherman, did not venture across the tidal lagoon to the sandbars where the one landing craft the Americans had left behind lay wrecked and rusting, holed by a 1940 obstruction and now the haunt of gulls who lined its weed-covered sides to watch for fish trapped in the hull. Evie Craddock saw them standing there as she tied up to the barnacled poles, slipped out of her skirt and singlet, and lowered herself into eight feet of slack water. There were no prohibitions about bathing now and in fine weather she came here every day. It brought Simon much closer and today she was in need of some kind of reassurance.

He had said nothing about the part he expected to play in the invasion but his extreme reticence had only increased her uneasiness. Before releasing her hold on the gunwale she looked across the ruffled water towards France, picturing what might be happening there, her guesses based on the scrappy content of the radio bulletins. They did not tell her much. To listen to the genteel voice of the announcer one would imagine the invasion was a kind of cross-Channel excursion, the picnic to end all picnics, with men wading ashore in shallows shouting like boys sent to play on a beach. She was aware, of course, that it was not like that at all, that over there, almost within sight it seemed, men were bleeding to death in the shallows and all was the wildest confusion.

222

Simon, if he was there at all, would have been ashore since first light, and she wondered, distractedly, whether there had been a second mention of glider troops in later bulletins. The thought made her push off and swim rapidly round the dinghy, as though ashamed of enjoying herself when Simon and hundreds of thousands of others were drenched in sweat and numbed by explosions. Then her commonsense caught up with her and she thought, "If he could see me he'd laugh—out here making a pilgrimage round the mermaid beat in his honour. I'll write and tell him what I did on D-Day." She lay flat on her back and let herself wash to and fro in the tidal wavelets. "He'll make it somehow," she told herself. "It's like Paul told me on the 'phone—Simon will make it in the long run or he wouldn't have got this far."

Simon had, in a manner of speaking, already made it. The Orne bridge was now as secure as the most optimistic of them could have hoped for ten hours previously when they cast off and came gliding in from the north-west to crash within fifty yards of the bridges over the little river and the Caen Canal.

The first twenty minutes had been the liveliest and, in some ways the most rewarding of Simon's military career and that career went back a long time now—to the day when he emerged from the hold of the Dutch collier to join the raggle-tailed Basques in a war that was already history. It was of this other war that he thought as he sat in the whistling glider awaiting the impact. You were not supposed to think of anything on these occasions but empty your mind so that the body was free to respond to reflexes rehearsed over the months of training for a single leap into the dark towards a specific objective. The leap was from the wreck of a Horsa glider. The objective a couple of bridges over two insignificant waterways near the village of Ranville, in Normandy.

And yet his mind persisted in making comparisons. Both wars, from his point of view, had been fought as an amateur, but this time he was an amateur with professional equipment at his disposal. Even the Bren gun he held was capable, in the hands of a trained man, of killing half-a-dozen men with a couple of bursts whereas, in Spain, he had counted himself lucky to carry a 1914 Lebel rifle with a stiff bolt action. The men beside him were amateurs, now as then. Tonight they were fresh-faced youngsters, keyed-up to a terrific pitch and probably terrified by the hazards of their assignment and yet, like himself, fortified by the certainty of ultimate victory, and this was half-way to survival. In Spain it had not been that way at all. Always they were staring over their shoulder at defeat, a mob of peasants fighting Italian armour and German dive-bombers in a contest from which the Democracies had stood aside, calling their cowardice non-intervention.

Well, here after so long was the beginning of the end, an invasion mounted on a massive scale and surprisingly he was part of it. And that in spite of having passed his fortieth birthday.

He heard the long, final swish of the glider and felt the grinding, bumping slither of its impact. Then training took over and his thoughts went tumbling back to the lumber room as men spilled out of the door and down through the shattered nosecap, shouting and leaping, whooping, prancing and firing haphazardly into the snake-belts of mist that hung above river and canal. Expecting to lead some thirty of them he was, instead, caught up in their tumult, and in the flash of exploding grenades images registered on his brain at the speed of a runaway film. He saw Lance-Corporal Gilson fire from the hip at the embrasure of a pillbox. He saw another man hurl grenades into a gun-pit. He saw a tall German soldier standing on the bridge itself, his mouth wide open but no sound issuing from it as a Bren burst folded him like a sack. And then there were his own tiny triumphs as he shot a man in the act of firing a Verey pistol and, seconds later, two more pounding back across the bridge. From the direction of the canal came the continuous wink of flashes and the roar of grenades and after that, from all around, a long, unaccountable silence. It was done, apparently, and so quickly that it was hard to believe. It had been like a noisier edition of one of the briefings, where every object seen here was a scale model glued in a frame. The only real difference was the dead, the man still holding a Verey pistol, the two fugitives at the far end of the bridge, and on the lip of the gun-pit his own sergeant, camouflage smock still smouldering from a phosphorous grenade.

Time passed and they pottered about in the gloom. "Consolidating" it was called but how did one consolidate fixed objects in the dark? Overhead he heard the throb of engines and glanced automatically at his watch. It was 3.20 a.m. and the noise would come from the Dakotas carrying parachutists to hold the heights north-east of Caen against a panzer counter-attack. Later he heard them rallying to the toot of an English hunting-horn. The sound had never stirred him as it seemed to stir other men, for he had forsworn foxhunting as a child. All the same it was odd to hear it away in the mist and he made a mental note to write and tell his father who, despite having been a Master of Foxhounds, had never learned to produce anything better than a despairing wail on the instrument.

Messages, most of them encouraging, came in from one source or another. The canal bridge was secure. The parachutists were assembling in the west. Casualties had been relatively light. Miraculously it was seen that their own glider had landed within fifty yards of the bridge. As it began to grow light, and they had to contend with nothing but a few snipers, abstract thoughts began to creep out again but they took no hold and skirted carefully on the edge of triviality. The hedge tear in his smock. The thick crust of dirt under his thumbnail. The foolishly upturned heels of the two dead men on the bridge. From the shelter of the gun-pit he could count eight German bodies. The British dead had been carried into the pillbox.

When it was quite light he could see the profile of the German with the Verey pistol and it was contemplating him that he came to terms with the curiously final reaction to the night that was gone and already receding into history, like the battles in Spain and the débâcle at Calais. For him, in a sense, it was over. There was no hate for the man spreadeagled on the bridge, or the inert grey forms of the others. All this time he had been sustained by a hatred that had driven him blindly along the years, and although it had moderated after his marriage to Evie there had still been enough to push him as far as this. But now it was altogether spent. Tomorrow or the day after they would roll on, he supposed, over the Seine, over the First War battlefields of Flanders, and ultimately over the Rhine, but it would be a campaign, not a crusade. The transition pleased him. In a way he felt purged and free.

The man at his elbow said, fighting a yawn, "They haven't shown up yet, sir. Taking their time." He meant Lovat's Commandos, scheduled to relieve them and already an hour-and-a-half overdue. "They'll be along," Simon said and as he

225

said it they heard, from down the road, the faint but unmistakable skirl of pipes so that Simon smiled, not from relief but at the juvenile enthusiasms the British injected into the sorry business of war. There had been that story about footballs punted across No-Man's-Land on the first day of the Somme offensive. There was the early morning toot of the hunting horn heard in the Normandy mists. And always, in every war, there was the moan of bagpipes.

He stood up and watched the men scrambling out of cover and moving across open country. Some of them were waving and cheering but most of them just stared. The green berets marched in with conscious panache, as if they were relieving another Lucknow. Their piper was playing "Blue Bonnets over the Border", a tune Simon had heard often during his long spell in the Highlands. Soon red and green berets intermingled and he overheard Lord Lovat apologise for being late, as though he and the Major had agreed to lunch together. "I must remember to tell the Gov'nor that too," he thought. "Amateurs, the whole bloody lot of us. But we look like beating the hell out of the pros and that's a damned sight more than we deserve, considering the way we went about it until a couple of years ago."

III

War, Claire was discovering, was an unreliable catalyst. She remembered the generalisations of 1914, when war had been proclaimed "ennobling" by poets, politicians and journalists, and she remembered how, not long afterwards, these same people had piously denounced war as "the final debasement of human currency". She was not, however, a diligent reader of leading articles, preferring to base her opinions on observation and instinct, and it seemed to her, now that the war was entering its sixth winter, its stresses were responsible for some dramatic changes in the characters of people around her.

Paul had changed very little but then Paul was Paul, the captive of a single idea and basically more conservative than any of the Tories he had campaigned against in the Liberal heyday. It was otherwise with his sons. If Margaret was to be believed Stevie had developed a new personality when he had switched from fighter-pilot to bomber-pilot whereas his twin,

Andy, had changed so dramatically that even casual acquaintances noticed it. He had gone to war a loud, cheerful extrovert and had returned, some three years later, a morose, truculent, glowering young man, quick to fly off the handle, silent and brooding when left alone. She didn't know what to make of him these days and neither, it seemed, did poor Margaret, who was having a difficult time with him.

Andy, Margaret told her, had not been soured by her involvement with Stevie. This was something that he had shrugged off and seemed to regard as no more than tiresome, and only then because it involved them all and governed their approach to him. He did not resent Vanessa either, in fact, in his lighter moments he appeared to be growing very fond of her. He had never, Margaret admitted under pressure, taxed her with disloyalty and when Claire, unable to believe this, had taken the risk of raising the subject with him, she found that Margaret was speaking the truth. "Stevie bought it, the old clot, so naturally I'll stand by the kid," he said, briefly. "As for Margy—we all make bloody fools of ourselves now and again and I'm no angel. Never pretended to be one."

And that was about as far as she got and sometimes she wondered whether the reconciliation she had achieved had been worth her cab fare from York to Criccieth. But then, she told herself, Andy's indifference was not all that surprising, for the younger generation had long since discarded the old values and invented for themselves an entirely different code of behaviour. What was more to the point was Andy's moodiness and Claire assumed this stemmed from his disfigurement and the limitations imposed upon him by his injuries. Margaret thought otherwise, saying that he would never perk up until he could reabsorb himself in the strike-it-rich brigade. "In that way he hasn't changed at all," she told Claire, in one of her confiding moments—"Stevie would never have gone back to scrap, or anything that meant keeping the kind of company we kept, or living in the places we lived in before the war. He would have gone for the open-air life, even farming maybe."

"Isn't it at all possible to steer Andy in that direction?" Claire asked. "Paul would probably set him up in one of the Coombe farms—my father's old farm for instance, as soon as these arty-crafty people move out and they will the moment the war finishes."

Margaret was not encouraging. "That isn't for Andy," she said, dolefully, "he's still interested in money for its own sake. He's already financed that one-legged speculator Shawcrosse he met in hospital and set him up next door for the duration. They hobnob most of the day when they aren't on the 'phone and are forming a company I believe."

"What kind of company exactly?"

"How would I know? He doesn't confide in me. All I know is that it's something to do with houses and land. Once upon a time he would have told me anything I asked but not any more, and I can't honestly blame him in that respect. He remembers. Before the war, when all four of us were living it up, I was never interested where the money came from, so long as it arrived in large, juicy dollops."

Claire sympathised with her. She lived in a vacuum between past and present. Her loyalty, perhaps her guilt, bound her to Andy, but she had seen through the sham of their pre-war marriage and its tawdriness, viewed in restrospect, dismayed her. Claire, who had always recognised its fairground glitter, understood this very well, but Andy was Margaret's problem and she could only wait for matters to resolve themselves.

They seemed to be doing this very satisfactorily as far as Simon was concerned. Claire had developed an easy undemanding relationship with Evie, who told her that Simon had also undergone a subtle change since his participation in the D-Day assault. To prove it she produced a letter she had received from him after the Allies had broken out from their beachhead and made their bid to win the war by Christmas.

"It will tell you a lot more than I can second-hand," she said, "and I daresay you'll read more into it than me because you knew his first wife and were around when he was involved in all those lame-dog campaigns. Anyway, read it, and tell me if I'm right about readjustment. I've only known him twelve months and I'm not all that bright, but it does seem to me that he's—well, mellowed a lot."

Claire laughed and said it was probably the prospect of having a wife to come home to, but when she read the letter she saw that the girl's instinct had served her well, and that Simon had indeed mellowed, so much so that there was hardly a trace of the smouldering young man Claire remembered in the period of political upheaval between the wars. She had always sympathised with his quarrel with the established order far more so than Paul, who regarded him as a bit of a fanatic, but she had never understood the masochistic pleasure he and that humourless girl Rachel seemed to derive from sharing the burdens (and sometimes the living quarters!) of what her father would have described as The Great Unwashed. All that, it seemed, was now in the past, and for the first time she detected tolerance and maturity in his outlook. *"I don't see this as a Left-versus-Right contest any more,"* he wrote, *"but as a kind of Sanitary Squad exercise! I've always lived for politics, and they've always presented a straight choice for me, as they did for Rachel, but since I got back here I've had to shift my sights for a variety of reasons. The prisoners we took after the break-through to the Seine aren't the Germans I remember, those arrogant, indoctrinated bullies, who bombed Guernica and threw us out of France, in 1940. Mostly they remind me of the kind of Jerry one met in Remarque's 'All Quiet . . .' The French too are not all 'gallant resisters', who have been running around with secret codes and homemade explosives ever since Dunkirk. Many did, of course, but others just sat and waited, and there were some who made a packet of money out of the Occupation. It isn't a matter of politics any more, but expediency. There are plenty of cruel bastards on the Left, as well as the Right. I had to threaten to shoot two of them yesterday, after they had shaved a seventeen-year-old girl because somebody pointed her out as someone who had once slept with a German. I've seen a lot of that since June and it isn't the kind of Democracy I've been fighting for ever since Spain."* Then came what was, to Claire, a frank admission of self-doubt and reappraisal. *"I'd more or less made up my mind to have a crack at getting into Parliament at the first post-war election but I've had second thoughts about that. I'm more interested in people than policies, so I shall look about for something where I can co-operate rather than legislate. Don't ask me what, for I don't know. We'll talk about it when I get home, and as the Daddy of the Company I'm at least sure of one thing—I'm right at the head of the demob-queue."*

Claire was so interested in his heresy that she took it upon herself to show part of the letter to Paul. She did not show him the final page that she ought not to have read but did, for she was always very curious to learn about other women's relationships with their husbands. What she read here encouraged her to think that dear old Simon, bless his air-conditioned heart, had at last found someone with enough cosiness and commonsense to make a grab at the bonuses of marriage in the way she had done from the outset of life with Paul and she was touched by the boyish endearments in the final paragraph. Evie must have realised she had read them but perhaps, in a way, she was glad for there had never been any secret between them that what Simon needed as much as a wife was an amiable mistress.

Whiz wrote one of her formal, slightly prissy letters from India about the same time and it was clear that she too was developing into a person with whom a conventional mother-daughter relationship was unlikely to survive the war. Claire found that she could accept this with equanimity for Whiz, alone among the Craddocks, pursued her objectives untroubled by emotional doubts. Ian, her husband, was now firmly entrenched among what the American Rangers called the Top Brass, and Whiz wrote as though this was no more than the right of a professional kingpin in a pyramid of amateurs. She had two children and a third expected, an announcement that caused Claire to comment, when reading her daughter's letter aloud to Paul, "She doesn't so much tell us these things as to make them public, like royalty!", to which Paul replied, with a chuckle (for his second daughter's pomposity always amused him) that a diet of curry must have gingered them up a little and if this happy state of affairs continued the Craddocks would contribute substantially to the population explosion the newspapers were prophesying.

Andy, Simon and Whiz Claire could adjust to without much difficulty, and even that curious, last-minute transformation of Stevie had been simplified by Margaret, but she knew little about Mary, or Mary's relationship with that genial oddity, Rumble Patrick. Mary had always been Paul's responsibility and Claire had never challenged his unrepentant favouritism of their eldest daughter.

Thus it was that she remained in ignorance of the slight shift in the balance of the former Periwinkle team, and the anxieties that had beset her daughter before that shift became apparent. Paul was not unaware of them but said nothing until the day Mary confided in him and shocked him by admitting that her principal worry over the last two years was not that Rumble would be killed but that he would outgrow his tribal loyalties to the Valley.

It should not have jolted him as much as it did. He

remembered Rumble's guarded admission at the time of the destruction of Periwinkle, a confession that he still cherished a curiosity about faraway places, but he did not appreciate the significance of this until the day he and Mary saddled the horses and rode over to Periwinkle to survey the prospects of rebuilding as soon as the authorities issued the building licence.

They spent an hour or so on the site but Paul noticed that Mary seemed preoccupied and not much interested in his proposals. He said, offhandedly, "You and Rumble do intend to return here, don't you? He isn't hankering after one of the other farms?" and she said, equably in the circumstances, "No Daddy, I imagine it'll be Periwinkle or nothing but until yesterday's mail I was half convinced it was going to be nothing."

He stared at her in amazement. Of all his children he had regarded her as the most permanently rooted and had often consoled himself with the fact that one at least had married someone who shared his own dedication to the Valley.

"Now what the devil do you mean by that?" he demanded. "Rumble isn't thinking of chucking the land is he?" and she said, patiently, that she had suspected so for some time past but that suddenly they were almost back to normal and this would be Rumble's last voyage if he could terminate his engagement as soon as his ship returned from the Far East.

He said, unhappily, "You and Rumble—you always seemed to me to belong. There's nothing wrong is there? I mean, nothing like the kind of thing that happened to The Pair?"

She smiled, kicking her feet free from the stirrups so that he saw her as a rosy-cheeked girl again, jogging along beside him after a day's hunting with the Sorrel Vale.

"It's not that kind of 'wrongness'," she said. "Rumble has his own rules and lives by them, pretty strictly I should say. I've never had an hour's worry about other women, even though I've only had him a month or so in more than two years. No, it's the gypsy in him I daresay, and also the fact that he married young—too young. I suppose I was to blame for that but you remember how it was that time he came home unexpectedly, when we were all so miserable about little Claire being killed."

"I remember perfectly," he said grimly. "Tell me the rest, providing you want to."

She said, surprisingly, "Very well, but we'll have to stop somewhere. The fact is he jumped at the chance of going to sea after the Germans bombed Periwinkle. In a way it was a last-minute reprieve and had the advantage of a built-in excuse to go with it. Farmhouse gone—prospect of seeing out the rest of the war as a lodger at the Big House—that didn't suit our Rumble's book at all! So he prattled a little about wanting to do his bit, like Stevie and Andy and Simon, and went off grinning all over his face."

"You mean you realised that at the time?"

"In a way I did, but I didn't admit it until after that one time he came home between voyages. I saw then that he wasn't really cured, that he had to see what was left of the world before he was ready to settle for Shallowford. I suppose I resented it in a way but I tried to make allowances. Like I say, he was a husband at twenty-one and a father a year later. He was also a Potter, and although the Potter generation you knew were content to squat in the Dell there's inherited wanderlust there, and always will be. Have you ever heard of a poet called James Elroy Flecker?"

"Surprisingly I have," he said. "I've got one or two of his poems in an Anthology."

"One called 'Brumana'?"

"Yes, the one where he realises that the pine trees that talked him into leaving England were damned liars. I liked that."

"Ah, you would," she said, "it's right up your street! Well, here's the connection—Rumble came across it in a magazine in a barber's shop in Auckland and it so fitted his mood that he sent the late Mr. Flecker home to do his dirty work for him!"

"How do you mean?"

She dismounted and he followed suit, sliding the reins over the cruppers and leaving the horses to crop the hedgerow grass in the lane that led over the shoulder of Hermitage Wood. She took out a letter that must have been a long time reaching her, for it was marked "June 7th, Sydney".

"You don't mind me reading it?"

"Good heavens no! Rumble couldn't write a love-letter! I settled for that years ago. Go on, read it, and then the poem he tore out of the magazine. It must have impressed him no end. When I last saw him *The Farmers' Weekly* was his literary high-water mark!"

He sat down on the bank and read pages of scrawl. The letter, it seemed, had been prompted by the D-Day news-bulletins and Paul got the impression that wide horizons had blurred Rumble's sense of geography, for he seemed to assume that Devon and the Normandy coastline were almost within hailing distance of one another and was in mortal fear of them being hit by stray shells. *"I feel,"* he began, *"the victim of a crazy practical joke! By my reckoning you are no more than a hundred miles north-west of the beaches, and here am I, polishing a gun I haven't fired for eight months and nearly thirteen thousand miles from the nearest Jerry! Remember to tell the Gov he was spot-on when he accused me of dodging the column! I was, by twelve thousand nine hundred miles!"*

"Is that what you meant? He feels out of it all, despite the Japs?"

"No, read from page four, the bit about Flecker. Read it aloud."

" 'I met an old friend of yours the other day. Name of Flecker—James Elroy Flecker. At least, I think he's a friend for the name rang a bell while I was browsing through a mag. in a barber's shop, in Auckland. It made me remember you before the fire at Periwinkle on a winter's night, with your "Just listen to this . . ." routine, and me trying to tot up a column of figures! I had to travel this distance to make the connection. Read the lines I've marked. It's how I feel right now and I couldn't have put it better if you had been right beside me. My God, I miss you and the Valley and can't get home quickly enough! Catch me straying out of Devon after the war and you can shoot me and start fresh with someone who can recognise a good thing when he sees one'."

Paul looked up quickly and saw laughter in his daughter's expression.

"Well," he said, "he may not write much of a love-letter but at least he doesn't beat about the bush," and Mary chuckled saying, "Read the poem and notice the bits he's underlined. I'll hold that in reserve for the rest of my life. A spare shot in my locker if he gets itchy feet in his middle-age!"

He read the poem and was moved by it, remembering very clearly some of the passages that had half-remained in his memory.

"Oh shall I ever be home again?
Meadows of England shining in the rain
Spread wide your daisied lawns . . ."

And

"Old fragrant friends—preserve me the last lines
Of that long saga which you sang me, pines,
When, lonely boy, beneath the chosen tree,
I listened, with my eyes upon the sea . . .
Oh traitor pines, you sang what life has found
The falsest of fair tales . . ."

He was chuckling himself now so that Mary chimed in with the final underscored passage—

"Hearing you sing O trees,
Hearing you murmur 'There are older seas
That beat upon vaster shores . . .' "

"Well, there you are. He's cured! But if he comes home quoting that poem you never heard of James Elroy Flecker and his traitor pines, understand?"

"I am not quite the bumbling old fool that you, your mother and your brothers sometimes take me for," he said, returning letter and poem and reaching for the bridle of the grey.

CHAPTER TWELVE

BOOBY TRAP

I

HE was by no means infallible. Even after forty-two years he was still capable of grievous misjudgments of character but he would admit to these with a kind of wry humour when he had got over the shock. Such an error was the one he made in respect of Noah Williams, Coombe Bay longshoreman, in the winter of 1944-45.

For a long time now the authorities outside the Valley had accepted his leadership and had never hesitated to delegate responsibility to him, sometimes with a readiness that made protest. For all that he would have resented them going elsewhere for help and advice, for he thought of himself as the God-appointed custodian of far more acres than he owned.

Coombe Bay jetty came within one of these areas for, although he had scattered properties in the village, the bay at the mouth of the Sorrel was not under his jurisdiction, particularly since the military had moved in to set up a gun-position there in the early autumn of 1940.

The gun was no longer there but the mock café that had housed it at the end of the jetty was still used as a Home Guard Command post. On this side of the estate and beyond it, where the sandbanks almost closed the channel at low tide, the military still had a network of weed-trailing beach obstacles that were sown in the summer of panic following Dunkirk.

Paul went down there two or three times a week, partly for the ride and partly to consort with one or other of his old cronies, Smut Potter, whose bakery was just along the quay, or Alf Willis, the wheelwright who had lost his sight at St.

Julien in 1917, but had refused to surrender the post of telephonist he had taken when the local L.D.V. unit was formed in the first spring of the war.

Paul was on the point of setting out for the village one gusty February afternoon when Claire called him back into the house to answer a call from the R.M. Camp on the Moor. It was Trubshaw, the adjutant, who gave him the gist of a message just received from the naval sub-depot at Whinmouth regarding a possible danger east of the landslip from floating mines. Neither the Navy nor the marines seemed much concerned.

"They're ours," Trubshaw said offhandedly, "and they're about as useful as fishermen's floats as far as coastal defence is concerned. Two of a dozen or so, laid outside the estuary early in the war. Judged on some of the stuff pressed into use about then they might even date from World War I. The Navy had orders to take them in months ago but you know Jack Ashore when it comes to paper work. They've probably been writing letters to one another about them since Dunkirk. Now they've recovered all but two that slipped their cables in last night's gale."

"Old or not they can still do a hell of a lot of damage. Has their position been plotted since daylight?"

"About an hour ago. They were drifting east towards the sandbanks at midday. Pretty well nudging one another I hear and moving out of our patch, thank God."

"Well, what the devil am I supposed to do about it?" Paul demanded and Trubshaw said, soothingly, "Oh, nothing, old boy, nothing at all. Just warn the civvies down near the quay. The Navy are coping. They're sending a cutter along. It's probably there now."

"Well, thanks for telling me," Paul said, unable to keep the irony out of his voice. "If the village has gone up in smoke by the time I've driven over I'll fill in a form and post it to the Admiralty."

"You do that, old man!" Trubshaw said genially, "and I'll back you up in triplicate."

Paul was not over-concerned by the news for his knowledge of the strong currents off the Bluff told him the scour would probably catch the mines west of the harbour mouth and push them on to the Conger Rocks two miles out to sea. There, at low tide, they would either explode harmlessly or half-submerge themselves on the eastern tip of the sandbars, and he assumed that a disposal unit was on board the cutter and equipped to defuse them on the spot.

His irritation stemmed from another source. He had not ridden for a week owing to an accumulation of work and had been looking forward to a trot down the river road and a canter home across the dunes before dusk. Now, he supposed, he would have to go by car, and turn the unclipped grey loose in the paddock. He unsaddled, gave the halter-end to Thirza, and climbed in the old station wagon that had replaced Claire's Morris as the estate runabout. He not only begrudged the loss of exercise but the petrol. Notwithstanding his Home Guard and agricultural allowances, the authorities were very miserly with their coupons.

He was just passing Mill Cottage, about half-way to the coast, when the explosion echoed up the Valley and its blast rattled his windscreen so vigorously that he was amazed it withstood the shock. The Valley was well accustomed to sudden bangs by now but this was a particularly heavy one. Feeling certain it must be one of the mines he pushed the accelerator as far as it would go. Then, as he rounded the last curve in the road, he saw the pall of brickdust rise over the village and shouted, involuntarily, "Good God, it's washed ashore!" and swept into the steep High Street, aware of scurrying figures moving towards the harbour at the double.

Down outside The Raven, where the dust-cloud was thickest, all was confusion and outcry. He scrambled out of the car and ran across to the quay where he almost collided with Smut Potter, hatless and coatless in the thin rain that had begun to fall as Paul set out.

"Tiz a bliddy gurt bomb o' some sort!" he shouted. "Us didden zee nothin' go over, did you, Squire?"

"It's a mine," Paul said, "one of two loose from Whinmouth. I just got word from the camp," and before Smut could comment he pulled him out of the mainstream of village women and children and into the porch of The Raven. "We've got to get all these people inshore before the other one drifts in and we've got to do it before we check for casualties. Who have you got to help?"

Smut's instincts as ex-poacher and ex-trench veteran showed at once. His blue eyes narrowed and his stocky body seemed to contract so that Paul saw him as he had first seen him, balanced on his toes ready to run.

"Be the other one handy then?" Smut demanded, and Paul said they had been close together when last sighted off the landslip.

"Then you take a good look while I put the fear o' God into these yer gawpers, Maister," he said and moved off, thrusting his way among the knots of sightseers and shouting, at the top of his voice. "Everyone inshore! Tiz a mine an' there's more of 'em out there!" Reaching in the glove box for his binoculars Paul saw him shoving his way along the quay and almost at once there was a general movement away from the water that began as a drift and ended as a mild stampede. At the same time the cob-dust began to settle and Paul, moving to the quay wall, was able to make some kind of assessment of the damage.

Fortunately, almost miraculously it seemed to him, it was negligible. The mine, reaching the harbour mouth on the turn of the tide, had drifted in on the swell and exploded against the wall of the jetty, blowing a gap ten yards wide. The mock cafe, at the end of the gimcrack structure, was now an island, and although its concrete walls seemed to have withstood the blast, its roof was stripped and its foundations had tilted so that it now looked like a grey box resting on a criss-cross of half-submerged pile. Apart from this, and a great many broken windows, there appeared to be no quayside damage and no casualties. People addressed him as he scanned the harbour but all he replied was, "Get off the beach. Get up behind the town," and trained his glasses on the grey waste of water between the shattered jetty and the nearest of the beach obstructions half a mile out to sea.

At first he could see very little. Rain continued to fall and visibility was bad owing to the mist that almost invariably accompanied damp weather at this time of year. Then, making a sweep of the sandbar, he saw the Whinmouth cutter and improbably it seemed to be anchored just outside the bar. He was trying to improve the focus when Noah Williams touched his elbow.

"They'm stuck," he said, with an element of glee in his voice. "They gone aground in shallow water and they'll have to bide until the tide's run an hour."

Paul lowered his glasses and stared into Noah's broad, gap-tooth face. "This is no time to be funny, Noah," he said sharply, for Noah had a reputation as a practical joker, but the longshoreman replied plaintively, "I baint 'avin' 'ee on,

Squire. They'm stuck I tell 'ee. You got to be right smart to catch that harbour at turn o' tide and they should ha' waited on for a spell. It happened bevore and I told 'em but they bliddy vorriners alwus knows best."

"Take a closer look yourself," Paul said, passing his binoculars but confirmation came at once, a rocket soaring from the cutter and arching its way over the western slope of the Bluff. The bomb-disposal team, it would appear, were themselves appealing for help.

"Well, for God's sake ..." Paul began, but Noah, taking the glasses said, "Tiz blowin' up rough too. They'd better not hang around out there, the gurt vools!" He might have been talking about a Nazi landing party.

Noah Williams, almost the last of the seafaring Williamses of Coombe Bay, was not a fisherman in the sense that his forbears had been. He still followed the trade of the sea but his status was that of a semi-amateur. He sold fish from his quayside cottage and in the summer he made some kind of a living conducting trips in the bay, but his intense dislike of salt-water was a local joke and had been ever since, as a boy, he had been almost drowned when caught in a summer squall off the landslip. His Uncle Tom and his brother Dan, who had been with him on that occasion, had been lost at Jutland but long before that Noah, basically a loafer, had all but renounced his ancestral calling. He still had a boat but he would never venture beyond the sandbars, and only then on a windless day. Even his summer traffic was carried by his only son, Jaffsie, who also did a little fishing.

Jaffsie, a young man with a slack mouth and a furtive manner, joined them now. For three centuries the Williamses had given their children biblical names and Jaffsie had been christened Japhet. Paul, who knew the personal history of everyone in the Valley, did not have much confidence in father or son.

Smut rejoined them, shoulders hunched against the rain. "I been the length o' the quay and give orders to keep everyone upalong," he said. "Voysey's takin' over in the High Street and they'll tak' more heed o' him than they will o' me. Be that bliddy cutter at anchor?"

"No, tiz aground," Noah crowed, "an' will be until the tide lifts her."

"Have 'ee spotted any more, Squire?"

"No. You've got the keenest sight of any of us. You take a look, Smut."

Smut took the glasses and began a methodical sweep of the little harbour, beginning at the foot of the Bluff and swinging the binoculars as far west as the landslip. Then he returned over the same field of vision and when he was two-thirds of the way round he stopped and remained rigid for nearly half a minute.

"Tiz there all right," he said at length, "low down, about dree hundred yards out. Take a bearing on what's left o' the jetty and you'll zee it bobbing like a bliddy gurt vootball."

For a long time Paul searched the area and at last picked up a small, dark object that he had previously assumed to be a piece of driftwood.

"Are you sure that's a mine?"

"Certain sure and 'er's goin' to drift in and strike within yards o' where t'other bugger went off. If you keep 'er in view you can zee the trailin' end o' the cable fallin' away from the bracket."

Paul tried again and saw that this was so. The mine was nine-tenths submerged but the trailing cable-end, bent in a wide loop, could be seen threshing mildly in the swirl of the tide a few yards to the right. From here the mine looked almost stationary. Paul said:

"How is the tide, Noah?"

"It turned less'n half an hour ago. Tiz slack out there now but it'll speed up any minute, especially if the wind gets up."

"Do you agree with Smut about where the other mine is likely to strike?"

"Arr I do," Noah said equably, "and a bliddy good job too. The Government'll 'ave to build us a new jetty, as well as pay for all the windows stove in, so us looks like makin' a praper ole profit out of it, dorn us?"

Paul considered. Contact would have to be made with the stranded cutter and a bomb-disposal expert brought ashore. The Naval sub-depot would have to be informed and everybody kept well clear of the beach. That, he supposed, was Constable Voysey's job and, as Noah said, the tide would take care of the cutter in less than an hour. All that was really necessary then was to keep the mine in view and get ready to bolt for cover when it was close inshore. He and Smut could do that and Noah or Jaffsie could get word to the crew of the cutter. The sea was choppy but presented no danger to a dinghy inside the bar.

"Go out and tell those chaps what's happening, Noah," he said, "If necessary bring one of the experts ashore."

Then, noting Noah's crestfallen look, "There's no danger, so long as you keep east of the jetty. Jaffsie will go along with you. You've got a skiff handy, haven't you?"

"Arr, I got a skiff, but they got one too. Why dorn 'em launch it an' row 'emselves ashore?"

"Because they zeen the mine explode and they baint spotted its mate yet," said Smut. "I daresay they'm zittin' cosy till the tide lifts 'em but you do like Squire says. They'm paid for their time and us idden."

Still grumbling Noah and Jaffsie slouched off to the boathouse and Smut, watching them go, muttered, "Baint no more good than a cold hot-dinner. Dan, his brother, would ha' been out there be now."

"I was just thinking the same," said Paul, with a grin and turned up his coat collar, tucking the glasses into his capacious pocket to keep them from misting. "Can you see that mine with your naked eye, Smut?"

"I can now I knows where her's tu."

"Then hang on here while I find Voysey and get him to tell Whinmouth what we're about," and he turned to recross the quay, heading for the rope Voysey had already placed across the High Street as a barrier.

He was only a few yards up the hill when he saw Voysey arguing with a fat woman on the fringe of the crowd and as he advanced the woman broke away, beating aside the constable's restraining hand and descending the slope at a trot. As she came closer he saw who it was, Pansy Willis, "Pansy-Potter-that-was", wife of the blind Home Guard telephonist who was her third husband. Paul had known all Pansy's husbands and had, in fact, been present at two of her weddings, the first to Walt Pascoe, killed by a Turkish sniper under the slopes of Achi Baba and later in the war to Dandy Timberlake, who had sired one of her children when she was still married to Walt. Despite promiscuity in and out of wedlock he had always regarded her as the best of the Potter girls. She had been a good wife to the ailing Dandy, a good mother to her children, and a real comfort to the near-helpless Willis in his middle-age. As she came slopping down the hill he noticed, even from a distance, that she was not her usual brash self and was clearly in some kind of distress for as she ran up to him she clawed at him for support, sobbing for breath and unable, for a moment, to utter more than a series of inarticulate sounds. He said, steadying her, "What is it, Pansy? What's the matter?" and Pansy, half reeling, gasped, "My Alf—I just heard—he's out there in that ole fort. *Do* something for God's sake, *send* someone out for him bevore 'er bleeds to death or drowns!"

For a moment Paul took it for granted that she was hysterical and talking nonsense, but when, writhing in his grasp, she pointed distractedly to the wrecked jetty, he realised that she might have information nobody had yet passed to him.

"*Alf is still in the post?* He was on duty when it happened?"

"They only just told me, the bliddy thickheads!" she wailed. "I took un over there when I come off duty in the bar and when the big bang come, and I see what happened, Nell Tremlett tells me he come ashore half an hour zince. But 'er didden, 'er coulden 'ave, because 'er baint home, an' where else could 'er be? I asked around an' nobody zeen him, *nobody!* He's out there, I know he is, and if he baint hurt he'll stumble an' vall among they ole piles!"

Paul said, "If he's there we'll get him. You're quite sure he was on duty when it happened?"

"Zertain sure. He was working on his ole switchboard. Fred Olver was going for him when it went off but then that vool of a Nell Tremlett told us he's come on back on his own. He could do that so long as he had the hand rail but 'er coulden have, or he'd *be* here, woulden 'er?"

It all seemed logical, the kind of mix-up that might easily occur in the few moments after a violent explosion. It was a case, Paul reflected grimly, of everybody assuming everyone else had done the obvious and as for Nell Tremlett, nobody would trust her identification for she had worn pebble glasses since she was a child. On balance it seemed that Pansy's fears were justified but was there time to check? In a matter of twenty minutes or so the surviving mine would be alongside the jetty and projecting underwater beams, splintered by the first explosion, would probably touch it off before it reached the main structure. If that happened, given that Willis had survived the first blast, his chances of surviving a second in the weakened structure of the block-house were not impressive.

"Let me think a minute, Pansy. There's another mine out there and the Naval boat can't reach it. Give me a minute to think."

She stopped talking and gesticulating, forcing herself to wait. She had acknowledged him tribal chief of the Valley for more than forty years and her faith was just about equal to the strain. His mind began to conjure with priorities, balancing the risks and the time element involved, but he realised at once that he could not do such a complicated sum alone. He needed the help and advice of a man of action and it would have to be Smut, for he could not imagine a man of Noah Williams' calibre undertaking the extremely delicate task of interposing between mine and jetty, and holding the boat steady while somebody searched the blockhouse and brought Willis out if he was alive.

He said briefly, "Come with me, Pansy. Smut and I will think of something, but there's no time to go asking for volunteers, no time at all," and together they hurried through the rain to the quayside opposite the jetty where Smut was still standing like a sentinel, his back to the village. In a few words he explained the situation and for once, having no constructive ideas and still not fully convinced by her story, he was content to leave it to a man who had been in and out of trouble the whole of is life.

Smut said, sucking his lips, "She's right. She must be right. Alf is mazed about that switchboard and he's out there all right if he baint backalong and he baint or I'd have seen him. Well then, there's two ways o' goin' at it, Squire, and tiz for you to decide. Do us go out an' fend off that bliddy Easter egg by catchin' hold o' the cable, or do us bank everything on bridging that gap and fishing Alf ashore bevore 'er strikes? Tiz one or the other, baint it?"

"No, it's both," Paul said for Smut's clear presentation of alternatives had aired his mind so that he began to form the basis of a plan. It wasn't much of a plan and he didn't think he had time to elaborate it. The mine was now appreciably closer the end of the jetty, rolling gently in the rising tide, and out of the corner of his eye he could see Noah and Jaffsie on the point of launching their skiff some seventy yards west of where they stood. He called, at the top of his voice, "Not there! Bring her this side!" and when Noah straightened himself and looked bewildered, he cupped his hands and roared, "Over here, man! Pick it up and carry it!" and his urgency must have conveyed itself to them for they bent and raised the light skiff as he turned to Smut and said, "If Noah and me can get to the blockhouse could you give us a few extra minutes by catching that trailing cable-end and stopping the drift? It's asking a lot I know, but there's no other way."

Pansy spoke up and Paul noticed that resignation had taken the place of panic in her voice. "If he won't, I will," but Smut said sourly, "Dornee talk so bliddy daft. You'd sink the skiff wi' your weight." Then, with a half-grin, "I'll do it but I doan reckon I could on me lonesome. It'll need two and it'll have to be Jaffsie. Anyways, I'd sooner him than his father."

"Supposing they refuse?"

"You leave the persuading to me, Squire. They'll back down on a gentleman."

By the time he had said this Noah and his son were within thirty yards, both bent under the weight of the skiff and oars. Smut hurried over and intercepted them and they lowered their burden to the ground. Pansy said, "What can I do then? I got to do *something*."

"You can tell the Constable what's happening and ask for volunteers if there are any able-bodied men in that crowd back there. Where are the nearest ladders, long ladders?"

"Back o' the pub, the boss keeps a twenty-rung in the yard in case o' fire. There's rope too if you need it, in the bran tub. Shall I show'ee?"

"I'll find them. Go up and tell Voysey and see if you can get someone to help, but I can't wait for them. We'll have to do the best we can right now."

She scuttled off into the High Street as the three men approached, Noah looking more thoughtful than Paul had ever seen him look although his boy Jaffsie was wearing the same slack grin.

"You knows what youm at, Squire," Noah said flatly, and Paul snapped, "Have you got a better plan? If you have, speak up. Every second counts."

"There baint a better plan," Noah said slowly. "Us've no choice, neither one of us. All the same—" and here he glowered at Smut, "there was no bliddy call for him to threaten me. You doan reckon I would have left Alf to get

244

blowed to tatters, do 'ee? I'd ha' done *something*. I'd ha' *tried!*"

The man's unaccustomed dignity shamed them both and Paul's memory, rippling back across the years, saw him not as Noah, the village layabout with the half-idiot son, but as all the dead Williamses who had plied their trade from this spot and lay in a string of two-tier graves in the churchyard, all but Tom and Dan, whose bones were coral now in the hull of a drowned battleship.

"There's a long ladder in The Raven yard," began Paul, "you and I could . . ." but Noah, still glowering, made a sudden, emphatic gesture and growled, "Bugger the ladder! You an' Smut can zee to that end of it. Me'n Jaffsie'll come in from the Bluff zide and zee if us can ketch that cable-end and hold un off for a spell, but fer Christ's sake doan hang about, Maister. The scour's getting stronger every minute an' us'll have our work cut out as it is. Come on Jaffsie, us'll launch un from the far zide o' the breakwater."

He and the youth picked up the skiff and marched off without another word and Smut, looking as chastened as Paul had ever seen him, drew his hand across his mouth without comment. They stood there long enough to see father and son crash down the shingle bank beyond the breakwater and then, turning their backs on the sea, they ran together through the open gates of The Raven yard.

II

The ladder was there, leaning against the roof of the old coach-house but Paul saw at a glance that it would be as much as they could do to carry it. They dragged it out and were emerging on to the quay when Voysey bustled up and behind him Fred Olver and Pansy. Behind Pansy was a tall Negro wearing the fatigue dress of the U.S. Army and Paul never did discover how he came to be there at that particular time but was grateful for his strength on his end of the ladder. In a staggering little group they ran diagonally across the quay to the short stretch of runway that sloped down to the jetty and it was only when they had begun to pick their way through the rubble that Paul remembered the boat. The rain was falling steadily now and visibility was shortening but the skiff was well in view, making its wide approach sweep to the west in choppy water. Without the glasses Paul could see Jaffsie at the oars and the thickset figure of Noah at the tiller. The mine was perhaps a hundred yards offshore, approximately equidistant between the boat and the blockhouse.

Voysey, notwithstanding his uniform, was awaiting a lead and it was Smut who gave it.

"If they catch and hold the bugger we can take our time. If they don't we'll never make it," he said.

"They'll catch it," Paul said and suddenly he had a vivid recollection of Noah's expression the moment before he bent to lift the stern of the boat. For the first time since Pansy had accosted him he felt confident of extricating Willis without the sacrifice of lives.

The ladder, long and cumbersome as it was, was too short to bridge the gap blown in piers and planking by the mine. The best they could do—and this was Voysey's suggestion—was to lower one end into the debris and rest the other on the last section of crossbeams where the jetty had been sliced as by a knife. The ladder then lay at an angle of about forty-five degrees and the approach beyond, across a tangled mass of beams and iron supports, was negotiable to an active man.

Voysey said, with a briskness that failed to conceal an exasperated dismay, "Do we all go over? And if he's there how do we get him down? He's not only blind, he's almost certainly unconscious or badly injured."

"We got to find him first," Smut said, but then the Negro private spoke up and Paul was surprised by the ordinariness of his voice, as though he had half-expected him to speak like a coloured character in *Huckleberry Finn.*

"I'll go across and poke around some," he said quietly. "Then I'll call for help, maybe."

They all looked at him with varying degrees of astonishment but he did not await their sanction or encouragement. Without even crouching he descended the angled ladder and picked his way over the rubble to the canting wall of the blockhouse. In a few seconds he had passed out of view behind the structure and Paul at once forgot him, turning to peer through the enclosing trailers of mist at the skiff.

It was no more than forty to fifty yards east of them now and being held almost stationary by an occasional flick of the oars. Noah was lying face down and full length in the stern, his gumbooted feet braced against the thwart on which Jaffsie sat, his arms, spread like an advancing wrestler's, projecting over the rudder-bar, almost as though he intended playing catch-as-catch-can with the black, spiralling object that bobbed and lifted about ten yards nearer the jetty. Smut, Voysey and the other man, Fred Olver, stared down at the scene as they might have gazed at some fantastic feat being performed for their entertainment in a circus tent. Nobody said anything. Everyone's concentration was riveted to the strange, crablike posture of the blubbery man in the skiff. They did not even shift their gaze to the mine. Their eyes were on Noah Williams and his half-crooked embrace of nothing.

They were brought out of this semi-trance by the Negro, hailing them against the wind from a projecting beam at the extreme right of the blockhouse. He was standing there silhouetted against the grey sky, holding Willis in his arms and his posture, Paul thought, was wildly improbable and grotesquely divorced from workaday life. It belonged in the coloured illustration of an adventure book he had read as a boy, something by Henty or Fenimore Cooper.

"He's alive and out cold," the Negro called, and forgetting Noah as readily as he had forgotten the American a moment before Paul followed Smut and Voysey down the ladder, leaving Fred Olver at the apex to steady it in readiness for the ascent. Just as he passed below the level of the debris Paul saw Noah's left hand flutter as he laid hold of the shredded length of cable. The boat was then no more than a few yards from the mine and the mine less than three boat lengths away from the jetty.

III

They did not relieve the Negro of his burden. He seemed to be a man of unusual strength endowed with an acrobat's sense of balance. With Voysey and Smut alongside him he picked his way over the rubble like a cat, needing no more than a touch or two on the elbow when his feet found the lower rungs of the ladder. Because of this Paul had leisure to glance through the shattered framework on his left and watch Jaffsie brace himself against the oars, so that the skiff swung slowly round in an arc and began heading out to sea.

It moved, Paul thought, with a terrible dragging slowness, so that he roused himself and shouted to the recumbent Noah, "Let her go and get ashore, man!" but Noah, if he heard, paid no attention to this advice but continued to sprawl with his face almost in the water and the splayed cable clutched in both hands. The mine, checked in its spiralling drift towards the end of the wrecked jetty, followed unwillingly, clearing the last beam by no more than a few yards. Then, ascending the ladder as one of a bunched group, Paul had no opportunity to follow its progress. Other people, Pansy among them, had joined Olver at the top of the ladder and Willis was lifted clear, Voysey venting his relief in a roar of disapproval as he realised the shore end of the jetty was now lined with figures, women and children among them. They all scuttled away with Voysey herding them like sheep, and the big Negro must have gone with them for suddenly Paul was alone with Smut watching the last scene in the drama as Noah, fifty yards seaward of the jetty, lowered the cable-end back into the water and rolled round facing his son who at once set a slanting course for the breakwater.

Smut, watching intently, voiced a thought that was in Paul's mind.

"He's got zense as well as nerve," he said grudgingly. "He's leaving her where the tide'll carry her 'way along the beach. Er'll blow off this zide o' the landslip and do no harm to nobody, except the gulls mebbe." But then, sensing perhaps that this was a wholly inadequate acknowledgment of what the Williamses had just achieved, he added, "Youm so bliddy wrong about people, Squire. I knowed Noah zince he was a tacker, and I woulden ha' bet a farden on him tackling a job like that, never mind doing it so quietlike. Buggered if I won't stand him a pint tonight if he shows up."

"You won't," Paul said, "I'll do any standing that's to be done, and it'll be a quart if he can take it," but at this Smut's grin returned to him for the first time that afternoon.

"You don't want to worry on that score," he said. "Noah baint a bible-puncher, like the rest of his kin. Noah Williams could drink the bliddy Raven dry if you give him the chance."

Huddling into their damp clothes they crossed the quay, their feet scrunching on shattered glass.

CHAPTER THIRTEEN

OUTPOST INCIDENT

I

RUMBLE's fears that the Valley might suffer further air attacks on account of its nearness to Normandy proved unfounded. By now the Luftwaffe was a spent force and although V-bombs, and later rockets, continued to keep Londoners on the jump, the provinces seemed to be groping their way back to a peacetime routine in that final winter of the war.

The Royal Marine camp was still in being but its complement had shrunk to a mere hundred or so. Many of those who had stamped and shouted on the square were now in Holland or the Far East, and not a few lay in graves beside the Scheldt, or along the approaches to Caen. Hit-and-run raiders were never seen now, only Polish-manned aircraft skimming over the coast like little silver hornets. Simon wrote saying he had an admin. job at Eindhoven. Rumble, travelling by slow stages, was on his way home across the Indian Ocean. Andy and his friend Ken Shawcrosse were still based in the tall Victorian houses at Coombe Bay but more often than not were away, leaving Margaret and the baby Vanessa to their own devices.

Claire, supposing her to be lonely, invited her to come and join Mary and the other children at the Big House, but she declined. It would be a nuisance, she said, to keep returning whenever Andy came home after one of his mysterious forays up and down the country. His Development Company was already in business and a little of his pre-war zest had returned to him. Margaret and the family generally welcomed this, but none of them cared much for his crony, Shawcrosse. They employed a blonde secretary, a hearty girl with a warm, built-in smile and Margaret hinted to Claire that they probably shared her as mistress as well as stenographer. Anticipating Claire's protest she said, "Now wait. Who the hell am I to complain of that? Besides, if it sweetens his temper I'll tuck them up in bed if they ask me nicely."

Claire said nothing. More than ever she was beginning to wonder if her brief essay in mending and making-do had not been a failure after all.

II

The valley did witness one further skirmish but it was between allies and took place one frosty morning in the Home Farm hayloft, whither Prudence Honeyman (née Pitts) had retired to settle for her PX goodies. It was a brisk, scandalous engagement, reminiscent of a much earlier era in the Valley when people made a rare fuss about this kind of thing, but although it did not involve a member of the Craddock family its repercussions were instrumental in breaking the long Honeyman tradition at Home Farm and causing Paul to redraw farm boundaries that had remained static for a generation.

One of the few Americans left in the Valley after the pre-D-Day exodus was Ed Morrisey, the barrel-chested sergeant in charge of the sub-depot in the goyle, about half-way between the landslip and Coombe Bay. He was on familiar terms with the Honeymans, for their's was the nearest farm and when, one morning in February, he received instructions to pack up and rejoin his unit, he decided to make a final attempt to collect dues skilfully withheld by Prudence for over a year.

What he did not know, it seemed, was that Prudence's husband Nelson had been keeping a close watch upon his regular and so far frustrated attempts to exact payment from the beneficiary, for Nelson had been married to Prudence for twelve humdrum years and knew her rather better than Eddy or anyone else in the Valley.

It had not been a successful marriage, although its failure was a secret from all but Paul, who knew most things of importance concerning his tenants, enough, in fact, to cause Claire to wonder why he was so unfamiliar with the domestic ebb and flow of his own family. The answer to this was that Paul had never taken his sons and daughters very seriously, whereas he automatically accepted responsibility for his tenants, and had done ever since buying the estate.

In the late nineteen-twenties, when she was growing up at Hermitage under the tolerant eye of Henry and her mother Gloria, Prudence Pitts had been the most sought-after girl in the Valley and at thirty-four she still had a good figure, bold, snapping eyes, and a mop of red-gold hair. Gloria had often despaired of getting her safely off her hands but then, to everyone's surprise, she had suddenly decided to marry Nelson, only son of old Honeyman, and one of the most conscientious younger men in the Valley. Nelson, slight, earnest and unoriginal, had been no more than a servitor at the court of Prudence but he was shrewd and it did not take him long to discover that the source of his luck was a false alarm on her part. Like the Potter girls before her Prudence had sampled most of the young men between the Whin and the Bluff before she settled on one in particular.

She was not, however, possessed of the Potter temperament, regarding men as swains and providers and not the means of passing a pleasant hour under the stars. To that extent she learned her lesson early in life and never made the same mistake again. She remained a flirt and many a man who had business at Home Farm in the last ten years had been encouraged to try his luck but, as in the case of Ed Morrisey, the prize eluded them. A kiss, a hasty fumble, a subdued giggle, was all they got in exchange for time and capital invested, and Sergeant Morrisey had been a steady investor since the first occasion Prudence had snapped her eyes at him and told him how she yearned for what she called "sweets" and he called "candy".

He brought her candy. Boxes and boxes of candy, together with "K" rations and towels and sheets representing scores of clothing coupons. He brought her tinned turkey at Christmas time and, when these yielded no more than a kiss or two in the barn, he produced several pairs of nylon stockings, now accepted in the Valley as a kind of down-payment on defloration. It remained, however, a strictly one-way trade. The missionary continued to distribute his beads but the native remained relatively hostile.

Morrisey was not desperate. He had access to several more liberal-minded girls in Whinmouth but by February 1945 he had come to believe that his manhood was at stake and decided to make one last attempt to vindicate it. He packed a large carton, choosing goods that were unobtainable, even in a community containing black market experts like Smut Potter and Jumbo Bellchamber, and drove his jeep over the sandhills to the Home Farm strawyard.

He did not make the mistake of telling Prudence that he was posted, or that this was his final visit. Indeed, he hinted at vast bounties awaiting her, underlining the hint by declaring that rationing would continue in Britain long after the cessation of hostilities. Prudence was impressed in spite of herself, both by the magnitude of his gifts and this threat of further shortages. In addition his visit had been nicely timed for Nelson, moments before Ed had appeared in the yard, had told her he was driving to Whinmouth to apply for extra feed coupons for his herd. She handled the packaged cartons as another woman might have handled pearls. "It's swell of you, Eddy," she said, "real swell!" Like all other women in the Valley she had imbibed American idioms along with American PX goods.

Eddy said, "It's cold out here. Let's go in the barn, honey."

They always went into the barn when he arrived with a carton but so far this had proved Eddy's terminus for Prudence was careful to leave the big door swinging open. She did so now but when he put his arm round her and kissed her in a way that Nelson had never kissed despite a good deal of encouragement on her part, she felt a bit of a niggard and wondered, a little apprehensively, how long this trade could be expected to continue at the present rate of exchange. She said, to his gratification, "I don't know how I could have coped this last year without you around, Eddy!" And then, "Did you pass Nelson on the way over here?"

"Yeah!" he said, hopefully, "heading towards the camp in his jalopy."

He would have added his persuasions then but reasoned that if an invitation was coming it was far better it should come from her, so he drew back a little, saying, "You sure are cute, baby! And you smell nice, too!"

"It's that perfume you gave me, the bottle your buddy brought back from France." Then, very cautiously, "Did Nelson see *you?*"

"I guess not. He was going in the other direction and all of a quarter mile up the road."

"Then let's go up the ladder," Prudence said, and was

surprised to find herself trembling. Eddy was getting on for forty and his poor condition had been a factor in him being left behind when the Rangers moved out, but he was up that vertical ladder in five seconds flat. There was plenty of hay up there and it was warm and dark, with no more than a shaft or two of winter sunshine penetrating cracks in the weatherboarding. She said, "You're a naughty boy, you really are! And don't think I believe a word about you being a bachelor!" Then, with a directness that rather shocked him, "You'll have to be quick before they wonder where we've gone."

Nelson had seen the jeep breast the last of the dunes, spotting it in his driving mirror as he approached the final bend in the farm track leading across the fields to the river road. It was no more than a glimpse but enough to decide his course of action. He rounded the bend, stopped, reversed and got out of the lorry, standing under the wall to plan his next move.

It was not the first time he had kept watch on them. Once or twice he had seen them embrace, his eye glued to the hingecrack of the barn door, but he had not disturbed them. A man could not be expected to stake his entire future on a kiss or two and a bit of scuffling behind an open barn door, but somehow, today, he felt very uneasy, having heard on the Valley grapevine that the U.S. depot on the beach was due to close. He left the vehicle where it was and went through the door in the park wall and across the western paddock, taking care to stay the far side of the hedge. Then, seeing no one in the yard but noting the bonnet of the jeep projecting from behind the barn, he moved quietly behind the byre and thus reached his usual observation post.

Nothing came within his range of vision except a pile of tools, a few bales of straw, and a muck-spreader, and this puzzled him so that he wondered for a moment if Prudence was settling accounts in the kitchen. Then he heard a stifled laugh and it came from immediately above, telling him that on this occasion Sergeant Morrisey had enlarged his bridgehead. He crept inside the barn and listened at the foot of the ladder. What he heard resolved his next action.

Among the tools in the corner of the barn was a mattock with a loose shaft and when he laid hold of it the head and shaft parted without so much as a rattle. Nelson was slightly built and below medium height and although, by now, he was fully charged with indignation, he knew that he was no match for the stocky sergeant. God, they said, looked favourably upon a worthy cause but there was another saying that He also sided with the big battalions and Nelson was a realist. He tightened his hold on the mattock shaft and ascended the vertical ladder step by step, taking his time about it and testing each rung for creaks.

Neither of them heard him and neither was positioned to see his head rise slowly above the level of the floor. He was more or less prepared for what he saw under the sloping eaves but it gave him a nasty jolt to have his gloomiest suspicions so convincingly confirmed. Prudence, it appeared, was at last giving full value for money and from the glimpse he got of her in his rush across the floor she was not finding the discharge of the debt irksome. Fortunately for her Eddy was the more exposed of the two and the heavy end of the shaft descended before either was aware they had company. Eddy shouted a picturesque oath and achieved a quick double roll, so that the second blow, aimed at his head, glanced off his padded shoulder and struck the back of his hand. Like a dancing demon returning to the pit in a miracle play he hopped the length of the loft and then, to Nelson's amazement, disappeared altogether having shot feet first through the hatch that was partially masked by hay.

He fell with a terrible crash and had not his exit been vertical he might have broken his neck. As it was he broke his right leg and lay bellowing like a calf, adding his yells to the piercing screams of Prudence who had somehow struggled to her knees and was embracing Nelson's gumbooted calves in the attitude of a drunkard's wife in a Victorian Temperance print.

It was a dramatic gesture but quite unnecessary. Nelson, appalled by the sergeant's yells and also by the speed of his exit, had no thought of striking her but was concerned only with the possibility of having committed murder. He was almost sure that he had and in the moment of terrible panic that followed he saw himself standing in the dock at Paxtonbury Assizes pleading the unwritten law. Then he managed to break free from his wife, leaving her clutching a pair of muddy gumboots, and the relief of seeing Sergeant Morrisey conscious and rocking himself to and fro at the foot of the ladder was stunning. He said, briefly, "Get down out of here you bloody whore and fetch Bernard and Jock. Say we were skylarking and he slipped. I'm going to 'phone ambulance and Squire."

She stared up at him and he thought he had never seen ̣nybody look so ridiculous, a woman in her mid-thirties, ̣neeling on a truss of hay embracing a pair of gumboots. Her skirt was rucked up to her thighs and her suspender clips were broken so that her stockings, stockings brought her by Eddy, had wrinkled down to her shins. Straw was clinging to her disordered hair and all the time she knelt there she continued to scream, so that it was not necessary to summon Bernard and Jock for they came running, together with Nelson's aged pigman, Walt Davey, who was thus able to give a lively account of the tableau that night in the bar of The Raven at Coombe Bay.

"There 'er was," Walt was to declare, "screaming 'er ade off, like 'er was mazed! And ther was the Yank, hollering bliddy murder at the bottom of the ladder! You never zeed zuch a carry-on, and then down comes Young Maister, white as a vish-belly, steps right over the Yank like he was a bale o' straw, and rins out to the vone! Well, us straightened him out as best we could, and Bernard put a splint on his leg, and then down comes the missis showing all 'er's got, and not giving a damn neither for 'er was that scared. 'Er stood looking at him for a minute without so much as a wink 'an then 'er zees us looking at *her* an' suddenly whips round and out and that's the last I zeed of 'er."

It was the best story told in the bar for a generation. They plied him with cider and he went on to describe the removal of the cursing, bellowing Yank to the Marine sickbay, but he was unable to tell them of the subsequent interview between Squire Craddock and Nelson Honeyman for it took place at the Big House, whither Nelson went as soon as the injured sergeant had been driven away. The result of that conversation, however, and others that followed it, was brought home to him when it became known that Nelson Honeyman and his wife—"Prudence-Pitts-that-was" as the Valley folk called her in the manner they referred to all girls who had married locally—were breaking their tenancy and taking a sheep farm in Dorset, and that Home Farm would now be run by Squire Craddock or one of his relatives.

It was no light decision for the badly shaken Nelson but although the Squire did his best to dissuade him from leaving his mind was made up by the certainty that the story had already passed into Valley legend, and also perhaps, by the attitude of his father-in-law, Henry Pitts of Hermitage.

Henry, called in at the second conference, was abruptly silenced by Paul when he broke out, "Tiz all a bliddy fuss over nought! You catches her under one o' they bliddy vorriners, an' you does what any man would do, lambasts him with a pick handle an' throws the bugger downstairs. But you forgot something after all. You didn't give my bliddy maid a tannin' 'er woulden forget in a hurry, and because you didden, and because it's too late in the day for me to do it, you'll never have the upper hand of 'er now. Giddon, when I was your age . . ."

But this was as far as he got, for Paul said, bleakly, "Hold your tongue, Henry. This is 1945 not 1895 and if Nelson lays a finger on his wife it won't do his case any good if the American prosecutes. He could, and probably would if he thought Prudence would back him up in court! Personally I think you're wrong to clear out, Nelson. These things are soon forgotten I can assure you, but for God's sake don't take it out on her until he's out of the country." He had never liked Nelson as much as his father but it saddened him to see a long family tradition broken by such a stupid incident. He went on, "Why don't you leave the American to me? I'll get in touch with his unit and tell them the facts and in the meantime you can think it over."

Nelson said glumly, "This Dorset farm is going cheap. You won't be able to buy it for double the money when the war is over and I'd like to get clear away from here, Squire. By now everybody knows what happened and everybody's sniggering behind my back."

"O' course they be," Henry muttered, "but they'd zoon stop if you took a beanpole to my maid like I said—all right Squire, us knows times 'ave changed, and everyone along with 'em, but I'm 'er father and she was always a bliddy handful, so why can't I have my say zame as you two?"

"Because it's a damn silly say," Paul told him, "and you keep away from her, do you hear?" Then, to Nelson, "Has she agreed to go to Dorset?"

"Not yet. I haven't told her. She's keeping out o' my way as you can imagine, but—well, I'd like you to discuss it with her while I'm seeing the solicitors. I daresay you could talk more sense into her than I could at the moment."

"All right if that's what you want," Paul said, although by

no means relishing the task and he left with a warning nod at Henry and crossed the paddock to the farm where he found Prudence drinking port and lemon in the kitchen. He said, briefly, "Nelson's been up at the house and told me and your father what happened over here. He wants to leave and take a bigger farm in Dorset. It seems he's had his eye on it for some time. How do you feel about backing him?"

She looked, he thought, unhappy and thoroughly ashamed of herself, and suddenly he remembered that she was one of his numerous godchildren. She said, slowly, "I'll make a fresh start with him if he wants to try." Then, "We've never really hit it off, Squire. I only married Nelson because I thought I was in the family way. To my mind that was worse than what happened with Eddy, but when he realised the truth he never made this kind of rumpus. Can you explain that?"

"It's very easy to explain," Paul said, recollecting that he had always had his suspicions about the marriage. "The first was a private matter but this makes him a Valley laughing stock and that's why he's determined to get out while he's got the chance." His resentment for her moderated as it always did when he was not faced with cant. These people in their early thirties were subject to pressures that had not been exerted on his own generation. The first war had damaged the structure of the old civilisation but it had not rotted it, as had the Depression and the years of drift that had resulted in Hitler. Back in 1917 and 1918 one had always felt one was fighting to preserve something worth preserving, that once things had settled down everything would be much the same, but this wasn't true any longer. The whole fabric of community and family life was in tatters and there did not seem to be much hope of repairing it. Would it seem such a dastardly thing to her to betray a colourless husband like Nelson Honeyman, trading a few sweaty moments in a loft for an armful of household goods that no housewife in the Valley would have wanted thirty years ago? He didn't think so. This kind of thing was in the atmosphere one breathed nowadays. It was in politics and business. It showed in the black-market traffic of men like Smut Potter and Henry, and in the business activities of his own son, Andy. Who the hell was he to condemn her for copulating with a Yank, when his own daughter-in-law had done the same thing with her brother-in-law and the passage of a year or so had resulted in his own wife's passive acceptance of the situation?

He said, "What's that muck you're drinking? Haven't you got a real drink to offer me?" and she crossed to the big dresser, returning with half a bottle of Scotch and poured him a few fingers.

"I suppose this is a bit more lease-lend?" he said glumly, and she said it wasn't but the last of half a dozen that Nelson had got from Stacey, the Whinmouth wine merchant, in exchange for a crate of eggs and a few pounds of butter. The information widened his area of tolerance and he said:

"That Yank could sue for assault and Nelson would find himself in serious trouble," but she replied, "Rubbish! Eddy would have to cite me as a witness and can you see me forgetting to tell the magistrates he got me up in that loft on false pretences?" He chuckled, then straightened his face. "I don't want you and Nelson to go. His father was farming here when I came and he was the third Honeyman to work the Home Farm. Will you be any happier among strangers?"

"That's for Nelson to decide," she said. "One farm is as good as another for my money."

There it was again, this rootlessness, this yawning renunciation of tradition and the claims of a community, and even Rumble had been infected by it to some extent. It was frightening to a man who would be sixty-six in June.

"What is it you *want*?" he asked, suddenly, "not just you but the whole lot of you who grew up here between the wars? What *means* anything to you?" She looked at him steadily and he was reminded of her great strapping mother, Gloria, whom he had seen courted, married and buried.

"Time to play," she said, with a candour that surprised him, "I don't seem to have had any since I was a kid. Soon I'll be forty and then what? Somewhere there must be fun around and I want a piece of it."

"What kind of fun?" he persisted.

"Every kind. A car that's not half a hearse. Travel maybe—there's lots of places I'd like to see before I die, good food in my belly after being made to feel like a criminal for using half a dozen of my own eggs in a pudding, and—well, let it pass!"

"No," he said, "we won't, what else?"

She looked across at him slyly, with a gleam of Henry's mischief in her eyes. "I suppose to feel a real woman now and again," she admitted. "Poor old Nelson, bless his heart, never had it in him to succeed in that direction."

"Did anyone else? Anyone special?"

"No, or if they did I've forgotten. I don't expect you to believe me but this was the first time I went off the rails. Really off them, I mean."

He believed her. Deep down, he suspected, she was as loyal as most of the young wives about the Valley, but she was also in open rebellion against the theft of her youth, not only by the war years but by the dullness of Young Nelson, and as if confirming this she looked at him with another flash of her father's mischief and said, "The war on one side, Squire, life isn't all acre yield and tractor hours, is it? We all know it isn't with you and God knows, you're dedicated enough."

"Now just how am I to interpret that?" he asked, smiling at her impudence.

"Well," she said frankly, "you've got a long family and you don't have any trouble with Mrs. Craddock."

He laughed openly at this and she laughed too, so that the tension that had been present in the room all but disappeared. He found his sympathy for her mounting. She was one of the prettiest girls the Valley had ever produced and he caught himself contemplating the opportunities Nelson must have neglected. "By George," he thought, "she's so frustrated I believe she'd welcome a man my age if I went the right way about it. That would really set the Valley by the ears!" But then, checking himself with a silent, half-humorous admonition, he said, "You can hardly expect me to give Nelson that kind of advice at his age. Do you think this has a bearing on you not having any family?"

"It might have," she said, "but I can't honestly say I feel deprived in that respect. It's a lot more complicated. I had a pretty good time before I was married and I've always gone out of my way to dodge that dowdiness that seems to creep up on most Valley women the moment they've hooked a man bringing home good money." A kind of defiance entered her voice as she stood up, leaning her weight against the black oak overmantel. "Men still look at me the way they used to ten years ago. Even men of settled habit do. But Nelson doesn't. I don't mean by that he isn't masculine, but there's something guarded about him. Maybe it's a Puritan streak, although some so-called Puritans I've met ..." and then reticence caught up with her and she completed the sentence with a shrug.

259

He stood up, feeling the conversation had gone as far as it could without some kind of deeper, personal involvement on his part, but honesty obliged him to make some final attempt at summarisation.

"Look here, Prudence," he said, "the real solution to this rests with you. This thing has been a hell of a shock to Nelson—it would be to any man who valued his self-respect— but it needn't be final and it could even be beneficial in the long run. He's a dour chap, like his father and grandfather, but he's very fond of you. I'd say more. He's damned proud of you, even if he hasn't shown it until he belted that Yank. You've been doing it effectively since you wore long plaits. My advice to you is—lay it on thick. If you don't feel any real remorse make him think you do, but don't overdo it either. That is, don't adopt the *mea culpa* approach. Go for him as soon as he gets back here and keep on going for him. Don't give him time to brood. Give him what you've never given him on account of his inhibitions. Make him sit up and say, 'My God, see what I've been missing!' Does that make sense to you?"

She was smiling openly now, not so much at the homily but at the exasperation with which it was delivered.

"It makes a bundle of sense," she said, "and what can I lose anyway?" Then, more soberly, "Do you go around giving this kind of advice to all your tenants?"

"No I don't," he said, relieved at her approach, "but I'm qualified to. In that Yank's shoes, fed up and far from home, I don't suppose I should have cared a damn about the niceties of the situation if I got the come-on sign from a girl like you."

He drained his whisky and moved to the door. "To return to the mundane," he concluded, "try that bigger farm and start fresh in new surroundings. This place will change but not as fast as you seem to want it. Leave Nelson to me and if you do find you're homesick, tell him to write. I daresay you'll come back in the end. Most of them do when they hear the clock ticking."

He went out and back across the paddock feeling better for the exchange. "What's really needed around here is a thorough stocktaking and some new blood," he told himself, "but I'm too old and too set in my ways to bother with it! Let her generation tackle it when they get tired of trapesing!"

PART TWO
CONDITIONAL SURRENDER

CHAPTER ONE

MARCHOUT WITH BANNERS

I

V.E. DAY celebrations, marked by an open-air lunch in Coombe Bay High Street, was the first communal event of the Valley in ten years. It was also, had Paul known it, the last but one of the sponsored, convivial occasions any of them were to witness, for the tradition, notwithstanding the importance of the occasion, was dying and had, indeed begun to decline as long ago as 1935 when the Valley assembled to celebrate the Silver Jubilee of King George and Queen Mary.

In the old days long before the Craddocks settled in the Valley, all national events of this kind were marked by a ritual that was obligatory on the part of every man, woman and child in the area, including babies in arms. Even the semi-feudal Lovells, who had preceded the Craddocks as Squires, had felt obliged to demonstrate local loyalty on national occasions. There had been, so Paul had been told, a very bibulous Trafalgar Supper, a costly (and destructive) Waterloo Bonfire Night, a rustic ball to celebrate the ascension of young Queen Victoria, and even a day of national mourning to mark the death of the Grand Old Duke, in 1852.

In his own time he had celebrated the coronation of King Edward VII with the first social event of his tenure, a grand ball and firework display in the grounds of the Big House, and there had been an even more spectacular jamboree and sports rally to mark King George's ascension, nine years later. Because he was essentially a traditionalist he went to some trouble and expense to organise this kind of festivity, a Victory Sports Meeting in June 1919 to celebrate the Treaty Signing, and the Silver Jubilee open-air banquet that really was a banquet and not a prolonged snack like today's event, but by 1945 sophisticated changes, and an accompanying falling off in enthusiasm, were not lost upon him and were not wholly the result of rationing restrictions.

For one thing, whereas all the other celebrations had been based on the Big House this one was staged in Coombe Bay, an indication that the fulcrum of the Valley had already shifted. For another, there was an atmosphere of enforced jollity about this event that had been absent from its predecessors. In 1911, for instance, he himself had taken part in a chariot race round the Home Farm meadows and teams of athletes, wrestlers and horsemen had travelled from as far away as Paxtonbury to compete for local prize money. There were no Paxtonbury folk here today and even the coastal town of Whinmouth was conducting its own celebrations in the square. Among those present, dutifully making merry at the long trestle tables, were many strangers, mostly evacuees from bombed cities, or families who had sought the imagined security of the Valley during the Baedekker raids of 1942 and 1943. Thirty, even twenty years ago, Paul had known everyone between the Heronslea boundary and the Bluff by their given names. Today he recognised barely one-third of those present, and when his eye did find a familiar face among the paper-hatted revellers it only reminded him of older faces and the half-remembered eccentricities of tenants and craftsmen now lying in neat rows behind Ypres, or in the churchyard behind the eastern façade of High Street cottages.

The hard core of the old community was well represented. Henry Pitts was there, guzzling cider by the quart, smiling his slow, rubbery smile, and exulting over the recent demise of Mussolini and his final public appearance on a lamp-bracket in Milan. Smut Potter and his French wife Marie were there, the one looking as waggish as in his poaching days, the other an unsmiling, rustling, black-draped mountain, as though she was still in mourning for her country's miserable performance in 1940. Bon-Bon, their only child was there too, home on leave from Germany where, they said, he had been one of the first to enter Belsen and had had the pleasure of locking one of the camp guards in a large refrigerator and forgetting all about him until the following morning. Dick Potter, the estate forester's eldest son was there too, miraculously intact after nearly five years in the Royal Armoured

Corps. Among the other tenants Paul saw Francis Willoughby, looking as old and bent as his preacher father had looked in King Edward's reign and Paul, reckoning his age, found to his surprise that he could give him a year or two. Young Eveleigh was present with his grey-haired mother, Connie, and his brother and sister, and so was the arty-crafty family from High Coombe, the elder among them looking disdainfully at this display of chawbaconry. Jumbo Bellchamber and his wife (Violet-Potter-that-was) appeared to be enjoying themselves for Paul heard Violet's shrill laughter and its note took him back more than forty years to a time he had seen her and her wanton sisters making periodical disappearances into the shrubbery on the night of the Coronation supper. Frail old Parson Horsey was still alive to pronounce grace, encouraged by Simon's wife Evie, without whose ministrations, Paul thought, the old chap would have died long since. For the rest there were a few of the old Coombe Bay craftsmen, a Tozer or two, a Stokes or two, but thinly spread among so many townees. His own family was represented by Claire, Rumble Patrick, home at last, his daughter Mary and her two children, and his daughter-in-law Margaret, but Andy was off on one of his piratical land surveys, Whiz was still in India, and Simon was with S.H.A.E.F. Headquarters in Belgium. John, his youngest boy, was also absent, for this was his first term at High Wood and there seemed little point in unsettling him so soon after his arrival.

Toasts were drunk, tables were cleared and blackouts ceremonially burned although this, the constable told him, was premature and could still lead to proceedings in court. As Chairman of the Committee he did his duty but his heart was not in the business. Towards evening, when the dancing began, he voiced his disappointment to Henry Pitts, who was watching the antics of a couple of sixteen-year-olds currently engaged in what looked like an African witch-doctor's dance.

" 'Jiving' they calls it," said Henry, "but it baint dancing be it? Back along, as I remember, there was on'y one point in taking a maid on the dance floor and that was to cuddle 'er up and veel cosylike as you moved around, but they doan zeem to 'ave that in mind, do 'em? They jigs about all over the auction but they stays apart-like as if they was afraid o' catching zummat! I dorn get it Maister, unless they'm workin' up an appetite fer after dark!"

Paul laughed, his first real laugh of the day.

"There's more to it than that, Henry. In our day dancing the polka or the bunny-hop was as close as we ever got to a woman in public and I suppose we took advantage of it. They don't have to watch their step as we did and can indulge in fancy steps if they feel inclined."

He left Henry pondering this and had a word with Young Bon-Bon, Smut's boy, who told him a little of the macabre shambles that had greeted his unit on entering Belsen. "Well, it's done with now, thank God," Paul said, "and I suppose it justifies the war, if that's what is needed. The more publicity it gets the better I'm pleased, but it still staggers me to discover that the Germans I fought against in Flanders could behave in that kind of way. Orientals yes, but not Europeans."

Suddenly he felt the urge to get away from them all and pay the dead of an earlier war the compliment of remembering them on such an occasion. Nobody else would—he could be quite sure of that—so he said to Claire, "When you're ready to go Rumble will drive you back. I'm going to stretch my legs for an hour or so. Don't wait up."

She didn't ask him where he was going because she guessed. She had noticed, earlier in the day, that he was in what she recognised as his "patriarchal mood".

II

Simon, as it happened, was not in Brussels for the celebrations but home in time to witness them in London, having been sent back with a report on repatriated prisoners. He found the responsible department at the War Office disinclined to sacrifice its holiday and attend to him so he wandered off, happily enough, to see the sights if there were any to be seen.

Like his father, he could detect the false note in the orchestra. It suffered, he thought, from its sponsors in rows of government offices along Whitehall where lived the men who had been handing down decrees concerned with lighting restrictions, rationing, careless talk and various other excuses for the exercise of bureaucracy for years on end. Now they had issued a final edict—"You will now celebrate, and no nonsense about it!"

He saw, with interest, a smartly-dressed Aneurin Bevan watching sailors splash in the Trafalgar Square fountains and then made his way towards the Mall where listless-looking crowds were drifting up and down in the hope that the King and Queen would reappear on the balcony of the Palace. There was a good deal of scuffling, some strident laughter, and some uninhibited embracing in Green Park, but the sense of compulsive enjoyment persisted, even when, in Piccadilly Circus, he watched an impromptu strip-tease act on top of some scaffolding over a subway entrance.

The crowd here was very thick and every now and again forlorn little processions, headed by some desperate character, would march away carrying improvised banners and using dustbin lids as drums. He wondered if the absence of real gaiety was due to the shortage of beer in the pubs and decided, sadly, that it probably was, because the English were never very good at spontaneous merry-making and needed at least three pints to shed their inhibitions. He remembered carnivals rather like this in Whinmouth when he was a boy, events that had seemed to revolve around half-a-dozen town drunks dressed as tramps or pierrots, whose antics were solemnly performed in the presence of solemn kerb-watchers. And then he had another thought, wondering if the damp-squib effect could be traced to years of underfeeding and deprivation, to say nothing of broken sleep and bombing. He had been present at the liberation of Brussels and had witnessed rejoicing that verged on hysteria, but then, the Belgians had something to celebrate. If London had been under the Gestapo for five years it was probable that the Cockneys would erupt as joyously as had the people of Paris and some of the other towns en route to the Rhine.

In contemplative mood he went down Haymarket, back to Trafalgar Square and then to Westminster again, where he looked across at the House and noted that a bomb splinter had struck and bent the upraised sword of the equestrian statue of Richard I. The bent sword diverted the current of his thoughts, so that it left the present and doubled back across the plain of history. Richard, he reflected, had no right to be waving a bent sword outside Parliament. The man had never given a thought to England, except as a milch-cow for his Crusade and his ransom. Simon de Montfort had a far better right to that plinth and surely the claims of John Pym, John Hampden and Tom Paine could not be ignored?

He moved along towards the bridge and stopped at the Boadicea statue to look back at the rambling, gothic building, remembering how much energy he had expended in the 'thirties trying to win entry there on behalf of Staffordshire miners, or Newcastle shipyard workers. What, he wondered, had driven him on, apart from the fanaticism of his first wife, Rachel? Had he really believed that a few men like himself, self-committed to the cause of the underprivileged, could change the face of British politics and usher in a new era? Looking back it seemed a futile gesture, for in 1940 it hadn't mattered a damn who was inside to rally the country. After the German breakthrough in the Lowlands everyone except a few eccentrics like Mosley had put their backs into it and here they were at the far end of the tunnel, with Hitler and Mussolini dead, Germany in ruins, and the Hammer and Sickle flying over the Chancellory in Berlin. What the hell would happen now, he wondered? Who would win the next election? And how was anyone going to set about the thankless job of redrawing European boundaries?

Abruptly, as though withdrawing from the argument, he turned away and went down Whitehall towards his Club. Whatever happened in the Commons now was still his business but not, he decided, his responsibility. War had taught him at least one important lesson—to limit his objectives and this, one way or another, was what he had resolved to do as long ago as D-Day whilst awaiting Lovat's Commandos at the Orne bridge. The question was how, and in what particular sphere? He had a degree but he also had a wife, and a child was expected in the autumn. The prospect of more politics, he discovered to his surprise, bored him. The process of disenchantment, beginning nearly ten years ago in Spain, was now complete, so that he could make an unconditional withdrawal from the hustings. He would never fight another election, not even if the party dug him out and offered him a safe seat. And this, he thought, had something to do with the sensation of coming home and was nourished by a yearning for the remoteness of the Valley.

It had been growing on him some time now, ever since the day he had seen Evie bob up from behind that beach-obstruction in Coombe Bay. Something akin to his father's extreme provincialism had seeded itself in him during that leave and had been enlarging its hold all the way from Normandy to the Ruhr. The difficulty was to find a useful place in that withdrawn society, for he knew himself well enough to realise that whatever he did would have to offer something creative. His father had found a life purpose in nursing thirteen hundred acres of English soil but his father, born in the heydey of Victorian imperialism, was not a self-doubter. For his part he could never be satisfied with farming, even in the purely administrative way his father had farmed and down there, in what was still a backward and isolated community, there were very few occupations independent of agriculture and tourism. He thought for a moment of the church, assessing the ready-to-hand advantages of its organisation, but he had no real belief in survival after death and no interest in religious dogma. Medicine did not attract him and neither did the law. One demanded serious dedication, the other an impersonal approach to people which he could never acquire. During his last leave he had discussed all these possibilities with Evie but nothing hopeful had emerged and now, he supposed, he was already half-inclined towards journalism, for at least some journalism was creative and there had been talk of a local paper going up for sale in Whinmouth.

It was, he supposed, within his means if he could persuade Paul to join him as partner, and for a moment the prospect of thundering out editorials about local car parks and sewage projects amused him, even though he saw it as a kind of surrender.

He was still weighing the pros and cons of newspaper proprietorship when he saw the boy, and at once he forgot everything else, for who could fail to be astonished by the sight and sound of a twelve-year-old in a crumpled Eton collar, gazing up at the pediment of Inigo Jones' banqueting hall and chanting,

> "He nothing common did or mean
> Upon that memorable scene
> But laid his head
> Down as on a bed!"

Simon was so struck by the piping voice that he did not immediately connect the quotation with the laughter that followed but then, looking closer into the eddy of pedestrians flowing down from the Cenotaph, he saw that the boy was one of a party of schoolboys in charge of a dried out little nut of a man, and the schoolmaster, catching his eye, said without irony, "Rawlins is speaking up on behalf of the majority. At his age all of us are Cavaliers! Reaction shows in the Fifth!"

Suddenly realising that he was lonely Simon smiled and begged to differ, admitting that he had been unrepentantly Roundhead from the Third onwards. Then the boys began to clamour for gory details of the execution and the little man, whipping off his steel-framed spectacles, said, "Ask Rawlins, he's obviously read it up," and Rawlins confirmed that, on this very spot, on January 30th, 1649, King Charles' head had been removed by a single blow and that "the blood had dripped through the planks of the scaffold by the pint."

"Extraordinary how they love blood!" the schoolmaster said, as though he had thought about it intermittently over the last fifty years. "They'll never forget Rawlins' touch of local colour but they've already forgotten the Grand Remonstrance and the Self-Denying Ordnance."

"So did you and I at that age," observed Simon, "and that, I imagine, has a direct bearing on what we're supposed to be celebrating."

"You have a point," said his companion, "but I daresay you've had enough of it."

"More than enough. I kept the boiler stoked up until D-Plus-Two but after that I began to simmer down. Do you mind if I ask you something? Isn't this an odd day to conduct a sight-seeing tour with that bunch in tow? It's not a responsibility I'd care for on V.E. night."

"A matter of killing two birds," said Mr. Chips, seriously. "After all, they're seeing history made, aren't they? We heard Churchill speak from the Air Ministry this morning, we've seen General Smuts go by, we've cheered Royalty, and we've taken in the Houses of Parliament, Scotland Yard and now the scaffold site of the Royal Martyrdom. Or the salutary end of The Man of Blood, whichever way you care to regard him."

It was as he said this, finishing on a long rasping sniff, that Simon caught the elusive familiarity of the man by the tail. He was so pleased with himself that he grabbed the schoolmaster by the shoulder, spun him round, and exclaimed with the greatest gusto, "I *know* you! You're Archie Bentinck! You were on the staff of High Wood when I was there, twenty-five years ago," and the little man did not seem displeased at having his identity shouted down Whitehall in the presence of his boys but smiled, shook Simon's hand, and said, "I am indeed, but please don't expect me to remember your name, or even murmur that your face is familiar. It isn't, for at my age all faces are alike. I never have been much good at recognising old boys. Only their style of essay distinguished them at the time—that and the wide range of excuses they made for various shortcomings."

"My name is Craddock," Simon said, curiously excited by the encounter, "Simon Craddock. I was there from 1917 to 1922 but you left before me. There was a ..." and he stopped, looking down at a boy who had strayed from the orbit of Rawlins' commentary and was staring up at him expectantly.

"A sharp exchange of views between me and that prig of a headmaster," Bentinck said, with another resonant sniff. "Yes, there was indeed. And I had the better of it. For here I am still hard at it, whereas that silly ass died of thrombosis years ago."

Mention of the headmaster during his five unprofitable years at the school drove a passage through the mists of Simon's memory. He remembered he had shared Bentinck's dislike of the head, a pompous, pretentious man, with high-falutin notions of dragging High Wood inside the select circle of schools where it could never be comfortable. There had been a long simmering row between the Head and Archie Bentinck, whose teaching methods were as unconventional as his appearance, and the boys, who had revelled in Archie's eccentricities, and had recognised him as a soft touch who enlivened history lessons by stray and sometimes slightly scandalous snippets of information, had been very sorry to see him go.

"You must be getting on," he said, "do you really mean to say you're still teaching?"

"A war-time stopgap," Bentinck told him, unable to conceal the pride he felt in his invincibility. "Apart from Merchant Bankers, the makers of armaments, and scoundrels who made five hundred per cent profit on the leaky huts we occupy at our temporary premises, I'm probably the only man of my generation who welcomed the war! I was dying of boredom when they called me back. To a private school of course. They wouldn't look at a man my age at the kind of place I taught after leaving High Wood."

271

"Are you taking this lot back tonight or are you staying over? The trains will be packed, won't they?"

"It's a two-day excursion," Bentinck said. "Around you stands the élite of St. Budolph's, the odd dozen who sold one hundred pounds' worth of savings stamps in a single term. The local Aldermen didn't think we could do it but we did and they had to fulfil their side of the bargain by footing the expenses of a V.E. jaunt. I think it rather rattled them when I 'phoned in our total."

"You haven't changed at all," Simon said, laughing, and his memories of Archie Bentinck became sharper every moment so that he could now see him, in shredded gown, perched on the end of the desk declaiming a favourite passage from "The Deserted Village", or obliterating the equations left on the blackboard by the maths master and looking as if this was a task he enjoyed. "Where are you staying overnight?"

"Guildford Street, by virtue of having a nephew who runs a small hotel there. Rawlins and two others are looking forward to sleeping in the bath. Incidentally, my nephew has been billeting Americans, so why not come back for a night-cap?"

"I'd be delighted," Simon said and they moved along to the Strand, the little man shouting, "Keep me in view and if any of you stray it's 23a, one minute's walk from the Russell Square tube entrance."

They were in Guildford Street in fifteen minutes and Simon, whose feet ached with so much pavement pounding, marvelled at the little man's energy as he darted about superintending the issue of cocoa and biscuits before shooing his charges off to bed.

"Would you mind telling me exactly how old you are?" he asked, when they were both enjoying a large whisky, and Archie Bentinck said, "Not now we're off the streets. I'll be seventy-nine next week but keep quiet about it or the boys might whip round and buy me another pipe rack. You can't be such a chicken yourself—let me see ... 1917-1922 ... you were eighteen when you left, twenty-three years ago ... wait a minute!" and he choked into his whisky. "I've got it! Craddock. Craddock S. A whole family of you somewhere in the West ... you had farms ... don't tell me."

"I won't," said Simon grinning, "but you're on course."

The schoolmaster subsided but continued to watch Simon's face with his alert squirrel's eyes. "Got it," he said finally, "and you didn't believe in it either, did you? There was that old boy—a conscientious objector—Norfield, Horsborough . . . some such name—and you got into hot water defending him after he was killed in France stretcher-bearing?"

"Horsey," Simon said, "and I married his widow."

"Good God," Bentinck exclaimed, proving that he could after all, be astonished. "It tallies, of course. You were another rebel and I really ought to have remembered you. There weren't all that number there. Not that I've anything against second-class public schools like High Wood, providing they make do with the material to hand and don't borrow the Eton Boating Song. There's still a place for them in the educational field but I was a misfit and it took me a long time to wake up to the fact. Once I did, and went back to the elementary day school, I was happy enough. They even made me a headmaster in the end. Galleywall Road Junior School, not all that far from here. It's in Rotherhithe."

"You not only enjoyed it, you still enjoy it."

"Enormously."

"Could you explain why?"

"It's a matter of temperament. All those secondhand traditions . . . all that esoteric slang . . . it seemed to me such a waste of good material. That was what the Head and I quarrelled about. We had diametrically opposed ideas about education. He wanted a production line of Doctor Arnold-type English gents and that didn't suit my book at all, and not simply because it was out-of-date even then. There's some promising stuff in places like Rotherhithe if you don't mind rooting for it. So many schoolmasters make so many mistakes about their essential function. After all, it's simple enough if you think about it. The job isn't to cut boys to a pattern, academic or social. It's to help them to develop individual personalities within the terms of reference we call civilisation. I did just that and I turned out some Tartars in my time. Three or four of them are doing a stretch right now but far more are doing well. Apart from that I like to think that a few of them are reading a book or two, or thinking a thought or two, that they wouldn't have been if I had stayed at High Wood. As for me, I've enjoyed the last thirty years of my life more than the first forty. You're not a regular, are you?"

"No, but I've been in since '39 and I'm due out the minute Japan packs it in."

"And then?"

"I was wondering that when I bumped into you."

"What did you do before?"

"Shouted in the wind. I fought by-elections, fought in Spain, was taken prisoner and had to be rescued by a Tory M.P."

"Are you going to fight at the coming election?"

"Not me!"

"But you chaps could scoop the pool this time."

Simon explained, reflecting as he did that there was a very strange phenomenon indeed—a professional schoolmaster who listened. By the time the level of their host's whisky bottle was appreciably lower he had told Bentinck as much as he would have told a close friend, but could not have said why. His memories of Archie Bentinck were vague but there was, within the man, an ability to probe that was the result of instructing generations of boys through successive eras.

He said, when Simon seemed to have finished, "Pity about you, Craddock. You've wasted a lot of time. Still, you're better equipped to start fresh than I was. I never had a proper degree, whereas you have, plus a good war record. Put in for a teacher's training course and do what I did. They'd never stand for you in a place like High Wood but you might be a spectacular success in a junior school. The thing you have to remember, of course, is that there is a far greater area of tolerance between grandfather and grandchild than between father and son and it's easy to see why. The one has ceased to expect miracles and the other hasn't had time to grow an impenetrable hide. Take a tip from me. After the age of eleven pass 'em on to somebody else to cope with. That way you'll keep some of your illusions."

"You really think I could start teaching at my age?"

"What the devil has age got to do with it? You've got a better idea of what life is about than some cocky young undergraduate with a swollen head stuffed with facts and theories. Give it a trial anyway. You'll find it a lot more rewarding than preaching the gospel according to Saint Keir Hardie, or trying to compromise between writing the truth and keeping the goodwill of local councillors who happen to be your advertisers. I'll tell you what. I've got a personal contact with the Principal at a Westcountry T.T. College in your area. Used to be a colleague of his before he took the job. I'll write to him if you like as soon as I get back. Or would you prefer to think it over between now and when you're demobbed?"

"I'll tell you what I'd like to do," said Simon, thoughtfully, "I'd like to 'phone my wife and do it right now. I lost track of you for twenty-five years and I don't want to risk it happening again. There's something weird about bumping into you tonight of all nights."

Luck was obviously running his way. In spite of jammed lines he made the connection in fifteen minutes, smiling at Evie's almost incoherent excitement at hearing his voice.

"I've just seen Uncle to bed," she said, "we've been down at the Coombe Bay V.E. Celebrations. I've been telling everyone you were still in Brussels. What are you doing back here? You aren't demobbed, are you?"

No, he told her, he was not, but to moderate her disappointment he assured her that there was no possibility of his being drafted out East. "It wasn't that I 'phoned you about," he said. "Do you see yourself living in a redbrick schoolhouse, putting iodine on grazed knees?"

"It depends. Redbrick you say? That rules out the Perrin-and-Trail hazards. Yes, if you were happy and settled I'd have no complaints. It's better than living over a shop and a lot better than sitting on a political platform beaming down at an audience who would sooner be home listening to the radio. What's headed you in that direction?"

"Far too expensive to tell you on the 'phone, particularly as we'll probably be cut off any moment. That's all for now. I'll write at length if I can't wangle a forty-eight hour pass."

"No wait. You haven't . . ."

He left it at that and rejoined a dozing Archie Bentinck in the lounge, nudging him awake.

"Write that letter, Archie," he said. "There'll probably be a stampede for teachers' training college places as soon as the big demob starts and for once in my life I'd like to be first on a bandwaggon!"

III

Paul would have denied it, and Andy would have derided it, but the truth was they were more alike in essentials than any of the Craddocks. Both had a steadiness of vision that

was strong, purposeful, and could at times be brutally obstinate; both had uncertain tempers. Paul, fortunately for
himself and others, had found his purpose early in life, and
succeeded in holding on to it through periods of boom,
slump, local disaster and two world wars. Andy was not so
fortunate. At twenty-one he had broken away to find a
purpose of his own, and although, to Paul, it had seemed a
very seedy one, it had satisfied him up to the time he rushed
into the R.A.F.

From then on, unlike Stevie, he had found another kind of
fulfilment. The hard, bright little machines he flew and the
challenge of wits presented by aerial combat, had absorbed
his zest and curiosity, so that, up to the time he was invalided
from the Service, he asked for nothing more, supposing that
he would ultimately drift back to his peacetime occupation
and get along as best he could with a relatively minor
handicap. He had not been (as Claire had expected him to
be) shattered by the news that his wife had been seduced by
his brother in his absence. He was astonished and, at the
outset, irritated by having to make another major adjust-
ment, but his relationship with Margaret, although eroded to
some extent, was not destroyed by the circumstances, as it
might have been in the case of a less tolerant man. Its present
weakness had nothing to do with Stevie. It was related to the
changes in society as a whole, for there seemed to Andy to
be very little left of the old world by the winter of 1943 and
months of hospital boredom had brought about changes in
himself, among them a readiness to admit that his affection
for Margaret had never had more than a physical basis.

It was not simply the result of a long cooling-off process.
Their world, the world they had shared with kindred spirits
like Stevie and Monica, had been buried under the rubble of
the blitz. Scrap was still in demand but its scavengers were
very different men from those Andy had haggled with in
dockside pubs and on provincial golf-courses. The Civil Service had moved in and taken over, as they had taken over
almost everything else in the country. Behind every rolltop
desk and trestle table was a faceless man who worked from
the book, who used set rules of procedure and who went
home at five o'clock to a wife in the suburbs. In almost every
case he was what had become known as "a Ministry man"
and this meant that he was immune to flattery and armoured
against bluff and bribes. You could not beat him or bully him

276

and he would have been outraged if you had suggested joining him. He was there by Government edict, entrenched behind mountains of forms and files, all needing a hundred different signatures in ancillary departments that seemed to Andy, in his quick, scornful, post-discharge survey of once-familiar terrain, nothing whatever to do with scrap metals, their source or their ultimate destination. It was this, more than his wounds, or the break-up of the old alliance, that convinced Andy Craddock there was no place for him in the present scheme of things and that he would have to make one and make one soon unless he was to go mad with boredom. The demand for scrap, his commercial instinct told him, would not last much longer and he had never had much doubt regarding the final outcome of the war. The old territory had been fenced off. He would never fly again. It therefore followed that he would have to break new ground and take advantage of the fact that he had arrived at the frontier in the vanguard of the gold rush.

He had other unquestionable advantages, chief among them capital that had accumulated appreciably during the last few years. He also possessed a trained ally in the person of Ken Shawcrosse, the ex-gunner. Shawcrosse, he discovered, was really no more than a buccaneer of the kind Andy had encountered by the score in the pre-war scrap world, but there was a difference. The dealers of those days had never sought to acquire the trappings of conventional society whereas Ken, and more particularly his wife, were greedy for them. They were snobs and made no apology for their ambition to be someone, to exert influence, to call the tune wherever they perched, and this intention was the mainspring of their commercial aggressiveness. Shawcrosse admitted this soon after he and Andy had registered their first company, Romulus Development Incorporated. The name, suggested by Shawcrosse, was a sneer at his own obscure origins and the buffeting he had received in the 'thirties.

"Rome wasn't built in a day, they tell me," he said, "but the joker who built it knew his business. His first job was to clobber the opposition and brother, that's me from here on! Before the war the Big Boys had it all their own way but now it's anybody's race. Did you ever read *Gone with the Wind*?"

Andy, who had never finished a novel in his life, said he had seen the film but Shawcrosse said, "It didn't come over in the film. There was the Wide Boy, Rhett Something-or-other, whose theory was there was more dough to be made out of a crumbling civilisation than a healthy one and he was right. This society was a regular carve-up before the war, where two per cent owned ninety-nine per cent of the property but now it's bust wide open. It'll never be the same again."

Andy said, "Are you a Bolshie, Ken?" and Shawcrosse had laughed. "I'm anything, old boy, anything that pays off in cash."

His attitude, in those early months of their association, was patronising but Andy gave him his head. He knew nothing of bricks and mortar, whereas Shawcrosse, reared in the world of small, readily-saleable property that was constantly changing hands, had familiarised himself with present conditions by a close study of local newspapers, sent to him during his long spell in hospital. His familiarity with requisitioning, building licenses, green belts, town planning and local government procedures impressed Andy from the outset, and so did the man's instinctive grasp of the essentials of any given situation requiring an indirect approach. He was like an ambitious ex-ranker sent by superiors to invest a small fortress, and would begin by considering the various merits of taking it by assault, resorting to the less costly method of sapping and mining, or solving the problem by bribing the garrison to open the gate at night. In every area they visited he seemed to know by instinct which method to adopt and the result was always the same, so that Romulus Development Incorporated soon found itself holding a mixed bag of assets, all the way down from a half-blitzed factory and accommodation land on the outskirts of market towns, to condemned workmen's cottages in built-up areas that had been falling down years before the Luftwaffe hastened the process.

There was an enormous amount of travelling and paper work to be done and all manner of calls upon people who, at first sight, seemed to have no place in a deal but whose goodwill was seen to be essential as time went on. Andy driving to and fro along the South Coast (an area favoured by Shawcrosse as offering the best post-war promise), met jobbing builders, city aldermen, town councillors, local government officers, country squires who reminded him of his father, farmers, rack renters, people who could speak hardly any English but owned sizeable chunks of England, and any number of Smiths and Browns guessing at the amount of compensation they would collect for a blitzed or derequisitioned premises. It was a strange, higgledy-piggledy world, in its own way as bizarre as Zorndorff's world of scrap, but Andy found it just as absorbing and sometimes exhilarating although, as he put it to Shawcrosse when they were prospecting a row of terrace houses half-demolished by a flying-bomb, they seemed to be staking a great deal of capital on an anticipated post-war rise in the price of site-values and the lifting of restrictive legislation regarding new building and renovation.

Shawcrosse, as always, had the answer. "The point is, old boy, restrictions won't be lifted for a long time but the man who holds the site holds the four-ace hand, even if he has to play a waiting game. I'm banking on most of these requisitioned premises staying requisitioned on wartime rents, so if you're looking for a quick turnover on the lines of pre-war scrap deals, stop looking. This is long-term investment—maybe as long as ten years—but in the end it won't be a matter of twelve to fifteen per cent profit. It'll be nearer a thousand per cent. I only hope to God the Reds do win the next election and keep their bloody regulations clamped on for years. That'll leave us sitting very pretty."

Andy, conditioned to a quick turnover, was not wholly convinced. "Suppose we end up holding a hundred thousand pounds-worth of sites and then run out of capital? I've already sunk all I've got into the Company."

Shawcrosse said, "Go easy, old boy. Do you suppose I hadn't worked that one out? We now hold round about sixty sites, plus the same number of houses capable of being patched up for the defenders of Democracy when they roll up in their civvy suits. The Government has to release a proportion of buildings and those who are too skint to pay our price will have to rent furnished. We haven't got any furnished? That's our next priority—round the auction rooms for the necessary. A couple of dozen rented houses in the right places—and I've made bloody sure ours *are* in the right places—will keep the old pot on the boil while things sort themselves out. If we need more cash there are always ways and means of getting the odd house derequisitioned. Fifty quid invested in palm-oil will take care of that, old boy."

Andy's movements were as rapid and uncertain as in the

279

heyday of the scrap empire. This was why Paul's V.J. letter took more than a week to catch up with him.

Andy pondered it a long time before passing it over to Ken, who was elated by its content. "So the old Dad has finally come round to it? He's handing over in advance, in the hope of doing the poor old Chancellor out of his death-duties! Well, good for him and good for you. Cash is nice to have but give me coastal land every time. It can't be pinched and it can't shrink in value like the poor old British quid. Nice little reserve, tucked away in the West."

"Too far West for your vacuum-cleaner," Andy said, but Shawcrosse made the fashionable deprecating gesture, shaking his head slowly to and fro and spreading his palms, Shylockwise. He was almost too quick, Andy noticed, to adapt to the current slang and tricks of expression.

"Don't believe it, old boy! With every twopenny-ha'penny clerk and plumber's mate owning a car it's not as far West as all that. Hang on to it, and see if you can't make it grow a bit if one of your brothers or sisters need a bit of the ready. We might even be able to use a slice like that Valley but not yet. Right now we stick to bricks and mortar within a bicycle ride of the nearest factory."

They plunged back into the mainstream of their activities. With the war in the East over, and everyone speculating on the long-term effects of Hiroshima and Nagasaki, their instincts warned them that they were only one jump ahead of the nearest pursuers.

IV

Paul's V.J. letter (that was how it was always referred to in after years), telling each of his children that he was ready to bet the Treasury he would attain the age of seventy-one, was the product of hard thinking set in train by his visit to French Wood just as dusk was falling on the Valley's celebration of victory in Europe. It was a good deal more comprehensive than the straight deed-of-gift suggested to him long ago by that sharp-nosed old pedant, Edgar Wonnacott, who had taken over his legal chores after the death of Franz Zorndorff, his father's partner in the original Thameside scrap-yard.

Paul had kept clear of lawyers most of his life, disliking

their bloodless approach to all human affairs. Up to the day of his death old Franz had kept a fatherly eye on the Valley's finances and on such capital as Paul did not plough back into the estate. Franz had sometimes given him good advice and had he followed it he could, at several turning points in his life, have reaped considerable financial advantage, but just as he edged away from lawyers he distrusted financiers and what he thought of as their whorehouse, the Stock Market. Indeed, in that respect his views approximated those of a Bolshevik.

He owned very few shares and had never, in the whole of his life, played the market, or spent five minutes studying *The Financial Times,* but his overall attitude towards money and moneymaking could not have been described as Puritanical, for most Puritans feel very much at home in the counting-house. It was, perhaps, a recoil from the original source of his acres, as though he could never quite remove the stain of the original fortune amassed by his father and that old rascal Zorndorff during the Boer War. He had always been conscious of having profited by the deaths of Boer children in the insanitary concentration camps on the Veldt, and the murder of his own generation in Flanders. This was why, on his return to the Valley in the autumn of 1918, one of his first acts had been to channel the whole of his wartime profits into the Valley and see most of it melt away in the agricultural slump of the 'twenties and early 'thirties.

Zorndorff had told him then that he was behaving like an idiot, that his few thousands were the equivalent of feeding one oat to a donkey, but he had persisted and Claire had encouraged him to persist. It might not be businesslike, she told Zorndorff and her cynical sons, but it was Paul Craddock, and she would have no part in persuading him to act against his instincts.

He was to suffer for his principle or, as some would say, his obstinacy, for as soon as agriculture began to pick up again taxation kept pace with its progress. By the end of World War II it was galloping well ahead, so that Paul often found himself in the position of a man of affluence who could find no one to change a five pound note. The Whinmouth bank manager, who knew him well, never pressed for a reduction of his periodical overdrafts and when what seemed to Paul staggering amounts were demanded by the Inland Revenue, cheerfully advanced him mortgages and other credits. When the war was virtually over, however, Paul realised that it was imperative to retrench and take some kind of action to stop the estate being bled white by the high rates of interest. It was with this in mind that he made an appointment with Edgar Wonnacott on what turned out to be the final day of the war.

Some time before that, however, he had been thinking in wider terms of a reshuffle of his affairs. He did not feel his age, or anything like his age and put this down to Devon air, plenty of exercise on foot and on horseback, and a lifelong limitation of objectives well within his ability to attain. He was, Claire said, very smug about his health and strength and the fact that he never caught cold or took so much as an aspirin. He slept well, did not suffer from rheumatism, ate sparingly and drank whisky when he could get it. He was also a heavy smoker of cigarettes but he had no cough and his wind was remarkable for a man of his age. He could still climb the Hermitage plateau or the Bluff in long, raking strides without much more than a grunt when he reached the summit. And yet, taken all round, he had lived a rough life and had been knocked about more than most men of his generation. He still limped slightly from the effects of a Mauser bullet in his kneecap, and twice since the Boer marksman had shot him down he had been seriously injured, once during the rescue of German sailors in Tamer Potter's Cove, in 1906, and again twelve years later during the final German offensive. Now, when the wind was in the east, his old wounds ached a little but it was not battles of long ago that reminded him it was time to get his affairs in order. It had much more to do with an acknowledgment of what he felt he owed the generation that had grown up between the wars. They had, he would say, given a damned good account of themselves. But for the energy and adaptability of people like Stevie and Andy (whom he had once thought of as near-decadent), and misfits like Simon, or scamps like Bon-Bon Potter and his cousin Dick, the Nazis would have got ashore and fought their way across his Valley. It was time, Paul thought, as he sat on the ridge of French Wood on V.E. night, that somebody faced up to this and it might as well be the landlord.

Below him, as the blue dusk stole in from the dunes, bonfires twinkled in a wide semi-circle, one big one at the R.M. Camp, smaller ones at Nun's Head and Four Winds, another on Coombe beach and the one he had just left in the High Street. The night was mild but damp, and the scent carried on the light breeze, was the smell of spring. From where he sat he could see the first drifts of bluebells in Hermitage larch coppice and the last of the primroses grew at his feet. On this plateau he could almost place the week of the year without reference to calendar or diary. Long ago he had memorised the sights, sounds and scents of successive seasons. In the spring the leaves were slippery underfoot, and in the autumn they whispered like children hushed by authority. The note of a snapping twig would tell him whether or not it held sap and he knew all the wild flowers and birds and small creatures who could be found here at different times of the year. He recognised too the sky signs over the Bluff where he could read the weather in cloud formation or degree of visibility. He thought, drawing on his cigarette, and welcoming the solitude of the wood, "I wonder who will take my place here in ten to fifteen years? The time will come when I can't even ride up here, when I turn my back on it for the last time and go home to die. Claire might outlive me by a few years but she wouldn't have to come this far to remember me. She could do that down by the Mere where she made her first clumsy attempt to catch me, or before the library fire, where we have spent so many pleasant, humdrum evenings. No, this place has always been more mine than anywhere else in the Valley and if I had any say in it I should like to die here as old Meg Potter died on the sand hills above Crabpot Willie's shanty."

The thought of the shanty redirected his thoughts to his wife and he remembered her very vividly as she had appeared to him one autumn evening there during a 1917 leave, a few days they had salvaged from that grim time and presented to one another as one might exchange simple, inexpensive gifts. He remembered how breathtakingly beautiful she had seemed to him standing naked in front of the fire, with the soft light of burning apple-logs reflected on her firm white flesh and unpinned hair, and shadows chasing one another the length of her rounded thighs and long, dimpled back.

The memory stirred nothing but silent laughter in him now, laughter and with it a flicker of complacency that their delight in one another had produced three sons and three daughters, to add to the one poor Grace had given him with

283

so much pain as long ago as 1904. The date reminded him of Simon's age and for a moment he thought of his children in two groups, five living and two dead. Then, detaching little Claire, Stevie, and the family postscript, John, he concentrated on the four who had weathered out this war and would now, he supposed, begin to think of settling down, as he had settled long before he was their age. Surely he owed it to them to offer some kind of inducement to do this, to put down roots and give those roots a chance to take hold of something, in the way every commemorative tree in this copse had rooted itself.

There was old Simon, the brainiest of them but still undecided what to do with his life. There was Andy, with his permanently-gloved hand and that dead strip of face. There was Mary and her Rumble Patrick, who would welcome any land coming his way. And there was the indifferent Whiz and her husband Ian, neither of whom he had seen for nearly six years. Whatever settlement was made would have to be an equal division among them. He had seen too many family quarrels begin in the Valley over a father's preference for one child or another, even when one member of the family deserved a larger slice of the cake. He could form some kind of company, he supposed, with four equal shares and himself as permanent Chairman but how could this be achieved without breaking up the estate into small, uneconomical units? Nothing would induce Simon or Andy or Ian to farm, although one or other of them might like to own a house and a plot of land in the Valley. Young John's patrimony could stay in pickle until he was twenty-one and that was still a decade away. Rumble Patrick might be persuaded through Mary to accept the vacant Home Farm as a gift, abandon the shattered Periwinkle, and join the two holdings in a single unit. As to Simon, his wife Evie, Andy, his wife Margaret, and Whiz and Ian, he couldn't be sure. They had earned something and one way or another they were going to get it without waiting for him to die. It was a problem to be put to Wonnacott as soon as possible. With this resolve he got up, carefully extinguished the butt of his cigarette, and stumped off down the winding track to the river road.

When he reached Codsall Bridge he noticed the stars, thrown across the arc of the sky like jewels scattered by a fugitive thief. He thought, as the damp of the river bottom probed his Boer wound, "I'd better ring Wonnacott and fix something up this week. That damned bullet nearly put paid to me before I set foot in this place, and Fritz's lump of shrapnel came even closer in 1918. I'm a good deal fitter than most men over the hill but let's face it—I've been luckier, and luck can run out, just as Stevie's did." An owl who lived in the elms at the corner of the park wall hooted as though confirming this possibility and Paul smiled into the gathering darkness, cupping his hands, blowing into the cavity, and giving such an accurate imitation of the hoot that the owl was mute with astonishment. By the time he had found his voice again Paul had turned in at the lodge and was half-way up the drive.

V

For once Edgar Wonnacott paid him a grudging compliment, expressing surprise that Paul had at last turned his mind to a possibility that most business men begin to consider on reaching the age of forty. Paul, not to be bullied by the old badger, said, "Damn it, Edgar, I've made my will, haven't I?"

"Yes and it's years out of date," said the lawyer, with one of his sour smiles. "I turned it out the day you 'phoned and your youngest child isn't even mentioned in it. If you are set on this Deed of Gift—which I'm not against mind you, for it's some kind of protection against penal death-duties—you'll have to scrap that will and draw up another. Before we go any further, however, can you trust your family?"

"Now what a damned stupid question," Paul said. "If I couldn't I shouldn't be here, should I?"

"I can't answer that," Wonnacott said, "it's something I have to take for granted on occasions such as this, but I always make a point of raising it. You'd be surprised to hear how some sons and daughters react to a covenant of this kind. I've known of more than one case where an indulgent parent has voluntarily stripped himself of all he possesses and then been shown the door."

"I'm not that kind of a fool and I don't have that kind of family," Paul told him. "I shall leave the house, grounds and Shallowford Woods in my own name. For the rest I had some idea of splitting it up as regards income yield, but stipulating that it wasn't to be sold off in my lifetime."

"You can't give something away and then lay down all kinds of conditions as to what the owner does with it," Wonnacott told him. "You could, however, make it over to a company, keep some of the shares yourself, and distribute the rest equally among your sons and daughters. It would have to have a secretary, of course, and would have to be registered in the proper way."

"All right, get cracking on it right away," Paul said.

"Wait a minute, Mr. Craddock. There would have to be a certain amount of preliminary reorganisation first. The fact is, you're heavily mortgaged and if you'll take my advice you'll clear off those mortgages and consolidate before bringing in other shareholders, even if those shareholders are your sons and daughters. That way the company will start life without a weight round its neck."

It seemed a rational point to make and Paul said so. "How much do the mortgages amount to?" he asked and Wonnacott said that they totalled just over nine thousand.

"Great God! As much as that."

"You've been paying a lot of tax lately and your rents have remained at Slump level. Sooner or later you'll have to raise them and start investing. Ever since I've known you you've spent as much as you earn, although I'll admit you've never spent much on yourself. It's all gone back into the estate. If restrictions and taxation hadn't prevented you from continuing to do that throughout the war, you would have had an even bigger overdraft by now."

Paul, sobered by the figure, asked, "What do you suggest I should do?"

"Contract," Wonnacott said, "providing you can find buyers. Why don't you sell off that eastern section, those three farms running down to Coombe Bay? With the money raised you could clear the mortgages altogether, hoist your rents all round—and don't tell me the farmers can't afford to pay more after the money they've been making lately and then form your company, with a small income guaranteed you for your lifetime? Have you got any private money I haven't heard about?"

"Two or three thousand in Government stock," Paul said, "and my wife got about as much from her father when he died. We could manage well enough. Periwinkle is due for a compensation grant but I don't really own that farm. My son-in-law was buying it when it was blown to blazes." He got up and went to the window, rubbing his chin. "I don't take kindly to the idea of slicing off the entire Coombe," he said finally. "Couldn't I dispose of isolated properties in Coombe Bay itself?"

"Certainly you could. It's as broad as it's long. My point was you aren't getting any younger and apart from raising capital it would reduce the area of your responsibility."

"I like responsibility," Paul said, "it's what's kept me going all these years. Go ahead with that company and the transfer of ownership aimed at dodging death-duties. I'll last another five years I promise you! In the meantime I'll send you a detailed list of all the Coombe Bay odds-and-sods and we can clear the mortgage with what they yield."

And so, in a matter of days, it was done, to Paul's mind entirely satisfactorily. He was astonished by the total figure produced by the sale of his Coombe Bay properties. Anticipating about twelve thousand pounds he actually received a net total of nineteen and even then Wonnacott told him he let some of them go too cheaply. Neither Paul nor his agent ever met the purchasers. They were, it seemed, intermediaries who bought properties, did them up, and resold them immediately. Wonnacott, accustomed to the measured pace of provincial business, expressed disgust at what was going on now that the war was over and ex-servicemen were demanding living space.

"Some of the places around here have changed hands five times in as many months," he growled. "They start out at about fifteen hundred pounds and the last in the queue hands over something in the region of four thousand." He looked at Paul cautiously for a moment, before saying, "If you were a business man, Mr. Craddock, I could put you in the way of making a packet."

"Out of youngsters who put paid to Hitler and his gang? No, thank you!"

"Oh, not necessarily that way," Wonnacott said but choosing his words carefully. "You could raise money on that timber of yours in Shallowford Woods and make another fortune out of building-sites where the woods touch the main road on your northern boundary."

Paul looked at him so bleakly that the lawyer shifted in his chair. "All right, let it pass but I wouldn't be doing my job properly if I didn't put forward these ideas. You wouldn't like anything of that kind to happen, I suppose?"

"Only over my carcass," Paul said, "and not even then, for I'm damned if I'd rest easy. Some of those oaks have been growing there since the Wars of the Roses and even the beeches are half-way through their second century. Who the hell am I to chop them down for cash and replace them with rows of little pink boxes? The next thing you'll suggest is we make a Lido out of the Mere, or hack a golf course out of Blackberry Moor."

"I daresay it will come to that," Wonnacott said seriously, "but not in our lifetime. You'd better sit down and listen to this covenant. I've called the company 'Shallowford Estates Limited'. Does that suit you?"

"Yes," Paul said, his humour restored by the man's obvious sympathy with his outlook, "it has a dynastic ring and my wife will enjoy the joke. She's always telling me I see myself as a biblical patriach!"

He settled himself and listened to the lawyer's sermon, marvelling at archaic words like "messuage" and "appurtenance", but the terms of the document were simple. Shallowford Estates Limited was now, nominally at least, to be administered by a board of directors, consisting of himself as Chairman, Simon, Andy, Rumble Patrick (representing Mary) and Whiz, who would serve more practical purpose on the board than her husband, for at least she had hunted the country. There were, in all, ten thousand shares, Paul holding three thousand, the remainder being distributed equally among the other four or their nominees. Claire was paid secretary and Young John, too young to hold shares, was named in the new will as heir to that part of the estate Paul retained for his own use or "enjoyment" as Wonnacott put it. All in all Paul left the office feeling that he had achieved something lasting, especially when Wonnacott reminded him of the amount of tax liability he had shed.

As he went to collect his car in Whinmouth Square he saw Smut Potter and Henry Pitts emerging from the Maltster's Arms, Henry wiping his mouth with the back of his hand, and at the same moment they saw him. "Us was just havin' a quick pint on V.J. Maister," Henry said. "Shall us go back and 'ave another?"

"No," Paul told them, "I've got an afternoon's letter-writing ahead of me. I've just come from Wonnacott, the lawyer. I've been forming a Company of the estate but don't spread it around until I've had a chance to talk to Rumble Patrick. He's one of the shareholders."

He saw that Smut was the more interested of the two. The floating of a private company, he decided, was beyond Henry's limited comprehension. Smut said, "Ah, us heard you'd sold off they Coombe Bay lots, Squire. Tell 'ee the truth, the Missus was on to me to tackle 'ee and buy our bakery. 'Squire'll let 'ee have it cheaper than he'd zell to a vorriner!' she said, but I wasn't 'avin' any. As long as I'm a tenant youm zaddled with all the repairs, baint 'ee?"

"Yes," said Paul, "but Marie was right. You could have had it cheaper if you had come to me. Who bought it? Do you know?"

"Not zo far I don't," Smut said, "but I baint bothered. They can't stick the rent up more'n a shillin' or two and they can't shift me so long as I'm a zittin' tenant."

"I ought to have given you the chance, Smut," he said, "but I left everything to Wonnacott," but Smut only grinned and said, "Aw, dornee worry, Squire. Us all knows you woulden diddle a Valley man but even you have to watch out for yourself these days."

"I never knowed Smut when he didn't," said Henry and then went on to talk with relish of the enormous blasting power of the two bombs that had just finished the war in the East. After they had parted, and Paul was driving up the hill to the crest of the moor, he thought it odd that a genial soul like Henry, who had been outraged by the order against fraternisation with the Germans after the 1918 armistice, should find so much pleasure in the thought of thousands of Japanese civilians being, in Henry's quaint phrase, "blowed to tatters" and supposed it had to do with the unspeakable way the Japs had treated their prisoners. "It's also the times," he told himself, "for everyone around here is getting tougher and tougher and Smut was right when he said a man has to look out for himself. After all, I'm doing just that, for this handing over of the estate to others is no more than a tax-fiddle and I've made damned sure of my own home and the woods behind it. I wouldn't part with those while there's breath in my body."

Then, as he coasted down from the moor and saw the silver thread of the Sorrel gleaming in August sunshine, he felt surprise and relief that he had lived to see yet another war relegated to the history books. In the summer of 1940 it had seemed impossible that one among them would have a chance to begin over again, as they had in the long, hot summer of 1919, but at least this war hadn't exacted such a fearful toll from the Valley as its predecessor. It had claimed one of his sons, and part of another; it had destroyed Simon's wife Rachel and Connie Eveleigh's husband; it had blasted Periwinkle to rubble and, here and there, in the Coombe Bay area, a familiar young face had been blotted out, but this was not an impossible price to pay for preventing some thick-necked German from establishing himself at Paxtonbury and sending his thugs to hammer on Valley doors in the middle of the night. What, he wondered, would happen now? Would there be the same optimism as there had been in 1919, when everyone had looked to the League of Nations to prevent the same thing happening again? He doubted it very much, for people—even simple countrymen like Smut Potter—had grown cynical and who could blame them? The best one could hope for was a long respite, long enough to last him out, and by then politicians and people generally might have learned a little sense. He stopped ruminating, put his foot down and hurried home to write his V.J. letters.

VI

The reactions, when they reached him, were interesting, for they emphasized the psychological differences of his children.

Whiz wrote in her usual formal prose, thanking him very politely on behalf of Ian and herself, and saying that when Ian retired he would "probably like to build a nice house somewhere on the estate and keep a couple of hunters". That was all; nothing about the farms, the crops or the machinery, so that it was clear from her letter that neither she nor her husband regarded themselves as anything but sleeping partners in the enterprise.

Simon's letter surprised him by its warmth and he was even more surprised by Evie's news, when she brought him the letter that had arrived from Germany, enclosed in one of her own. Simon, she said, was to be demobilised in a month and go straight into a teachers' training college, and when Paul asked what kind of job he would seek when qualified she said he would apply for a post at a local elementary school, in Paxtonbury perhaps, or Whinmouth.

"That's not very ambitious, is it?" he said and she told him Simon had lost interest in party politics, notwithstanding the recent triumph of the Left. All he seemed to want now was to live in the country or by the sea and do some kind of worthwhile job, and perhaps write in the holidays. It looked as if he was going the right way about achieving these modest ends.

"You think so too, don't you?" she said, clearly anxious to have his approval, and he said that he did, adding, "I think Simon will make a damned good schoolmaster. The income from the company should help you along, providing, of course, that you don't go in for a family of my size."

She looked down at her thickening figure with satisfaction and he thought again how lucky Simon had been to meet a girl like her when he was tired, disillusioned and getting on for forty.

"I don't suppose we'll run to that," she said, "we started too late, but I daresay I'll add one or two more to your score before I'm through. I mean to try, anyway. Simon is marvellous with kids. What are you hoping for this time?"

"A girl," he said emphatically, "and as like you as possible, my dear," and she kissed him and left him reading Simon's comments on the formation of the Company. They were more generous than those of his daughter Whiz but here again it seemed unlikely that Simon would play more than a passive part in the Board room.

Andy wrote from London with enthusiasm, giving as his opinion that it was a first-class idea on somebody's part (clearly he found it difficult to believe it had been Paul's) and should "save him a packet in the long run". He had, he said, a number of ideas for increasing the estate income but he would not enumerate them until he had sounded out the others.

Paul, smiling grimly, was not in much doubt as to what those ideas were. "It wouldn't surprise me if he didn't want to build a blasted hotel on the Dunes," he told Rumble, "but if he does he'll have to wait a year or two before he starts browbeating me about that. I don't mind parting with income, but any changes around here are going to be strictly agricultural, and not so many of those if I can help it."

In the event the only immediate change resulting from the

formation of the Company occurred at Home Farm. Rumble Patrick and Mary moved into the vacant farmhouse that autumn, taking in the much smaller unit of Periwinkle and bulldozing the ruin that had begun to look like the monument of a dead generation, with mitre-shaped walls pointing to the sky and a riot of nettles, trefoil, dock, campion and tall yellow stichwort jostling for space in the kitchen where Rachel had died four years before.

Paul and Rumble went over there to see it done and Rumble winced as the great lumbering machine crashed through into the fireplace, like a mastodon stalking prey. Paul, hoping to reassure him, said, "You'll soon have Home Farm as cheerful as this place when you and Mary married and moved in," but Rumble said, glumly, "Sure we will, and it's a better farm in every way, but I didn't build Home Farm, Gov'nor! It was there two hundred years ago."

"I know exactly what you mean," Paul said. "You don't like parting with the tools you handled when you learned your trade. That's the male equivalent of a woman's feelings about her first lover, but there's another way of looking at it."

"Such as?"

"The way one ought to learn to look at everything inanimate. The soil is still here and every particle of it is alive. Bricks, mortar, tools, cob, thatch are all expendable. Even if they serve you a lifetime they're only a loan, like the pictures and china and furniture I've accumulated up at the house. In the end what happens to it? A stranger walks in and carts it away but you can't do that with this," and he bent down and picked up a handful of dry, red soil, letting it run through his fingers and ricochet from the toecaps of his gumboots.

Rumble grinned, his humour restored. "This Company you've launched," he said, "I don't know how it'll work. There's built-in rivalry to begin with—you and me, a couple of nostalgic sentimentalists, Andy and Whiz, who think of places like the Valley as sites rather than farming land, and finally old Simon, conditioned over the years to juggle with abstracts. Won't we fall out over fundamentals?"

"I daresay," Paul said, equably, "most family concerns do but they survive when other enterprises don't. Blood is still thicker than all that champagne they guzzle at business luncheons."

"Good old Gov," said Rumble, laughing, "long live the

feudal system," and he went down the slope to have a closer look at the bulldozer's progress, leaving Paul to sift the last dry grains of soil in the hollow of his hand. "Long live the feudal system," he muttered, "and not all that much of a joke either. It served its purpose a damned sight better than the one we have now, where policy decisions are handed down to us by civil servants. They'll take us over lock, stock and barrel in the end, I suppose, but not yet, not quite yet" ... and he waved good-bye to Rumble and went down across the long tussocky slope to the foot of the Hermitage plateau.

CHAPTER TWO

ROUTINE RECONNAISSANCE

I

ON the first Saturday in August, 1947, Paul Craddock saddled his aged grey, vintage horse of the Valley, and set out on his first circular sweep for nearly a year.

Most of the interval had been spent far from the Valley and this, in itself, had been a local talking-point through the long and excessively severe winter, for it had not gone unnoticed by Shallowford originals that this was the first time Squire Craddock had spent more than a fortnight out of sight of the Sorrel since 1918, when everyone but his wife had given him up for dead. Paul had, in fact, surprised everyone, including himself, by taking his doctor's advice in February and setting off on a world cruise via Gibraltar, Suez, Tasmania, across the Pacific to San Francisco and Vancouver, then over the Rockies to Montreal and home by the *Queen Elizabeth* to Southampton.

Early in the New Year, when snow began to build into twenty-foot drifts on the eastern slopes of the moor, and the Sorrel froze harder than it had in the lifetime of Henry Pitts and Smut Potter (both of whom could remember more hard winters hereabouts than the Squire himself) he had gone down with bronchitis, his first real illness, discounting war injuries and accidents since boyhood. It had frightened Claire very much to hear him wheeze as he sat reading before the library fire and there had been some brisk exchanges in the kitchen when she had seen him lumber out into the stableyard and hoist his saddle on to Snowdrop's unclipped back.

By mid-January, when the Valley was cut off from Whinmouth and Paxtonbury by almost Alpine walls of packed snow, he was in bed with a temperature of a hundred and four degrees, and even the aged Maureen Rudd, who still attended a few of her original patients, expressed anxiety to the family and called in a specialist. Within twenty-four hours of the specialist's arrival, however, Paul unexpectedly rallied and asked Claire what all the fuss was about. She soothed him with invalid talk that at first made him very irritable but then, fortunately for everyone, reminded him of the days shortly before their marriage when she had come rushing back to the Valley to nurse him through injuries received in the sea-rescue off Tamer Potter's Cove. His memory of the occasion, it seemed, was extraordinarily vivid and it pleased him to see her sitting over by the tall window again after all these years. He said:

"Funny thing, I remember opening my eyes after Maureen operated on me on the kitchen table for those broken ribs, and wondering how you and poor old Grace had changed places. It was summer then. The sun played games in a wisp of hair behind your ear. I remember watching it for a hell of a long time before I spoke. Then you got me some tea and played that tuneless piano we had in the dining-room, remember?"

"In great detail," she said, having to make a big effort to hold back tears of relief, for she had been more frightened than she cared to admit.

After that he mended very quickly and Maureen was able to talk him into a Mediterranean cruise for the early spring but somehow—after being informed that an overlooked insurance policy for nearly two thousand was due—the jaunt had enlarged itself into a world tour and because, at that time, he had to be humoured, Claire pretended to be enthusiastic and everything was arranged in a great hurry so that they were basking in Sicilian sunshine by March.

It was getting on for half a century since he had been so far afield and Claire had never even been to Calais, so that to their astonishment they began to enjoy themselves, particularly when they reached Egypt and took the traditional camel-ride to the pyramids, and then, in a hard, dry heat that never scorched the Valley, sailed down the Arabian Gulf and across to Colombo, and on to Hobart where Claire had a very hospitable cousin holding high rank in the police force.

Paul liked Tasmania because it had so many physical

similarities to Devon and they stayed there nearly a month before moving on to Samoa where he paid his respects to the late Robert Louis Stevenson, and after that to San Francisco, a city that appealed to him as a sparkling, vigorous place in great contrast to the more sultry parts of California they visited. He also enjoyed his trip across the Rockies although he told Claire that mountain scenery of this kind made him homesick for the tree-hung hills of the Westcountry. This was his first admission of homesickness and she was glad they were well on their way home, for although he now looked as tanned and fit as she ever remembered, she sensed that he was getting restless and had noticed that he needed no provocation to bring the Valley into their conversation.

She said, when they sighted the Eddystone "Well now, there you are, and I don't imagine we'll ever catch you west of Plymouth again," and he replied, fervently, "By God, you won't!" and then, hastily, "Not that I haven't enjoyed it, old girl. It was time we shook the straw out of our hair and I'm not at all sorry we went." But from that instant he was in a ferment to be home and the Valley could hardly have put on a better show for him, for the long, hot summer he had predicted was longer and hotter than anyone remembered, to offset a winter that had been longer and colder.

As they drove down the slope of the moor to their first sight of the Sorrel he was like a boy returning home from his first term at boarding school and when, early next morning, she saw him foraging in the cupboard for his riding breeches and tall boots, she did not have to be told what he intended doing but said, hiding her smile, "What time lunch?" and he replied, "Any old time. I want to have a good look round and get myself up-to-date! I'll probably make do with a sandwich and a beer in The Raven."

She could indulge herself in a long chuckle the moment he had clattered out of the yard and said to Mary, who had dropped in for breakfast, "He's been on a lot of day excursions in the last few months but he'll get a bigger kick out of this one than his trot around the Pyramids on a camel." Then, forgetting him, she pumped her daughter for all the family gossip and spent a pleasant hour or so hearing progress reports on her numerous grandchildren.

Paul walked the grey across the field paths to the door in the park wall that he always thought of as "The Postern" and dismounted to pass it. It had been relatively cool in the paddocks but out here, facing the open fields of Four Winds that stretched as far as the dunes, the full strength of the morning sun struck his face and flies began to pester Snowdrop so that he flung his big head to and fro. Eveleigh's harvest looked very promising from here, acres of wheat nearest the river and further over barley and rye. The early summer months must have been exceptionally hot to produce such results and Paul reminded himself to ask Rumble to tell him how many hours of sunshine they had had since April. He could only recall two summers in his life when the sun had this strength at 9 a.m., that of 1902, the year he had settled in, and later in 1919, when he had returned to a depopulated Valley after the war. He was sorry for Snowdrop, but for himself he always enjoyed a blazing sun and as he went along under the park wall he made his usual observation of the pattern of wildflowers growing there, huge glowing dandelions like picquet lines of miniature suns, splashes of crimson campion, honeysuckle he could inhale from the saddle, yellow toadflax, vetch, yarrow, and the one that few thought of as a flower but had always impressed him as majestic—the huge, gently nodding umbrellas of cowparsley, a growth that Gypsy Meg had dignified by the name of "Ladies' Lace". It was a fine show but he supposed farmers like Eveleigh and Rumble Patrick never thought of it as anything but a vast crop of weeds. The river was down to a trickle and the mud along the margins was baked hard and seamed by a thousand cracks.

He crossed Codsall Bridge and stopped for a moment to greet Young Eveleigh, now not so young, for he must be at least twenty-eight although he was still a bachelor. Bob Eveleigh, not a notable conversationalist, confirmed his hopes of a bumper harvest and as he rode on down the lane Paul wondered if the young man was conscious of standing on the exact spot where his father, in local parlance, "had been blowed to tatters" in February, 1942. He thought not, for the Eveleighs, one and all, were an unsentimental breed who concerned themselves with the present. Connie was pleased to see him and came out wiping her hands on her apron, asking conventional questions about his travels.

"I didn't see anything to compare with this, Connie," he told her and she said that didn't surprise her for he was generally reckoned a stay-at-home, but if someone gave her the opportunity to sail round the world she would soon be off and away. She told him about her younger children, the boy studying accountancy in Bristol, the girl, married to a G.P.O. telephone engineer, who had presented her with a grandson "looking exactly like a snap I kept of Harold at the same age". He rode on, wondering at his abiding interest in such trivia, keeping the river on his right as he ascended the long heathery slope of the moor to the abandoned R.M. Camp, still, he noted, a blot on the landscape and the abode of squatters Andy had urged him to send packing last autumn.

There were about half-a-dozen families living in ruinous Nissen huts, presenting the same kind of picture as the Potters of the Dell forty years ago. One of the men, a pale, unshaven Londoner, with an accent that Paul placed as Hounslow or thereabouts, looked at him apprehensively, but when Paul smiled and nodded he approached hesitantly, his wife and two or three children peeping from the hut door-way.

"Hasn't anyone at Whinmouth done anything for you people?" Paul asked. "It must have been damned cold up here last winter," and the man said, sulkily, that it was at least a roof and a stove, and that everyone here had their name down on the Council lists but were told, whenever they went into the town, that there were scores of local residents ahead of them. He looked at Paul speculatively, trying to assess his interest in the situation, and finally added, "Couldn't you ginger 'em up a bit, sir? I wouldn't care to spend another winter up here. If I'd have known what we was in for in that bloody desert I woulder let old Rommel chase the Wogs round Cairo, and good luck to him!"

It was, Paul reflected, a perennial problem. He had heard almost identical comments from trench-veterans in the early 'twenties and it did seem monstrously unjust that a man who had devoted years of his life to saving the country from a thug like Hitler could be at the mercy of tinpot officials when he demanded a home for his children. It was no use asking the fellow why he had left his own area and wandered down here among strangers. There were probably any number of reasons, all of them complex. He could have chased them off last year, he supposed, and that might have compelled local government to do something on their behalf, but somehow he hadn't the heart when their spokesman had called on him and asked for time. Instead he had turned a blind eye to the little community, ignoring Andy's advice "to boot the buggers off". He said, "How many of you are here? How many units?" and the man said there were now five, nineteen people in all, eleven of them kids. "I'll have another go at the Housing Committee," he said, "but in the meantime make some kind of effort to keep the place tidier and if the constable calls refer him to me."

The man thanked him and he rode away feeling shamed. "That's patronage if you like!" he told himself, "and a generation out of date. But what else could I say? It wasn't as if any one of them up here is ready to learn farming, and I wouldn't wonder if most of them aren't layabouts who wouldn't stick at a job in the cities!"

The encounter took a little of the brightness out of the morning and, as he crossed the edge of the moor and headed past the scar of Periwinkle, it struck him as ridiculous that civilisation could evolve, when necessary, the means of destroying a city the size of Hiroshima with a single bomb and then fall flat on its face when asked to find homes for five English families. The answer, he supposed, was an economic one, for Japan had been blasted because the Japanese had threatened commerce and these people did not constitute a threat. So long as they kept out of sight and didn't brawl or steal they were nobody's business. They talked a great deal about the Welfare State these days and he supposed recent progress had been spectacular in some areas, but it obviously took more than talk at Westminster to vanquish the good old British slum mentality and make people admit their responsibility towards the inevitable misfits. There was a time when he would have made an issue of the squatters but his days of political campaigning were over. Someone else could worry about the solution. At sixty-eight he hadn't all that much time left to enjoy the sun, the wildflowers and the distant prospect of Shallowford Woods.

Away in the distance he saw Rumble Patrick at work with a baler but checked an impulse to ride the fly-pestered grey across open country and turned inland, noting that the rubble of Periwinkle farmhouse had now been carted away and that the site showed on the hillside like a filled-in shell-crater. It was shadier under the spur of Hermitage Plateau, so he skirted it and headed up Hermitage Lane towards the beckoning shadow of the woods. At the last swing gate north of the farm he saw Henry Pitts and his greeting widened his old friend's rubbery smile by at least two inches.

"Giddon, youm back!" Henry shouted, gleefully. "Us'd begun to reckon you an' the Missus would stay outalong," and suddenly his smile shrank beyond its normal width and he said, "You won't have heard the latest about my David's caper, will 'ee? Now youm back 'ee won't waste no time plaguing 'ee again."

Paul remembered then that David had made an offer for the freehold of Hermitage and had been referred to Andy, who had told him brusquely that the Company had no intention of selling off more land. It was something Paul had forgotten, thinking it could wait for the Company's next quarterly meeting, but now it occurred to him that there must have been a meeting during his absence so he said, "There's not all that hurry, is there? I'm willing to consider it if he's really made up his mind and can pay us a fair market price. I wouldn't sell to a stranger but David is different. He was born on the place! Didn't Andy tell him to hold his horses until I got back?"

"No, 'er didden," Henry said, sourly to him, "'er showed him the door and zed there was no chance of David nor anyone else buying freeholds," and it seemed to Paul that he would have liked to express himself even more forcibly but did not do so out of regard for their long-standing friendship. He said:

"You mean they had a row over it?" and Henry said this was so, and that David came back saying he was going to emigrate to Australia where a man could hope to die owning the land he had worked in his lifetime.

For the second time that morning the sparkle left the air. First the squatters and now David Pitts and his son Andy snarling at one another in his absence.

"David isn't serious about emigrating, is he?" he asked but Henry said he had already sent for brochures from Australia House.

"I told him not to act like a bliddy vool until you was back," he said, "but now his ole gran is dade he'll go if he's got to bide yer as a tenant. He's always had it in mind to own Hermitage, mind you. I never did, nor my ole feyther either, but they young ones is diffr'ent. *Your* boy's diffr'ent. They doan zeem to be able to give an' taake zame as us did, backalong."

"Well, tell him to throw those damned brochures in the fire," Paul said. "We'll have a Company meeting in a week or two and he can rely on me to back him if he's keen to buy. I don't know why Andy should be so bloody-minded about it. This Valley is only a fringe interest of his. He's got far bigger fish to fry and some of them stink to my mind."

Suddenly Henry looked cheerful again. "Would 'ee tell un that now?" he said, and without waiting for assent he put his finger in his mouth and produced a piercing whistle, so that the chunky figure of David emerged from Hermitage copse some fifty yards away.

"You damned old rascal, you must have seen me coming," Paul said, laughing, and Henry admitted as much so that Paul, reflecting that the ambush was reminiscent of earlier days, felt that the situation was now resolved and told the red-faced David that he could come over and talk figures as soon as he had had an opportunity to discuss the matter with Rumble Patrick and Andy.

"There now, what did I tell 'ee?" demanded Henry, rounding on his stolid son as though he had been a surly child of five. "Tiz the Squire who gives the orders round here, so hang they ole papers you got in the bliddy privvy, where they belong."

David said nothing at all but Paul could see that he was relieved. He went off up the slope slashing at thistles with his stick and Paul, struck by the dissimilarity of father and son, said, "Do you know what it is about them, Henry? They don't laugh any more, that's their trouble. The only one of mine who can really see a joke is Simon and he couldn't until those boys of his began rubbing his corners off down at the school," and he touched Snowdrop with his heels and passed gratefully into the deep shadow of the lane that ran under the southern edge of the woods.

II

Up among the big timber the summer scents were far stronger than on the plain and the muted orchestra that he always listened for here at this time of year reached him as a subdued clamour as he picked his way down to the Mere. The surface was glacial and over on the far side he could see some of the older beeches reflected in elaborate detail. The air was full of rustlings and hummings, punctuated every now and again by the flutes of the blackbirds, or the squawks of moorhens concealed on the islet. By the time he had ridden the length of the sheet of water his humour was quite restored and he was further gladdened by the sight of old Sam Potter, now the oldest of the Shallowford originals, who had lived on here alone after the death of his wife Joannie in the autumn.

Sam, the eldest of the Dell Potters, had been his woods-man for forty-five years and Paul supposed that he would now be making plans to live with one of his children, Dick perhaps, who had replaced that arty family at High Coombe, or Pauline, whose birth Paul had almost witnessed in this cottage the year he bought the estate. Sam, however, had other ideas, as he soon advertised saying, with a humility everyone else on the estate had discarded, "Was 'ee thinkin' o' givin' me marchin' orders, Squire, now Joannie's dade and I draws the pension?"

"Well now that you mention it I'm surprised to see you here. It must be very lonely for you, living in this place all alone."

"*Lonely?*" Sam's expression came as near to flat contradic-tion as Paul could remember. "God love you, I baint lonely. Not that I doan miss the ole woman. I do, 'specially in the evenings, but a man can't be lonely out yer so long as he can get about and I'd far zooner bide than move in as lodger wi' any one of 'em. They'd 'ave me, mind. Pauline would do for me, and I daresay I could earn board and lodge up at High Coombe wi' Dick, but I'd zooner bide if it's all the zame to you. Will 'ee be wantin' the cottage for someone younger?"

"No, of course I won't," Paul assured him, glad to have at least one local landmark confirmed. "You can live here as long as you like and I'm not thinking of getting another woodsman in any case. There's precious little game to keep and the woods can look after themselves, the same as they were doing long before you and I arrived on the scene." And then it occurred to him that this was tantamount to saying that Sam had never justified himself all these years, so he added, "You've more than pulled your weight ever since I gave you the job, Sam. If you slack off a bit now don't imagine I'll complain. It might seem odd to you but these woods have always meant more to me than any acres that pay rent. As long as you keep the rides open and there's a refuge handy for everything in the Valley that needs one, I'm satisfied. That's about all I ever wanted out of this part of the estate, so let's leave it that way and you can go on paying peppercorn rent for that cottage of yours."

It was a pleasure to watch Sam's embarrassment as he stood by Snowdrop's head, scratching a large brown mole that divided the furrows of his cheek. Sam, he reflected, had never had much in common with his father, mother, his poacher-brother Smut, or his numerous sisters, for he lacked their independence and cheerful impudence. He had always reminded Paul of a rural character out of another century and his presence here was a small buttress against change. He said, suddenly, "How do you put in the day, Sam? I mean, apart from clearing fallen timber and cutting the brambles back?" and Sam said, "I got the chicken to zee to, and a bit o' cookin' and cleanin', for Joannie liked the place scoured and 'er woulden 'ave it otherwise. But the best times is early on, when I watch the varmints."

Paul remembered then that a "varmint", to Sam was anything on four legs that came down to the Mere and he remembered that, unlike most keepers, Sam had never erected a vermin pole and seldom carried a gun. Somehow he must have sensed that Paul, never much of a sportsman, subscribed to his live-and-let-live theory hereabouts. Apart from hunting foxes (and refusing to dig them out) Paul had rarely killed for sport or the pot. He always thought of the wild life on this side of the woods as tenantry.

He said good-bye to Sam and took the winding path to the head of the Dell where the sun blazed out again and he saw that Dick Potter was due to start reaping in High Coombe's west-sloping fields beyond the last of the trees.

He was relieved to see a real Shallowfordian back in the farm where Claire had been born and where, on an airless summer morning such as this, she had first appeared to him as a laughing girl offering him a plate of pikelets, and holding his hand longer than necessary when their fingers touched. "She had made up her mind to get me from the very start," he reflected, grinning, "and that madcap first marriage of mine must have set the whole Derwent family by the ears. Old Edward, her father, was a crusty old chap but one of the best farmers in the Valley, and I still can't be sure Dick Potter will stick at it after all that trapesing about the world in the Forces. However, he can't do worse than that bunch

303

we had here during the war," and as he thought this Dick Potter, and his lifelong chum and cousin, Bon-Bon, Smut's boy, left their tractor stuttering in the yard and came across to him, asking with a frankness that old Sam would have considered impertinent, "if he and Mrs. Craddock had been gypped by the Wogs in Port Said". Two generations ago, Paul thought, nobody working up here would have heard of Port Said, but two world wars had improved their geography and simultaneously widened and narrowed their outlook. They were more sophisticated than their grandfathers but their travels seemed to have left them even more contemptuous of foreigners.

He told them a little of his travels and asked if either of them had heard or seen anything of the former tenant, who had gone off owing a quarter's rent. "Not a butcher's," Bon-Bon said, "the poor bastard was stuck with the kids. You heard his Missis—the one who was always painting when she wasn't giving birth—ran off with a Yank? Imagine that! And her turned forty and as broad in the beam as that grey of yours."

"I'd heard she had left him," Paul said, feeling a little sorry for that idiot Archer-Forbes, "but I didn't know it was for a Yank. It wasn't the same one who caused that trouble over at the Home Farm, was it?"

"Giddon no," said Dick Potter, chuckling, "this one was a darkie. He must have had something her old man didn't have, in spite of all those kids. Come on Bon-Bon, time we got weaving. This summer has been a real scorcher, Squire, and it looks like staying that way."

He left them roaring away on their tractor, trailing blue exhaust and reflecting that he might have been wrong about the seriousness of the younger generation, for obviously here were a pair who were not weighed down by their responsibilities. "Funny thing," he said to himself, as he crossed the border to Deepdene, the middle Coombe farm, "you think you know it all and then you suddenly realise you know very little about anyone. Noah Williams and that mine, Andy's attitude to those squatters, David Pitts getting it into his head to sail off to Australia, Sam Potter content to live out his days watching otters and badgers, and now a middle-aged woman with a large family running off with a buck negro. Sometimes life is as good as a pantomime about here but the townsman still thinks of us as a bunch of rustics bogged down in mud and tradition."

He was in for a bigger shock when he clattered into the yard of Deepdene, expecting to be greeted by old Francis Willoughby. Who should be sunning herself in the porch but Prudence Honeyman—"Prudence-Pitts-that-was"—and she seemed surprised that he was surprised, for apparently Rumble Patrick had promised to write informing him that Francis, defeated by his asthma, had retired in April and that Nelson Honeyman, homesick for the Valley after only three years "abroad" in Dorset, had sold up, applied for the Deepdene lease and been granted it, Simon and Rumble having obtained Andy's agreement over the telephone.

"Well, I'm delighted to see you back," he admitted, thinking how handsome she looked and how much more sure of herself than when he had last seen her after that ludicrous incident in the Home Farm hayloft, "But surely Deepdene isn't large enough for Nelson? I thought he was ambitious to make money."

"He was," Prudence said, "and he did. We sold that Dorset farm and stock for more than twice the price we paid for it. One of those expense-account farmers from London turned up, Nelson asked a silly price and he paid it, without batting an eyelid. It's something to do with their tax but don't ask me to explain it. We heard old Francis Willoughby was packing it in so Nelson decided he'd like to come back and see what he could make of this place. After all, Francis made money here, mostly with beef cattle of course, but Nelson's sticking to sheep. He did very well out of them over there," and she pointed in the general direction of Dorset.

He said, a little diffidently, "Er . . . how *are* things between Nelson and you, Prudence? You were very frank the last time we talked," and she said, with a laugh, "Yes I was, wasn't I? Well, I'll be frank again, Mr. Craddock. That business with Eddy Morrisey showed a profit. Nelson has never been quite the same since and I don't mean by that he throws it up at me. He never has, not once."

She paused a moment and Paul noticed that she wasn't quite as brazen as her local reputation implied for she was blushing. She went on, however, "I more or less told you what our trouble was—that time you tried to sort us out? Well—how can I put it? There isn't that kind of trouble any more. I suppose the shock of that silly business helped. Not only

Nelson but me, too. I'm not tarty-minded, you know, or not so long as I'm not taken for granted, the way I was up to that time. He spends more now, takes me out and about a bit, buys me things without me having to hint. What I really mean is—I'll always settle for a quiet life, so long as it's not too quiet if you follow me!"

"Indeed I do," he said, smiling and reflecting that, in some ways, she was not unlike Claire. She had plenty to offer, and provided it was accepted with enthusiasm she could jog along contentedly enough, even with an unimaginative creature like Nelson. All she really looked for was security and to be admired and needed. For the rest, things could be left to take care of themselves.

"Where is Nelson now?"

"Gone to Paxtonbury to buy a smashing new car. Can I make you some coffee?"

He was tempted but pleaded appointments in Coombe Bay and moved on, comforted by the thought that stability had returned to this side of the estate now that Dick Potter and Bon-Bon were at High Coombe, and a Honeyman was installed at Deepdene. This area had always been the weak spot in his defences and still was to a degree, for he was worried about Low Coombe, a perennial source of anxiety ever since old Tamer's days. Brissot, the French Canadian who partnered Jumbo Bellchamber, had been a good farmer but the Cockney had never regarded the farm as much more than a bolt hole after the First War. Now that Brissot had retired and gone back to the home he left in 1914, Paul couldn't see Jumbo managing on his own, especially with a woman like Violet Potter for a wife. He knew that they had all been coining money during the war and were still in cahoots with Smut Potter and his avaricious French wife, Marie. Both Jumbo and Smut ran big cars and spent whole days at National Hunt meetings. They also went up to London for a binge every now and again, and the farm was beginning to look down-at-heel.

He descended the winding path through thinning trees, his thoughts returning to characters who had used it over the last half century—savage old Tamer, Gypsy Meg, the Timberlake boys who had come courting the Potter girls, and Jem, the Bideford Goliath, who had once held sway here with the two eldest Potter girls as his wives, and children of doubtful parentage swarming all over the Dell. Then, as he approached the clearing where the farmhouse squatted, he heard the roar of a powerful engine and was just in time to see a long, blue car shoot off down the track. Jumbo, standing at the porch, looked a little disconcerted, as though he might be asked questions concerning his visitor but Paul made no comment. Rationing was still in force, but if Jumbo was still active in the black market there was not much point in lecturing him years after the collapse of the Third Reich.

Jumbo said, guardedly, "Heard you was back, Mr. Craddock," and Paul wondered at the infallibility of the Valley jungle-drums and asked how Jumbo was faring now that his partner had left, and what kind of crops he intended raising in the cliff fields further east. The Cockney was more than usually evasive. His wary eyes—a rifleman's eyes thought Paul, recalling how Jumbo had once shot four Uhlans out of the saddle like ducks at a fair—roved the Dell, and when Paul enquired after Violet he said, carelessly, "Lazy old slut's gorne ter Whinmouth to 'ave a nairdo! She's there twice a week."

Paul said, on impulse, "Do you ever regret settling here, Jumbo? Don't you ever hanker after London?" and the man replied, as though suspecting a trap, "No. Woulden want ter live there no more. Like a bit o' country, alwus did," so that Paul had a glimpse of the original Jumbo playing cricket with a piece of wood and a rag ball in some smuty park near Southwark. Bellchamber, his instinct told him, was certainly uncomfortable about something. But he was not curious and rode down the track to the river road where he passed Mill Cottage, once the home of Hazel and her baby son Rumble, now much in need of renovation but capable, he would say, of housing a squatter if one of them could be persuaded to buckle down and earn a living from the soil. He made a note of this and pushed on across fields shimmering with heat to the head of Coombe Bay village where he had once owned property but, on looking about him, was glad it had passed to other hands.

There were changes here every month now as the place continued to inflate itself into a community somewhere between Bognor Regis and one of those Westcountry coastal villages trying to qualify as a terminus for day-trippers. Old cottages had been ripped down and replaced with flat, greyish shops that looked like the blockhouses they had once built along the Transvaal railway, except that they had chromium-framed windows and were hung about with rubbishy merchandise and jazzy signs painted in hard, gilt lettering. There were several small cafés flanked by tinplate advertisements for soft drinks and brands of cigarettes, a window full of "handicrafts" that included ashtrays contrived out of tortured knots of wood and pixies made from twigs and acorns. There were painted seashells and one or two wishy-washy watercolours trying to get themselves adopted as calendars, and lower down the hill was a shop called "The Olde Spinning Wheele" that set Paul wondering why everyone who tried to give the impression he was practising an ancient craft should find it necessary to add a couple of "e"s to his signboard. The Raven, always a nondescript pub, now looked like a child's attempt to build a Tudor barn out of black sticks and cardboard and the whole place smelled of fish, varnish and hot rubber.

The season was in full swing and Paul marvelled at the number of people attracted by all this clutter. Familes trudged up and down the hill, large pink mums in navy slacks and dads in shirtsleeves and cheap Panama hats. The children, some of them blistered but all of them well-fed and chubby, seemed never to have seen a man mounted on a horse before, for they shouted and pointed with every indication of excitement. Then Paul saw the new Rector, Mark Portal, chatting to an elderly hiker who looked as if he had stepped out of a pre-war *Punch* with his khaki shorts, deerstalker, and enormous rucksack. He reined in to pass the time of day with the parson whom he hardly knew, for Old Horsey had died a year ago and had not been replaced until the week before Paul's winter illness. The professor-type hiker moved on and the young Rector called, "Top of the morning, Squire," with professional heartiness, but noting Paul's bleak look, added, with a grin, "I'm sorry, Mr. Craddock, but it gives me a lift to call somebody 'Squire'. It puts me back in a world of free blankets, private pews and long, thundering sermons aimed at maintaining the status quo." Paul wondered if the fellow was getting at him but decided not, for he had an open face and humorous eyes. He said, "How are you liking it here? Is there anything I can do? My responsibility in the village has been whittled down to your rectory and the Boer War memorial tablet in the church. Wait a minute, I'll get off, I can't talk down to the cloth in this high-handed manner," and he dismounted, looping the grey's bridle over his arm and edging into the kerb to make way for a motor-coach crammed with the day's quota of sightseers from Paxton-bury's hotels. The smell of seaweed, always so strong about here, was banished by the whiff of exhaust and he could not prevent himself saying, "If this is progress then number me among the primitives."

The Rector chuckled. "Yes, I heard they were your senti-ments," he said, "and actually they're mine too, but I dare not advertise it. My father had a latter-day Oliver Goldsmith living in Northamptonshire when I was a boy and the local Squire managed to keep even the railway at bay until 1899. He was a dedicated hunting man."

"So was your predecessor-before-last, Parson Bull," Paul said. "He drove himself into the ground foxhunting and between you and me he was one of the biggest old rascals around here."

"I heard that too," Portal said. "There's a photograph of him in my study and he looks like a warrior bishop about the time of the Peasants' Revolt. I wonder how he'd cope with my kind of parishioner?" and Paul said that it would be interesting to watch him herding them to evensong with his long, leather whip that produced cracks capable of carrying across two fields and a covert. Portal said, thoughtfully, "It's a matter of adjusting, I suppose, but frankly the speed of it all has left me breathless. I'm only thirty-nine and I've seen an incredible amount of change in that time. You must have seen a great deal more. Is all of it vulgar?"

"Not by any means," Paul replied, taking a sudden liking to the man. "When I came here first there were some fearful injustices, a great deal of filthy housing, too much cruelty to children and animals, and old people living on about a shilling a day. There was an old woman called Coombes who lived in that cottage—or where a cottage once stood—she used to dry her tea-leaves on a piece of board to make them last a week. There was a family of nine who were all swept away by typhoid in a single summer due to polluted drinking water. We've got rid of that kind of thing, but somehow I can't help wishing we'd managed it more gracefully. Will you and your wife come to dinner one day next week? That was obligatory in the old days but you won't upset me a bit by declining."

Portal said he would be delighted and they fixed on Wednesday, after which Paul swung himself into the saddle and went on down to the quay where he turned right, hoping to escape his involuntary role as one of the Coombe Bay holiday attractions. Half-way along the quay, however, he pulled up short outside Smut Potter's bakery, astonished to discover that it was no longer a bakery but a half-gutted shop in the process of conversion into a Continental-type café. Iron tables were already stacked in one corner and the store had been demolished to make room for a drive-in car park. It was not his concern any longer, for he had sold the property when the Company was formed, but all the same it surprised him. He had always thought of Smut and Marie as permanent Shallowfordians and found it difficult to believe that they had made enough during the war to retire. Then Smut came out of the yard pushing a handcart loaded with part of his oven and gave Paul a cheery greeting. He too must have been listening to Valley drums for he said, "Us yerd you was backalong. Did 'ee see the boy on the way down?"

"You mean your boy, Bon-Bon?"

"Giddon no, *your* boy. The townee one, Andy."

"Andy has been here today?"

"Just left," Smut said, "come to zee how us was gettin' on with the new place."

A thought occurred to Paul. He said, "Was he driving a big flashy car? A blue one?"

"Yes he was," said Smut, "a real corker. Cost him nigh on dree thousand, or so he said. Do 'em pay that much for cars in London?"

"You'd be surprised what they do up there," Paul said, vaguely, for his mind was occupied with the reason, if there was a reason, for Andy's abrupt departure from Lower Coombe half an hour before. Thinking back it seemed to connect with Jumbo Bellchamber's hangdog look and his reluctance to chat, as though he was anxious to prevent Paul from knowing Andy had been there. He said, briefly, "Look, Smut, what the hell *is* going on around here? This place is changing overnight and there's a smell about it I don't like. Do you own those premises of yours now?"

"Not me," said Smut, readily. "I rent 'em, zame as I did from you. This café lark is Marie's idea, but the new land-lord is backing her. Not that I'm against it, mind. There's a packet o' money to be made in season the way things is going yerabouts."

"Then who is the new landlord?"

"It's a Company. Your boy could tell you more about it than me. Chum of his is the Chairman, one-legged chap called Shawcrosse. He was the one who bought it, and all them other lots you sold off a year or two back."

The name had an elusive familiarity but Paul, after chasing it a moment or two postponed pursuit until he could talk to Andy whom he supposed had gone to the house to await his return. "What the devil is this chap Shawcrosse trying to do? He'll never make a Blackpool out of this place. It's too far from the main road and any expansion east is blocked by the Bluff. Come to that, he can't even expand inland, for there he runs smack up against our border. Have you ever actually met him?"

"Not me," said Smut again, "he's too bliddy toffee-nosed to pass the time o' day with my sort but your boy can tell you about him. He lived next door to him for a time, back end o' the war, when they was both upalong."

Paul remembered then and his disquiet increased. Shawcrosse—a chap about Andy's age or a little older, who had lost a leg in the Western Desert and had rented one of the tall Victorian houses in Cliff Terrace for his convalescence. He remembered him now, a smooth, outwardly affable type, with ginger hair brushed straight back and a mincing little wife who wore shoes with heels like poniards.

"So that's him? A speculator I wouldn't wonder. Well, there's nothing I can do to stop his gallop even if I wanted to, so good luck with the café, Smut, and give my regards to Marie."

He rode on down the quay and up on to the dunes, leaving Smut to dispose of his oven that he supposed would now go for scrap if people still wanted scrap. The sun sparkled on the great sheet of blue water between the beach and the sandbanks but Paul did not notice it. Deep down he knew himself to be disturbed but would have found it difficult to say why, for on the whole his ride had been reassuring. There had been changes, some of them startling changes, but then there always had been, even in his earliest days, and one soon got used to new patterns and new faces. Deliberately, as he walked the sweating grey over the soft ground towards the ford, he marshalled his thoughts, beginning with the squatters and moving on to David Pitts' determination to become a freeholder. Old Sam Potter was a fixture and so, it seemed, was his son Dick at High Coombe. Then there was the pleasant discovery of finding the Honeymans established at Deepdene but the pattern began to change as he descended the Coombe and approached that noisy little sham resort at the mouth of the Sorrel. Jumbo Bellchamber was up to something, and so was this fellow Shawcrosse, and he suspected that Andy had a finger in the pie somewhere along the line. They had better, he thought, bring it out into the open right away and he rode up the drive and into the stableyard expecting to see his son's three-thousand-pound car parked behind the house. It was not and when Claire came out to tell him that lunch was on the table she added that Andy had 'phoned from Whinmouth and she had invited him over but he said he had another engagement.

"Is anything the matter?" she asked, noting his frown, and he told her no, or not that he knew of, but he had just made a resolution to keep clear of Coombe Bay during the summer months. Then he remembered the Rector and warned her that he was coming to dinner, and after that he told her rather more of his conversation with Prudence Honeyman than he had intended, for somehow he needed to switch his mind to lighter subjects. She said, as he knew she would, "Well, I'm glad. And I'm surprised too, for that girl deserved someone more positive than Nelson. She ought to have had half-a-dozen children by now," to which Paul replied, "She would if I'd had anything to do with it."

"Don't be so damned greedy," said Claire, "and don't preen yourself that you could have satisfied two of me, even in your lustiest years."

"Ah," he replied, the small cloud lifting in her comfortable presence, "that's true enough but who, apart from Brigham Young, could hope to achieve that? My observation was academic, I'm not complaining."

"I should think not," she said. "Here, get on with this and fill me in with the local chit-chat," and she handed him a vast plate of ham, cold chicken and salad prepared by Mary and warned him that there was a trifle and clotted cream to follow.

CHAPTER THREE

BASTIONS FOR SALE

I

PAUL never outgrew his initial embarrassment at having to preside over the meetings of the Shallowford Estates Company.

Sitting at the head of the library table, flanked by sons, a son-in-law and daughter, he felt himself to be playing a part in a charade at a Christmas party, and when he told Claire that he felt amateur in the role, she said, cheerfully, "Well, it always makes me a little edgy but if there's an imbalance at those meetings it's in your favour. Simon always votes with you, and you and that Rumble Patrick rehearse your approach to every item on the agenda before Andy gets here."

"Yes, and he always arrives with Whiz's proxy vote in his pocket, don't forget that."

"What of it? He keeps her in the picture and you don't. As a matter of fact, I'm surprised that he takes the business as seriously as he does. It must seem very small beer to him these days. If you want my opinion he does it out of loyalty to you and the others."

"I'd like to believe that, old girl, but knowing our post-war Andy I rather doubt it. Sometimes he reminds me of my father in his early scrapyard days, and then again, of your father when I was married to Grace. How does he get on with Margaret these days? Does he ever tell you?"

"I don't ask," Claire said. "At sixty-four I've learned to let well alone."

She did not add that she often regretted her part in the wartime reconciliation but he was not really interested in Andy's matrimonial affairs, as she realised when he replied,

313

"That's it! That's what I ought to have done—let well alone."

"You mean you're sorry you formed the Company? But you told me only a month ago it was saving you two thousand a year in tax!"

"There are worse things than paying out half your income in tax."

"Tell me one."

"All right, I will. Seeing this entire Valley raped the way they've raped that village on the coast! It isn't parting with acres I resent—I'm advocating we sell Hermitage to David Pitts at today's meeting, but David is a farmer not a speculator. Suppose they got a real foothold and started a rampage on our side of the river?"

"How could they do that when we own all the freehold?"

"I don't know," he said doubtfully, "but I do know that everyone associated with this Company except Mary considers me fossilised. Maybe if the money offered for sites was tempting enough . . ."

She interrupted with a snort of indignation. "Nonsense! If any one of them tried to cross you in that way they'd have me to reckon with."

"But you haven't got a vote."

"No, but I've got a vitriolic tongue when I care to use it. If I thought Andy, Rumble, Simon or even Mary was using your generosity to spoil your old age, you'd hear my protest from one end of the Valley to the other."

At the time the promise was lighthearted. She thought of his anxieties as symptomatic of the worries he had always harboured for a place that had taken and used his life as ruthlessly and as exclusively as it had. And yet, within less than a month, she was called upon to make good her promise.

The initial meeting, held within a month of their return, provided some lively exchanges but was not, on the whole, an acrimonious one for it was soon clear that Andy's eagerness to run the squatters off the moor would be effectively checked by Paul's tolerance and the half-extinct embers of Simon's Socialist fires. Paul told them about his encounter with the ex-Eighth-Army man, and of the trouble strangers faced in getting a local council to take their housing applications seriously. Andy said, flatly, "Look, don't give me that ex-service line. You never heard me bleat about this, did you?" and he held up his gloved hand, the first gesture he had ever made to draw attention to it.

Simon said, quietly, "You started with advantages those squatters don't have. You ended the war with money in the bank and the land you're talking about was handed to you on a plate. Don't be so bloody vindictive about those poor devils out there. Do you imagine they would be pigging it in a Nissen hut if they could find a real home?"

Paul sat back smiling, content to leave it all to Simon, who was better qualified to conduct this kind of argument. But Andy did not make an issue of it. He said briefly, "Well, if it was left to me and to Whiz we'd have them off in a brace of shakes. As it is, let the Gov'nor take it up with the local housing committees. We pay enough in rates, God knows."

Paul promised to do this and they went on to agree upon renovations to Mill Cottage, installations at High Coombe, and the new rent to be fixed for the Honeymans at Deepdene. Then Paul resurrected the matter of David Pitts' application to buy Hermitage and saw Andy glower.

"I told him while you were away that you were absolutely opposed to selling off freeholds," he protested when Paul, to everyone's surprise, admitted having told David and his father that the latter could buy Hermitage if he could find the money. "I consulted Rumble here and he agreed." Andy turned to Rumble for confirmation. "That's true, is it?"

"Yes it is," Rumble admitted, somewhat uncomfortably as Mary turned to him, "but I've been a freeholder since 1935 and thinking it over mine was a hypocritical stand to take. I see David's point of view very clearly but I always got the impression the Gov'nor was dead against parcelling up the estate. That was the reason I agreed to say no."

"I was and I still am," Paul admitted, "but you're a member of the family and David, besides being a first-rate farmer, is the son of my oldest friend in the Valley. It makes a difference."

"Nothing makes a difference when you're in business," said Andy and Claire saw the live side of his face twitch.

"It makes a difference to me," Paul said shortly, "and it's time you understood that."

"What's he prepared to pay? That's the real issue," said

315

Andy, and Paul reported that Henry had agreed to help and that the bank would come across with a substantial loan.

"I'd be prepared to sell for £8,000" he said. "That's allowing about two-five for the farmhouse. The stock, or course, is his own."

"It's not enough," Andy said, brutally. "Up it to £9,-500."

Paul flushed and Claire thought he was going to lose his temper but he restrained himself, saying "What do the others think? I presume you're acting for Whiz as well as yourself?"

"Whiz is like me," Andy said, "she'll want as much as she can get."

Rumble Patrick did a little sum involving the acreage of Hermitage and the price per acre that agricultural land was fetching. "Nine-five is top price for land about here," he said, "and I daresay one of the stockbrokers looking for a tax-fiddle would pay more if we advertised, but part of Hermitage is rough land, especially those fields behind French Wood. I'd say a fair price was £8,750 and I know David would pay that. He did damned well there during the war—at least Henry did, with all the black market traffic that went on. I daresay they've got more salted away than any of us."

They put it to the vote and the compromise price was carried. After that tension ebbed and the men spent an hour or so passing the bottle and discussing general matters while Paul 'phoned Henry and got his acceptance of the price and agreement to complete by January 1st.

One of the more rewarding aspects of the post-war Andy was that he could peel off his board-room toughness as soon as the agenda sheets had been collected up and the ash trays emptied, a job, Claire reminded them, that always seemed to fall to the unpaid secretary of the Company. He told them something of the property world in London and elsewhere, of the sudden popularity of farm land among business men seeking escape hatches for heavily-taxed profits, and of the world in which he moved now that he was engaged in property deals all over the country. Paul, although not approving, was impressed by his expertise and wondered if he had inherited his techniques from his grandfather, who had made his pile out of scrap metals, or whether he had acquired them as part of the tactical training given him by old

Franz Zorndorff in the years after he and Stevie had broken away to make their own way in life. He remembered the initial interview he had had with them in this very room and his disgusted comment at the time—"From scrap to scrap in three generations ... !" Zorndorff, he knew, had always admired The Pair, and in a way he could still admire Andy, who found no difficulty at all in adapting to the cut-and-thrust of post-war commerce, so different in pace, method and even equipment to that of his grandfather's era. The boy's war injuries never seemed to bother him and it was possible to forget, watching him, that his left arm ended above the wrist and that the skin down one side of his face had been grafted from his buttock.

Musing, he dropped out of the conversation and watched them, collectively and individually. Andy stood apart, the only one among them who had really kept pace with the gathering momentum of the cntury. Rumble Patrick was closest to Andy, for at least he had mastered the technical advances of the last two decades and was applying them to his profession, whereas Mary was happy in the role of a dutiful wife of a type that Claire had never been, not even in her most complaisant moments. Then there was Whiz, who sometimes showed up to side with Andy and somehow managed to give the impression that money was vulgar and yet, when it came to taking some, could be tougher than Andy who was always as interested in the game as the profits. Old Simon, as usual, was still the odd man out, but a far more integrated odd man than in his barn-storming days, when he had campaigned alongside that first wife of his. He was obviously in the right profession now and happily immersed in the short-lived enthusiasms of youth and passing on, in his own amiable way, all the lessons he had learned from two wars and a ten-year slump. More and more Paul found himself subscribing to Simon's creed of watered-down Socialism, an attitude of mind rather than a political faith, and one, he felt, that the old Liberals of pre-First World War days would have understood and tried to practise today. Thank God the boy had found a wife like Evie Horsey, who cheerfully mothered his boys in that asphalt playground at Whinmouth and was content to stitch costumes for the pageants and plays Simon was always writing and producing to supplement his text-books. He was very popular there, Paul understood, not only with the boys but also—surprisingly—with the School Managers and parents. He had, at forty plus, at last found his niche and was even beginning to look like a schoolmaster with his long, narrow face, thinning hair and hunched gait.

The meeting broke up with boisterous good-byes and Andy roared off down the drive in his absurdly luxurious car, while Rumble Patrick and Mary stumped off across the fields to the Home Farm. Simon, watching them go, said:

"They don't change much, do they? I remember seeing them wander off like that when they were about nine! Mary's pregnant again, I see. How many grandchildren will that make?"

"Eight," Claire said, "unless you've got any news for us," and Simon said that he had and that their second child could be expected round about January.

"Well, you're all coming up the straight," said Claire, "and not before time. Whiz has her three, Mary two and one in the oven, there's your Mark and another to come, and finally that lovely child Vanessa, whom you could describe as a kind of combined effort, for Margaret tells me Andy spoils her terribly."

She would never have said this to Paul, but the relationship between her and Simon had always been relaxed. He said, "I'm glad. That's how it should be, but collectively we haven't made much of a showing against your six and the Gov'nor's seven, have we?"

"There's time enough," she said, "providing you don't reduce sex to a kind of algebra, as people seem to be doing if you read the newspapers nowadays."

He laughed, kissed her and drove off in his third-hand Humber. He never seemed to care what kind of car he owned or what kind of clothes he wore. Even now, after all these years, his preoccupation with abstracts reminded her vividly of Grace Lovell, his mother, whom she had once hated but had eventually come to understand and respect.

II

The crisis came a few weeks later when Andy rang and asked if they could convene a special meeting to consider a proposal he wanted to put to them. He would not say what the proposal was, only that it had reached him in a roundabout way and was sufficiently important to merit general discussion. Paul said he would arrange it and the date was fixed for the first day of October, Whiz writing to say that she couldn't attend as she and Ian were due to preside over a passing-out ceremony but that Andy had agreed to act on her behalf.

"What do you suppose that boy is up to now?" Paul grumbled, at breakfast. "Does he want us to spend David's purchase price on a whole lot of battery houses, or a new road to serve the Coombe Farms? I never see the point of making money the way he and his kind make it. The minute they have it they find something fresh to spend it on."

"That's what it's for," Claire said, "and you're the right one to preach I must say. When I think of all the money you've poured into the stretch between the Bluff and the Moor. What did old Franz used to call it—Craddock's 'Slough of Despond'?"

"At least something useful re-emerged from mine, enough to beat two U-boat campaigns and raise a lot of healthy people. All Andy raises are office blocks that look like bloody great greenhouses, housing estates beginning to sprout T.V. aerials, and a lot of layabouts who seem to live off the rates."

She laughed, as she usually did when he took one of his bad-tempered swipes at post-war trends. "My God! Listen to the man who talked my Tory father into voting for Lloyd George. Come on, help me prepare the board-room, and whatever Andy proposes count ten before you jump. I daresay it's something that'll do the Inland Revenue out of a hundred or so and if it is I'm in there rooting for him."

They had no agenda for there was nothing that couldn't wait upon the December meeting. Andy, when he drove up, looked subdued and this impression was confirmed when he began, in response to Paul's invitation, to say what he had in mind.

"You're probably going to blow your top at this, Gov'nor. But before you do remember I'm making the proposition with the idea of ensuring any money that flows into the Valley flows our way as well as other people's."

"Every time I hear you use that word 'money'," said Paul, misquoting Goering, "I want to reach for my gun. However, go on and I'll try and judge the proposal impartially."

"It leads back to that chap Bellchamber in Low Coombe," Andy went on, for some reason preferring to look in Rumble

Patrick's direction. "The fact is he's very eager to buy his freehold. Maybe it's catching."

Everyone was surprised but no one more than Paul, who had never thought of Jumbo Bellchamber as anything more than a kind of First World War squatter. "*Bellchamber* wants Low Coombe? And he approached *you?*"

"Indirectly, yes."

"Why did he do that? I was over there a month or two ago and he never so much as hinted at it."

"I'm not surprised. He probably thought you'd knock him down for daring to suggest it."

A shutter flicked in Paul's brain and showed him something he was not over-anxious to see. He remembered Jumbo's evasiveness on the last occasion they had met, and then the glimpse of a big car shooting off down the Dell track. He remembered, too, Smut telling him that same morning that Andy was in the Valley and how he had expected to find him up at the house but had been told by Claire that he had 'phoned from Whinmouth saying he was otherwise engaged. He said, carefully, "You've seen Bellchamber yourself? You've already discussed it with him?"

"That's right."

They were all watching now, sensing the tension between father and son.

"*When,* exactly?"

"Does it matter when?"

"Yes it does. Was it the day after I came home from abroad?"

"It might have been."

"It damn well was. I saw your car. And you shot off like a bolted fox the moment you saw me riding down the Coombe on Snowdrop."

If Andy was rattled he did not show it. He said, evenly, "It was me all right. I went there to find out exactly what was going on and I did find out. As a matter of fact I've seen him since."

"And what was 'going on', as you put it?"

"Look, for God's sake Gov'nor. I'm not fifteen and I haven't been at your cigars. This is supposed to be a Company. All I'm trying to do is steer it towards the jackpot."

"Get to the point, Andy."

This from Claire, looking flushed, as she usually did when

320

obliged by her position as secretary to witness a family row as a neutral.

"I'll get to the point if he'll let me. Jumbo Bellchamber is prepared to buy Low Coombe, the tattiest farm on the estate, for half as much again as David Pitts is paying for Hermitage freehold."

Rumble was the first to speak. He looked stunned, and no wonder Paul thought, for he had worked hard since he was a boy without assembling half that amount of capital.

"Over twelve thousand? For Low Coombe, half of it rough grazing, and a third of the other half blackberry bushes running wild? Where the hell would Jumbo Bellchamber get his hands on that kind of money? Has he won the Pools? Or ploughed up buried treasure?"

"That was one of the things I checked on," said Andy, calmly. "He can pay. That and more if necessary."

"But why? That's what I'd like to know. *Why!*"

Rumble was red in the face and Paul couldn't be sure if his flush was caused by astonishment or by resentment that a slut farmer like Bellchamber had earned that kind of money in five years of a national food shortage. He had a right to be angry, Paul thought. All the time the Valley black marketeers had been shuttling to and from the premises of local butchers and dairymen Rumble had been one of the idiots keeping their petrol lines open at the risk of his life. He said, "That's something we'd all like to know, Andy. *Why?*"

"Certain people are backing an idea of his that will make money a good deal easier and faster than it's made by farming. It's tied in with that expansion in Coombe Bay, and if we block it in the north-west it will happen in the east beyond the Bluff, where there's an alternative site just as good as Jumbo's and even nearer the sea."

"A site for what? For housing?"

It was Simon who asked the question and Claire saw that he wasn't angry but troubled, almost certainly more on Paul's account than his own.

"No," said Andy, "the County Council wouldn't approve more housing sites in that area yet. Sooner or later, of course, they'll have to, and accommodation land will be released in ten and twenty acre dollops. But right now we can actually stop proliferation by selling to Jumbo because he's on to a good thing. A camping site, with a maximum of fifty caravans and probably twice as many tents. He'll put in

321

latrines, incinerators, and probably one temporary shop to sell gear, dairy products and tinned stuff. The choice is very simple. We sell and pick up more than three times what that tip is worth. Or we don't sell, and a camping and caravan site opens up anyhow a mile or so further east, on Lakeworthy's land. That's the alternative. Kick it around among yourselves."

"It's bloody scandalous!" roared Paul. "I haven't heard a whisper about a camping site over there. I always understood a thing like that had to be thrashed out very thoroughly in a local and a County Council before you could build shanty-towns on coastal land."

"It has been thrashed out, Gov'nor," Andy said, "but not much of it in public. Most of it is done in committee and the backers I'm talking about know their business. I daresay they've got their stoolies planted here and there."

" 'Stoolies'? What kind of jargon is that?" Paul demanded, glad to be able to direct his fury on something specific and Andy grinned as Rumble said, pacifically. "Take it easy, Gov'nor. Andy means stool-pigeons—tame Councillors on their side, either on Whinmouth U.D.C. or Paxtonbury R.D.C.

"Both if they know what they're about," said Andy, "and don't assume naked bribery comes into it. It's usually an old-pals act. That's the way it goes nowadays, but maybe it always did."

"It damned well didn't," Paul said, warmly. "There was a time when local landowners were consulted before something like this was rammed under their noses."

Claire said, sharply for her, "Calm down, Paul, and don't cloud the issue. After all, you could have got yourself elected on a Council any time over the last forty years but you never bothered. Maybe it's a pity you didn't." She turned to Andy, mildly enough for him to mistake her for an ally. "You seem to know a great deal about this, Andy. I accept the fact that you're familiar with backstage jiggery-pokery, and also that you went to some pains to get this information in advance, but do you actually know these backers of Jumbo's?"

He looked at her squarely. "Not well enough to stop them," he said, "but well enough to appreciate that they're people who don't move in unless they're sure of themselves. It seems that they picked on Jumbo. Jumbo certainly didn't seek them out."

"Couldn't we lodge objections?" asked Simon, and Andy

said they could, both as a Company and as individuals. Several residents in the district would object but it would serve very little purpose, except, possibly, to delay it a season. "Too many people are likely to benefit," he explained. "All the farmers round here and every tradesman within a radius of five miles. As long as the camp conforms to certain sanitary and siting regulations there are no grounds upon which any effective objection can be based. Coombe Bay is growing fast, and so is Whinmouth. There's even talk of a coastal road connecting the two and that would lead to a compulsory purchase order involving us."

"Very well," said Claire, who seemed to have taken matters in her own hands, "tell us exactly how you feel about it and don't hold anything back. I'm sure everyone wants to know precisely where they stand and don't interrupt him, Paul, wait until he's finished."

"It's easy enough for a child to understand," Andy said, trying to keep a note of exasperation out of his voice. "Sooner or later we're going to have either housing or a caravan site on our eastern boundary. You can fend it off for so long but with everyone screaming for homes, and all this emphasis on youth clubs and outdoor activities that produce new industries—caravan-building for instance—the pattern of places like this has to change and it will change, no matter how far people like the Gov'nor dig their heels in. It's not change for the sake of change, either. It's made inevitable by factors like the population explosion, rising wages, and holidays with pay—especially holidays with pay. Places like this can't survive any longer on agriculture alone. They've got to develop as holiday centres whether they want or not and they're lucky if they can keep light industry at arm's length. Even as it is, with every coastal town expanding like mad, the younger generation are still moving out in search of jobs, in search of more sophistication if you like. I don't have to tell you how many men agriculture is losing every year. The figures are there in *The Farmer's Weekly*, for anyone to read. Well, that's point one—more housing or something less permanent and purely seasonal, like a caravan site. Point two, who makes a profit out of it? Us, or someone standing on the touchline, like that smallholder Lakeworthy the far side of the Bluff? We could let the site ourselves, of course, but the Gov'nor wouldn't stand for that in a million years and for once I'm with him, because Bellchamber doesn't know what he's in for with all the sanitary regulations and all the moonlight flits he'll have to cope with! My advice, for what it's worth, is to squeeze the last drop out of him while he's in a position to pay."

There was an uncomfortable silence. Perhaps everyone was waiting for Paul to speak but he said nothing because it seemed to him that others, younger than him, should have their say first. Rumble Patrick looked at Mary, paused, and finally said, "Well, that's straight enough, Andy, and there wasn't much hot air in what you said. It's logical, or most of it is, and although none of us are keen to see even a third-rate farm like the Dell pack it in and earn its living out of campers, we could use that twelve thousand to stop the same thing happening to the rest of the farm. Twelve thousand, carefully spent, could make our holdings the most efficient and productive in the county."

It was, Paul thought, qualified approval, and although he accepted Rumble's logic he flinched from the prospect of being obliged to move over for men like Bellchamber, for Bellchamber's backers and, behind them, jobbers who seemed to have infiltrated into every legislative body in the land, people who never would give a damn for the soil that fed them and who didn't know a stoat from a weasel. He said, sourly, "Simon? You anything to add to that?" and Simon said he hadn't but would vote with Paul on grounds of sentiment.

It was Claire's cue to step in again. She said, "For Heaven's sake . . . don't let's split down the middle on a thing like this. Andy doesn't want that, it doesn't mean enough to him financially, and I'll not sit here and watch you totting up your share values and measuring them against one another just to find out who pips who. This might be a business but it's also a family. Do one thing or the other but do it unanimously. Throw it out of court, or agree to sell and let Bellchamber wheel his caravans in, so long as we write into his contract that he leaves our side of the Dell Wood untouched as a screen. After all, we've had bigger camps than his in the Valley twice in my lifetime and they didn't give us claustrophobia. Andy was right to bring it up in this way. You'll admit that, won't you, Paul?"

Paul roused himself with difficulty. "Yes, I'll admit that, and I'll also admit that we could retrench with another twelve thousand in the kitty but I can't pretend that I'm philosophical about it. It seems to me that even this is only the thin edge of the wedge and for the first time in my life I'm going to ring what's left of my place with warnings against trespassing. I've never gone in for close-paling fences, broken glass on walls, or barbed wire. I didn't have to, because people used to be born with a sense of fitness and an appreciation of a decent bit of landscape, but now it's different, different in every way, and they'll find I can prove as prickly as those others are smooth and slippery. You can sell to Bellchamber but don't ask me to sit here hammering out the conditions of sale. I couldn't stomach that. It might turn my mind in the direction of spring-guns and man-traps and I believe they've been taken off the statute-book!"

He pushed back his chair, got up and walked out through the garden door. Claire called "Paul!" but he didn't reply and Rumble said, "Leave him, I'll talk to him later." Simon said nothing, sitting hunched with his hands in his pockets until Andy said, glumly, "And where does that leave us? God knows, I knew he'd take it pretty hard but it isn't the end of the world—just a few tents and caravans, half a mile away and still out of sight . . ."

"Get some kind of proposition on paper," Claire said, "and make sure that you put in that clause about leaving the timber our side of the wood." She got up and followed Paul on to the terrace.

III

Perhaps Margaret was alerted by his expression as he came in or by the way he listened apathetically when she told him Shawcrosse was awaiting him in the study. She had lost touch with him lately and the only real point of contact between them was Vanessa, to whom he was very devoted, almost as though he regarded the child as the one remaining link with the boisterous days before the war when business deals of the kind that obsessed him still had acted upon him like champagne rather than drugs. It was not like that any more. The chasm between them could not be traced back to the small fissure caused by her association with Stevie or he could never have made a cult of Vanessa, buying her ponies, tossing her up and down, teasing her, laughing with her, and whisking her off to places like Fortnum & Mason's to array her in expensive, and to Margaret's mind, show-off clothes. She had no complaint to make regarding his attitude towards herself. He was always kind if abstracted, invariably generous, and very occasionally, when he was idle between deals, he would make love to her in a way that recalled, very fleetingly, the extrovert Andy of the 'thirties. It was, she supposed, as good a marriage as most people of their generation enjoyed. There wasn't much sparkle about it but there was no acrimony either, and certainly no bitterness on his part that Stevie had given her the child who was capable of interesting him as she could never do again.

She wondered about this a great deal, toying with all kinds of theories that led ultimately to a single theory. The end of the tie torn loose by Stevie's death had somehow reattached itself to Vanessa, by-passing her altogether, so that there was not much more than tolerance between them but it was tolerance that stemmed from gratitude for the presence of the child. She wondered sometimes if things would have been different if they had had children of their own but there was not much prospect of this now and he did not seem interested in the possibility. Whenever he did use her, and it was not very often for he was away from home most of the year, he did it as though reassociating with a discarded mistress, or an old, complaisant girl friend of his youth whom he had met after an interval of years and taken to bed in an effort to recall old times. She realised that she was as much to blame for this as he was. The few short months spent with Stevie in the little house under the wood had changed her expectation of a relationship between a man and a woman seeking fulfilment in one another's company. Magically Stevie had become a different person after that first encounter in London but Andy, although undergoing many outward changes, had remained basically the same, a roving buccaneer who became bored and irritable after more than forty-eight hours ashore.

She had never made any secret of the fact that she disliked Shawcrosse and Shawcrosse's mincing little wife, Rhoda, and now, for a moment at least, it looked as if he shared her impatience. He said, sharply, "He's here? He doesn't take much on trust, does he? How long has he been waiting?"

"About an hour," she told him, "I gave him a drink and *The Times*," and then she left him to go about her business, wondering why he was jumpy, and what lay behind his peevish comment on Shawcrosse's presence. Soon, however, she forgot the incident and drove off to the riding stables to fetch Vanessa. It was never any good wondering what went on in Andy's mind. It never had been any good, not even in the days when she and Monica had been sucked into the whirlpool of their scrap-market activities. It was not until a month later, when she happened to go into the study in search of blotting paper, that she stumbled on a corner of the jigsaw puzzle his life had become since he had left the R.A.F.

They had rented a large, detached house on the outskirts of Whinmouth, one of the many rented houses she had shared with him in the last thirteen years. Like all the others it was not a home but a plushy perch, with a large, well-kept garden, a sun lounge, and between-the-wars furniture that made her homesick for the black oak of "*Ty-Bach*". He had a large, pseudo-Regency desk with innumerable drawers, all but one of them locked, so she opened the central drawer hoping to find the blotter he sometimes used. Finding it there she lifted it out and thus uncovered the plan.

It was a large, mounted tracing that she recognised as a detailed plan of the coastal belt between Nun's Head and Shallowford Bluff. Every farm, field and coppice was marked in and named.

There was no special reason why she should be interested but she picked it up nevertheless and carried it over to the French windows, forgetting the blotter as partial awareness of what she was holding edged into her mind. Paul, her father-in-law, had a map just like this in his estate office adjoining the library and had proudly displayed it to her the first time Andy brought her to Shallowford House just before they had married. He told her then that he had drawn it when he was a young man and had added to it as the years went by, and changes were recorded in and around the farms, the tracks, and green blobs of woodland.

But the plan she was holding was really two plans. One was the original, or rather a fair copy of the original, and the other a detailed record of recent changes within and without the estate boundaries. It struck her then that some of the features on the map must be speculative for there was a road hugging the coastline all the way from Whinmouth to Coombe Bay and she knew that there never had been anything more than a footpath over the dunes following the southern boundary of the estate.

There was another new feature shown, a great, shaded patch, rectangular in shape, reaching from the river road half-way up the Dell and this was overprinted with the words, "*Shawcrosse Holiday Camp*". This surprised her, not only because a holiday camp was apparently scheduled to be built inside the estate, but because she could not imagine a man like Paul Craddock doing business with a spiv like Shawcrosse.

She took the plan back to the desk, laid it down and rummaged among other papers in the drawer. They were mostly copies of letters written on the notepaper of Shawcrosse & Craddock, Craddock Development Company, or Vista Homes Limited, only three of the names Andy used in his complicated network of ventures. It was not necessary to study the letters. She found a memoranda sheet with a paper-clip clinging to it and recognised it as the key that had been affixed to the plan. It told her as much as she wanted to know.

This was the Shallowford Valley, not as Paul saw it, or as anyone else had ever seen it, but how it would look when Shawcrosse and Andy had finished with it. The ruthlessness of the exercise, already well started it seemed, stirred an indignation within her that made her feel physically sick. She sat back in his swivel-chair for a moment, closing her eyes and making a great effort to concentrate. Then, with deliberation, she compared key and plan, relating the initial capital letters—"A", "B", "C", etc., to coloured twins on the map. "A", shown in blue, was property already acquired by one or other of the companies in Coombe Bay and there seemed to be a great deal of it. "B" was the holiday camp, absorbing one of the Shallowford farms and spreading, in the shape of a spur, to the cliffs east of the Bluff. "C" was labelled "*Proposed New Road*" and after it, written in pencil, were the words, "*Est. time compt'n., Sept. 1950*". There were various other features, a hotel half-way along the road and a housing site on the Moor but she did not study these in detail. Suddenly the pattern became very clear indeed. Andy, as the dominant director of the family company, was the inside man operating on behalf of Shawcrosse, and perhaps some of the other vulpine characters who occasionally called at the house for a drink or left cryptic messages when Andy was out.

It was like finding oneself involuntarily caught up in a

conspiracy to defraud or, even more frightening, witnessing a back-alley attack on an unsuspecting victim and being faced with the choice of intervening or looking the other way. Sitting there, glancing from map to key and key to map, she was stunned by his betrayal, remembering that his access to this property had been a free gift, a shy acknowledgment by his father of his war-service and perhaps also a form of recompense for his physical injuries. She did not try to persuade herself that it might not be a conspiracy at all, that everything on that map was known and approved by Paul, by Simon, Rumble Patrick and the others. It had the hall-marks of a secret treaty and somehow it carried not only Andy's signature but the unmistakeable stamp of Shawcrosse. But if she had wanted further proof it was there to hand, in the carbon copies of letters exchanged between Andy and Shawcrosse and between Andy and his sister Whiz. It was the tailpiece of one of the letters to Whiz that told her something else. Not only had Andy acquired his sister's shares more than a year ago, but had apparently tried and failed to buy Simon's, for Andy had written to his sister: ". . . *Simon wouldn't sell. He seems to think it would upset the Old Man and I daresay he's right, so don't make your sale to me public until I give you the okay. No sense in getting his back up to that extent, and Simon won't say anything about my offer. He doesn't know, of course, that you and Ian have already sold out."*

Margaret wondered vaguely if Whiz had any clear idea of what was really going on, and also how much Andy had paid her for her shares. She knew very little about Whiz, recalling her only as a rather formal little madam, who had wrinkled her pretty nose at Margaret's Welsh accent when they first met. But it didn't matter about Whiz. Andy was the central figure and behind Andy, like a puppeteer, was Shawcrosse, jerking strings to make the Craddocks dance. As she thought about it other pieces of the jigsaw came to hand; snippets of conversations, that hangdog look of Andy's when he returned from the Big House, the visitors he had from time to time, among them the farmer Bellchamber who, she remembered, was the tenant of the holding now labelled "*Shawcrosse Holiday Camp*".

She sat on sifting the pieces and enlarging the pattern until the exercise disgusted her and she got up, stuffed plan and letters into her handbag and went out to the car. Five minutes later she was climbing Whinmouth Hill to the crest of the moor.

Claire heard her out in silence, scanning the plan for a long time and then asking odd and seemingly irrelevant questions. When was Andy expected back? Where was he at this moment? Where was Vanessa? Did Andy ever talk about Stevie? How much of his affluence was real, how much reposed in mortgaged property? Margaret answered as best she could but all the time she was wondering why Claire didn't summon Paul, who was working in the estate office across the hall. At last she put this to Claire, admitting that her intention had been to pass the information to Paul straight away and let him take any action he thought fit without informing Andy but Claire said, quietly, "I'm very glad you didn't. It was wise of you to tell me first," and then, "I'm not blameless you know. I've sensed that something very odd was going on for a long time and I ought to have challenged him outright. As it is you've got yourself involved and I don't like that. How can things be the same between you when he knows you've been poking among his private papers and bringing them over here?"

"It isn't that important," Margaret said, "not to me at all events."

"To Vanessa it might be."

Margaret was silent a moment. Then she said "No, not to Vanessa either. I wouldn't want Vanessa to grow up in that atmosphere and Stevie wouldn't have wanted it either. Or not the Stevie I knew at "Ty-Bach".

"You see what comes of meddling," Claire said. "You knew from the beginning it wouldn't work, didn't you? That time in Criccieth, when I bullied you into making a clean breast of it and giving Andy a chance?"

"I never saw it as anything but the best of a bad job," she said, "but what do any of us know about what goes on in other people's heads?"

"I know what goes on in Paul's," Claire said, "and if this isn't handled cleverly it'll scar him for life. You say Andy is due back tomorrow? Do you know what time?"

"I never know what time. He just shows up, sometimes alone, sometimes with one of his cronies."

"Then let's hope he's alone this time. I'll come over after breakfast, just to make sure."

"What will you do?"

"I don't know, it depends on so many things. On his attitude and my instinct mostly, but I'll be there. I'm not going to let you face this alone. And don't ever imagine I'm not grateful, Margaret. Right now I wish you were my daughter as much as I wish Andy wasn't my son."

They went out to the stableyard where Margaret's car was parked and as she got in Margaret said, "There's just one thing more. That Mill Cottage down on the river road, I noticed they were doing it up and rethatching. Is it for rent, or is it earmarked for one of the estate workers?"

"It was," Claire said, "but if you need it for a cooling-off spell you can have it, I'll make sure of that," and as she said it her mind conjured up a picture of another forlorn young woman who had found refuge there years and years ago, at the time of the First War. The woman was Hazel Potter, the half-wild postscript of the Potter family, and Hazel's child was now her son-in-law. She thought, as she watched Margaret drive away. "It's odd the way people and buildings and situations resolve themselves in this place; Four Winds, the Codsalls, the Eveleighs and tragedy; Periwinkle, the bombs, and Simon's wife; High Coombe, and me, and my brother Hugh when he tried to double-cross Paul in the way Andy had done; and now Mill Cottage, restored just in time to provide a sanctuary again." Then she went in and up to the room that had been Young Claire's that she used as an inner tabernacle, keeping everyone else at bay. She took with her the tracing and the letters. Without fuss she sat down and studied them, line by line and word by word.

IV

When lunch was cleared away and still Andy had not returned or telephoned, Margaret said she would drive down into the town and collect Vanessa who had been having a dancing lesson at a little Academy in the Y.W.C.A. Hall. Claire was glad to get her out of the house. It gave her a better opportunity of putting her apology for a plan to work, and it seemed to her that confrontation without Margaret in the offing would be less complicated.

She was luckier than she had hoped. Within fifteen minutes she heard Andy's car send the gravel flying as he drove up with his inevitable flourish, slammed the door and ran up the porch steps carrying his worn briefcase. Watching him through the study window she could see him objectively, as a teenager storming into the Big House with Stevie at his heels, a couple of freebooters returning to base for a meal and a chance to plan the next foray. He was heavier, of course, and all that scar tissue hadn't improved his looks, but he still dressed with the same assertive flashiness, expensive camel-hair coat, carelessly knotted silk scarf, yellow gloves and handmade shoes, as though he used his clothes to proclaim the shallow prosperity of his enterprises. She thought, distractedly, "How the devil did an uncomplicated man like Paul Craddock sire a pair of prancing stallions like Andy and Stevie? Where does it come from, this obsession to be top-dog and prove it every minute of the day? It couldn't have come from Paul's scrapyard father—he was always bullied by that old rascal Zorndorff, and my father wasn't greedy for anything except the acres he ploughed!" He came into the hall in what seemed to Claire to be a very good humour, calling, "Margy? You there Margy?" and when Claire moved into the study doorway he looked first baffled and then alerted, perhaps by her presence within reach of his desk. Then, already bluffing, he threw down his coat and brief case and said, "Had lunch? Vanessa around?" and she told him that Vanessa was at dancing class and that Margaret had just gone for her.

"I'll fix myself something," he said, "come into the kitchen and yarn while I eat. I've just driven two-fifty without stopping. She's a honey, that car. Why don't you talk the Gov into getting one? Is he going to potter round the Valley in an Austin for the rest of his life?"

"I don't know," Claire said, carefully, "maybe he'll push the boat out when he capitalises on what's left of the estate," and he gave her a shrewd look and said, "What's cooking? Why are you up here?" and then brushed past her into the study and saw the tracing and the letters on the desk and the centre drawer of his desk open.

It did not take him more than a few seconds to recover and she marvelled at his sangfroid, wholly assumed but more than adequate to absorb any amount of recoil. It was, she supposed, a trick of the trade acquired over the years. He said, with a shrug, "You've rumbled it, then?"

"Yes, I've rumbled it. I always brought you and the others

332

up to regard the act of reading one another's mail as one of the shabbiest things one person could do to another but there are exceptions. I'm glad I got the chance to read yours."

He went over to the desk and studied the plan for a moment. He did not so much as glance at the letters.

"Well," he said, lighting a cigarette and blowing smoke through his nose, "that's that! I knew there would have to be a showdown sooner or later and I daresay it'll be a more civilised one with you than it would be with the Old Man."

The word "civilised" irritated her but only momentarily. She said, "Is it part of the new creed of the civilised to sell their own kith and kin to strangers? Providing the price is right? Does *anything* go nowadays?

"Pretty well anything," he said, "but if that's your approach I might just as well try and have a final go at converting the Gov'nor. No sense in the two of us rehearsing is there? I have got a point of view, you know."

She gave herself a moment or two to bite back the obvious retort, one of several that occurred to her and he watched her, smiling with the live side of his face, so that anyone not aware of his facial burns might have mistaken his blandness for mockery. She was familiar with the distortion and today it set limits to her anger. She said, "Very well. If there is an explanation, any kind of explanation, I'd be interested to hear it," and sat down in his swivel chair.

"I dropped a broad hint at the last meeting," he said, "but nobody noticed."

"I noticed. That's why I'm here. All that talk about young people drifting out of the Valley in search of jobs and kicks. That was the hint, wasn't it?"

"It's happening," he said, "and in places like Coombe Bay it's already happened. Everybody still there depends entirely on the holiday trade. Without it there wouldn't be a hundred people left in the village. Are you going to deny that?"

"It isn't what we're talking about," she said.

"You mean the devious way I went about it? Well, what alternative was there? You ought to know, you've been married to the Old Boy for forty years."

He had been well in control of himself up to now but suddenly he became very emphatic. "An industrialised country doesn't stand still. It can't or it would go bust in a single generation. That was true when we stopped feeding Europe a century ago and it's even more true today. We live by importing food and exporting manufactured goods and we've been doing that for the last eighty years but there are still people like the Gov'nor who can't or won't admit it, and naturally they get hurt when it hits them between the eyes. I'm sorry about that—in a way I admire him, always have admired him, but for far different reasons than the middle-of-the-roaders like Rumble Patrick and Simon admire him. He can't help being the kind of person he is any more than I can, or you can, but he has to pay the standard price for the privilege of trying to turn back the tide. He has to get his feet wet every now and again!"

"Can you honestly say he hasn't done a wonderful job of work since he came here half a century ago? Are you even qualified to say whether he has or hasn't? You didn't know this place until he'd put years of his life into it but I did. I knew it in an absentee landlord's time when most of the people about here hadn't got a good roof over their heads and shared outside privvies and pump water. Don't talk about him as if he was antedeluvian. He doesn't deserve it. And he certainly doesn't deserve what you've done to him."

"He'll never understand what I've done or tried to do," Andy said, "and for that matter I don't suppose any of you will but I don't give a damn about that. All I'm interested in is making sure that when he is taken for a ride he gets paid for it. That's been the general object of the exercise as far as I'm concerned. Do you think Shawcrosse would have paid twelve thousand for that tip of Bellchamber's if I hadn't twisted his arm?"

"But can't you see that he isn't the least bit interested in money? If he had been do you suppose he would have ploughed a fortune into the Valley and then given what was left to people like you? This Company, this Deed-of-Gift nonsense the lawyers talked him into, do you really believe he did it to save tax and dodge death-duties? It wasn't that way at all. It was a gesture—*his* kind of gesture, to people like Stevie who lost his life, and people like you who were bruised and knocked about. He didn't have to do it. He could have sat back and let the whole lot of you get on with it and be damned to the speculators, and the Exchequer and everyone else who is trying to turn his dream into a nightmare. Oh, I daresay that sounds fanciful to you but he does have a dream, he's always had it, and it isn't a selfish dream either.

334

He fought for it and worked for it and if the times have overtaken him it isn't your place to lead the stampede."

"I never did lead it," he said. "As a matter of fact, most of the time, I've been trying to head it off."

"By ranging yourself with people like this man Shawcrosse, whoever he is."

"Shawcrosse isn't anyone in particular," he said stubbornly. "Shawcrosse is just a symbol. There are hundreds of Shawcrosses, thousands of Shawcrosses, and most of them have eased themselves into places where they can call the tune! The departmental offices concerned with the future of places like the Valley are stuffed with Shawcrosses and there's a baker's dozen of them—half of them builders—on every sizeable town council. They've got dreams that he doesn't even know about and wouldn't understand even if he did know. But in ten years' time he'll find that out, and then it'll be too late, because the only power the Shawcrosses respect is the power of money. By then, unless he capitalises and reinvests the way I've been urging him to do, he won't have any money and not much land either. He'll have been bled white by tax and sewn up with legislative tape. They'll serve him with forms and requisitions and anything else they've got in their bloody pigeonholes. And even if he doesn't change the rest of the Valley will the moment they spot a chance of making big capital gains. You'll see a stampede then all right and who will be heading it? The Pittses, the Honeymans, the Eveleighs and the Bellchambers. The whole damned lot of them, one after the other, and they won't wait around to say good-bye either, because their kind of loyalty was spent long before I came on the scene. It didn't survive the First War and if you don't believe me ask anyone of them how much they made out of the black market when I was in the Desert."

He obviously believed every word he said. He was not, she decided, excusing himself, or softening her up in the hope that some of his arguments would be passed on to Paul when she got home. She said, distractedly, "You don't believe in anything, do you? *Nothing.* Nothing at all. When did you stop believing, Andy?"

She never learned how he would have answered that question and she would have liked very much to have heard it from his lips. Just then a door banged somewhere outside and then, surprising them both, Margaret was there in her hat and coat and with a red suitcase in her hand. She said, addressing Claire, "Will you be long? Vanessa's out there and I don't want her dragged into it."

For the first time since he had come into the house he looked nonplussed. It was not her words or her suitcase that disconcerted him but her act of addressing Claire as though there was no one else in the room. Claire saw him flush and the colour, restricted to the live side of his face, reminded her of a reflection in warped mirror. Then the colour died away and he said, without moving, "Where the hell are you going? How do you come into this?" and looked back in Claire's direction as though she could supply the answer.

"I don't know what Claire's been telling you," Margaret said, "but she probably didn't explain that I came across that tracing and those letters when I was looking for some blotting paper. I took them to her at once. It seemed to me I owed her and your father that much."

"If you have prejudged the issue go where the hell you like," he shouted, "but don't take Vanessa out of here on account of a damn silly family squabble." Margaret did not move as he took a step towards her, however, but said, in the same level tone, "I'll take Vanessa where I like. You're not her father and have no say in what happens to her, Andy. Stop shouting at me and get yourself a drink." Then she went out and Claire, after hesitating a moment, followed. He walked behind as far as the front door and then stopped and when she reached Margaret's car and saw Vanessa perched on the back seat among other suitcases, Claire turned her head and saw him standing at the library window watching.

She said, in a low voice, "Are you sure about this, Margaret? It's not your quarrel you know," and Margaret said, easing herself into the driving seat, "I'm sure. I only needed something like this as a pushover," and let in the clutch.

Vanessa said, equably, "Are we going to Nan's?" and when Claire confirmed that they were she said, "Good! Gramp will let me ride Spotty to Saturday's meet. If I stay on he'll probably let me poke about the coverts a bit, unless they find straight off."

"I'm sure he will," Claire said, "but don't argue if he keeps you on the leading rein like last time you went hunting with him."

It was more or less as he had prophesied, except that his time schedule was over-optimistic. The face of the Valley was changed not in ten years but in seven.

Andy had spoken of an army of Shawcrosses and of their plans, of private men with private swathes to cut, and public men with reputations to make or to guard, one eye on the local editorials, the other on the ballot-box, and also of faceless men at the disposal of both groups for the price of a little deference.

Andy had warned her that Paul would not even understand their motives if they were spelled out to him and here again he was right. These cohorts did not use Paul Craddock's dictionary. They called things by strange names. A row of red-brick houses, with slated roofs and bearded gnomes surrounding small concrete rock-pools, replaced a row of thatched, cob cottages burned down as fire brigade exercises, and this was called "Modernisation". A concrete swimming-bath, built within a hundred yards of the sea was called "An Amenity". A road, flanked by hoardings advertising tyres and Coca-Cola was "Marine Access", although only a potential suicide would use such a road without a girdle of chromium and pressed steel about him.

The transformation was not dramatically achieved and always the eruptions were strictly localised. It was as though the miles separating Whinmouth and Coombe Bay ran across a corrupted body and no one could be sure where a boil would gather or where the skin would pucker and change colour. The initial eruption was along the eastern edge of the Coombe where all the trees were felled and all the hazel-bushes and gorse ripped out and carted away, and in their place multi-coloured caravans were parked in neat rows, with here a corrugated-iron privy, there a squat, cast-iron incinerator. Beyond them, mushrooming between Whitsun and September, stretched the tents and between tents and caravans they built a wainy elm bungalow, selling camping gear and presided over by Bellchamber himself.

That was in the late spring of 1948. Other amenities followed in quick succession.

A housing estate grew up on the western slopes of the Bluff and the gulls who lived in Tamer Potter's Cove soon had access to three hundred dustbins. The swimming-pool, pride of a Rural District Council based as far away as Paxtonbury, dominated the quay, and there was another just like it at Whinmouth. Hard tennis-courts were carved out of the Undercliff and the number of shops in the steep High Street increased to thirty-eight, nine of them seasonal cafes, four of them gift shops, one a supermarket.

There would have been no sense in developing on this scale whilst confining the twin approach to the village (by footpath over the Dunes, by track following the course of the Sorrel) to the access of other days. This would have been to create a ghost town under the Bluff. In 1950, again as Andy had predicted, a compulsory purchase order prefaced the arrival of the bull-dozers and their sun-tanned operators, humming snatches of *Oklahoma* hit tunes, made short work of the undulating stretch of sandy soil and couch grass between the southern tip of the Moor and Crabpot Willie's goyle, then on over more level ground to the first houses of Coombe Bay. This road was for coastal traffic, and approaches to the sea were channelled below it through three short tunnels, giving on to the beach. The plantation of Douglas firs that had crowned the head of the goyle fell to the scream of mechanical saws in less than a week.

On route to Coombe Bay, but a mile or so nearer Whinmouth, the triangle of freehold separating the Shallowford and Heronslea estates was aquired by Shawcrosse himself who began building a hotel there before the road was finished. He called it "Hotel Majestic", and in his advance publicity he advertised a private beach but there was a storm over this in Whinmouth Council and he had to retract. That part of the beach was already leased to refreshment hut proprietors and Whinmouth ratepayers saw no reason why they should sacrifice a source of revenue to a stranger.

But the coastal road was not enough. Coombe Bay needed direct access to the main road to Paxtonbury and after a great deal of discussion it was decided to re-surface and widen the road that was already there, the river road that slipped down from the Moor, rounded Hermitage plateau, and ran past Codsall Bridge to the ford that had given the estate its name. Paul fought this "amenity" tooth and claw and there was a Public Enquiry but he lost the day. A local poll, organised by Shawcrosse, resulted in a landslide victory for the progressives, two thousand and seven votes to four hundred and eight. The road went through. By 1953 it was

necessary to challenge two streams of traffic if you wanted to
walk or ride from the Big House to the beach, unless, of
course, you used one of the coastal road tunnels, where the
summer traffic, rumbling overhead, sounded like a south-
westerly beating on the shore.

Andy had been right in yet another respect. Most of the
locals soon came to terms with the changes and among the
first to do so was Henry Pitts, whose land ran right down to
the inland road. It was about here, back in 1904, that he had
left his plough and run across two fields to gape at the first
motorcar he had ever seen and had bolted for safety when
Young Roddy Rudd, son of the agent, had restarted his
engine. He did not bolt now, for although there was a great
deal of noise there was not much movement, especially at the
height of the season. Cars and coaches approached Coombe
Bay in procession, progressing in short, stuttering jerks. There
was plenty of time for Ellie, Henry's busy little wife, to sell
plums, cut blooms, apples and even strawberries from a stall
erected at the end of Hermitage Lane, although her stepson,
David, disapproved so wholeheartedly of her clientele that he
sold out in Coronation year and carried out his threat to
emigrate. His father, who had financed him as a freeholder,
did not try to stop him this time for he appreciated his
motives.

"Let un go if he's a mind to," he told Ellie, "for there's no
bliddy future in raising corn nor cattle in all this fume an'
racket. Tiz like a bliddy motor-rally yer from July 'till September but us shoulden complain should us, midear? Not
when us can cut out they middlemen and zell direct to the
public."

There was a rumour that Henry would eventually sell a
string of roadside plots for ribbon development but he never
did. Either he had too much sympathy for Paul or he lacked
a sponsor on the nearest Town and Country Planning Committee.

By the time the tepid Coronation festivities were over the
estate had become a tight-waisted island, bounded by the new
coastal road in the south and the new four-lane Paxtonbury
road in the north. To the east, the Coombe having been
punched out, the two holdings of Deepdene and High
Coombe ballooned in the direction of the county border. To
the west, with Hermitage gone, the rough rectangle compris-
ing Home Farm pastures and Four Winds still formed a

buffer that protected the Big House itself and the wilderness of Shallowford Woods.

As long as the two paddocks and woods were left to him Paul found he could tolerate the changes and, to an extent, he slowly adapted to them, for whenever he rode now he turned inland, pushing into the heavy timber or crossing Henry's fields to the moor. There had been talk of building bungalows up here but it came to nothing and Paul claimed no credit for parrying this left hook of the Whinmouth U.D.C. It was parried by the War Office, far away in Whitehall, who had already fattened two generations of cannon-fodder on these slopes and decided to hold the pasture in reserve until they were convinced that the next war would be fought without benefit of spit-and-polish techniques perfected in the heather.

Between 1953 and 1954 there was a lull. The builders, it seemed, had run out of options, or the department had used up their ideas. But towards the end of the latter year the assault was commenced again and this time Paul and his rump of diehards realised it would be a fight to the finish, for the threat came from the north, where Paxtonbury's civil airport had been constructed out of the ruins of the old Polish airfield.

It seemed that longer runways were necessary and the airport authorities acquired a clutch of meadows that took them right up to the main road, beyond which the northernmost clumps of Shallowford Woods began, a mile-long plantation of oak, beech, ash and sycamore. It was not the best timber on the estate—that lay lower down, beyond the Mere—but a speech by a Paxtonbury Councillor, claiming that the nearness of the trees constituted a danger to aircraft, made it clear where the next blow would fall. When Paul flatly refused to fell a single tree the fight was on.

For once the garrison had allies and Paul could call in The Men of the Trees, and other rural preservation societies. Several public meetings were held and there was a sharp exchange of letters in all the local newspapers, but it was not until his youngest son John, currently studying for a science degree at Bristol University, made a close study of Green Belt legislation aimed at protecting roadside timber, that victory seemed possible and the airport people drew off to ponder new strategy.

The respite was doubly welcome to Paul. Not only did it

save his trees, at least temporarily, it also restored his faith in the solidarity of the family, so badly shaken by Andy at the time of his abrupt withdrawal from the Company. Piecemeal presentation of Andy's case by Claire, Rumble Patrick and even Simon, had not done much to mellow Paul's view of his son's enlistment with the enemy. At first an almost Victorian situation developed so that it was considered bad taste on anyone's part to mention Andy's name. Later, when it was learned that Andy had disposed of all his interests in Shawcrosse Enterprises and gone to live in the States, it was possible to persuade Paul that his son's equivocal attitude to local development did not quite qualify as perfidy and he learned to accept it as a by-product of his son's long apprenticeship among rascals living on their wits. Subconsciously, therefore, he began to think of Andy as someone who had contracted a skin disease whilst taking wholly unnecessary risks in a sewer.

Claire and the others were more generous, accepting the fact that Andy had, however mistakenly, sincerely believed that he was acting in the family's best interests. By the late nineteen-forties there was already a desultory exchange of letters between them and the exile, but Margaret never returned to him and Paul could always rely on a sympathetic audience when he referred to his son as "that bloody Quisling".

This did not mean that Margaret shared Paul's committal to the status-quo in the Valley. Her severance was a voluntary withdrawal from the mock-marriage imposed on her by family pressures at the time of Stevie's death. She had rejected Andy's way of life as profitless and found a healing stillness at Mill Cottage, three-parts of a mile along the road between Shallowford lodge-gate and Coombe Bay. The traffic did not worry her. She was a sociable person and the occasional motorist seeking water for a boiling radiator, or respite for a car-sick child, helped to counteract the isolation of the cottage. She adapted to grass-widowhood more easily than she had anticipated. At forty, she discovered, it was possible to get along without a man, so long as she had Vanessa, Vanessa's pony-tailed friends and easy access to Claire, to Mary, and to Simon's wife, Evie. It was easier still when Simon obtained the headship of a new school in Coombe Bay and he and Evie left Whinmouth to live a mile or so down the river.

After settling into the cottage she began to take an interest in gardening and soon the two little patches, one at the front, the other climbing the steep slope to the edge of the half-naked Coombe, became an obsession. She spent whole days out here growing a variety of plants and doing her own potting in a greenhouse Paul built for her alongside the old shed at the top of the half-acre. She never bothered to get a divorce and Andy never sought one, although he sent her money regularly, asking and receiving news and the latest snapshots of Vanessa. Paul, visiting her occasionally, thought it strange that an attractive woman of forty should be content to lead such a withdrawn life at this forlorn outpost of his crumbling empire and once asked her point-blank if she ever contemplated putting the past behind her and perhaps marrying again. Her answer touched and amused him. "I've been 'married' twice," she said, "both times to your sons. I wouldn't want to marry outside the family and the only male Craddock left is Young John!" Then, half-seriously, "He's growing more like the Stevie I remember every day. Did you realise that?"

"No," he said, very decidedly, "I didn't. John is one on his own and in some ways the sharpest of the litter. Like Stevie indeed! How the devil can you say that? Poor old Stevie had his points, but all the time I knew him there was never a pin to choose between him and Andy."

"Ah," she said, with the Welsh lilt that always intrigued him, "but you never met the real Stevie, did you now?" and then refused to qualify the comment but directed his attention to her lupins, declaring them to be the most spectacular ever grown in the Valley.

He went off across the sloping field in one of his half-rueful, contemplative moods, thinking not so much of the past, as he did more and more now that he had passed his seventieth birthday, but of the present in relation to his sons and daughters, alive and dead. Every one of them had been born in that stone and timber house set on the ridge under the woods but if what Margaret said was true each of them might have had a different mother and a different father. Stevie and little Claire were dead, and Andy was lost to him; of the others only John, the tailpiece, came close to establishing the relationship he had looked for in a son. The forging of this friendship between a man of seventy and a boy in his teens had been one of the few rewarding aspects of these last, hard-fought years.

VI

It had all happened rather haphazardly, beginning during a chance visit he paid to John during his last year at school. The boy was almost eighteen then and his record at High Wood was the most impressive of any of the Craddocks who had gone there. Paul gathered that he not only found the assimilation of knowledge easy but had proved to be that very rare phenomenon at an English school—someone who could make an excellent showing at games but could also win scholarships.

He was due to go up to University in October, and although Paul found it difficult to rejoice in the prospect of any young man reading for a scientific degree, he already knew enough about John to appreciate the many-sided aspect of his interests and enthusiasms and did not see him as someone likely to devote his life to evolving new methods of blowing the world to smithereens, or inventing a new killer epidemic in the national interest. For this was how he had come to look upon all scientists of late, a conspiracy of experts lacking moral responsibility and divorced from the humanities, idiots who not only helped to proliferate devilish weapons but, in their less dedicated moments, invented the mass-produced gadgets and plastic rubbish exhibited in the gift shops at Coombe Bay. He was willing to admit that he was extremely prejudiced in this respect but there was nothing he could do about it, even though, in private moments, he sometimes saw himself as a latterday Henry Pitts, who had fled from his first motor and inveighed against the introduction of tanks to the Western Front.

He discovered, to his relief, that John intended to specialise in zoology but was already well advanced in physics, so that he was puzzled as to the precise direction in which the boy was heading and responded eagerly when John suggested they should take advantage of a cancelled rugger match and walk across the spur of Exmoor on which the school was set.

He had always liked it about here, a wild, lonely spot where the constant changes in cloud formation suggested that the crust about the outcrops of granite was as molten as the day the plateau had heaved itself out of the sea. He said, after showing John the spot where he had told Simon of the death of his mother in France, in 1917, "I've always enjoyed a visit here. If I didn't live in the Valley I'd buy myself a hill-farm on one of these slopes and watch the light fade over Lundy, instead of the English Channel."

John said, chuckling, that he was quite incurable, and would have been far more at home in Elizabethan England than in the middle of the twentieth century but added, half-apologetically, "Not that I don't go part way with you, Dad. I always have you know, a good deal further than any of the others, not excluding Rumble Patrick."

The boy's admission warmed his old bones and they stopped by common consent at a drystone wall that ran diagonally across the moor like a miniature ruin of Hadrian's barrier in the north.

"How far is part-way?" he demanded. "Come now, admit that you've always regarded me as someone with the outlook of a small-time squire about 1760."

John said, with a boy's seriousness, "*No*, Gov! You're much more than that. You won't take a damned thing on trust until it's worked itself into the national bloodstream, but people like you are progressive in your own way and that's what I like about this country. You and Andy offset one another and provide an essential balance. Menzies—he's our history master, that one with pebble-glasses—has an obsessive theory about it and although we often rag him on that account he's managed to inject it into most of the Sixth by the simple method of tireless reiteration. He says that your kind of caution is so widespread among the English that it produces a steady percentage of inventive rebels in every generation and that's how the Industrial Revolution began, sons improving on their fathers' essentially sound methods and then, at about fifty, becoming conservative themselves and producing another reaction."

"Interesting," Paul said, and meant it, for he had often thought along these lines himself when reading beside a winter fire. "Does this chap Menzies say where we got it from, or why it's peculiar to these offshore islands?"

"Yes, he says it's a racial accident, Celtic romanticism, Roman organisation, Saxon preoccupation with agriculture, Sandinavian obsession with the sea and finally Norman know-how. Successive invasions produced a kind of five-decker sandwich and you're living proof of it. I suppose, knowing you, inclined me to take 'The Menzies Theory' on trust. What I mean is, you resent change like hell but you always end up by adapting to it and rescuing some of the pieces. The Valley's proof of it, proof of compromise I mean, and compromise—old Menzies again—is a basic English virtue. Two things could have happened to Shallowford under any-one else. It could have clung to feudalism and atrophied years ago, or it could have turned itself into a cash-register, like parts of the Lancashire and the Welsh coasts. But be-cause you were there, directing the traffic so to speak, it didn't. In the end it not only kept most of its charm but its essential usefulness."

"Well," said Paul feeling more gratified than at any time since Andy's betrayal, "I must say it's a relief to have one's lifework understood by at least one member of the family," and he went home to tell Claire that her conception of John in middle-age was probably the most rewarding mistake she had made in her life.

Claire was encouraged by the friendship she saw de-veloping between them. For her part she had always been wary of her youngest. He seemed to know so much, including what she was thinking most of the time, and his range of interests bewildered a person like herself who had never had more than one. As time went on Paul and John hobnobbed together whenever the boy was at home. Paul's gain was twofold. He not only used John as a bridge between the extremes of the two generations but also as a source of up-to-date information that enabled him to score points off the opposition. It was John, in fact, who was behind the important victory that saved Shallowford Woods.

By 1954, when he was in his third year at University, the Paxtonbury Civil Airport had grown into one of the most important in the West and the power of the men behind it increased with its expansion. The local M.P. was enlisted on their behalf and the threat to the northern half of the woods grew more and more menacing as questions were asked in the House, and a pressure group went to work on the Ministry. There came a time, in the early autumn, when he was almost ready to concede defeat but then, at the last moment, John organised a sally that not only relieved the pressure but ultimately raised the seige altogether. It was made possible by John's affiliations with the new mass media, television.

On leaving university John surprised everyone except Paul by choosing a television career. Paul, now enjoying the advantages of an inside view, could see how the manifold threads of the boy's obsessions over the years led naturally in this direction and recalled his wartime expeditions across the Valley with box camera, butterfly net, binoculars and other impedimenta. John's degree and natural charm enabled him to infiltrate into this half-technical, half-creative world without difficulty, and one September morning he appeared in the drive with a camera team, announcing that he "had the answer to the airport zombies in one!"

"My potential boss has a blank spot to fill in a national programme early in the New Year," he told Paul, without preamble, "and he's looking for something he can resell overseas as tourist bait. The overall theme is the English landscape and English customs and if we get good enough coverage we can stir up the National Trust, the Coastal Preservation boys, The Men of the Trees, and God knows who else is prejudiced in your favour. Once it's been seen all over the country and is passed on to the Castle-and-Cheesecake Department, we shall have a strong hand to play. Who knows? The airport boys might even get the chop!"

Paul, who had had to familiarise himself to the slang of successive decades, stumbled over the identification of "the Castle-and-Cheesecake Department" and John explained that it was the Government department responsible for promoting British tourism. "They pack," he said, "a very hefty punch because tourists are dollars and as we're always in the red this is important."

A little more questioning elicited the information that the team intended to film the entire Valley, including many of the items that passed for amenities, and produce a half-hour feature emphasing the changes that had already taken place and the importance of retaining what was left of the natural beauty of the Valley. Paul thought it a splendid idea and rode around with the team, even starring as a mounted leftover from the Edwardian era and enjoying every moment of it.

John said the feature would be called "*The Green Gauntlet*" and described how the title had suggested itself during an aerial survey.

"This Valley, from a thousand feet, *looks* like a gauntlet," he said, "a great, finger-spread glove, made of green and rust-coloured leather. It's all wrinkled and seamed, and the two predominant colours are unevenly spaced, blotches of both appearing here and there but without any plan. We shall use aerial shots, of course, and they show in our favour, for the only jarring notes are the new buildings around Coombe Bay. The tongues of the woods, for instance, are the original colour of the gauntlet, a faded green and they form the fingers. There's the gimmick angle too, of course, throwing down the gauntlet to the developers."

His enthusiasm and technical discipline was about evenly matched and when Paul saw the first run-through (that John called "rushes"), he was very impressed. Somehow they had distilled the magic of the place into a pictorial potion, so that most of the elements that had contributed to his lifelong love-affair with these few square miles were there to be sipped. The ranks of the old timber marching down the ridges to the Mere. The Mere itself, enclosed by evergreens and starred with the islet and the ruin of the Folly. The rooted farmsteads of High Coombe, Deepdene, Four Winds, and Hermitage. The mellow look of the Big House with its steep, curving drive flanked by chestnuts. The winding Sorrel and its ox-bows. The open dunes, now confined between two busy roads. And finally the gentle curve of the coast from the landslip to Tamer's Cove, taking in the sandbars and the Bluff. It was all there. The only thing lacking was its colour.

They had good weather and finished shooting in less than a fortnight and John himself wrote the commentary. On New Year's Eve Paul and Claire sat in front of their television screen feeling as nervous as a couple of amateurs on an opening night but as soon as the first few feet of film unfolded Paul lost his anxiety in admiration, not only for the subject matter but for its originator.

"By God," he exclaimed, when the last notes of the 'Greensleeves' backing faded, "that boy's a bloody genius. He ought to be Prime Minister!" and Claire laughed as heartily as she had laughed in a long time and said that maybe he would be but as John was unlikely to take office until he was middle-aged neither of them were likely to be invited to Number Ten.

The end result was more satisfactory than any of them

could have hoped. The feature received praise from a number of critics and the preservation of the Sorrel Valley became a Westcountry topic for a week or so. There was no more talk of felling the Shallowford oaks and soon it was being canvassed that new runways were to be built pointing east-west, instead of north-south. Paul, making a cautious reconnaissance on the far side of the main road, saw to his intense relief that several meadows running parallel with the highway were now being surveyed. He said, on his return, that the woods had had an even closer shave than in 1915, when Government agents had come to him screaming for timber, and that he intended to give John a sports car on his twenty-first birthday in a fortnight or so. Claire made a convincing show of sharing his sense of delivery and, being in such an ebullient mood, he did not notice her air of abstraction.

He remembered it later, much later, when he would have done better not to have remembered it at all.

CHAPTER FOUR

CAVE-IN

I

THAT winter the rainfall had been well above average and the Sorrel was in spate earlier than was usual, its waters running tobacco-brown from early November, its ox-bows flooding to the edge of the new road and over it at places where the banks had been cut back to make a low embankment. What had once been the Codsall stubble fields, south of the road, were flooded to a depth of about a foot by Christmas and flotsam carried down by moorland streams and the fast-flowing rill of the Coombe, floated out to the foothills of the dunes.

Paul, walking or riding along this road and sometimes crossing the sloping field to the screen of trees that was now his border with the Shawcrosse Caravan Camp, or "China-town" as he preferred to call it, noticed the weight of water coming down the Coombe and estimated that its volume had quadrupled since the felling of so many trees and the removal of so much brushwood from the eastern side of the Coombe, for about here the water had always been absorbed by thick undergrowth and for many years now the Coombe stream had been jumpable at any point between the Dell and Mill Cottage.

It was no satisfaction for him to see that the danger of big-scale erosion he had warned them about at the time was now apparent, even to a layman. They had not listened to him when he had tried, in their own interests as well as his, to set limits to the wholesale clearance that began before the first caravan was hauled up the one-in-four gradient of Coombe Lane. They had just gone right ahead with their clawing and rooting and digging until the only trees left was the screen written into the contract at the suggestion of Claire, who had been raised on a Coombe farm and knew the freaks and features of the long cleft better than anyone in the Valley, with the possible exception of Smut Potter and his brother Sam.

As the winter rains continued Coombe rill enlarged itself into a miniature Sorrel and its overspill raced through the culverts they had built under the road about fifty yards east of Mill Cottage. They were big culverts, capable of handling a large volume of water, but more than water was coming down now and twice the R.D.C. Surveyor's department had to remove tree trunks and a build-up of stones, branches and jagged lumps of concrete washed down from the camp site.

Paul, watching their operations, warned the foreman to take a look higher up nearer the old Potter farmhouse, where the shoulder of the hill was a wilderness of small red craters, starred here and there with tree-stumps, so that the place reminded him of the quagmire west of Pilckem Wood in the Ypres sector. It had the same tortured look of an area stripped of vegetation and robbed of its natural drainage system, and if much more rain fell it would soon be impassable in gumboots or by tractor. He didn't care much what happened up here any more. They had made their mucky bed and they could lie on it, or drown in it for that matter. But any serious erosion in the Coombe would have a chain reaction upon Four Winds' pastures across the river, and might even cause serious flooding at the ford outside his own lodge gates. Young Eveleigh thought so too, and insisted the Council foreman looked at his fields. Nothing was done about it, although later Paul learned that the Surveyor's department had telephoned Shawcrosse and Bellchamber, urging them to sandbag and revet the widest section of the rill two hundred yards above the road.

Paul, far from satisfied, got Henry Pitts and Smut Potter up there and both sucked in their lips on surveying the widening area of slush on the eastern side of the Dell. Smut said, "Old Tamer knew a thing or two about the Dell. Woulden 'ave a bush trimmed yerabouts. 'Twas moren' our skins was worth to cut wood this zide o' the stream. Tamer always reckoned the on'y thing that stopped the bliddy hill shredding away was thicky tangle, reaching from the cliff fields to the river road."

"Tamer was dead right," said Paul, "but seeing that I don't own a yard that side of the stream what can I do but warn them about it?"

Henry said, thoughtfully, "You still own Deepdene an' High Coombe, dornee? A vine ole mess us'll 'ave if the brook turns 'erself into a river bigger'n the Sortel. Four Winds would be under dree foot o' water but they'd be starved o' water upalong come a drought. If I was you, Maister, I'd zee the bliddy County Surveyor meself an' give it to 'un straight."

"I might even do that," Paul said and intended to, but in the whirl of preparing for John's coming-of-age party he forgot about it, for it was a long time since they had had a big family occasion up at the House and both he and Claire were out of touch with the kind of entertainment young people seemed to expect nowadays.

The birthday fell late in January and all the preceding week Claire was busy helping Mary and Simon's wife, Evie, decorate the house. She enjoyed these occasions usually but lately she was feeling her age and left the strenuous work to her daughter and daughter-in-law, who enlisted Margaret and some of the grandchildren in making the ground-floor rooms look festive and prepare for more overnight guests than Shallowford House had entertained since before the war.

Two days before the party, at about eleven in the morning, she left the others planning the menu in the big kitchen and took her coffee into the double room west of the hall where, as was usual on these occasions, the partition dividing the drawing-room and dining-room had been removed and most of the heavy furniture cleared or pushed back for dancing.

The girls had, as they said, "gone to town" in here, and the place was hung with evergreens from floor to ceiling. A rostrum had been erected for the dance band, the floor had been waxed and all Paul's china had been taken upstairs for safety. His pictures had been left, however, for the walls would have looked patchy without them and as she sat sipping her coffee, listening to the sounds about the old house, she contemplated Paul's favorite acquisition, a portrait of a lady in a blue headdress that was supposed to be a genuine Lely and was one of the few original items he had bought at the Lovell sale, in 1902.

She remembered so many occasions when this room had

rocked with noise and laughter. There had been the original sale, the second occasion she had met Paul without realising he was already mooning after Grace Lovell, and there had been the Coronation supper-ball later in the year, when she had been convinced he was going to propose to her but had proposed to Grace instead. Later, in happier days, there had been a succession of Shallowford parties here, and after that a second Coronation dance for Edward's successor, in 1911.

During the First War the room had been put to more sombre use and twenty beds had been wedged in here when Shallowford served as a convalescent home until 1918. Later still Simon, The Pair, Mary and Whiz, had all had their twenty-first birthday parties here and on two other occasions her daughters had received their wedding guests on this threshold.

It all seemed an incredibly long time ago, and as she sat there, thinking of the coming-of-age of her youngest, she reminded herself that she had already entered her seventy-third year. It was enough to prompt her to heave herself up and glance into the gilt-framed mirror hanging over the marble mantelshelf.

As usual she was able to persuade herself that she did not look her age. She had given up the struggle to keep the grey from her plentiful hair and had settled for a blue rinse. Her skin was mercifully free of wrinkles and her plump, slightly pendulous cheeks had resisted the sallow shadows of most of her contemporaries. Her eyes were still clear and her figure, although inclined towards stockiness, was far from shapeless so that she walked without the slump of the Potter girls and others who had grown old in the last decade or so. She thought, contemplating the coming celebrations, "I suppose it's some kind of achievement to have survived to attend the coming-of-age of a son born after his mother was fifty, and still be game for a dance if anyone asks me! It's a pity Paul and I can't slip away after midnight and go down to Crabpot Willie's shelter, as we did half-way through The Pair's coming-of-age in 1929. He was just fifty then and I was forty-six, and we were both so full of champagne that we had our own kind of celebration down there and could have taught those youngsters a thing or two I wouldn't wonder." Then she remembered that Crabpot Willie's shanty had been cleared to make way for the new coastal road and this blunted the edge of her complacency so that she reached up and touched her hair to trap a stray wisp over the temples.

Then it came. For the second time that week. For the fifth time in the last three months. A paroxysm of pain starting in her back, shooting into her left shoulder and running the length of her upraised arm. It was so awful that it made her gasp and stagger, so that she clutched at the edge of the mantelshelf and hung there, head bowed, teeth clamped to her lip as the tide of agony gushed down to her finger-tips and then, recoiling like a spent wave, retreated as far as the shoulder, swirled around for a moment and left her trembling body as suddenly as it had appeared.

She stood quite still for more than a minute incapable of thought of any kind but marshalling every nerve in her body to prevent a scream that would bring others clattering into the room. Then, moving very slowly, she returned to the table and sat beside her empty cup, realising that she would have to confess to Maureen after all, and do it before the party so as to get something to guard against a spasm on the night when she might spoil everything for everybody. She waited another few minutes and then got up and went into the hall, asking the Coombe Bay operator for Maureen's number and waiting, tapping impatiently, until Maureen's gruff voice said, "Doctor Rudd. Who is it?"

For more than forty years now it had been a joke between them that Claire never consulted her unless she was pregnant. Maureen, who seldom congratulated anyone, had often remarked upon her health, matching it against Paul's power to survive the injuries he had collected in the way of bullets, shrapnel and broken ribs throughout this life. But today Maureen was not joking and her face did not relax, as it usually did, when she finished her examination. Perhaps she was conscious of this for she turned her back on Claire on the excuse of washing her hands and stood there looking, Claire thought, very old and tired and helpless.

She said, "All right, Maureen, you don't have to find the right words. It is angina, isn't it? I've been telling myself it was chronic rheumatism ever since the first time, last year."

"Why didn't you come then?" Maureen said, without turning, and Claire was touched by the break in her voice. In all the years she had known her she had never seen Maureen shed a tear for anyone, not even her own John Rudd when he had died in the room above a long time ago.

"I honestly did think it was rheumatism at first. Then I thought maybe I'd put something out and was pinching a nerve. It was only the time before last I was sure and after that I put off thinking about it. The thing is, what's to be done?"

Maureen turned round and faced her, having got herself under some kind of control. She said, "Very little's to be done at your age, any more than it would be at mine. You could go on for years, depending upon the kind of life you lead. Angina isn't nearly as predictable as most people imagine, at least I've never found it so. It's a killer in the end but Old Aaron, the reed-cutter, had it for the last fifteen years of his life and he was eighty-eight when he died. He would have been dead at seventy-three if he hadn't given up cutting reeds and taken to carving model schooners in his porch. The truth is, Claire, the party is over but you can still go on watching it. From now on you don't do a damned thing impulsively, not even lift a basket, or walk upstairs. You think about it, plan it, and you'll have to tell Paul at once."

"Not before John's coming-of-age. That's only forty-eight hours away now."

"Well, forty-eight hours won't make much difference. I'll give you tablets, of course, but for God's sake take it easy the rest of this week. Don't do a damned thing but beam at people and don't join in any of their games on the night. For that matter don't imagine you can play strenuous games of your own either."

Claire could smile at this. "Run along with you. What games do you think we could play at our age?"

"Knowing you nothing would surprise me," Maureen said, and then, with a show of her occasional warmth, "we've all got to die of something. I haven't found my label yet but it won't be long now. I'm an old fool to think I can go on diagnosing at my age. Not that I blame myself about you, for I haven't examined you since before the war. I'll make an appointment for you to see Hilary Wescott, in Paxtonbury, the day after the party, but you must tell Paul the truth before then. You'll get that pain now and again but not too often to bear, and I do mean that." She looked at her speculatively. "You don't want to hear all the technical details I hope?"

"No. I'll tell you something though. I'd far sooner this than cancer of the womb or breast. That's always been my secret horror."

"I know," Maureen said, "it is with most women, particularly those who have enjoyed themselves the way you have."

She went over to the latticed window and looked out on the winter landscape, still soaking up a thin, never-ending rain.

"We neither of us can grumble, I suppose. It's been a long time, and most of it fun. You feel that, don't you?"

"Yes. It's only that I can't imagine how he could cope without me. He's been very close to violent death twice since I've known him and I suppose that's the reason I've always taken it for granted that I should be the one who would have to cope. The thing is, nobody ever knows for sure, do they?"

Maureen turned slowly and regarded her steadily. "You've taken it far better than most," she said, "but then again, why not? You've had a much better run for your money than anyone else I know. Will you tell the family, eventually?"

"Not likely!" Claire said, "I wouldn't even tell Paul if I could trust you not to."

"It would be unfair not to," Maureen said, "and you'll realise that if you think about it. I'll get hold of these tablets by tonight and deliver them personally. You'll be up at the house for supper I suppose?"

"No, I won't," Claire told her, "I've promised to baby-sit for Margaret who is coming over from the cottage to plan the ceremonial with Mary and Evie. Put them in an innocent-looking package and leave them in my desk."

"I'll do that," Maureen said, heavily. And then, "What do you mean, baby-sit? That child Vanessa is turned twelve, isn't she?"

"She has her leg in plaster after a fall out hunting last Saturday. I don't think it's all that serious but she'll have to miss the party and anyway she hates being left alone." She paused a moment, then went on. "Vanessa and me, we've got a rather special relationship. Very different from all the other grandchildren. I suppose it's the circumstances, although I've never asked Margaret how much she told the child about Stevie."

"I knew about that special relationship. I keep my eyes open. She isn't very robust, is she? In spite of all this gallivanting about on horses."

355

"She's my favourite," Claire said, and left it at that.

Maureen said, "I'll pop in to look at the decorations and slip the tablets in your notepaper drawer. I'll do something else for you too, I'll be there when you tell Paul if you'd like me to. It might help him to accept it without a lot of fuss." Suddenly she crossed the room and kissed her on the forehead, a gesture so uncharacteristic that Claire was taken by surprise.

"That was the whole truth, wasn't it?" she asked, and Maureen replied "Yes, it was. There was a time when I would have bluffed but that was long ago, my dear. The rest depends very much on you."

II

It was still drizzling when she climbed carefully into Margaret's two-seater at dusk and slowly negotiated the sharp bend in the drive. Margaret said Evie would drop her off at the cottage about eleven and Claire could then use the little car to return home. The slush in the lane, she warned her, was ankle deep and if she drove the station wagon it would get stuck turning.

At the bottom of the drive, for no particular reason, she stopped and looked back. Here, at the half-flooded ford, darkness pressed in on all sides but higher up the rise, beyond the last of the chestnuts, she could see an orange glow spreading from the terrace where all the lights were burning as though John's party had already begun. For a moment she sat looking at them, wondering if this was the last party she would ever attend at the Big House.

Her fortitude had increased during the afternoon with so much bustle going on around her and everybody simmering with subdued excitement. It was interesting, she thought, how a family occasion like this exposed the sameness of successive generations. Her own children, and more still their children, pretended to indifference towards family junketings, as though they had no strong family ties but the atmosphere up there now was really no different from that of the old harvest suppers and coronation soirées. Only the externals changed. The tunes the band would play tomorrow night would have a different rhythm and their lyrics would have some of the sentimentality ironed out of them. The style of dancing would be different, with less proximity between partners, and the horseplay would be less inhibited, but all the essentials were there, the sense of anticipation associated with fun and frolic, laughter and swift embraces in the dark corners of the house. It had all happened before and it would go on happening for ever, because that was what life was about, although one had to keep reminding oneself of this when reading newspapers or watching television.

Maureen had been right. She had had her innings and enjoyed it far more than most people she knew. Paul had had his too, but she doubted if he would admit it as cheerfully as she did for he made the worst kind of invalid and sometimes took himself as seriously as a hanging judge. Not with her, thank God! Never with her, and that, she supposed, was what she had had to offer all these years, a sanctuary and distraction from all the stresses of his life. Beyond that nothing very much, except to present him with a rather fractious brood and nourish his pride in his virility.

The party was over Maureen had said and from now on she was a spectator. Well, she wasn't so sure about that, or not as long as that agonising pain stayed away. She had, she supposed, been sentenced to death in that little lodge just inside the gates a few hours ago but it hadn't even sobered her, much less depressed her. Perhaps she had known, subconsciously, since last September, when it sent her reeling for the first time and she would have screamed for help if she hadn't remembered just in time that Paul was so tragically obsessed by the certainty that they would reduce his Vally to an islet, hemmed in by speeding cars and zooming aircraft. As it was she didn't know how much to believe of Maureen's qualified assurances but it didn't seem to matter all that much anyway. At seventy-two only the luckiest had more than a small handful of summers ahead of them and she had never wanted to live on for the sake of living, like old Mrs. Timberlake, who had been born the year of Trafalgar and had died more than a century later a mumbling, toothless, shrivelled old nut. That wasn't living. Living was all that had happened to her since she came storming back into the Valley on hearing the news that Paul Craddock had been calling for her whilst Maureen O'Keefe (as she then was) had been setting his bones after that shipwreck in Tamer's Cove.

Before that life had been pleasant enough but humdrum up

at High Coombe with her gruff old father and her horse-faced sister, Rose. It hadn't really begun to crackle until he had opened his eyes and seen her sitting in the window alcove in that ridiculous V.A.D. uniform, posing as a nurse on the strength of a few evening lectures at Guy's Hospital. Then, only a week or two after, the fuse had begun to splutter and the rocket had soared. Within a month he had proposed, while they were swimming in the landslip rock-pool and it was high time too for, at his instance, she had shed a monstrously ugly bathing costume and bathed in the nude, although he had kept his promise about minding the horses and looking out to sea.

She was remembering so much today and enjoying remembering. "A good run for her money" Maureen had said and it had been a fantastic run, and it wasn't over yet! The years slipped through her memory like a film, most of the images blurred but a few of them startlingly clear and distinct. Their two honeymoons in Anglesey, separated by twenty-six years. The Coronation visit to London in her prime, spoiled by that terrible suffragette riot outside the Houses of Parliament. Her one clumsy flirtation with that Kitchener-Army staff officer—she had even forgotten his name—that came close to getting her hide tanned when she blurted out the truth. And the rest? Long hot summers and long dark winters, enlivened by Heaven knows how many Christmases and Hallowe'en Parties and Guy Fawkes bonfires. The election campaign that he almost won but mercifully lost. A house full of noise and children. The stableyard full of sleek, restless hunters when the Sorrel Vale met there every first Saturday in November and every Boxing Day. Rooms full of flowers from the garden and the soft flutter of apple logs in the library grate. The smell of baking in the big old-fashioned kitchen that she was always intending to modernise but somehow never did. The smell of lavender on sheets and the smell of a man when she opened her eyes at first light on a spring morning and slipped from his embrace. The terrible, though never wholly despairing months he had been missing in France, and the joy of having him home again, only slightly the worse for wear. Marvellous, all of it. Who was she to complain about a few sharp spasms and the certainty of a speedy exit at the end of it all?

She eased herself round and let in the clutch, inching the car forward very slowly when the lamps reflected floodwater half-way across the road. She took it quietly and easily, in case there was more flooding on the stretch to the cottage but there was only an inch or two, although the noise of water roaring through the road culverts was deafening. She reached the cottage and backed carefully into the lane, grateful for the porch light Margaret had left burning, then climbed the five steps to the latched door. At the sound of its click Vanessa called from the living-room. "Is that you, Nan?" and Claire said it was and went in to find her propped up on a settee, her injured leg resting on a humpty. The lamplit room looked very cosy and suddenly she was glad she had escaped from the Big House. Vanessa had repose and tonight she needed repose more than Maureen's tablets.

"Is it still flooding out there?" Vanessa asked. "The river was right over the road at high tide this afternoon," and before Claire could reply, "Do you want to watch telly? Or shall we just drink tea and talk?"

"We'll drink tea and talk," Claire said, laughing, and thought how cuddly Vanessa looked with her shining nut-brown hair in its fashionable pony-tail and her freckles looking more definite than they really were in the glow of the lamp behind her.

"It's an awful bore this happening just before the party," Vanessa said. "I was jolly well looking forward to it I can tell you. John said I could invite as many as I liked, so I sent invitations to everyone in the Pony Club. Now they'll all turn up and I won't."

"Oh, I daresay we'll get you there somehow," said Claire, "and after all, it isn't everyone who breaks a bone over a hairy fence. You'll be one of the principal attractions."

"I'd sooner have shown what I could do at rock'n'roll!" said Vanessa. "Put the kettle on, Nan and then I'll introduce you to someone special. A real *discovery*."

Vanessa was always making "real discoveries". Once it had been Schubert, another time Renoir, and then again Grace Darling, the lighthouse heroine or a stray book of reminiscences by R. L. Stevenson. Today it was a modern poet, John Betjeman, whose love-affair with the suburbs had caught her fancy. Claire was not entirely unfamiliar with Betjeman for Paul had been impressed by his outspoken criticism of the modern compulsion to tear down old buildings and replace them with functional monstrosities. She mentioned this as she was putting the kettle on but Vanessa exclaimed, "Oh, he's much more than a *preserver*, Nan! He takes tiny, trivial things, and tiny, trivial people who seem dull but aren't because he shows you the pathos about everything. Just listen to this," and she read a sad little poem about a clergyman's widow in a furnished room, and then an even sadder one called "The Cottage Hospital", all about dying.

They were not, perhaps, morale-boosters but in her present mood Claire was more impressed than she would have been.

"Read me some more," she said, pouring their ritual tea. "Doesn't he write any cheerful poems?"

"Oh, yes," said Vanessa, "sometimes he can be ever so funny—you know—in a *nudgy* kind of way. Listen to this one, beginning "Come, friendly bombs and fall on Slough," and she read a poem that Claire thought would have pleased Paul, for it expressed much that he felt about current values.

"I think your latest discovery is wonderful," she said, "and I'll tell you what—give Grandpa a collected edition of Mr. Betjeman's work for his next present. He'd be thrilled to think someone of your generation understood his point of view so well. Have you ever written any poetry yourself, Vanessa? Somehow you always give me the impression that you might one day." Vanessa looked a little embarrassed and said, "I've never told anyone else, not even Mummy."

"You mean you *do* write poems?"

"Well—bits, when I get an idea. But I'm never satisfied with them. As soon as I try and make thoughts rhyme they seem forced and not *private* any more, as though somebody had said, 'Bet you couldn't make it scan and *sound* like poetry!' They're in that attaché case on the dresser, a little blue notebook."

Claire got the book and handed it to her, smiling at Vanessa's concentrated frown as she thumbed through the pages and said, "There. That one isn't bad but don't dare read it aloud."

"You read it," Claire urged. "Poets should always read their own poetry."

Vanessa hesitated but finally reached out, cleared her throat, and said, "Do you remember that funny little kindergarten I went to in Whinmouth years and years ago?"

"It couldn't have been all that time ago."

"It seems a long time ago. I was only five. Well, it was

360

kept by three old maids and I was thinking about them the other day. They were terribly old-fashioned but nice. What I mean is, they didn't really teach but they did make school something to look forward to and that's a terrific achievement if you think about it. I thought I'd—well—pay them a tribute, especially as they all died within about a year of one another when their school closed down. They kind of propped one another up you see, so that when one went they all went."

She cleared her throat again and began to read. "It's called 'Kindergarten'."

" 'Miss Adams, Miss Ball and Miss Parminter-Beech
Wherever you are there is chalk within reach,
You were different in method, in looks, and in name
But in many respects you were almost the same.

" 'You each wore your hair in an old-fashioned bun
And each of you rationed the moments of fun,
Each sat on a dais and instructed us while,
You smiled the same "let's-make-an-effort-now" smile.

" 'Miss Adams, Miss Ball and Miss Parminter-Beech
Wherever you are there is chalk within reach,
For, quick as you were with your morning, "Look sharp!"
God Himself wouldn't venture to teach you the harp.

" 'Miss Adams I see you with mock-severe look,
Making well-rounded "*O*"s at an alphabet book,
Miss Ball with abacus and bright-coloured beads
She forsakes to attend to our "May-I-go . . . ?" needs.

" 'But the one who still flatters my memory well
Is Miss Parminter-Beech with her lavender smell,
And the "scraps" she declared only triers could earn
But which everyone got at the end of the term.

" 'What did you earn in those faraway days?
It couldn't have paid for a new pair of stays
That creaked when you rose to admonish a caper
Or serve out the crayons, the paints and the paper.

" 'I think of you still when I hear the word "teach"
Miss Adams, Miss Ball and Miss Parminter-Beech,
Are they kind to you now? Was it true when they said
That the last one to die went out of her head?' "

Vanessa looked up as she laid the book aside but was only in time to see Claire's back as she whisked the tea-things into the scullery. She withdrew because she did not want to find answers for the questions Vanessa might ask if she saw tears in her eyes and in any case they had nothing to do with the suspended sentence Maureen had pronounced on her a few hours ago. They were released by the poignancy of the child's observation and her instinctive appreciation of the empty past of the three old ducks she had written about. In a way, Claire thought, the immature verses emphasised the difference of Vanessa, the separateness of her psychological make-up, and the circumstances of her conception and birth, bound up with the pathos of Stevie's death and the putting of a term to the fulfilment he had found in the arms of the child's mother. It also emphasised her own part in that bizarre episode, of her long weeks of anxiety ending in that interminable train journey up north only to find Stevie dead, and after that the long haul over the mountains to find and comfort Margaret in that nursing home on the bleak Welsh coast. But it did more than that, contrasting her own richly-endowed life with the drabness of the lives of Miss Adams, Miss Ball and Miss Parminter-Beech, who had probably never had an opportunity to weigh the disappointments of life against the bonuses of producing a family and having a husband who could be stirred to laughter and desire by the worn clichés of love.

She managed to say, "I think it's terrific, Vanessa. I honestly do."

Vanessa made some kind of reply but what it was she was unable to catch, for at that moment a long, rumbling sound reached her like the gust of an enormously powerful gale and the cottage shuddered and bucked like a horse frightened by the sudden flap-crack of a haystack tarpaulin.

At first she thought she must be fainting and made a grab at the edge of the sink, but the sink came away in her hands and crashed down on her right foot, numbing it completely, and as she lurched into the circle of lamplight she saw the table on which the lamp was standing slide forward and fall with a crash, and beyond it the wide-eyed expression of Vanessa as she rolled past the fireplace towards the window, her mouth open in a scream that was lost in the confused uproar that had grown out of the original rumbling sound.

Claire's first conscious act as she staggered into the room was to grab the long, heavy torch she had brought with her and had put down on the dresser, and automatically she switched it on so that the powerful beam was directed at the chaos on the far side of the room. At the same moment her brain cleared, the power of coherent thought rising like a swimmer shooting to the surface to find herself jostled by an ocean of flotsam.

She knew then, more or less, what had happened. The great hill that rose behind the cottage had moved, sliding towards the road and the river, and in the same moment she knew why this had happened and cursed the fools who had stripped the Dell of its vegetation and left it naked and vulnerable to every stream descending from the tableland behind.

As though goaded by rage the instinct of self-preservation reasserted itself and she hobbled on her damaged foot across the canting floorboards, kicking at objects that got in her way but keeping the beam of the torch fixed on the mass of broken furniture wedged in the window aperture where she could still see Vanessa's head and shoulders and her angled leg encased in plaster, looking like a short white stump crowning a pile of rubble. She shouted, above the thunder of the landslide and the hiss of water. "*Wait!* I'm coming! Hold *on!*" and glanced over her shoulder to see whether the overturned lamp or the logs in the shattered grate had started a fire to add to the horror.

There was no flame and no smell of smoke. The weight of cob, the avalanche of mud, or both, had effectively doused fire and lamp-oil, but instead a tide of sludge seemed to be rising to her waist and as she struggled against it the window frame burst outward with a prolonged crash of glass and crackle of splintered woodwork. With a tremendous effort she tore herself free from the glutinous embrace and reached Vanessa, and at the same moment she saw a means of survival directly ahead, where the trailing roots of a tree that had fallen on the cottage, crushing it like a cardboard carton, pointed towards the river at an angle of about thirty degrees to the ground. She even recognised the tree as the solitary oak that had stood about half-way up the garden at the back, and had, she remembered, a little house in its first fork built by Jerry, Mary's child, when he had spent a week staying here while his parents were away.

If the remains of the little house were still there, if the fork itself was intact, and if the roots of the tree remained embedded in the ruins of the cottage, it offered some kind of refuge for both of them and she raised her arm to direct the beam through the jagged aperture and along the short, thick bole of the oak. The probing end of the shaft caught the fork and showed its exact position, about eight to ten feet above the flood and the swirl of wreckage, and at once Claire realised what had happened, and why the tree was so angled, for its branches must have been trapped in the granite outcrop on which the cottage had been built. It would, she thought, survive a great deal of pressure, no matter how heavily the hill pressed on it, for its own weight would have wedged it among rocks stripped of their topsoil. If they could reach that fork they might hang on until help arrived.

She said, clutching hard at Vanessa's shoulder, "Are you hurt? Can you move?" and Vanessa said, between gasps, "My leg . . . the bad leg . . . it's caught . . . !" and then her body relaxed and she lost consciousness.

She turned the beam on the short column of plaster rooted in a variety of things, a chair, a small oak coffer, an assortment of sodden rugs and bricks from the chimney-piece. She began to scrabble, gripping the torch under her chin and using both hands, and finally freed it from debris so that she was able to inch forward until she was crouched about two feet above Vanessa and could make some kind of attempt to drag her through the tangle of roots that all but blocked the window. It was terribly hard work but she made some progress, even though she dared not let go of the torch, and had to work with one hand and sometimes her teeth and knees. At length, however, they were free of the roots and she felt rough bark under her knees, and after that, straddling the trunk and moving an inch or so at a time, she found she could drag Vanessa upward and outward towards the fork.

It had stopped raining but the wind was strong and rank with the smell of fresh earth and sodden cob. During a pause for breath she swung her torch in an arc to reveal a scene of unimaginable desolation, a world of uprooted trees, tangled briars, and man-made objects from the cottage or other dwellings. On her right was Margaret's car that she had left in the lane, its radiator poking from shining slime like the snout of a shark, and to the left, nearer the village, she could see what looked like a caravan, its stovepipe projecting at a crazy angle. Towards the river there was no debris, but a great swirling mass of water and the hill must have stopped sliding for behind her there was now comparative stillness, only the steady roar of water surging through the culverts that ran under a road no longer there.

By now, using reserves of strength she would not have believed she possessed as a young woman, she had dragged Vanessa about twenty feet from the window and her torch picked out some bent six-inch nails that had held Jerry's tree-house to the fork. A few planks of the nest remained, affording some protection from the wind and behind these she crouched, one arm encircling Vanessa, the other clutching the torch.

By straining across Vanessa she could read the luminous dial of her watch. It had stopped at five minutes past eight and Margaret would not even attempt to return until ten. She tried to calculate how long an interval had passed between her watch having stopped and now but she could only guess. The struggle to free Vanessa's foot and the slow journey up the tree might have taken ten minutes or an hour.

The roar of the water was getting louder and its level seemed to be rising but perched up here, only a few feet above the brown swirl, it was very difficult to judge. Far away to the left she could see a few twinkling lights pinpointing Coombe Bay but in the other direction, towards the lodge gates, there was nothing but windy darkness. She thought, without resentment, "Well, this is it, and it's odd that it should happen today of all days. 'A good run' Maureen said, 'might last for years, like old Aaron the reed-cutter, depending on the life you lead'." But now it didn't depend on anything but the temporary security of a fallen tree and the strength of the Sorrel current. Just these two factors, nothing else at all.

The distant lights appearing on the right showed like wavering globes, as though a large fish, with stupid, yellow eyes, was swimming slowly and carefully downstream. A moment or so passed before she recognised the eyes as headlights and then they stopped moving but remained pointing in her direction, about a hundred yards nearer the ford.

She began to shout but soon realised that she could not hope to compete with such an uproar, so she stopped shouting, threw a leg across Vanessa to brace her against the trunk, and turned the torch towards the stationary lights. Very deliberately she began to flash. Three short, three long, three short, a signal she didn't even realise she had learned as representing the letters S.O.S. in morse code. She pressed the finger button of the torch over and over again, three short, three long, three short and then, to her astonishment. the car-lights began to respond and as they did the car edged away, retreating up the road towards the ford.

She thought, "The road is obviously open to within about a hundred yards of here but it won't be for long. Soon the flood, searching for lower ground, will wash back towards the ford unless the banks give way on the other side of the river and all the Coombe water floods across the stubble fields. Or perhaps it depends on the tide, in which case, if it isn't ebbing now, it will be too late no matter how quickly they get here." And then another and more terrifying thought occurred to her. Irrespective of the arrival of rescuers how long could she hang on up here, even if the flood did not rise, even if the tree did remain jutting out over the water like half a bridge? And if she fell Vanessa would go too, unless the child could be secured somehow.

She isolated this last "if" and began to consider it calmly and logically, using a part of her brain beyond the cells numbed by shock and terror. Maureen had said, do nothing impulsively, plan every action, even the lifting of a basket or a walk upstairs. She would indeed, and the first thing to plan was how to ensure Vanessa remained wedged in the fork, without having to be held there by a woman of over seventy with angina.

She turned her torch towards the cottage and what she saw there reminded her of the rubble she had shifted to free Vanessa's leg. There might be some kind of fastening back there although she could not imagine what and the chances of finding it had to be weighed against the terrible risk of leaving the child while she searched. She balanced the risks carefully and finally decided to act, but before she began her descent of the trunk she wanted to assure herself of the fact that Vanessa was not, in fact, already dead, and slid her hand

366

under the child's sodden jersey, exploring the area to the right of her left breast. The beat of the heart was unmistakable and she spent the next minute of two wedging the body further into the fork. If Vanessa stirred while she was gone nothing could prevent her falling but this was another imponderable and there was nothing to be gained by taking it into account. Moving an inch at a time, and still straddling the bole as though it was a horse with a bad reputation, she eased herself down to the roots, where there was at least something to clutch and therefore less danger of rolling into the water. She did not test its depth, knowing that it would be at least six feet, for the ground outside the window had sloped away very sharply and there might even be eight or ten feet of water below, depending upon how much top soil had washed into the Sorrel.

Miraculously she still had the torch, and even more miraculously its battery continued to work. She clawed her way through the screen of roots and directed the beam downwards. Almost at once she gave a cry of satisfaction, for there was the upended sofa, with part of its webbing still attached to it, and a trailing end just within reach. She grasped it, wound it round her free hand and began to tug, at first gently, then frantically as the tacks resisted the rupture.

It came away very slowly, perhaps six inches at each tug but at last it floated free and she gathered about eight feet of the tough, fibrous fastening. Then, trailing it behind her she began her return journey up the sloping trunk.

It seemed to her the tallest tree in the world, taller than one of those huge redwoods she had seen in California, taller than the giant Douglas fir that had once stood at the top of the orchard but had been felled many years ago because, Paul said, its roots were exposed and it promised to come down on the greenhouses. All the time she kept the beam directed on the fork, spotlighting the white blur of the plaster on Vanessa's leg and when at last she could reach up and touch the child's shoe she was so thankful that she remained motionless for more than a minute before making the supreme effort to draw herself into the fork.

There was no hope of cutting the webbing. The best she could do was to fasten one end to the deeply embedded nails, driven there by young Jerry and then, holding the torch clamped between chin and breast, wind it round and round one of the branches and under Vanessa's armpits, knotting the loose end to the butt of a sawn-off branch a few inches lower down. She was so intent upon the task that she did not notice the wavering approach of lights, this time from a different direction, and it was fortunate that she was not diverted. The moment the last knot was tied she felt the first exploratory probes of pain.

This time it was so terrible that it blotted out everything else—Vanessa, their chance of rescue, the landslide, the tree, the roar of water below. Everything was submerged in the great surge of pain that shot from her back to shoulder, then down her left arm like a jet of molten lead directed at wincing flesh.

The pain was totally absorbing. While it lasted she was not conscious of movement and confused shouting away in the darkness beyond the wrecked cottage, or the snail-like approach of light on the shoulder of the hill behind the garden, but then, as the pain moderated, she experienced an almost dreamlike sensation of relief and on the threshhold of this liberating trance she heard, or thought she heard, Paul's voice calling her name, calling it loudly and clearly over and over again.

Then, as though amplified a hundred times, the steady roar of the water became deafening and everything about her began to toss and thresh on the surface of the flood. And after that nothing, only the long sough of the wind, strong enough to absorb every sound in the Valley.

III

Their uneasiness increased when they rounded the last bend leading to the stretch of river road on which the cottage stood. Already Simon had slowed the speed of the Vanguard to about three miles an hour as they moved through six inches of overspill and listened to the crackle-swish of twigs and brushwood caught up in the wheels. He stopped about a hundred yards short of the cottage, saying it would be asking for trouble to drive any further. If the engine died they would have no alternative but to wade all the way back to the lodge in the dark.

"I can't even turn here," he said, "I shall have to reverse. Thank God the Gov'nor had those white flood-posts put in all the way along."

The roar of the Sorrel on their right was so loud that Evie had to shout in his ear.

"I can't see the cottage. We're not even near it yet," and the statement alerted him because he had often fished along here as a boy and would have thought he could have pinpointed his position to a yard. And yet she was right. The white hump of the cottage should have shown up in the path of the headlights but it did not. On their left was the gleaming bank of the sloping meadow between the paddock and the western side of the Coombe, and on their right a seemingly limitless waste of water.

It was the unfamiliar note of the torrent that gave him his first clue. It seemed to come from further afield, as though road and river were separated by an appreciable distance rather than yards. He said, "Wait, I'll test it for depth," and got out, the flood reaching to his shins and the surface under his feet more yielding than it should have been.

He edged forward in the beam of the lights but he had not gone far when he came up against a wild tangle of brushwood. He tried to scramble beyond it but, to his bewilderment, the ground on his left rose steeply so that it was almost as though he was clawing his way up a bank. Then, directly ahead, he saw the wink of the torch flashing its signal and a partial awareness of the situation came to him, expressing itself in a yelp of dismay. Sloshing back to the car he shouted, "There's been a landslide! A bloody great landslide and they're beyond it, signalling for help!"

Margaret seemed stunned but Evie said, "We've got to get to them. We've got to get to them somehow!"

"We can't, not from here. Nobody could. We'll have to reverse back and get help."

Margaret said with a groan, "Vanessa—she can't help herself—her leg's in plaster! Let me try ..." and she threw open the car door but Evie reached over and grabbed her by the shoulder. "If Simon can't, you can't. You'll drown out there. If they're signalling they're still all right—they're almost certainly upstairs."

Simon said, sharply, "Shut that bloody door and watch out for me—I'm going to back" but before he threw the car into reverse he answered the signal, three short flashes, three long, three short.

They kept him on course over nearly a mile of reversing. The posts helped—about a foot of each was still showing—

and Evie shouted directions from her side. It needed a tremendous effort of will not to accelerate but Simon took his time. Nothing would be gained by ditching the car or stalling the engine and having to walk. At last they reached the ford, crossed it and made a U-turn. Then, in forward gear, the car shot up the drive and skidded to a halt in the forecourt.

From then on it was Paul who took command and they deferred to him, for he was on his home ground and a situation like this had always seen him at the hub of affairs, working without haste and certainly without any hint of confusion, bringing his intimate knowledge of the tract between the Bluff and the Whin to bear on problems of approach and method.

He said, as soon as Simon had briefed him on the situation, "One thing's clear, we can't go at it direct until it's light. We'll have to do the best we can without more help—just the three of us, you, me and young John. The girls must stay here but one of them can go across to Home Farm and tell Rumble to contact Henry Pitts, Eveleigh and any men they can get together." And when Simon said, "Damn it, Gov'nor, there's the 'phone," he said, gravely, "You can try it but I'll lay you a thousand to one it's dead. A slide like that would bring all the poles down. You won't be able to raise Home Farm or Coombe Bay."

Simon marvelled at his steadiness, at the way he grasped the essentials of the task. Then he remembered that Paul had been a community leader here a very long time and that he had faced approximate situations not once but a dozen times over the years, the first of them the day Simon had been born when he had ridden through a gale to Four Winds and had been the first to find Arabella Codsall sliced to death with a hay knife and her crazy husband swinging from a beam.

Watching him going about his preparations Simon swore to himself that he would never undervalue Paul again, that this was, and always had been, a job that few men he had ever known could perform with anything like the same despatch and efficiency. Evie, equipped with a bull's-eye, set off on foot across the paddock to alert the Home Farm. There was no danger in that direction, he told her, for the farmhouse lay this side of the road and the ground fell away sharply to the south. All the same, she was to follow the paddock palings, even though it meant another half-mile.

"You can lose your sense of direction in the meadow," he said, "and might run against something Rumble has left lying around." In the circumstances he spoke very quietly and decisively so that nobody questioned his decisions. He gave Margaret something to occupy her mind, sending her off to put hot-water bottles in the beds, light fires in the bedrooms and after that to prepare soup.

"Make up the stove and hang blankets on the clothes-horse," he added. "They'll want to be fed first and there's nothing like drinking soup while wrapped in a warm blanket after a shock and a drenching." Simon expected him to comment on the cause of the landslide but he did not. He just went about things methodically, almost as though he had been planning it for days.

Young John said, "We've got a torch apiece. We can cross the field and work our way down the lane. Shall I go on ahead? I can get there far quicker than either of you." But Paul said, quietly, "No, John, we'll stay together, the three of us. And we won't walk either. We'll take the landrover and go by way of Hermitage Lane, branching off along that track under the woods. Then we'll have transport handy when we find them and the benefit of headlights providing we're lucky enough to get down the lane."

They were factors that Simon, with all his army training, might have overlooked—handy transport for the rescued, and light to work by. A few moments later they were off, John driving and the landrover carrying a coil of rope, rugs and a metal ladder that opened out to twenty rungs. They went down the drive and turned right instead of left, moving along under the park wall until it joined Hermitage Lane and climbing it to within about two hundred yards of Henry's place.

"Couldn't we pick up Henry now?" Simon asked, but Paul said no, it wasn't worth the wasted time. Three could do nearly as much as four and Rumble would have others on the scene within the hour.

There was no evidence of the slide up here under the woods and the track, although very muddy, was negotiable. In ten minutes they had struck the head of the narrow lane that ran up from the river road to the south-eastern corner of the woods and as John eased the vehicle round, Paul said,

"Steady now, we don't know where the slide began. My guess is it's much lower down but there may be fissures as high as this. Let me get out and walk ahead."

He got out and Simon with him. Together they began to descend the slushy surface of the lane, pointing their torches beyond the creeping headlight beam of the landrover. In five minutes more they struck the first big change in a familiar landscape, a great mound of freshly-turned earth, as though someone had ploughed a giant, diagonal furrow from east to west. Paul judged that they were now two-thirds of the way down and within eighty yards of the cottage but they couldn't be sure, for their lights fell on what looked like a twenty-foot earthwork, and the rivulet on their immediate left had grown to a torrent that skirted the lower ridges of the new escarpment and then fell directly on to the flooded road. The water echoed flatly as it came down, the sound telling Paul that it was cascading into appreciable depths. He stopped for a moment, directing his torch to the crest of the mound.

"We'll have to leave the landrover here," he said, "but keep the headlights on and don't lose touch. We've got to go up and over, no matter how liquid it is. Bring the rope and leave the ladder against the bonnet."

They did as he bid, moving like a couple of privates under the eye of a general, and then, with Paul in the lead, they advanced into the soft soil and forced their way up the face of the giant slide.

It was heavy going on the north side but they kept moving, sometimes sinking to their knees. Once over the summit the mud was even less solid and sometimes rose to their thighs, plucking at their gumboots and causing them to flounder and curse. They made progress, however, and half-way down they saw the tree and the cottage or what was left of the cottage.

The tree was a sturdy elm, probably about seventy years old and because it had not stood in the direct path of the avalanche it had remained rooted in the bank, mud enclosing its bole to within a few feet of the lower branches. Approaching it and paying out the rope they sank to their waists, but Paul fought free of this porridge as soon as he grasped the lowest bough and was able to fasten the rope as an anchor for further descent. John said, fearfully. "There's no sign of life down there, Gov'nor. The back part of the roof is smashed in and the rear walls are down," and he waited for his father to comment.

"They'll be at the front," Paul said and bracing himself against the rope cupped a hand and shouted, "Claire! We're coming down!"

They stood waist-deep in the mud and waited for a reply but none came. All they could hear was the frenzied roar of the Sorrel tumbling down to the sea and after thirty seconds or so Paul said, huskily, "Stay here, John, and bring the ladder if I shout for it."

"Let me go down first."

"Do as you're told, boy," he said and John nodded, taking hold of the anchored rope and helping them pay it out as they slipped and slithered down the still-moving mass of mud to a lip of stones that marked the northern edge of the garden.

It was just possible, down here, to stand on the remains of the thatch and the slices of cob that had been the walls of the kitchen and scullery. Moving from beam to beam and probing with their torches they called and called again, and when no answer came from below they gave the rope a twist round an angled beam-end and kicked their way through the rubble, Simon advancing with mounting desperation so that Paul, still calm, said, "Easy, boy. We won't help by bringing the whole damned lot down on us."

A moment later they were in the chaos of the living-room and their torches centred on the spread of roots in the aperture. For the first time since he had returned home with the news of the landslide Simon sensed desolation in the man who was stumbling and probing among the mush of carpet and shattered furniture that had built up under the window. He said, with authority, "Stay here, Gov, and let me do the looking," and without waiting for Paul's assent he crawled through the roots, pushing his torch ahead until its beam rested on the small figure lashed to the fork by strips of webbing. He called over his shoulder, "It's Vanessa. She's here, tied in a tree ... it's okay Gov'nor, she's fastened there." Then, despair lifting his voice an octave, "Claire. Where are you Claire?" as he edged out along the trunk and clawed at the fastenings holding the child in the "Y" of the lower branches.

Paul said, so quietly that Simon had to incline his head to hear him, "Is she alive? Can you tell?" and when Simon said he could feel her pulse and began chafing her, he heard Paul scrambling back over the ruins of the scullery shouting to John to bring the ladder. Then he was back in the room again and when he saw her stir he suddenly became excited and leaped up shouting, "*John!* The ladder! Hurry! Come over the roof!" Subsiding again, as though ashamed of his outburst, he said, "You say she was *tied* there? Out on that tree?" and Simon, still chafing the child's hands, mumbled, "There's no one else out there, Gov. I'm sorry ... sorry ..." but could add nothing more.

John came scrambling over the roof and they heard the thump of the ladder, neither of them pausing to wonder how the devil he had managed to drag the cumbersome thing this far but then, as Simon rose, cradling Vanessa in his arms, he saw Paul crawl into the aperture and cast the beam of his torch in a wide arc over the water. They had already eased Vanessa through the hole at the back and were beginning to ascend the first rungs of the ladder before he rejoined them, reaching forward to steady Simon's shoulders. He said, "Tied there ... Must have dragged her there ... God knows, it's a bloody miracle ... *I* couldn't have done it. Neither could you or anyone else, not with the place falling about her ..."

They said nothing, concentrating on the tricky task of inching the child across the ladder that John had placed as a bridge between the remains of the thatch and a perilously insecure mound of cob a few yards beyond. They managed it somehow and dragged themselves back along the rope as far as the elm, with Vanessa balanced on their shoulders and Paul abreast of them, lending his shoulder as a staff whenever either of them needed it. When they reached the landrover he gave another series of despairing shouts but the answer came from some way above them, where there was a confused flicker of lights at the top of the lane.

Simon said sharply, "Take Vanessa home, Gov'nor. There's no sense in staying now help has arrived. I'll pilot them down there and we've got the rope and ladder. Drive him back, John. And see what you can do to rouse Whinmouth. Drive there by the moor if necessary, or try and 'phone from somewhere en route. God knows, there might be dozens of casualties in that caravan park on the other side of the Coombe."

He stood beside the bonnet gesturing and watched his father's authority ebb so that John was able to coax him into the landrover where he sat hunched and silent, the child across his knees. Then, as Rumble Patrick and one of Eveleigh's men appeared out of the darkness, John revved and began to back up the lane, the tyres fighting for a grip on a wash of loose stones in the gateway. Rumble Patrick asked no questions. With Simon and Eveleigh's man he dragged at the floundering tail-board until the vehicle was wrenched round and moved off up the lane to where two other cars were parked at the junction. Henry Pitts waddled out of one of them, swathed in an enormous greatcoat that John recognised as super-annuated Home Guard issue. He said briefly, "Stay here and keep contact, Henry. We've got Vanessa but mother's still missing," and then swung left and lurched off into the darkness.

Henry Pitts stood there with his mouth agape, watching the tail-lights until they disappeared and then turning to look at the bobbing lights lower down where Simon, Rumble Patrick and Eveleigh's man were scrambling over a wilderness of liquid mud.

"Christ A'mighty," he said aloud, "to think it should ha' come to this. Claire Craddock gone. Carried away by a tide o' mud in her own bliddy vields."

Suddenly he felt very old and helpless so that he blundered back to the car, groped in the glove box for a flask and sucked down two great mouthfuls of whisky and water. He recorked the flask, wiped his mouth on the back of his hand and sat glumly to await reinforcements. Sitting alone in the darkness he remembered another such night down in Tamer's Cove, when the whole lot of them were engrossed in work of this kind. But that was in the splendour of their youth and nothing had seemed too difficult or depressing. It was, he reflected, almost exactly half-a-century ago. The wonder of it was that of all that team he and Squire Craddock were present for the encore.

CHAPTER FIVE

COUNTER ATTACK

I

THEY recovered her body the following afternoon. It was caught in a tangle of briars nearly a mile below the landslide, just short of the choked bridge where flotsam was piled twenty feet high and the Sorrel, in its furious search for the sea, had turned aside to flood half the houses and shops of Coombe Bay High Street, some of them to a depth of ten feet.

She did not die alone that night. The Coombe Bay constable, shouting a warning to sleeping householders, was caught by a wall of water between two of the shops and washed as far as the quay where the torrent tore through Smut Potter's café leaving a hole ten yards wide. Down here, in one of the few original quayside cottages, an elderly couple were drowned in their beds and in the new red, brick houses, where the block stood in the path of the diverted mainstream, five other people died, two of them children.

It was astonishing, people said when they surveyed the two-mile path of the torrent that the death roll was not higher. Thirty houses had subsided when the tide rolled back the floodwater in the small hours and several caravans, mercifully empty, were swept from the eastern side of the Dell and carried in the path of the slide as far as the river bed.

Nine dead, damage estimated at a hundred and seventy thousand pounds. It was enough to put the Valley on the front page of the nationals for the fourth time in fifty-one years and bring newspapermen and television teams flocking in from London, Bristol and Plymouth to record the devastation and interview survivors. A short-lived, out-of-season boom followed the night of terror. Hotels and boarding houses reopened to accommodate the Press and a Paxton-bury disaster fund was opened for the families of victims and the hundred-odd homeless. People living as far away as Rome looked curiously at the ruin of an English village half-inundated in slime and temporarily isolated by the two arms of the Sorrel, the one following its original course when the bridge arches were cleared, the other, the wayward one, cutting through the new housing block, a huddle of cottages behind the High Street, and on into the bay via Smut Potter's café and the old quayside.

Simon, plodding about among the muck and debris after his school was closed, likened the desolate scene to some of the towns he had passed in pursuit of the Wehrmacht to the Seine, places like Caen and Le Havre, but the defilement of this end of the Valley worried him less than his father's silence.

When they told him she had been found he seemed neither surprised nor relieved but looked at them under his grey, shaggy brows and listened politely, as though to a report of a relatively trivial occurrence at one of the farms, a burned rick perhaps, or a Dutch barn unroofed by a gale. The Whinmouth doctor said it was the effect of shock, but Maureen, who knew him far better than his sons, understood that it was a more complex and deepseated reaction, involving not only Claire but the Valley as a whole, and that, in any case, he would be likely to see his human and material loss as one for all the time she had known him he had identified the Valley with his wife. His withdrawal, she thought, was caused by his attempt to come to terms with this quirk in his character and that whilst others would see it as a coincidence to him it was nothing of the sort. There was a kind of inevitability about it that, to an extent, buttressed him against grief, at least for the time being. She did not try to explain this to anyone because it was far too complicated. The only person capable of understanding it would be his daughter Mary, and she had her own grieving to do and her own pride to sustain her.

As more and more reporters arrived and people began to talk freely, the story of the manner of Claire's death half-leaked and they began to plague him for details. A village destroyed by a landslide and a torrent was first-class copy, but a bonus human story—a seventy-two-year-old grand-mother sacrificing her life for an injured grandchild was a golden peg on which such a story could be hung. They picqueted the Big House hour after hour and the restored telephone hardly ever stopped ringing, and had it not been for the presence of Simon and John, both with first-hand experience of newspapers and T.V. coverage, they might have overwhelmed him. As it was they preserved his isolation, dribbling a fact here, a recollection there, so that their reticence did not result in acrimony.

Then, down in the village, they began to talk of his involvement with the developers and also plan for a mass funeral, so that pressure, instead of dwindling as the days passed, continued to mount, and Simon had to make a clearcut decision about the funeral as well as bear the brunt at the inquest. His evidence, and that of John's, was concise. They said as little as possible about the night sortie that they and Paul had made from the edge of the woods, and this was easier than they would have supposed for by now the issues were getting blurred and attention was redirected to the Coombe Bay area, to Shawcrosse's stripping of the Dell and the supreme folly of cutting two new roads either side of an unpredictable watercourse.

He took no part in all this, keeping very much to himself and seeming to agree when Simon told him he had arranged for Claire to be buried privately the day after the eight other victims were laid in the churchyard. Simon, handling him gently, was worried by his passiveness. His grief did not rise to the surface and he told Maureen, who had pronounced Paul little worse for his terrible exertions on the night, that he was worried about the weeks ahead, when the impact of all that had happened would fall on his father like another landslide. It was then that Maureen made her decision and went to him with the truth. The effect astonished her, who knew most of his secret thoughts, as much as it astonished the others.

On the fourth day after the disaster, the day before the big funeral, winter borrowed a day from spring, as it sometimes did in the Valley, and those few gleams of sunshine came to Maureen's rescue and to his.

They told her that he had gone out soon after breakfast and climbed the upsloping orchard behind the stableyard to the stile that looked down on the lane and it was here that she found him, knowing full well why he was here, for it had been one of Claire's favourite spots.

She eased herself into his thoughts by this route, reminding him of how he had come to her during Claire's second pregnancy, complaining that she had taken to getting up early in the morning and walking here barefoot among the bluebells and late primroses. He smiled, slowly, saying, "I remember very well, because you told me morning dew had never been known to cause an abortion," and then she smiled too and said, directly, "Simon and the others are wondering if you would like to see Claire. I told them I'd ask you."

He took his time answering but finally said, "No, I won't see her. I daresay some of the older people in the Valley will raise their eyebrows at that but I've never subscribed to that tribal rite of tiptoeing into the presence of the dead and speaking in whispers, as though they might be embarrassed by what was said. I can't imagine Claire wanting me to look at her any other way than through my memories. They're pleasant enough, God knows, and I daresay they'll last me out." Then, looking almost fierce as he stared at her under heavy, arched brows, "She wasn't disfigured in any way, was she?"

"Not in any way at all," Maureen said. "Once the mud was washed away she looked her usual 'safe side of sixty'," and he said, with relief, "That's good. She was as vain as a peacock about her looks."

"It wasn't so much vanity as insurance against losing your interest." She hesitated a moment longer. "She wasn't drowned, Paul. I can't prove it of course, but let me say that in my opinion it was extremely unlikely. She was almost certainly dead when the water closed over her and took her half-way to the coast."

He looked so startled that she went on very hurriedly, telling him the full truth about Claire's visit to her the morning before the flood, and when she had finished she was so flustered by the blankness of his expression that she said, uncertainly, "Well, Paul ... it seemed to me you should know. What I mean is ... she must have realised exactly what she was doing clambering up and down that tree trunk, getting those fastenings, and hanging on there in all that storm and wind. Perhaps a person in that situation with a helpless child would do what she did instinctively, or at least try to do it, but to me, knowing her heart condition, it was

379

nothing short of a miracle. It was also a deliberate sacrifice," She paused. "Is that how you see it?"

He said, at length, "Yes, that's how I see it and that's how it was. I'll tell you something else, Maureen. I always loved the girl—once I got adjusted to losing Grace that is—and I was always damned proud of her looks and fine figure, but this is something different. What I mean is, it makes Claire a different person, someone whom even I didn't know, and that after living with her for half-a-century. I wonder how many V.C.s were dished out for that kind of act in the two wars? It makes me proud of her in a new way."

She knew that he had not finished, that he had something else to tell her and she was right. After a moment he went on, without looking at her. "There's another way of looking at this business and it keeps returning to me. It's the curious completeness, almost *rightness* of that kind of death in that particular place. She was Valley-born and all her life she stood by me in a fight for and against the Valley but I don't mean by that a fight against outsiders. The Sorrel and all the soil that came down on her weren't outsiders. Neither was the heavy rainfall at the back of that landslide. These things have always been part and parcel of our life here. In a way we've always been fighting them, trying to tame them, trying to make them work for us. Somehow it doesn't seem so bad to go down fighting in an old cause. Hazel, Rumble Patrick's mother, was killed by a honking staff car near that cottage, and poor old Grace was killed in a foreign land by a foreign bomb. But Claire was luckier than either of them. If she had to go soon, then it was a wonderful thing to have a chance of doing something as useful as that at the final moment. I'm glad you told me, In fact, I'll never cease to appreciate it," and he pressed her hand.

"You mean it helps that much?"

"More than you can know," he said and suddenly he turned on his heel and went down the orchard with his old, measured-yard stride, and across the stableyard into the house. She thought, following him, "He's a queer one and no mistake. When do you ever stop learning about someone? God knows, I thought I knew them both but it seems I didn't. In all these years I've only managed to lift a corner of the curtain."

But even Maureen was not prepared for the end-product of the talk they had leaning on the orchard stile.

He called Simon and John into the library as soon as he entered and sent for the others as well. They realised at once that he was himself again as soon as he said, pouring them and himself whiskies, "Right. None of you have to creep about the damned house any more. What time is that funeral fixed for tomorrow?" and when Simon said it was scheduled for 3 p.m., and likely to be televised, he added, "I've had second thoughts. Claire ought to be part of it. This is a Valley occasion and she was very much a part of the Valley. She wouldn't care to be buried quietly and discreetly, or not in the circumstances. Somehow I'm suddenly sure of that. Could you make the necessary alterations at this stage?"

"Why yes, I suppose so," said Simon, doubtfully, "providing you're sure that's what you want."

"It is," he said, "and I'll get around to telling you why, but not now because there's something else I want to do. I'd like to make some kind of statement to those Press chaps. I'd like to do Claire justice. Yes, I know, it cuts across what you thought I'd want but there it is, and unless it's going to upset the rest of you I'd like to get the record straight. How much have they printed about things like Claire tying that webbing round Vanessa?"

"Bits and pieces," John said. "We played it right down. Even the coroner thinks you waited by the landrover when Si and I went down to look. That's why you weren't called at the inquest."

"Well, it can't make much difference now," Paul said, "and what the hell have any of us got to hide? She didn't just die of exhaustion out there, and she wasn't really caught by the flood. She had angina, pretty badly Maureen says, and she must have realised precisely what she was doing all the time. I'd like that generally known unless, that is, it's going to embarrass either of you, or Mary, or any of the others.

They were silent as Rumble Patrick slipped into the room, and behind him Mary, Margaret and last of all Maureen. "It's all right," Maureen said, "I told them the same as I told you," and John said, slowly, "You don't *mind* this sort of thing being broadcast, Gov?"

"No, I don't," he said emphatically. "Why should I? Why should any of us? She did something astounding and why should it be passed over? I've told Maureen that I'm damned proud of her, and I imagine you are too. It helps me a lot and if you'll let it, it'll help you. I'd like Vanessa to know the truth about it when she's up and about. God knows, she wouldn't have had any chance at all if Claire had thought of herself."

And so it was done, and the full story appeared in the morning papers, and nine coffins instead of eight were carried along the improvised duckboard track from the mortuary to the plot behind the church that Shallowfordians still called "Overspill".

Never before had so many strangers witnessed a Valley funeral, and never had so many flowers been passed hand to hand from van to grave-side. Only the male Craddocks were present for it was a tradition that no female Craddock attended a funeral, and Paul, noticing John's troubled glance when he gazed round at the phalanx of spectators, touched his elbow and said, "It's all as it should be, John. Nothing that has ever happened here has been private. It wouldn't have caused your mother the least concern. We're still a community here in spite of everything, and four of those other people were born and raised in the Valley."

When the simple service was over and the crowds began to disperse, Henry Pitts sidled up and said, nodding towards the obelisk raised by the German Merchant Marine over Tamer Potter's grave, "Do 'ee remember the last time us had this kind o' caper up yer, Maister?" and Paul said he remembered very clearly, and had been thinking of it all day for it seemed to him very strange that two tragedies, separated by fifty years, should have had so many similarities.

After that he stayed close to Henry, drawing comfort from the comradeship that had helped them both through the years and together they looked out over the devastation of the Village and the new course of the Sorrel.

"They'll soon get around to clearing it up and rebuilding, I imagine," Paul said. And then, making his first and last reference to the cause of the landslide; "Maybe it'll teach them something, Henry. Maybe, if we raise the matter of replanting, someone might listen to us next time." But Henry, made cynical by the years, said, "Maybe, but I woulden bet on it, Maister."

II

Andy did not fly home for the funeral but wrote saying he intended leaving the States and returning to the U.K. in the spring and that he would contact them on arrival. A week or so later a second letter arrived from him, addressed to Paul, and marked "Personal", so that Paul did not open it in front of Margaret, now living at the Big House, but carried it away to his study as soon as breakfast was over.

It was, he supposed, something in the nature of an *amende honourable*, for the boy was clearly distracted by the circumstances of Claire's death and his indirect contribution to the changes at that end of the Valley. In spite of his isolation he was, Paul noted, still very well-informed about everything that was going on and Paul wondered how much the others had told him or, indeed, whether Margaret herself had let slip that the disaster had been caused by stripping vegetation from that part of the Coombe. He hoped not, for he felt no rancour now, wishing heartily that Andy had sense enough to realise as much, "I'll sit down and write him a cheery letter when I feel more up to it," he told himself, but the weeks went by, and the effort of adjusting to the emptiness of the bedroom and the library chair accounted for most of his waning energy. He mentioned Andy to Margaret once or twice, and even to Vanessa when she told him all she could recall of that last evening at Mill Cottage. The child seemed more interested than her mother, who merely said, "We still keep in touch . . ." but so offhandedly that he let the subject drop and turned the conversation to Vanessa's future.

Until then Margaret had taken it for granted that she would have a more or less formal education, but after reading some of her essays and verses Paul ventured an opinion that the customary five-year spell at Paxtonbury Convent School might be improved upon and in the end they managed to get her into Dartington Hall where, Paul was informed by Mary (the family authority on such matters), Vanessa's creative impulse would be encouraged. That same spring she went off happily enough, and within a day or so of her departure Andy returned to the Valley after an absence of more than five years.

He did not make his presence known and did not even inform them he had landed. He had urgent business to attend to and wanted it settled to his satisfaction before he made peace with the family. It was with this in mind that he hired a small and, for him, very unostentatious car and drove by a roundabout route to Coombe Bay churchyard to visit Claire's grave. He was far from being a sentimentalist but he went there for all that. It was as though he wished to include her in the reconciliation.

The sight of the nine fresh mounds and the debris of so many wreaths among clusters of fresh flowers, stirred him more than he had been stirred in a very long time He stood there reading the inscription on the temporary headstone and then, hands in pockets, lounged across to the wall overlooking that section of Coombe Bay where the Sorrel had carved a new channel to the sea.

Desolation persisted down here despite the nonstop work of earth-moving machines and the dumping of hundreds of tons of soil and rocks along the old course of the river. Like his brother Simon he found himself equating the rubble-strewn acres with the wrecked towns he had seen during the war and then his gaze crossed the river and the new dykes, finally resting on the bald, eastern half of the Coombe where the sun glittered on zinc or glass at what was left of the caravan park. He went down into the town and talked to one or two of the workmen, posing as a stranger and learning things about the flood and its repercussions that he had suspected but had been unable to confirm until now. Then he got in his hired car and drove back along the coastal road to keep an appointment with his father's solicitors. That same evening, about eight o'clock, he 'phoned his former partner, Shawcrosse, from a hotel booth.

Shawcrosse sounded glad to hear from him and could hardly wait to give him an up-to-date report on Shawcrosse Developments Ltd.

"We've had our teething troubles," he assured Andy, "but we're over them now. You were a B.F., old boy, to let the family scare you off in that way. What started as an outsider looks like coming up the straight ahead of anything I've ever done in this bracket. Why not come over for the odd noggin? Rhoda will be tickled to death. She always had a yen for the strong silent types, old boy."

He seemed not to realise that he was talking to the son of Claire Craddock, washed down the Sorrel a few months ago among the debris of his holiday camp, and Andy did not remind him but said he would come over right away and had a proposition that might interest Shawcrosse. Then, having collected his brief case and downed a stiff brandy, he drove out along the Whinmouth road to the big double gates of the

Shawcrosse home, a large, detached house built between the wars and garnished at a later date with Carolean-Cum-Tudor embellishments.

Shawcrosse, shaking hands with his customary man-to-man emphasis, greeted him enthusiastically, calling to Rhoda that he and Andy wanted a business chat "before the social yakkity-yak began". He showed Andy into a large study that reminded his visitor of a room one of the pre-war scrap kings might have window-dressed in the hope of impressing a customer with a public-school background. The desk was as massive as Mussolini's, the fitted carpet tickled the ankle, the pictures, all very modern, suggested framed wallpaper designs executed by a heroin addict. Andy said, by way of acknowledging the furnishings, "You've come a long way, Ken. Is it as far as you hoped when we first met, back in Tunis?"

"Can't grumble," Shawcrosse said genially, "but it hasn't been all beer and skittles, especially since that bloody shambles over at Coombe Bay. Take a pew, old boy, that's what they're for," and he flung open a military chest saucily converted into a cocktail bar, saying, "Don't tell me. I know your tipple. Make a point of remembering things like that."

"Great God," thought Andy, "he talks as though it was still 1942 and he was three weeks out of an Officers' Training Unit. Are there many like him still around?" and it sobered him to reflect that he had spent so many hours in this man's company or that he had associated with him in any way at all, even over the telephone. Everything he said and did was phoney. The way he lifted his glass and leered as he gulped. The clothes he wore and the pub-talk gambits he used. The desk he sat at and the curtains he had chosen. Every last thing about him was as counterfeit as a deep-freeze dinner sealed in cellophane.

He said, taking his drink, "Let's get to the point. I haven't very long. That proposition I mentioned, I don't think you'll need to chew on it. All I want is a plain 'yes' or 'no'," and he opened his brief case and took out a folder he had collected from the Whinmouth solicitors an hour or so ago.

Shawcrosse looked down at it and blinked once or twice. "I'll say that for him," Andy thought, watching closely, "it doesn't take him long to get the message," and Shawcrosse said, meeting his eye, "So you want to buy your way in again? No hard feelings, old boy, but it's too late for that.

385

You held good cards and I didn't ask you to throw your hand in."

"No, you didn't, Ken. All the same, you'll take me up on that offer. It's for the Coombe Farm holding, every acre you bought north of the river, the farm I steered your way, remember?"

"Good God, of course I remember. I'm not likely to forget a thing like that but you aren't such a clot as to imagine a bit of flooding and that cliff cave-in has turned the place into a hot potato are you?"

He turned the document over, running an eye down the last page of single-spaced typing and as he did this Andy saw the blood surge into his neck where it bulged over the collar of his shirt. "*Twelve-five?* The price we paid for it? Oh, come on, you must be kidding! I'll get planning permission there eventually. As a matter of fact I've already got it, over on the village side. They don't do business that way in the States, do they?"

Andy said, snapping the catch of his brief case, "Don't look at it as a straight sale, Ken. Try and see it as hush-money. I could get it for a lot less if I was greedy or vindictive, but I'm not. All I want is the Coombe, and I'm not even knocking off the odd thousand for the slice that fell into the river and drowned my mother, a copper, an old couple, and a bunch of kids."

He had not expected violent reaction to the threat and there was none. For a moment there was no reaction at all, a deepening of that brick-red flush, so that he thought, "Why the hell does he wear his collar so tight? Do his self-delusions run to kidding himself he's still twelve stone instead of fifteen?"

Shawcrosse said, taking a careful sip of his whisky, "You know a lot better than that, Andy. Where the hell have you been? Running a crap game in the Chicago stockyards? Or watching revivals of bootleg films on the telly? I'm sorry because I got along with you better than most people. I can only imagine you've been hitting the bottle too hard," and he got up, crossed the room and opened the door. "No hard feelings," he said.

"None at all," said Andy but without moving, "and no Public Prosecutor either, providing you sign that bill of sale. I've already written the cheque," and he took an envelope from his pocket and laid it on the desk.

Shawcrosse closed the door again but remained with his back to it. "What the hell are you talking about? You're in every fiddle we operated right up to here. If they gave me a five-stretch they'd give you a sixer."

"I doubt it," said Andy, "I wasn't in that bloody great fire you had in the Enfield warehouse and that's the fiddle I think of when I think about you. And in any case, do you think I give a damn what happens to me? I've no kids, and my wife thinks I stink. I've got brothers and sisters but if I walked into a room where they were assembled conversation would be reduced to the weather. I've no friends either. You were the nearest I ever came to having one, after my brother Stevie got the chop. You'd be surprised how little a man in my situation cares where he ends up, or what happens to him. It might even be interesting to mix with the big-time crooks instead of our kind."

The flush above the collar had spread a little, flooding the smooth pink skin on Shawcrosse's pendulous cheeks. From across the room Andy could hear the whistle of his breath in his nostrils. Suddenly the interview shamed him, as though he had been caught helping Shawcrosse scrawl obscenities on the wall of a public lavatory. He said, "For Christ's sake. I'm not bluffing! I've just come from that churchyard and that bloody awful village of yours. I'll give you two minutes to sign and cut your losses, or I make a precis of everything I can prove about what went on between the time we were demobbed and the time we split up. I'm not putting the bite on you, not really. All I want is the Coombe farm. The rest of it, those places nearer the sea, aren't worth having any more."

Shawcrosse came back slowly to behind his desk and took another look at the folded document. "You're mad," he said. "You're just bloody mad enough to do it, aren't you? And it's not liquor either. They've hooked you on something more lethal in the last year or so."

"Let's say I hooked myself. You've got a pen there, haven't you? The one you use for signing all the planning permissions on the councils?"

Shawcrosse made no reply. He signed the document in two places, pushed it back across the desk, picked up the envelope containing the cheque and stuck it in his pocket without looking at it.

"Get to hell out of here," he said, "and I hope you die of cancer in the bowel."

"Far more likely the liver," Andy said, and putting the bill of sale in his brief case he turned and let himself out. Rhoda, Shawcrosse's wife, came gushing across the hall as he fumbled with the catch of the front door. "Andy . . . wait . . . It's been so long . . ."

He did not look at her but swung the door open and went out on to the lamplit porch. Before she could follow he was half-way down the drive.

His watch showed him it was still only a few minutes to nine so instead of swinging left to Paxtonbury he turned right, skirted the old town and found the "B" road that led to the moor. It was dusk now and a warm night for April. Up here he could smell the sea and the whiff of wild onion that drifted off the dunes when the wind was right. His need for a drink, overpowering when he left the Shawcrosse place, had left him and he kept so light a touch on the accelerator that the speedometer hovered around twenty. Slowly, like the effect of vodka, warmth spread to his belly and on the crest of the moor, just before he began to dip down to the junction of the old dust road he stopped and lit a cigarette, watching the smoke lose itself in the light air.

From here he could just see the lights of Coombe Bay at the very end of the Valley, and between there and the moor some of the familiar landmarks loomed in the dusk. Four Winds farmhouse to his right, Hermitage to his left, and beyond Hermitage the blue-black blur of the woods. French Wood reared up on his immediate left, and below him the narrow blade of the Sorrel swept in a broad arc from the lower slopes of the Moor to the nearest meadows of Home Farm, re-emerging half-a-mile on where it ran between the Coombe and Codsall's stubble fields. He was well over forty now and yet he could not remember an occasion when he had stopped to contemplate the Valley in quite the same way. Either it had never occurred to him or he had never had the time. He thought of Stevie riding knee to knee with him across this part of the moor during a Boxing Day hunt when they were about seventeen, and then again of the time when they had equipped a third-hand motor-boat for a trip to France but had got no further than the sandbar to be rescued by Coombe Bay fishermen. He thought of Margaret too, and how he had first brought her here one icy, February morning, the night after he had abducted her from that stinking little hospital in Wales. And he thought of Vanessa, Stevie's kid, and her brown curls and big grey eyes—"mild as a heifer's" as Claire had once said. Well, here it all was, or what was left of it, and at least he had something to offer in the way of a coming-home present that the old Gov would value far above any of the junk he had thought of buying in New York or Chicago. He carefully extinguished the cigarette butt, remembering as he did how fussy Paul was about carelessly-strewn cigarette ends up here. Then he let in the stiff clutch and coasted down the hill to the junction.

Lights were burning on the terrace when he changed down to tackle the last gradient of the drive but nobody heard the car and nobody came out. He closed the car door silently and walked along the flagstones as far as the library but although the fireplace lights were on, and a small fire was burning in the grate, the room was empty so he moved along to peep through the window of the adjoining room that had always been the estate office.

Paul was there and it made him wince to see how old he looked, even though he still held himself straight and worked without glasses. He was writing in some kind of ledger as fat as a family Bible and his hearing must have been unimpaired for suddenly he stopped writing and stood erect, cocking an ear as though he had detected the scrape of feet outside. Beyond him, clamped squarely to the wall, was an oil-portrait of Claire that Andy remembered had once hung in the main bedroom. It showed her sitting on a sandstone rock down at the goyle, with her head thrown back as she reached across her breast to loosen the shoulder-strap of her blue costume. Andy remembered that it had been a present to his father on his sixtieth birthday and yet she looked no more than about forty-two or three, and although, when the story got around, the family had laughed at her vanity, they had all admitted that it was a wonderful likeness and the Gov had been so proud of the painting that he treated it like a Rubens. Affection for the lonely old man made him choke so that he remembered his longing for a drink, one of Paul's really stiff drinks of Irish whisky that he kept for special visitors in the library cupboard.

He called softly, "Gov! It's me. Andy," and Paul swung round so quickly that Andy regretted he had not made a conventional entry. Then he saw that the old man was jerky with excitement and crossed the little office so quickly that his elbow caught the ledger and spun it round on the hook-and-eye drawing-board. He flung open the garden door and pulled Andy into the room, holding him by the shoulders in a grip that proved he was not so old and tired as he had looked through glass.

"God bless you, it's wonderful to see you, boy," he said. "Why the devil didn't you tell us . . . me . . . Margaret . . . Rumble . . . they'll all be delighted . . ." and he looked as if he was going to run across the library, fling open the door and summon the entire family. Andy said quickly, "Hold on, Gov . . . wait until I've had time to look at you. Christ, you're spry for—what is it—seventy-five?"

"Seventy-six on June first. And you don't look so bad yourself, although you've put on a stone or so, haven't you?"

"It's not from the grub in the States," Andy said. "Tasteless, every damned mouthful."

"What will you drink?" Paul asked. "Drop of old Irish?"

"I was standing there thinking about it with my tongue hanging out," Andy said, and when his father turned his back he slipped the bill of sale from his brief case and said, casually, "Prodigal's peace offering. I didn't squander all my patrimony on the husks that the swine eat."

He watched the old man raise his glass and then lower it again, curiosity showing in the lift of the heavy, tufted eyebrows. He said, with a hard swallow, "*The Dell?* In my name?" and Andy said it was all buttoned up and that he had bought it back for the price Paul had received from Jumbo Bellchamber seven years ago.

He had never seen the old man so bemused or embarrassed. He kept looking at the typescript, then at Andy, then back at the typescript, fumbling for words and finding none, so that Andy said, for something to say, "I figured you could plant there again . . . half-grown soft woods, so that you'll live to see them. Neither you nor I can wait around for oaks and beeches to grow but you could put in a few for the kids. I was up there this afternoon and it looked so bald. Then I had this idea."

Paul found his tongue at last. "It was a wonderful idea," he said, fighting to keep his voice steady, "the best idea you ever had," and then he dropped the paper on the floor and threw his arms round him, holding him close for a full half-minute. He had never embraced any of his children like that before, not even Mary.

They had to plan the initial approach to Margaret. She was over at Home Farm, Paul told him, but was due back any minute. "You stay here and I'll go and meet her when the car lights show in the drive," and then he seemed to want to talk about Vanessa, and her prospects at Dartington, but Andy steered him back to Margaret, saying "You'd better brief me, Gov. Is there any chance at all of Margy and I having a third go at it?"

"I don't know," he said unhappily, "I honestly don't know. We're friendly, and since the flood she likes to fuss me, but she never did talk that kind of shop with me, only with Claire. She took a terrific knock over Claire. They were very fond of one another."

"And you?"

"I managed to ride it out. I don't think I should if it had happened any other way but pride—at a time like that—well, it helps more than you'd think. It was a terrific show she put up down there, just the kind of show Stevie put up when he brought that A.G. home in one piece. Whenever I get low I remind myself of that, and also of the fact that, according to Maureen, she wouldn't have had more than a year or so with that heart of hers."

They finished their whisky and Paul asked if he would like another but he refused. Then, as the white glow of headlights showed on the rhododendrons, he said, "Wait here," and went out. There was no shuffle in his step. He still walked like a middle-aged countryman crossing frozen furrows in heavy boots.

She slipped into the room alone when he was in the act of pouring himself another whisky. He was astonished by the absence of change in her. Her brown hair still trapped the gleam of the centre light and her skin was as smooth and unblemished as the day he had grabbed her by the shoulders as she straightened his pillow in the hospital and kissed her wide mouth, with the sour-faced sister three beds down the ward. He would have expected her to put on weight, for, although small-boned, she had always inclined to chubbiness, but her figure was as neat as when she was twenty. Only her large brown eyes indicated maturity.

She showed none of Paul's initial embarrassment but said,

quietly, if a little huskily, "Hullo Andy. Good to see you. We'd practically given you up," and he did not know whether to take this as a rebuff until she added, "Paul told me you had got him the Coombe back. That was a nice thought and I'm just as glad as he is about it. Not just the fact that he can pass it on, as he always wanted to every yard of the Valley, but because you remembered that. Has he told you about Vanessa?"

"Yes," he said, "but it's about us I came, Margy. I owed him the Coombe anyway but if you and I could pick up the threads again it could be important to him and Vanessa."

"Is that why you'd like to try?"

"No," he said, "I only said that as some kind of inducement to you, I imagine."

"Well?"

She wasn't giving him much help but he had not come here expecting any. He said, "I've been around, and I'm not saying I haven't had the odd tumble or two but none of them meant a damned thing. I couldn't get you out of my system any more than I could Stevie. In the old days there was you and Stevie and Monica and business, and business was a lot of fun at that time but isn't any more, just a habit. The women I took to bed over there, and even those I played around with, before we broke up, were less than a habit, just a means of filling time when all the offices were closed and 'phones rang unanswered. Do you believe that?"

"Yes," she said, "I believe it. As a matter of fact I've always believed it."

"Does that mean you don't give a damn any more?"

"It doesn't mean anything of the sort," she said, "but who was I to bellyache? I moved over to Stevie didn't I? And you didn't seem to hold that against me."

"I never did," he said, "but I always had the impression there was something left over for me, particularly after I got used to being back, and showed you that I liked having Vanessa around. Was I wrong about that? Did old Stevie make a grand slam?"

She said slowly—"There's never been anyone else—just the two of you, and, as I told Claire, sometimes you didn't seem two people, even after Stevie changed and you stayed the same. I could have made a go of it after the war if you hadn't been so obsessed with what you were doing and creeps like Shawcrosse. I kept waiting for a chance to make that clear to you, Andy. I daresay I could now if I made up my mind to it."

Suddenly she straightened up and the drag left her voice so that he saw her for a second or so as the girl of long ago. She said, "Let's face it, Andy. There was never much between you and me but strong physical attraction but it was enough then and could be again. God knows, in the last few years I've thought about you often enough, wondered how you were doing, what you were up to, and what kind of women you went around with."

He said, without looking at her, "You don't make anything more than casual contacts with people after the age of thirty or so. You lose the knack of making yourself matter, or finding something in them worth cultivating. It's been that way with me a long time now. I'm damned lonely and I'm going to get lonelier. I never found anyone or anything that came near replacing the old set-up. I suppose I took it for granted that you had by now."

He paused, hoping she might volunteer information on the use she had made of her isolation, but when she said nothing but only looked gumly at the floor, he crossed to her and put his sound arm on her shoulder. "I'd like a chance to try again. I'd make it up to you somehow, but God knows, I don't want to put pressure on you."

"Pressure?" Her head came up. "There now. There's a silly thing to say ..."

As always under the stress of emotion, the Welsh lilt returned to her voice so that she seemed to him as young and irrepressible as the day they had met. Her eyes still brooded but he noticed a familiar twitch at the corners of her mouth and it encouraged him to go on. "I'll tell you something else, Margy. I'd get a hell of a kick putting physical pressure on you right now."

"Ah, would you?" She was half-smiling now and it crossed his mind that she was probably egging him on in the hope of getting some of her own back. The doubt was sufficient to make him lift his hand from her shoulder but surprisingly, she reached out and seized it, pulling him round so that they stood with no more than an inch or so between them. The gesture, and the slight trembling that communicated itself to him through her fingers, elated him out of all proportion to its promise. For a moment they stood there, facing one another, and then, with a shrug that implied an eager readiness to jettison the past, she said. "Talk ... all this old talk. What's got into us all nowadays that we have to explain everything, take everything to pieces? You're back, aren't you? You're sick of trapesing then, and I'm sick of making do, and living my life through Vanessa. I'm not that old yet, Andy bach," and she threw her arms round him and kissed him on the mouth in the way he had forgotten but now remembered.

More than anything she could have said or done the kiss renewed him, stripping away his drabness and taking him back so far and so swiftly that he remembered the first occasion she had failed to elude his awkward grab when he lay trussed in her dingy little hospital twenty years ago. He said, thankfully, "By God, Margy, I needed that. I really needed something like that by way of a welcome," and she replied gaily, "Me too. It'll do for a starter," and she opened her bag and foraged for her lipstick. He looked past her at his father's decanter. For the first time in months he could contemplate liquor without craving it.

CHAPTER SIX

ABSORBING THE ENEMY

IN some ways these were the most rewarding years of his life and certainly the most tranquil.

Age, and enormous experience, enabled him to deal with people and problems more objectively than had been possible in his young and middle life, and although eighty on June 1st, 1959, he continued to enjoy splendid health. There was something else that mellowed him a great deal. He found that he could take the storms and triumphs and frustrations and controversies of the years and winnow them through a wry and retentive memory, setting the grain of commonsense and kindness on one side and discarding the chaff of prejudice and partisanship. It was his ability to do this that buttressed him against a prevailing mood of national pessimism and self-doubt, caused (so pundits assured him) by the effort and sacrifices of two world wars, and the loss of an empire.

Just as he had always seen the fruitfulness of the Valley reflected in the flesh of his wife, so he now saw the overall shift of pattern in national life adapt to the new pressures but without losing the more important of its basic values. Of course, he was very biased in this direction, and those who remained of his generation challenged the thesis, but he had the advantage of day to day contact with a horde of grandchildren and god-children, and they nurtured his essential tolerance, so that he refused to join in the headshaking of the over-sixties when pop art cut a swathe into culture, when the sputnik bleeped its way around outer space, and the cult of permissiveness rained volleys of custard pies at the Establishment across the television studios. He told himself that he had seen it all before, or something very like it, and reminded himself that, for all his anxieties, the Valley was still more or less intact and the British still the secret envy of other nations. His argument was simple. One did not, he would say, go out of one's way to mock an old lady who had been by-passed by the mainstream of life; one left her alone, or sniggered behind her back, but today, when almost everyone was busy abusing Britain, it was clear that they did so because they envied her her superb mastery of the art of compromise.

This proved, of course, that he was still an unrepentant chauvinist and he made no apology for being one but managed to hold his own against his exasperated descendants because his arguments were genially expressed and his memory diabolically accurate.

"I can recall all that European cackling at the time of the Boer War," he would tell them, "but in the end what happened? We had the Boers fighting for us against the Germans."

He was something of a prophet, too. Outraging Vanessa, and Simon's son, Mark, by defending Eden's Suez policy, he told them, "We shall soon have a peck of trouble with that fellow Nasser," and he was right. Later on, when the Profumo scandal blew up in the faces of the Tories, he warned his Tory friends that the Puritan streak in the British would do them more harm than any number of Opposition broadsides, and he was right again. They continued to chuckle over him, declaring that his mind had atrophied about the time Rupert Brooke wrote "The Soldier", but they always enjoyed his company nevertheless.

They had called him Young Squire once and then Squire, but now it was Old Squire, and this he accepted as an ironical compliment in days of coastal traffic jams, sonic booms, the Beatles, four-letter words, and hi-fi recordings of compositions that had been scored, he would remind them, in days when the creative impulse could get along without the help of gadgets.

He had one or two violent prejudices that never were exorcised. One was official tolerance of things like the strip club and the fruit-machine; another was the "with-it" parson, trying so fatuously to get into step with the times and making himself and the cloth ridiculous. A third was the tendency on the part of all Governments to subsidise vast armies of civil servants and rule the country from Whitehall without taking into account provincial prejudices. A fourth was the regular appearance of jockeys, cricketers, pop-singers and reformed rabble-rousers in the honours lists. But these were not more than eccentricities and a man could be forgiven a few eccentricities when he had passed his eightieth birthday.

Perhaps the occasions when he could best hold his own among the youngsters were those when he rode out on Saturdays between November and April with the Sorrel Vale Hunt, for he was still to be seen a field or two behind the thrusters and a coppice ahead of the laggards. He was the only one of the original Shallowfordians who still hunted and was now riding his fourth grey, not counting the skewbald he had hunted between the wars. He would pound along with Rumble's son Jerry and sometimes Vanessa or Simon's son Mark, showing them the best short-cuts, or gaps offering a dignified alternative to a "hairy fence". He knew, it seemed, every puddle and every bunch of dock leaves between the Dunes, the Woods, the Bluff and the Whin, and visitors uncertain of the direction to take during a fast point, would shout, breathlessly, "Keep an eye on Old Squire. He'll get us there." And he always did, with or without mud on their backs.

He had other absorbing interests now and the chief of these developed from his lifelong appreciation of good china, old silver and moderately-priced oils. Under his hand the interior of the Big House took on a subdued splendour, for Claire had never bothered what she sat on, what she ate from, or what she hung on walls. Good quality pictures began to appear in the bedrooms and on the landings, a few of them sure to appreciate in value he told them, and in his hunt for a good piece of eighteenth-century walnut, or a George II soup ladle, he built a solid bridge between himself and his prodigal Andy who, to everyone's astonishment, acquired large, rambling premises in the Cathedral Close, Paxtonbury, and opened an antique shop to which he brought his aggressive initiative so that it soon became one of the regular calling places of tourists and, more particularly, The Trade.

Both he and Andy enjoyed their flirtation with The Trade. Andy was amused by the hamfisted tactics they used, prowling about in hard-faced couples and denigrating everything they wanted to buy. Paul liked their easy patter ... ". . . pity it's got a chip," ". . . pity there aren't two," and the inevitable ". . . not all that 'right' Gov'nor, been married up with something." Often, in the late 'fifties and early 'sixties, he and Andy could have been seen at country-house sales, where they evolved a technique in opposition to the bidding of what Andy called "The Get-together Boys". Margaret, seeing Paul draw closer to Andy, extracted a good deal of satisfaction from the reconciliation for her own relationship with Andy had mellowed. Andy not only showed excessive devotion to Vanessa (now serving as a journalist on a small-town newspaper and secretly writing a novel about Byron), but seemed also to have found his way back to the boisterous days of their marriage so that she could always tell whether or not he had had a good day at the auctions by his approach as a lover.

One night, after they had been energetically pursuing their lost youth, he surprised her very much by telling her that the harmony she had achieved with his mother was understandable because they were temperamentally as alike as he and Stevie had been. When she asked him to elaborate he said, with a grin, "The only thing that ever mattered to either of you was to be needed and regularly man-handled. Claire never really gave a damn for any one of us, except that kid-sister of mine who was killed in that air-crash, and after her Vanessa. My guess is that all she was really interested in was the Gov, and the way he looked at her, especially when she took her clothes off. My God, 'dutiful' wasn't the word for her. You could sense the difference in her every time he came stomping in from the fields or from hunting. She positively fluttered."

"I don't flutter," Margaret said, indignantly, although secretly conceding there might be something in what he said, but he replied, "Not yet, but you're coming on nicely, Margy. I see now why I went looking for a wife in Wild Wales." It was that kind of relationship these days—warm, lighthearted, relaxed. Approaching the age of fifty it was all she asked for.

Another compensation Paul found in his old age was music. One Christmas they bought him a radiogram and a stack of records, and he would play them over and over late at night as he sat before the library fire with a favourite book on his knee. He never read a new book now, preferring something he didn't have to take on trust, but he bought a

new record every time he went to Paxtonbury or Whinmouth. His taste was very catholic. If you went along the
library passage at night you were likely to hear Mozart,
Haydn, Dvorjak, Strauss, or even Mario Lanza bellowing
songs from *The Student Prince,* but whatever it was it had
some kind of eighteenth to nineteenth century flavour, for
this was one of his favourite ways of retracing his footsteps.
The other was his irregular rounds, sometimes ridden in vile
weather, so that Mary and Evie and Margaret would scold
him for taking chances but not seriously, for they knew he
had the toughest hide in the county.

He took Andy's advice about replanting the Coombe. By
the end of the decade the landslide scar had healed and could
only be seen as a faint discolouration, west of the Dell, where
a small forest of spruce, larch and Norwegian fir half covered the slopes. Here and there he had planted a few oaks
and beeches, telling young Jerry, Rumble's son, that when he
was his age the trees would amount to something.

Jerry, to Paul's delight, applied for the lease of Low
Coombe and under Rumble's direction rebuilt the old cob
farmhouse and ploughed up the meadows where Shawcrosse's
caravans had once stood. It gave Paul tremendous satisfaction to reflect that Old Tamer's grandson was back in the
Coombe and making it yield more than any Potter had ever
succeeded in doing in the past. Sometimes, when he rode out
there, he could recognise the old rascal's rolling gait in the
young man's walk and see yet another ancestral trait in the
sharp, half-truculent look that greeted him when he clattered
up the loose stones of the approach.

Over at Home Farm Rumble Patrick and Mary prospered
although, to Paul's mind, Rumble was still too experimental
to develop into the kind of farmer old Honeyman had proved
to be in pre-First World War days. They had three other
children besides Jerry but Mary told him that Jerry was likely
to prove the only dedicated sodbreaker in the brood.

Over at High Coombe Dick Potter, unpredictably, had
modelled himself on his stolid father Sam, instead of his
Uncle Smut, and seemed happy enough, ultimately marrying
a long-legged agricultural student, ten years his junior, who
presented him with an addition to the family every eighteen
months. Hearing the clamour every time he passed this way,
Paul remembered the bawdy dictum of Doctor Maureen who
always declared that a young woman had only to set foot in

the Valley to become pregnant. He did not know whether the size of Dick's family proved her theory. The Potters, generation by generation, had always been prolific.

Lower down, at Deepdene, the old Willoughby Farm, Nelson and Prudence Honeyman stayed on, Nelson forsaking sheep and building up a first-class Guernsey herd, Prudence opening a riding stable with horses bought at the sale of Claire's sister Rose, in Gloucestershire. Paul approved of this heartily, for he enjoyed watching her cavalcade of youngsters tit-tupping through the woods and daring one another to jump fallen logs on bored ponies. It took him back to the days of long ago when Rose had run a riding school at High Coombe, and nowadays he hoarded his satisfied memories like doubloons.

Over at Hermitage Henry Pitts, like himself, was long past active participation in any kind of husbandry but he had an efficient manager and a couple of brawny women who had learned their trade in the Land Army during the war. Henry pottered about but he was becoming increasingly fat and the only thing about him that called to mind the Henry of Passchendaele was the slow, rubbery smile that was never effaced, not even by his jeering contempt of "they ole contrapshuns", by which he meant every piece of machinery, industrial or domestic, that had appeared on the market since 1913.

Early in 1961 Henry fell sick and took to his bed and when he seemed likely to die Ellie, his second wife, sent one of her women across to the Big House with an urgent message. Paul was at his bedside within the hour and commiserated with him concerning the absence of his son David, who was now farming in Alberta and had not been summoned. Henry, his great blubbery face still holding the wide, gap-toothed grin that was as familiar to Shallowfordians as the Bluff or the Sorrel, rejected his sympathy. "Giddon, Maister," he said, huskily, "tidden no odds. Davey's got his own matters to 'tend tu and us never did relish the notion of zeein' 'em all standing round the baid, trying not to think of 'ow much was coming their way zoon as the poor ole toad snuffed it."

Paul had heard Henry refer to hundreds of Shallowfordians as "poor ole toads" but had never thought to hear him apply the phrase to himself and it made him sad to reflect that his oldest friend in the Valley must, indeed, be on his way out. Henry, for his part, was willing to concede this but without sacrificing his grin. "Truth is, Maister," he wheezed, "us 'ave diddled 'em pretty smartlike, you an' me, when you think on that bliddy old mudbath in Flanders, and all they bliddy aeroplanes that come near blowin' us to tatters twenty-year after that. I made eighty-zix didden I? And I baint gone yet."

He was gone, however, before the spring, and Paul, attending the popular funeral in the Overspill, reflected that he was now virtually the only survivor of the old brigade, for Smut Potter had died the previous year, after having opened a betting-shop in Paxtonbury with the proceeds of an insurance policy, and his brother Sam had died about the same time. The transition from old to new faces, however, had now become so gradual that Paul was beginning to think of comparative youngsters like Rumble Patrick and Nelson Honeyman as veterans.

Eveleigh—still "Young Eveleigh" to Paul—made a great success of Four Winds, once the unluckiest farm on the estate, winning prizes at County Shows as far away as Bath and Hereford. Connie, his mother, lived on in one of the cottages and the only worry in this corner was Eveleigh's bachelor status that must have bothered his mother for she confided to Paul that she was "on the lookout for a nice wife for the boy", saying it as though she was thinking of taking the 'bus to Paxtonbury to buy him a pair of gumboots. He said, musing "I wouldn't bother if I was you, Connie. Funny thing about the mating instinct in the Valley. It's usually the girls who make the running and corral the men like bullocks. You only have to think back a bit to see my point. Old Arabella Codsall cornered Martin in this very kitchen. And you were always the brains behind your boy Harold, just as Joannie Potter ran Sam, and that Frenchwoman took over Smut when he was cut off behind Fritz's lines and hid out in her bakery. I could give you plenty of other examples. There was my Whiz and that Ian of hers—she picked him cold-bloodedly from the entire male field of the Sorrel Vale Hunt, and there was my Claire, who didn't give me up even when I married Grace Lovell. She was the best example of all, because the summer I came here, long before you were born, she took me on what I thought was an innocent ramble down by the Mere and came damned close to seducing me. And me only weeks out of hospital."

Connie was very intrigued by this story and asked for more details but he called her a nosey old woman and wouldn't elaborate, except to say, "Leave it to natural selection. Some smart young filly already has her eye on your boy, I wouldn't wonder."

He was right yet again. That summer, whilst showing a prize bull in the Vale of Evesham, Farmer Eveleigh was carefully singled out by the daughter of one of the judges, a very pretty brunette in her late 'twenties who had, so they said, been a model and had actually played small parts in films.

Connie, caught on the hop, was not at all sure that the girl would prove the right kind of wife for a dedicated farmer living in the remote provinces but Paul, after looking her over, said, "Damn it, Connie, you're even more old-fashioned than I am. What kind of woman do you want? A slabsided, rosy-faced milkmaid, with a tie-on bonnet and hands the colour and size of hams? Farmers' wives don't come that way any more. They go into Paxtonbury once a week for a hair-do, and if you saw them driving their Hillmans and Wolseleys to a Point-to-Point you'd think they were young duchesses. That girl might set local tongues wagging but she'll also lead women's fashions and I wouldn't be surprised if she isn't well dowered into the bargain."

They had an old-fashioned local wedding, disposing of seven dozen bottles of champagne, for Eveleigh's bride, with a townee's starry-eyed approach to the country, pretended to fall in love with Coombe Bay's fourteenth-century church, and decided to marry there instead of on her home ground. Actually her choice was dictated by the fact that in her own locality lived hundreds of ultra-smart and highly sophisticated women, whereas down here she was certain to create a sensation. Bob Eveleigh, knowing little of women, thought her preference a good omen and told Paul, in a rare burst of confidence, "Judith seems to think a local wedding will help to play her in because she doesn't know a soul around here." Paul, not so easily hoodwinked, still thought of Judith as showing good sense.

He did not go as far as Coombe Bay very often nowadays, except to attend an occasional function at Simon's school where the boy ("the boy" was approaching sixty) seemed to have established a close personal contact with all the new families who had drifted there after the flood damage was repaired and the western half of the town rebuilt. Then, to his own surprise, Simon got a headship at a new school in Whinmouth and comparative freedom of action enabled him to develop theories about the processes of educating under-sixteens. You would often see him, with some of his boys, at the local police court and even an inquest, or out on the cliffs examining the geological strata at the landslip, and every Easter he took a party to Paris and sometimes headed a summer jaunt to Normandy or Flanders. He "got up", as he said, an astonishing variety of object lessons, including visits to Stratford-on-Avon, tours of the Civil War battlefields, and even a trip to the Eddystone lighthouse. He spent his own money freely and lived on overdrafts. It seemed to Paul, however, that he not only enjoyed himself but aged very gracefully.

John, the most eccentric of the family, made a modest reputation for himself in television, specialising in the kind of programme Paul liked to watch, "*The Source and Course of the Thames*", "*A Cobbett on Wheels*", "*The Rape of Staffordshire*" and kindred subjects, all presented with a whimsicality that softened a sharp social comment on John Bull's transition from farmer-industrialist to bankrupt ex-Imperialist. John, having more humour and rather more tolerance than any of the Craddocks, was able to strike an exact balance between missionary and clown and his pro-gramme received good ratings, but when Paul tried to pin him down on objectives he was evasive and said, "For God's sake don't label me, Gov'nor! The one thing I can't wear is a label. Just say I make a living the most entertaining way I know."

When he was twenty-four he married, without saying a word to any of them, and during the first leg of a touring honeymoon he turned up with his bride, a quiet, softly-spoken girl, with a slim figure, jet-black hair and an air of decorum that placed her, in Paul's mind somewhere between Jane Eyre and Mrs. Copperfield. When he got over his astonishment he was delighted. She was exactly, he told himself, the kind of wife suited to a free-ranging, self-contained person like John, but he was astounded when John told him that she had been married before to an actor whom she had just divorced on grounds of cruelty.

"That's why I kept it dark," he said, "for this chap is well-known as a sick comic and a notorious lush."

"What's a lush?" Paul asked and John explained that it was an alcoholic and that Anne, his wife, had taken a beating during the two years she had tried to cope with him.

"Where the devil did you run across her?" Paul asked, curiously, "She doesn't strike me as an actressy type."

"She isn't," John said, "do you think I'm nuts enough to marry an actress? Good God, I'd sooner marry a woman-journalist. At least she could be professionally useful. As a matter of fact, I met her in an all-night chemist's shop near Shepherd's Bush. I went in for a hangover cure and we got to talking about the effect of booze on the soul. She had some interesting things to say on the subject, one thing led to another and we short of chummed up. You know how it is."

"I don't," said Paul, indignantly. "People didn't pick their partners like that in my day. Was *she* there for a hangover cure?"

"Good Lord no," said John, laughing, "she was working there, as a dispenser. It was that that did it, really. She looked rather sweet in her little white overall and I've always had a bit of a yen for chemists' assistants. They all look so competent and almost all of them are shy-violet pretty, in Anne's kind of way."

Paul gave up. It sounded so casual, rather like he or Claire might have chosen somebody to partner them in a waltz or a turkey-trot, and he contented himself with saying, "Well, she is pretty and I must say it is a relief to hear a girl with a subdued voice." And then, to his relief, he discovered that her father had been a veterinary-surgeon and that she knew about horses, so he showed her the Valley from the saddle on a golden September afternoon, reflecting, as he rode along, that he had been singularly fortunate with his in-laws. There was Rumble Patrick and Evie and Margaret, and now this shy little thing, and between them they more than offset Whiz's patrician-type husband, Ian, and that daughter of the Archdeacon, Monica, who had turned her back on Stevie during the war and indirectly caused all that upset between the boys.

He had no favourites among his grandchildren and god-children in the way that Claire had favoured Vanessa. He would sometimes, however, contemplate the impressive list of their names and birthdates in the old estate diary that was still clamped between the hinged covers of the Bible that old

George Lovell, his predecessor, had used to camouflage his gallery of local nudes. There were so many of them now— for seven godchildren dated from his first decade in the Valley, and after them came Simon's three, Stevie's one, Mary's four, and Whiz's five. It was difficult to believe that there had been a time when he had felt cheated of descendants.

Maureen Rudd, still known in the Valley as "The Lady Doctor", lived on until the summer of '62, when she was eighty-eight. She died, to Paul's great regret, in Edinburgh, at the home of her son who had been named for him back in 1912, and Paul much appreciated Paul Rudd's gesture in sending her back to be buried in Overspill, among so many of her old patients.

It was, as it happened, the last funeral he attended in the Valley and because it was a warm, sunny day he lingered after the other mourners had dispersed and took a look at the higgledy-piggledy array of mounds and headstones both here and in the older part of the churchyard.

He found he was able to do this without sadness for none of them seemed dead to him, not nearly so dead, for instance, as the Valley men who went west in Flanders between 1914 and 1918 and even these he indentified with trees in French Wood.

He pottered about here a long time, looking at Old Tamer's memorial, at "Preacher" Willoughby's grave, at the Eveleigh plot where lay Norman, of Four Winds, Marian his wife, and their children, Harold and Rachel. He stopped for a moment at the fresh mounds representing Henry Pitts, Smut Potter, Sam Potter and several others, including the older graves of Parson Horsey and his predecessor, Parson Bull, whose headstone was garnished by a particularly insipid angel, the sight of whom, had he met her in the hunting field, would have caused old Bull to bellow one of the oaths he reserved for those who got between him and the fox. Paul contemplated the angel a long time, smiling to himself and thinking how Maureen Rudd and her husband John, or Henry, or Smut, would have appreciated the incongruity of the memorial had he been able to share the joke with any one of them.

Then, whistling under his breath he went through the lych-gate and got into his car. One last memory pursued him as he backed into the lane abutting the High Street. It was here, at this lych-gate, that his first wife, Grace Lovell, had tried to persuade him to withdraw his proposal a few months short of sixty years ago.

CHAPTER SEVEN

SNOW AND GARRISON ALLIANCES

I

THEY were nearly all home for Christmas 1962, so that Paul, chuckling in private, suspected that Mary or Simon had asked each of them to make a special effort because this might be his last. He did not think it would be, and neither was it, but those final days of December and the months that followed were to provide him with a uniquely awesome aspect of the Valley. It was the hardest winter he could recall, the hardest, they said, since records had been kept. Snow held off until the late afternoon of Boxing Day but the ground was already under a hard frost and hunting had to be called off. By the next day, when everyone was getting ready to leave, the snow lay in eight-foot drifts under the banks. Twenty-four hours later the Valley was a sealed white stocking laid between sea and the shoulder of the woods.

This, in itself, was not unique. Several times in living memory the Sorrel had frozen hard enough for skating and often, in the last six decades, wagons had been unable to tackle the steep, winding road that skirted the moor between the main highway and the river. But now the coastal link between Whinmouth and Coombe Bay was also cut and the new tarmac road lay buried beneath four feet of snow, with banks of up to fifteen feet in the hollows under Whinmouth Hill.

It was, Paul thought, a magnificent sight as he took a constitutional down the drive and along the iron-bound margins of the river. Nothing had passed or could pass this way since the last eight-hour fall and a great blanket of virgin snow stretched as far as the eye could see, with the sun hanging like a tangerine over the long sweep of the woods.

Only French Wood, resting on a steeply angled spur, reared itself out of the enveloping sheet like a young colt in the act of standing upright, and Paul eyed it with satisfaction for it now showed as a real wood and not a coppice and the trees here, none of them much more than forty years old, had done remarkably well considering their exposed position.

It was difficult to get used to the silence. Always, even in high summer, the Sorrel hummed a lively tune about here and when Four Winds pastures were shrouded in mist and soggy with mud you could still hear the suck of cows' hooves in the socketed soil. The wind was usually gossiping in Home Farm elms but today the wail of a single gull carried right across the Valley, a plaintive acknowledgment of the world's inability to go about its business.

He thought, "My God, but I'd like to make the rounds today and see it all again," but he realised that this was impossible, for the grey's hooves would ball up and bring him down before he had ridden as far as the lodge and he was too old to attempt the circuit on foot. He compromised, however, by retracing his steps through Home Farm strawyard (where Mary's two youngest were tobogganing down the incline of the aeroplane field), cutting across the paddock to the orchard, and thence to the back lane that ran the length of the woods.

Up here it was sheer magic. Drifts had filled the cutting and frozen hard so that it was possible to walk across almost level ground to the first of the big beeches and the oldest of the oaks. The birds were already tamed by hunger and several of them had succumbed to starvation. Robins, bright-eyed and ridiculously puffed, followed him hopefully, skipping from twig to twig and setting the long icicles flashing ruby red in the heatless rays of the morning sun. He went down again for some scraps and Margaret and Andy, who were staying on for a few days, returned with him to the stile carrying a basket of pasties. Sparrows, finches, rooks and one crow coasted in for their share and before they left they strung strips of fat on the apple boughs for the tits, Paul counting four varieties.

Margaret, watching him, cautioned him against catching cold and he told her not to be an old woman and that he had never minded snow in the Valley so long as passing traffic didn't convert it into yellow slush.

"Mother couldn't stand it," said Andy, suddenly, and Paul

408

agreed that this was so, and that Claire had been an April-October person, although he did not see why, seeing that she had always had more flesh about her than any of them, even in her early twenties. Then they all three went in and drank a hot toddy and Rumble ploughed his way across the paddocks to borrow suet, bringing with him a warning that there would be a great deal of lending and borrowing before this lot was over, because isolated farms like Hermitage and Four Winds would be unable to replenish stores in the way still available to farms within easy walking distance of Coombe Bay.

Rumble was both right and wrong. Requests for help soon came from Ellie Pitts, who lived on at Hermitage, and from the new Mrs. Eveleigh, having her first experience of rural isolation in Four Winds. Both, it seemed, had exhausted their larder stocks over Christmas and not anticipating anything like this had delayed making a dash for Paxtonbury. Rumble, trying to deliver a few essentials, got as far as Codsall Bridge in his tractor but there the trailer had to be unloaded and its contents carried by hand up both farm lanes.

By the evening of the next day even a tractor trip was out of the question for snow had fallen steadily for another twelve hours and communication between the farms ceased except by telephone and the occasional message delivered on foot.

It was as though, before he was quite through, the Valley gods, older and more capricious than Jehovah, were eager to show him everything in the celestial repertoire. He would have thought that they could not surprise him but they did and he enjoyed being surprised, for it gave him yet another opportunity of exercising his suzerainty over the community, just as he had on so many previous occasions at times of drought, flood, cattle plague, slump and war.

His estate office became once again a battle headquarters, with its stream of telephone calls and red-faced runners who came in and out blowing on their fingers and stamping their boots. He got a load of cow-nuts for Jerry hauled up the Coombe by sledge, groceries for Prudence Honeyman and Dick Potter by the same means, and then mounted an emergency rescue on behalf of Home Farm lambs. He got a vet to High Coombe by dictating over the telephone a means of access from the nearest point of the main road and over the north-eastern corner of Shallowford Woods, pinpointing a list of landmarks that nobody but himself would have remembered, much less been able to describe in recognisable terms. He did all kinds of things within the immediate vicinity of the Big House, including making a snowman for Mary's youngest and co-operating with Andy and Margaret, marooned along with him, in a nonstop mercy mission among the hundreds of wild birds picqueting the orchard and stableyard.

"My reward for these terrible exertions," he told Andy, "will be to have every damned raspberry and gooseberry stolen by them in the summer. Repairing those fruit cages is one of the jobs Claire and me and old Horace Hancock have been putting off since 1914. Now I'm the only one alive to do it and I shall have to buy what fruit I need from tenants." He revelled in every moment of the exercise for not only did he enjoy his usefulness but also the sense of the Valley drawing together as an interlocked community that had been such a feature of his early days here. The peak of that terrible winter, however, was not scaled until mid-February, when he conceived and organised the airlift.

II

Nobody, not even the gloomiest among them, had expected it to endure so long without the least sign of a break in the weather. Soon communication between the farms, even on foot, became very difficult and it was essential to keep in touch with headquarters and one another by daily exchanges of information over the telephone. No milk had gone out of the Valley since the New Year and the surplus was being fed to the pigs, the only living creatures in the Valley to benefit from the freeze-up. Thousands of eggs lay in their square cartons awaiting collection and soon proteins began to run short, particularly at Four Winds and Deepdene, where Eveleigh and Nelson Honeyman maintained sizeable herds. It was after watching bales of hay being dropped by helicopter to New Forest ponies on his T.V. set that Paul, saying nothing to anyone, made a calculation of the most urgent needs at these two farms and then added a few hundred-weight of poultry food, mostly for Jerry at Low Coombe, who specialised in hens. Then, to Andy's amazement, he blandly suggested telephoning the County Agricultural Office at Paxtonbury and laying on helicopters.

"Good God," Andy said, "they'll never wear that, Gov." But they did, and within forty-eight hours the "choppers", as Andy called them, were sailing in over the desolate slopes and dropping carefully-packaged supplies ordered in Squire Craddock's name from Paxtonbury suppliers who had snow-plough access to the R.A.F. training base further along the coast.

He watched them arrive like a boy gazing up at his first aircraft—"Almost gobbling with glee," as Andy told Margaret that lunchtime, adding, with a grin, "I'm glad we got marooned out here along with him. I wouldn't have missed it for a tax-free year. It's absolutely fascinating to see all the threads leading back to that office of his, just the way it did when I was a kid growing up here."

And then Paul came in, his face glowing and his eyes bright with mischief as he said, sitting down to a plate of Margaret's vegetable stew, "Well now, I never thought to see the day when I could watch those damned things earn their keep. My God, I wish old Henry Pitts had lived to see them arrive with their cattle-cake and pellets. I can imagine his long whistle of surprise and his 'Gordamme, Maister, they vound a praper use for they bliddy ole contrapshuns after all, didden 'em now?' "

The helicopters came in again an hour before sunset, pivoting on the Coombe and hammering their way across the sky. Andy, watching them remembered that he had never flown a helicopter but had always wanted to. He wondered if he could manage one with his artificial hand and then re-called Douglas Bader and his tin legs in the Battle of Britain days. The only regrets he ever had nowadays centred on flying.

The frost held on until the first days of March but when the thaw set in it seemed to happen very quickly. By the end of the month the only reminders of the ten-week siege were pock-marked drifts under north-facing and east-facing hedge-rows. The wind was still keen but Paul, standing on the half-moon sweep outside the porch to see Andy and Margaret make their belated departure, could sniff the spring and said he hoped she wouldn't dawdle south of the sandbars.

That same afternoon he threw his favourite Souter saddle across the fretful grey and rode across the sloping field to the woods, feeling his way cautiously, as though it was his first excursion here. He got as far as the rusting remnant of the

411

German bomber on the downslope to the Mere but had his work cut out to hold his horse on a tight rein because the gelding had been brooding in loose-box and yard ever since Christmas. It wasn't time yet, Paul decided, to have a thorough look around, so he trotted back along the lane to drink a cup of tea with Ellie Pitts at Hermitage, and discuss the last few weeks as two old soldiers might talk of a campaign that had just ended in triumph.

The right moment came about a month later, when the last of the mottled drifts had blown away and green shoots of new grass were revealed beneath them.

This time he made ready for a longer foray, filling his hunting flask with whisky and water and descending the drive between the two rows of candlesticks (for that was how he had always thought of the prim chestnuts in either paddock) turning left instead of his customary right, and making his first call on Jerry at the Dell.

Before he reached there, however, he had to ride along the path of the landslide and pass the naked foundations of Mill Cottage and was pleased that he could regard them without a pang. In bright sunshine, with the hedges full of dandelion, campion and stitchwort, he did not feel isolated from Claire. She was still somewhere close at hand, in the salty tang of the breeze blowing in from the Dunes, or in the green-gold fastness of the beech hedge to his left. The Sorrel was down to its normal width, despite the enormous amount of melted snow it must have carried down to the sea in the last few weeks, and its current was singing again as a variety of river birds flitted among the iris stems of the ox-bows. Low down on one of the very few original elms about here a blackbird sang and high above him, centred on Codsall stubble fields, a lark entered into competition but soon withdrew from the contest.

That day he paid a visit to all the Coombe farms, complimenting Jerry on his progress here and telling him that it was a relief to be able to ride into the Dell without having to fortify oneself against a stream of piteous supplications, such as his grandfather Tamer would utter every time he saw Squire approaching. Jerry introduced him to his new resident couple, man and wife, who shared his quarters in the rebuilt farmhouse and Paul, reckoning the boy's age as he invariably did on these occasions, thought it high time he got himself a wife like Young Eveleigh, over at Four Winds.

At Deepdene the Honeymans made him very welcome and Prudence, as saucy as ever he thought, thanked him with a kiss for his help during the Big Freeze. He stopped long enough to tell her the joke he had made about her father's probable reaction to the arrival of helicopters over the Valley; then he went on up the winding, perfumed track to High Coombe, remembering it was here, in this yard, that he had first glimpsed Claire when she came tripping out to offer him and old John Rudd, the agent, sherry and pikelets on his first tour of the estate. The memory of her, a laughing, blushing beauty of nineteen, was so vivid to him that he hardly heard what Dick Potter and his wife had to say but in any case it would have been difficult to hold a conversation from the saddle while all those Potter children were making such a racket behind the barns.

He came then to his favourite stretch, the drop down through the north-eastern corner of the woods, past the rhododendron forest under Hazel's cave, past the empty cottage of old Sam and Joannie Potter, to the edge of the Mere, still and silent in the sunshine with the trees lining the far bank beginning to show green and the bracken on the islet a cluster of sere, brittle fronds shot through with white undersides of new growth.

It was here, just opposite the islet and its ridiculous Folly, that his memories of both Claire and Grace were most poignant, so that he stopped for a moment shading his eyes against the strong sunlight and luxuriating in the past as a man might relax in a soda-bath after a day's hunting. For all that he was still able to laugh at himself, murmuring, "I'm always remembering now ... almost minute by minute," and then, "Why not? It's about all a man can do at my time of life and in a way it's a compliment to the pair of them, the brazen hussies," and he smiled a slow, vain smile at the memory of tumbling Grace about on that islet one hot summer day, and doing the same for Claire on the very spot where the grey was standing. His eye caught a pair of wrens flirting in the hazel bush a short way up the track and he thought, "And that's about the size of it. Survival, like the time we've just come through, then renewal under the sun. By God, I'd give an arm and a leg to start all over again."

He touched the grey with his heels and rode on over the shoulder of the woods to Hermitage Lane, and thence to Four Winds where Eveleigh's smart, city wife made a great fuss of him, although her cheek-to-cheek kiss lacked the warmth of Prudence Honeyman's lips. He noted, however, with a degree of interest that he had no business to express, that she was pregnant and thought, as he rode back across Codsall Bridge to make a final call on Rumble and Mary, that old Maureen had known a thing or two when she made that time-honoured crack about the fertility of the Sorrel Valley.

III

There were two family weddings that year, each bringing him the promise of great-grandchildren—"a rare privilege" as he told Margaret, on their way to see Whiz's eldest married to an almost exact replica of her father Ian when he had stood beside Whiz in Coombe Bay church back in the 'thirties.

It was, he thought, a rather stuffy wedding, despite the money Ian and Whiz had lavished on it, but then this branch of the family had always been a little bit stuffy and he supposed it made for variety when one remembered the kind of antics The Pair and Simon had practised in days gone by.

The guests in and about the huge marquee were garnished with gold lace that Andy, cynically enjoying himself, called "scrambled eggs", apparently a sardonic R.A.F. term for high-ranking personnel. The act of cutting the wedding cake with the bridegroom's sword fascinated Paul. What, he asked himself, would an R.A.F. officer do with a damned great sword throughout his professional career? He felt obliged to comment on it.

"Damn it," he said to Margaret, who was sitting next to him, "they didn't even use ironmongery of that kind in the cavalry after that first brush with the Uhlans, in August, 1914," but Margaret, giggling, shushed him and told him to behave, and so he did until they got him into the car and set off for home. Then he made Andy swerve by reciting a bawdy wedding toast that had shocked Big House guests as long ago as 1907, when Doctor Maureen was marrying old John Rudd.

He was, they told each other, becoming a bit of a handful on social occasions, having reached an age and seen enough to claim the privilege of saying precisely what he liked, but somehow, the older he grew the more lovable and amusing he became, so that people like Simon and Mary and Andy and Rumble Patrick, who could recall his cross-carrying moods and his harassed "Elizabethan look," were often shocked into laughter by his candour.

"You wouldn't think a man could change in his mid-eighties without becoming senile," Simon told his wife, "but the old Gov has and somehow it suits him. I wish Claire had lived to see it. She always thought he took himself and his precious Valley too seriously. It would have given her no end of a kick to see him sitting in that marquee knocking back his champagne and treating that Air Vice-Marshal as if he was a tenant behind with his rent."

An even happier occasion was the wedding that followed in the first week of June, the week of his eighty-fourth birthday. This was his second entry in the race for the first great-grandchild for Vanessa, who had been working as a freelance journalist in London, suddenly appeared with a minor celebrity in tow, a jolly, broadshouldered young man, who had not only published two historical biographies—"popular history" he called it to isolate it from academic work—but had also represented Britain at the Olympic Games as a long-distance runner.

He was called by the somewhat off-putting name of Hugo Pychley-Cook, but there was nothing stuffy about *him*, Paul decided, as soon as Vanessa left them alone and they got into a lively discussion on Lord Cardigan, the leader of the Charge of the Light Brigade. Paul found Mr. Pychley-Cook very much to his taste, a great, jovial extrovert, who was clearly head-over-heels in love with Vanessa. And who wouldn't be, he thought, when he saw her sail up the aisle on the arm of Andy.

Margaret began to sniff as the service began and Paul, who had never had the slightest patience with women's tears at weddings, turned a frown on her but remembered just in time that she was probably thinking of poor old Stevie and patted her instead, and for a moment their eyes met and he felt he could have used a sniff or two himself.

They had the reception at the Big House, the scene of so many notable occasions and Paul played host in a way that made Mary smile so that she said, in an aside to Rumble Patrick, "He's absolutely terrific on days like this. I remember how warm and gay he was when I was waiting for the

415

car to take me to church, and how relieved he was too when he realised I wasn't in the least jittery."

Rumble, knowing how this comment would please the old man, passed it on when they were waiting for Vanessa to change, and Paul said, with the merest hint of a quaver, "By George, Rumble, I remember as though it was yesterday. She was the prettiest bride I ever saw, including today's. Funny thing though, she had me puzzled, because she was the most retiring of the lot but when she went out of that door she might have been on her way to a hair appointment. Wouldn't even accept a small brandy and didn't need one either." And then, with that candour for which he was now famous. "Been a good marriage—you and Mary. Best of the lot in some ways. But why the hell am I telling *you* that?"

"I'm damned if I know!" said Rumble, chuckling, "it's a bit late in the day to start selling Mary to me. I took an option on her when I was nine."

They all crowded out into the forecourt to speed the young couple on their way and reserved for him the honour of being the last to embrace the bride before she sidled into the car. "Stick it, Gramp," she whispered in his ear, "and put all your money on me for the first male in the fourth line of succession!"

He remembered that and thought about it when he was having his nightcap in the library late that night. Claire had been very shrewd in assessing Vanessa when she was still a toddler, he thought. The girl had all the exuberance of The Pair when they had surged out of this room to seek their fortunes, but something extra that stirred him deeply. It was a leavening of Claire's warmth and sensuality, plus any amount of "Derwent commonsense". He raised his glass to her and to that jovial young giant of hers, and in acknowledging them he acknowledged the promise he saw (and so many failed to see) in their down-to-earth generation.

"I daresay they've as many faults as we and the parents had," he told himself, "but there's at least one they lost on the way down the years and that's humbug. No bloody humbug about that bunch and I must say I find that refreshing."

Tired, but pleasantly so, he finished his whisky and went slowly up the shallow stairs to bed.

CHAPTER EIGHT

TERMS OF CAPITULATION

I

THEY could not interest him in the 1964 general election. His time for partisan politics, he said, was long past and thank God for it, for it ought to be obvious to any man of sense that the rhetoric of "that jaw-factory on the Thames" had spent itself in issues like Women's Suffrage, the General Strike, and the débâcle of Munich. There was no point in taking it seriously in this day and age, when members trotted in and out the division lobbies like strings of circus ponies. If "those Labour chaps" thought they could make a better go of things they were welcome to try and at least the tiny majority would keep the professionals on their toes. The only politician he had ever respected was Jimmy Grenfell, Liberal M.P. for the Valley for so many years, but in the end even Jimmy had retired from Westminster disillusioned, telling him that, notwithstanding the fuss and blather up there, the country really ran itself and always had, ever since provincial communities had wrung charters from bankrupt Plantagenets.

What interested him much more, they noticed, was Churchill's final illness and this surprised them, for they had taken for granted until then that he had never subscribed to the Churchill cult, not even in the war, but had continued to regard him as a firebrand of Lloyd George's stamp, with the trick of focusing public attention upon himself at times of crisis and then retreating into a corner to growl at nonentities who trod on his corns.

They were, it seemed, quite wrong about this, for in the last few years he had succeeded in identifying Churchill as the embodiment of a number of essentially British character-

417

istics, so that he lifted him high above the clamour and set him up as a tribal symbol, like the Union Jack, pre-First World War dreadnoughts, roast beef, Gilbert and Sullivan, and village cricket.

They were not quite sure how this had been achieved for, in his time, Paul had been a vehement champion of the Left, Right and Centre, depending upon his private reading of the national pulse. Simon could recall him sympathising with Churchill over being made a scapegoat for the Gallipoli failure, then rejecting him during the 'twenties and early 'thirties, and later still applauding him for his pre-war truculence and his wresting of the Premiership from "that umbrella chump" Chamberlain, but his enthusiasm did not survive the famous "Gestapo" speech of the immediate post-war period. Simon supposed that, as time went on, Paul came to revere Winston as one of his few surviving contemporaries, for they had been born within five years of one another and this fact alone must have elevated him in the eyes of a man extremely reluctant to discard anything from the past that might prove useful in shoring up present and future.

However it was he listened eagerly to all the bulletins when Churchill lay dying and was moved by the spectacle of long queues waiting in the cold to pass through Westminster Hall at the Lying-in-State.

When the day of the funeral was announced he said to Simon, "God knows, I haven't often felt the urge to go to London, haven't been near the damn place in years, but I'd give a good deal to see that funeral. It's the end of an era, *my* era, but there it is ... I suppose I must watch it on T.V."

"You'll see more of it there than standing in the cold," Evie told him but he said, a little querulously, "It's not the same. It's never the same. That's the trouble nowadays, everything has to be 'instant'. Instant soup, instant sex, instant politics. Watered down, the whole dam' lot of 'em. Well, you can't produce instant emotion in a man of my age. Actually being there and seeing that piece of pageantry would be an experience worth having, I can tell you."

It was the day after that that Simon received a surprise call from the managing editor of a group of Westcountry newspapers to which he had contributed ever since his return to Civvy Street. The group had been allocated a seat in St. Paul's, one of a hundred issued to the world's Press, and the

418

journalist selected to represent the West had been involved in a car accident so that Simon, as a proven feature writer, was offered his place.

"I'm not looking for straight reporting," the editor told Simon over the 'phone. "Everything that can be said about Churchill has been said in the last fortnight. What I want is a feature written by someone with a sense of history. I can fix it in a couple of hours if you'll cover it for us. You can collect all the bumff from our Fleet Street rep. and he'll arrange a car. We shall have people covering the route of course. All we want of you is two to three columns on the atmosphere at St. Paul's."

Simon, secretly flattered, accepted and it was only when he was in the act of telling Paul the news over the 'phone that he remembered his father's comment the night before. "Look here, Gov," he said impulsively, "how would you like to come up with me? I wouldn't suggest it but I can run you to the City, pick you up again as soon as the service is over, and I'll have a car to drive you back to the hotel. At least you'll get a grandstand view, I'll make sure of that."

Paul said, with an enthusiasm he took no pains to conceal, "You're a trump, Simon. If I won't be in the way I'd be delighted to come with you. We'll stay at that hotel Zorndorff lived in for nearly fifty years. There's a man there who had reason to be very grateful to Franz and I've kept in touch whenever I've had to stay in town. I'll book for two nights and you pick me up when you're ready."

He went upstairs and rummaged in the drawer of his tallboy, looking for something he handled once a year, his clamp of medals, that his sons referred to as "gongs". Having found them he contemplated them thoughtfully in the waning light.

There were seven of them, two South African decorations, his M.C. and Croix de Guerre, gained during the St. Quentin and the Chemin des Dames fighting in 1918, his general service and victory medals and the Second World War medal awarded for Home Guard service. For the first time in all these years he took pride in them but whether to wear them or not, that was something he would have to think about. Carefully and slowly, the way he did everything nowadays, he packed a night case and filled his hunting flask with brandy and water.

Simon's hired car dropped him off at the bottom of Fleet Street and Simon pointed out the offices where he would collect him after the service.

"Go in and wait if you feel cold, Gov'nor," he said. "I daresay you can get a first-class view from the window and I've told the London rep. to expect you. It's still only eight-forty-five and you've got at least three hours to kill. I'd feel happier if you stayed with the car but it has to go in the official park and if you go with it you won't see a thing. Now you're okay? You're sure?"

Of course he was okay. It was cold, bitterly cold, but mercifully dry and he was well bundled up, with top coat, scarf, fur gloves, woollen underclothes, and two pairs of socks. In addition he had his flask and his medals, and a glow of anticipation that spread from his ribs to the extremities of his body. He had no intention of watching the procession from the window, or its progress down from Westminster on a television screen, for it was not the procession he had come to see. It was the people, and by that he did not mean the notabilities. As soon as Simon's car had sped on down the hill between the two phalanxes of spectators he set out in pursuit, aiming to get as close to St. Paul's as possible. But first, to fortify himself, he had a quick swallow from his flask in the shelter of a doorway.

The crowd was very orderly but the first thing that struck him was that it was not a gathering of mourners. Neither was it the kind of assembly he remembered on other State occasions he had witnessed, the second Jubilee, when he was a lad of eighteen, the coronation of King George V in 1911, and the Victory Parade of June, 1919. Those had been national celebrations, of the kind in which the British, for all their alleged restraint, had delighted. The mood here was something he had never sensed among English people, a compound that defied accurate analysis, for it had about it elements of solemnity, good-temper, gaiety, inevitability, awe, and an overall sense of achievement, as though they were here to witness something half-way between the completion of an enormous national shrine and the pageantry that would attend the burial of a mediaeval king.

It was, he decided, a very elusive mood indeed and the only constituent entirely absent on the streets was grief, even the pseudo-solemnity that passes for grief at the funeral of a paladin or a city father.

He edged down behind the four-deep pavement crowds until he could get a glimpse of the forecourt and steps of St. Paul's. Because he was tall, and carried himself very straight, he could see over the heads of most and he found a spot within a stone's throw of the statue at the foot of the steps where the knot of sightseers between him and the roadway were short, with shoulders hunched against the wind. It consisted of a sallow little man, his sallow little wife, and three children with almost traditionally authentic Cockney accents. The youngest kept asking, "When's he coming, Mum?" and Mum made the same reply over and over again. "Soon, Ernie, soon." They had, it seemed, an inexhaustible supply of thermos flasks and the steady consumption of tea obviously worried the father because he said in a low voice, "You'd better go easy on that, Lil, or they'll be fidgetting to go somewhere and they can't, not 'ere."

He stood there arching his neck and stamping his feet, taking it all in and distilling it methodically, the way he winnowed the seasonal impressions of the Valley. They were all, he thought, very patient and orderly, and friendly without being pushing, for the woman offered him a drink from the cup of the latest thermos flask and when he smiled and shook his head, tapping the pocket that held his flask, she nodded, almost as though he was the eldest of her flock and thus qualified for something stronger than tea.

Round about ten o'clock they started arriving, car after car sliding up to the foot of the steps and their doors were discreetly opened by a bevy of smart girl redcaps—he had not known such a unit existed—so that he forgot the cold and the tea-swilling family in watching the history of the century unfold in a steady procession of V.I.P.s

The first he picked out was the striking figure of De Gaulle, whose kepi made him think of the rout at Chemin des Dames and then the solid figure of General Eisenhower, whom he had always thought of as a man of compassion, so unlike the blockheads who had initiated the wholesale slaughter of the Somme and Passchendaele. Then, advertised by a long ripple in the crowd, the Royal party arrived and he watched the slim figure of the Queen ascend the broad, shallow steps as the flank guard of dismounted Lifeguards brought their swords to the salute and Prince Philip said something to Prince Charles who nodded and turned his head to look. Even from this distance his sharp old eyes caught something else that he supposed the watchers took for granted, a smile directed by the Queen Mother at the person who handed her out of the car. He liked that very much. It confirmed his opinion of her as a person of warm dignity and expertise, who knew instinctively how to radiate the good manners one expected of someone whose whole being was concerned with the mystique of ceremonial.

The huge doors of the Cathedral kept opening and closing and he supposed the people inside must be very sensitive to draught. Mounted policemen on well-mannered bays pivoted gracefully as car-bonnets nosed within inches of shining bits. The trim little redcaps kept advancing and retreating as new arrivals appeared. The stream of cars and chauffeurs deposited their passengers and then disappeared without trace, as though whisked out of sight by the wave of a conjuror's baton. It was astounding—the smoothness and synchronisation of the entire operation and he thought, "It's like something that's been rehearsed once a week by many generations. Nobody will believe it when I tell them." And then he remembered that he wouldn't need to tell them because they would have seen it all on television and more besides. But that wasn't the same, somehow.

He could not have said why it was not the same until his ear caught the first far-off notes of the "Dead March" but then he knew, because everyone around him heard them at the same time, and a tide of tremendous but curiously controlled excitement swept up Ludgate Hill, making itself felt like a long, sighing breath that challenged the penetrating probe of the cold air they were breathing, and as everyone round him cocked an eye to the right the notes closed up to form the terrifying finality of the measured rhythm, and the sallow dispenser of thermos flasks said, in the voice people used in church, "There, Ernie, it's coming," and the child hopped and pranced as though his father's fears were about to be realised.

It passed like a carefully unrolled carpet, a great strip of patterned colour and, in what seemed to him, a stupendous silence, despite the measured tramp of so many boots, the thud of the music, and the faint rattle of the gun carriage where the wheels passed over the specks of grit in their path. It was a spectacle of a kind he had never seen before and never hoped to see, and he stood very straight, his seven medals trapping a ray of winter sunshine as the guardsmen formed up alongside the coffin and expertly transferred its terrible weight to their shoulders. The pallbearers went ahead in a loose group, Attlee, looking like an old but indomitable Chinese mandarin, relying upon the discreet elbow-touch of Eden, Macmillan walking on the outside, hunched against the cold, and somewhere there so many others who had been stirred or exasperated by the slurred exhortations of the man now resting on the shoulders of the straining guardsmen.

The very passage of the cortège up the steps toward the slowly-opening doors was the finale of an epoch that no film producer, however talented and inspired, could conjure out of celluloid and stage carpenters. It was as though, in that moment of time, a century of human experience peculiar to these islands and to the people standing about him, was being taken out of the stream of history and stored away with all the other experiences assembled in that place, the Great Fire, the Duke of Wellington, Trafalgar, the Jubilees, and the latest of them, the fire-blitz of 1941 when, on a rare visit to London, he had made his way here and seen the enormous bulk of St. Paul's standing almost alone amid acres of blackened rubble. His taxi-driver, equally impressed, had said, unconscious of bathos, "*Marvellous*, ain't it? Bloody marvellous," and that, he thought, was as good an estimate as any. It *was* marvellous. *Bloody* marvellous! Every last aspect of it, all the way from a cavalry charge at Omdurman to St. Paul's.

He turned, giddy with cold or emotion, and let himself be carried along down Ludgate Hill to an Expresso bar where he drank two cups of scalding coffee and then crossed the road to the newspaper office to await Simon. He experienced no sense of anticlimax but instead a kind of emotional repletion that revealed itself in a slight unsteadiness of gait on the steep stairs and a breathlessness that had nothing to do with the cold or his age. He sat by a singing gas-fire thawing his toes and taking another sip or two from his flask. Overhead, like the rush of wild geese down the Valley in autumn, aircraft of the R.A.F. swept in salute, and down by the river he heard the defiant whoops of ships' sirens.

He was engaged in piecing together impressions to form a whole and the process was familiar to him, the method smoothed by the sixty-three years he had spent in the Valley.

What he sought, as he sat there musing, was a compendium of British virtues, some kind of justification for the intense national pride that brought a sparkle to his eyes, and he assembled it like a man building a utensil from odds and ends that had strayed within reach. There was dignity there, expressed in a pageantry that some might feel verged upon the ridiculous but it was not ridiculous because it was motivated by impulses worthier than pride—by respect and by an unconscious groping after traditions that had survived the passage of centuries. There was courage, too, of the kind he had witnessed so often in Flanders and in the Valley when hostile aircraft flew in from the sea. And underneath it all there was patience and kindness and wonder, expressed in the voice of the mother—"Soon, Ernie, soon," in her diffident offer of lukewarm tea to an aged stranger, and in that taxi-driver's involuntary tribute to the indestructibility of St. Paul's—"*Marvellous* ain't it? Bloody marvellous."

The assessment brought to him a sense of belonging that he had never felt in these noisy crowded streets, a comfort that he had never found in religion or the promise of survival after death. He was at one with that strange, growling volcano of a man now on his way to Oxfordshire, and with all the people who had witnessed his passage, and there was immortality enough in this fellowship and in the loins of his sons, daughters and descendants.

Somewhere close at hand a typewriter clacked, perhaps recording what he felt about what he had seen or something like it. For what was going on to that page was quarried from English thought dressed in the English tongue.

III

That, towards the end, was his self-analysis as a patriot. His final self-assessment as patriarch and man was more complicated and he delayed making it for a long time.

The rest of the winter passed quietly. He was still able to get out and about, and twice rode the grey to a meet, although he only stayed on an hour or two for he tired very easily now and sometimes his chest gave him a little trouble, so that the young doctor who came in from Coombe Bay, warned him to cut down on his cigarettes. He did not take the warning seriously, telling the doctor that a man within weeks of his eighty-sixth birthday was not obliged to cut down on anything.

"I'm not one of those drooling old buffers who want to make a century just to get a telegram from some flunkey at the Palace and have a lot of relatives goo-gooing over a cake I can't digest," he said, and the young man had looked flustered until Paul invited him to help himself to a whisky from the decanter.

"I wouldn't have had to tell that to either of your predecessors," he said, with a dry chuckle. "Both Maureen, and before her old Doctor O'Keefe, expected a tot of Irish every time they came to read my pulse. Matter of fact the old doctor died of it, running away from blue monkeys so his daughter told me."

He was not ill but he was not himself, not even when the spring came round and he could make his way down to the lodge, or potter about the rose-garden that Grace had conjured out of the tail of the east paddock. Simon, seeking information from the doctor, was only moderately reassured.

"Nothing specific," the man said, with the patronage inseparable from his profession, "just anno domini. There's a whisper under his ribs. He had a couple smashed at one time, didn't he?"

"Yes," said Simon, "but that was 'way back in 1906, when he was injured fishing sailors out of the Cove."

"It's the weak spot in his overall defences," the doctor said, "but allowing for that, a bullet through his knee, and a lump of shrapnel calling for the kind of surgery that shows under his hair, he'll do very well if you can get him to take it easier and switch to a pipe."

Simon, without actually disliking the man, could not find much confidence in him and talked to Evie about getting one of Maureen's specialist friends in from Paxtonbury, but she gave it as her opinion that Paul wouldn't thank him for it so he let it go until word came that the old man had taken to his bed with bronchitis.

He was obliged to give up his smoking then, for the cough resulting from a puff or two made his eyes water and his old bones rattle. Andy, visiting him at weekends, found him testy but far from helpless, and as the days lengthened and May sunshine came flooding into his room he became restive, pottering about in his old-fashioned dressing-gown, dismissing the nurse they found for him, and appearing downstairs the week of his birthday when he seemed almost himself apart from that cough.

A week or two after his birthday they brought him the news he had been awaiting. Vanessa had won the great-grandchild race, and produced a nine-pound boy on the anniversary of her wedding. She only just kept her promise. Two days later Whiz rang from Ross, to say that she was a grandmother. The close finish amused him but he was glad Vanessa had won because it would mean more to her and her jovial cross-country runner than to Whiz's daughter and her poker-faced husband.

He lugged out the estate diary and leafed it through, losing himself in memories as he read of droughts and crop records and Valley gossip, some recorded in his own writing, some in Claire's. Before he put it away again, however, he made the two entries and totted up his live descendants, making a tally of twenty, covering three generations.

"Well, that's not so bad, old girl," he said aloud, as though Claire was present and hanging upon the answer to the sum, "but it's amazing there aren't twice as many when you think of it."

Then, the book still open before him, he took a nap, and John and his wife Anne, one-time dispenser of hangover cures, came in at teatime and woke him up, saying they were down for the week. On seeing what he had written in the diary that afternoon they told him the score was likely to be twenty-one by the end of November. For once they succeeded in surprising him and he said, defensively, "Must be my eyesight. Wouldn't have missed a thing like that a year ago. Your mother was the one, however. Regular Sherlock Holmes when it came to babies. She sometimes spotted them in advance of the mothers," and Anne said, not for the first time, that she always regretted not having known Claire because she sounded so much fun.

"She was," he said, "in more ways than I can tell a woman your age."

John's visit, and the fact that it brought Andy and Margaret and Simon and Evie into the house four times that week, had a far better effect upon him than any amount of cough mixture and tablets, so good in fact that John, after a private consultation with the others, cancelled a week's holiday in Cornwall and decided to stay on, for the weather promised to be hot and he and Anne enjoyed water-skiing in the bay. Paul went down there with them once but the excursion tired him so that he spent the next day in bed and seemed listless or contemplative—they couldn't decide which—the morning after that. Simon came about midday announcing a day's holiday and they asked Rumble and Mary to look in for tea at four-thirty.

About two hours before that, however, he sent for Simon, who found him sitting on the edge of the bed in a pair of khaki drill slacks.

"Damned stuffy in here, boy," he said, "open the windows a bit wider," but when they were open as far as they would go he said. "It's still airless. Somewhere up in the eighties. Should be a bumper harvest. Must make a note to ring Young Eveleigh and Jerry on their prospects."

"Rumble will be over for tea," Simon said. "He'll know all there is to know, won't he?" and Paul said, so quietly that he seemed to be talking to himself, "Rumble ... Rumble could fix it. He'd understand too, I daresay."

"Understand what, Gov'nor?" asked Simon, relishing neither the sound nor the look of him and Paul said, with a note of apology, "Sorry, boy, I was thinking ..." and then, more decisively, "Get Rumble over here now and tell him to bring the landrover. I've a fancy to go where I can breathe. It's all right, nothing to get upset about. I only want him to take me up to my perch for an hour or so. I'll be back for tea and I'm damned if I'll have it up here on a tray. I don't want to waste weather like this in bed. No damned sense in doing that at my time of life. Go on, Simon, there's a good chap, 'phone Rumble and ask him to bring the Landy."

Simon, without confiding in the women, did as he was asked but privately took John on one side and said, "This is a bit dicey, kid. He wants to go up to French Wood this afternoon, just as he wanted to trail down to the bay the day before last. I think he's got a feeling that if he takes to his bed he won't get up again and it's beginning to frighten him a little. I can't remember him looking that way before."

John said, deferring to a brother thirty years his senior, "You're the boss when he's not around and it's up to you. Knowing the Gov, however, he'll do anything he wants to do, so maybe you'd better humour him. Is Rumble coming?"

"On his way. I told him what I told you but he says he's

often taken him up there in the last year or so. Apparently you can drive to within fifty yards of the crest now."

"Then that settles it. It's a Valley rite of theirs, and they must have decided to let us in on it. Tell the girls and I'll get him ready."

But when he entered the bedroom John found that Paul had got himself ready. He was wearing, apart from khaki slacks, an old grey sweater and a pair of heavy brogues. He was also in the act of lighting a cigarette and said, in answer to his youngest son's mildly reproachful glance, "I know, I know, but I felt like one. It's the first in forty-eight hours," and he inhaled with pleasure, looking, John thought, like a defiant fifth-former surprised by a master in the Smokery behind the lumber-room trunks.

Rumble and Mary drove up in their green landrover a few minutes later. He had been harvesting an early crop and his face was the colour of ripe barley. He looked, Paul thought, splendidly fit and he wished more of his family spent their time in the open. John was showing the benefit of a week's water-skiing and skin-diving but Simon looked like a man who spent most of his life indoors and Andy, he recalled, had looked his fifty-six years last time he was over, although Mary did not look her fifty-four. She said, kissing him, "Rumble says you want to drive up to French Wood. Why don't you wait until after tea, when it's cooler?"

"Because everything will have quietened down by then and I like to see it at full stretch," he said. "Apart from that trip down to that damned Lido, in Coombe Bay, I haven't been beyond the lodge in weeks. I like sun. Always did. The stronger the better."

Perhaps Mary had been forewarned by Rumble, or perhaps she caught the eye of John. However it was she made no further protest but watched him clamber unaided into the high seat beside Rumble and then went in to talk to Anne and Evie about his tiresomeness. "He simply refuses to adjust to old age," she said and Anne replied, "Good for him. Thank your stars he isn't a hypochondriac, like my grandfather," and they went on to talk about children and forgot about him. But Simon did not, finding it difficult to rid himself of the memory of a spent old man, sitting on the edge of the bed with his weight resting on his hands and his gaze on something that only the very old could see.

Rumble drove slowly down the drive and turned right at

the lodge, hugging the shade of the park wall as far as the junction of Hermitage Lane. The Sorrel was reduced to a trickle and almost silent but the birds about it were noisy enough and colour flamed both sides of the road, forget-me-nots, yellow iris, purple loosestrife and meadow-sweet on the left, and higher up, on the right-hand bank, Paul's old friends the foxgloves, constellations of bright yellow dandelions and buttercups, cowparsley, purple orchis, cinquefoil, bedstraw, greater celandine, speedwell, trefoil and scarlet poppy. It was, thought Paul, a tremendous show, far more rewarding than any horticultural display in a flapping tent, and he said suddenly, "That bank—first thing that ever impressed me about here, the day old John Rudd brought me this way from Sorrel Halt all those years ago. I saw my first kingfisher that day, and there's another."

Rumble, making a sharp turn up the lane did not see the bird, but said, grinning, "There's not much you miss, is there Gov'nor?" and Paul said no, or not so long as he was mobile, and then remembered to thank the boy for leaving his work at this busy time of year in order to drive an old bag of bones to his favourite roost.

They passed through an open gate about two hundred yards short of Hermitage, where Ellie Pitts' foreman was tinkering with a tractor and then over the shoulder of the pasture known as Undercliff, making for the trees at the rear of French Wood where there was a track negotiable in dry weather.

The gorse between here and Hermitage Copse dip was ablaze and between the great yellow clumps grew acres of heath and heather. Rumble said, "Old Henry, and David after him, made several attempts to root out that stuff and enlarge this pasture but they never made much progress, did they?" and Paul replied, "No, thank God. A man can clear too much on his holding and it begins to look like a suburban allotment, if he isn't careful." Then, after a pause, "Don't let them make too many changes when I'm gone, Rumble, You'll have to go along with the times, of course, but leave all the big timber and don't monkey with French Wood, or places like that wildflower bank down by the river."

"Well I can vouch for Home Farm, and our Jerry will take care of the Dell," Rumble said, as they nosed into the central ride that divided the plantation, "as for the rest, that's up to

429

Simon. He'll have the main say in what goes on, won't he?"

"If he wants to," said Paul, glad that Rumble did not make the usual deprecating noises about him lasting indefinitely, that some might have felt obliged to make. "This is far enough. I can make it on my own to the ridge, and don't hang about like a chauffeur waiting for me. I'd like to sun myself up here for an hour. Go back to your work, boy, and send one of the others for me around four-thirty."

Rumble was not surprised by this abrupt dismissal. It was the fifth or sixth time in the last few months that he had been summoned to take the old man within reach of the crest and he knew that at no time in his life had Paul needed company up here. All the same, he stayed and watched him go, walking slowly along the level ground to where the trees ended. Then, seeing him lower himself into the hollow of the sawn elm that the Hermitage foreman had converted into a makeshift seat at his request, he backed between a rowan and a silver birch and drove back the way he had come.

IV

The air up here was less humid than at river level but the murmur was continuous, an undulating chorus that he always listened for in woods at this season of the year, the long, gluttonous song of summer, of bees hard at work on curtseying stalks and the prolonged twitter and rustle of birds in the thickets. You could, he thought, almost hear things growing.

Up here, from April until August, blackbirds and thrushes sang all day but they were difficult to spot in the complicated sun-patterns of the leaves and he could see none now, although he did see a jay, betrayed by its bright plumage, and after that a green woodpecker rapping away at an old beech, one of the very few original trees on the plateau. He had always liked this industrious bird, whose search for insects exposed signs of decay to an observant woodsman like old Sam Potter, who had called them by the country name, "yaffle", because of their derisive laugh. He watched the "yaffle" pursue its fitful, circular search, passing out of sight on the far side of the trunk and then reappearing, prospecting the bark like a conscientious carpenter searching out a fault in the structure of a wall. Then a swift flashed out of the wood and he followed its flight down the steeply-angled slope to the curve of the river. The lightest kind of breeze touched the stiff-ranked grain of Four Winds' meadows, turning them into a sea of molten gold, and then passed on and up the escarpment to lose itself in the wood at his back. Its passage reminded him of a snatch from a poem he had learned at school and he murmured it aloud,

> " 'All along the brimming river
> Little breezes dusk and shiver . . .' "

"Good that," he thought, "that chap Tennyson knew what he was talking about."

Away beyond the cluster of Four Winds' outbuildings he could see the hyacinth-blue rim of the moor, with none of the camp scars showing now, and to the far right, just within range of his eye, the faint rectangle marking the site of Periwinkle that had never quite harmonised with the soil surrounding it, probably because of the noxious chemicals in that damned bomb they had dropped there. He thought about Periwinkle a moment and what had emerged from it after he had created it out of the old Hardcastle freeholding and leased it to poor old Will Codsall, killed in the Loos sector in 1915. It had earned its keep he supposed, first as a refuge for Will and his Elinor—Elinor-Willoughby-that-was— then as a starting point for Rumble Patrick and Mary in the days when Rumble's head was full of undigested theories. His first grandson had been born down there, and almost killed there a few years later, but now it was no more than a scar on the boundary between Four Winds and Hermitage. It had served its purpose and been reclaimed by the Valley, as would every other man-made monument in time.

The sun warmed him through but the haze in the Valley set limits to his view. Ordinarily he should have been able to glimpse a strip of the bay between the landslip and the goyle, where Crabpot Willie's shanty had once stood, but today it was invisible. Only the upper bastion of the Bluff showed on the left and between that and the spur on which he sat, the sun shining on the seaward curves of the Sorrel. His eager gaze dropped a point or two so that he could just make out the clump of new trees growing down the western side of the Coombe. Following their march to the level of the river road he picked out the narrow slash of the lane that ended in the site of Mill Cottage.

The memory of what had happened there returned to him, poignantly this time, for suddenly, inexplicably after all this time, he felt a great surge of loneliness that could not be assuaged by the thought of a houseful of sons and daughters-in-law awaiting tea for him back at the house. He enjoyed their company and their comradeship, and he liked to watch the high spirits of their children, but they were not his generation, the last of whom had dropped away in ones and twos, leaving him a Crusoe on an island of time. He was filled with a great longing to see Claire, to reach out and touch her, to hear her voice and catch the sparkle of her eye as she looked over her shoulder at him while tugging a comb through her hair, and the yearning was strong enough to revive a little of his resentment against the spoilers whose greed had been powerful enough to move a hillside that had stood still since the days when the Sorrel was five miles wide and the haunt of dinosaurs.

The small flame of anger burned itself out in a matter of seconds. When he looked that way again he could not even detect the place where the landslide had occurred. In the shimmer of heat the long slope of the Coombe looked as it had always looked in summer, a squat green lizard with its tail in the river.

He thought, idly, "What's it all about? What difference would it have made, if I'd spent my life anywhere else?" and he fell to contemplating all he had put into the Valley and all he had taken out. It was a very long and complicated balance sheet but that did not bother him, old and muddled as he was, for it was an exercise in accountancy that he had practised daily for more than sixty years.

He thought first of the debit side, of his disappointments and frustrations, of the farms and the people he had seen go sour—old Martin Codsall killing Arabella with a hay knife and then hanging himself with baling cord, the fact that not one of his four sons had shared his active interest in the place but thought of it as a kind of summer retreat or, at best, a family base to bring their children at Christmas and holiday times. He remembered his first wife's openly expressed contempt for the narrowness of a life lived between the Whin and the Bluff and her renunciation of himself and the Valley before he was twenty-six. He remembered the ravages of two wars, the wholesale slaughter of Valley men in France and, twenty odd years later, the wanton deaths of people like Rachel, Harold Eveleigh and his own son, Stevie. He remembered other, lesser plagues, foot and mouth epidemics, storms, droughts, crop failures of one kind or another, the long trek across the desert of the Slump when farms were two a penny, and the final blow that had robbed him of Claire in his old age.

But there was another side to it, thank God, and it was as well to dwell on this, the rehousing of people who had lived in squalor when he came here the reclaiming of hundreds of acres of wilderness that had paid a high dividend when the country was reduced to seige rations, all the marrying and procreating that had gone on down there over half a century, and all the laughter and junketing attending the special occasions they had celebrated as far back as Edward VII's coronation. You had to balance the good with the bad, the positive against the negative, and in the end, even when viewed objectively, the first far outweighed the second. If he had never set foot in the place how would it look at the moment? The whole strip of coast would be sown with red and white dolls' houses and nothing would be growing there except a few front-garden roses and a few back-garden vegetables. Some of the farms, like High Coombe and Low Coombe, would have long since disappeared and in their place would be caravan parks and maybe a hoarding or two. The woods would have been thrown, the axe eating into standing timber year by year, until nothing remained except moss-covered stumps. The Mere, if it survived at all, would look like the Serpentine on a busy day. He had stopped this happening and had bent most of his energies towards conservation, but he had also developed and expanded within the limits of his pocket, so that people like the Potters and the Eveleighs and the Pittses and the Honeymans had been encouraged to live useful and, in the main, enjoyable lives, or more useful and more enjoyable than they would have lived under the patronage of someone like that scoundrel Shawcrosse, or Sydney Codsall, his predecessor, who had also tried to usher in an era of ugliness and urban sprawl. On the whole, and making full allowances for his stubbornness, he had succeeded. It was a pleasant verdict to arrive at on a hot summer's afternoon when a man's eighty-sixth birthday was behind him.

It was then that he spotted the hare, one of the largest he had ever seen in the Valley, and the sight of it sitting there, its long ears raised an inch or two above the young bracken fronds, gave him not exactly a fright but a feeling of unease, for he remembered that there were many legends about hares in the Valley and all of them were associated in one way or another with bad luck. The hare was not looking in his direction and he must have been well to the windward of it, for although its nose twitched it looked as placid as a cat dozing in the sun. What was that story Old Meg or her poacher son Smut had told him about a Valley witch who turned herself into a hare every night? Something about a silver bullet they made from a crooked sixpence, so that the hare could be stalked and shot, and in the morning they found the old woman dead with the crooked sixpence in her heart. How many such legends had they told him over the last sixty-odd years and how persistent they were, passed on from generation to generation as faithfully as ancestral traits like the Codsall streak of violence, the rolling Potter gait, the Pitts' grin that had missed David and reappeared in Prudence Honeyman when she reached middle-age? How timeless everything was or everything except the body that one used to go about the business of life, working, planning, eating, mating and then disintegrating with a certainty no other human experience could match?

He stared fixedly at the hare, so fixedly that when it moved, bounding out of the bracken and shooting off at a tremendous pace across the escarpment, he gave a great start that jolted his bones and set him coughing so violently that he had to grip the bark of the elm with one hand, using the other to grope in his pocket for his handkerchief, his eyes misting so that the whole vista below slanted and blurred.

He got hold of the handkerchief but the paroxysm was so violent and so persistent that he had no power to raise it to his eyes. The cough jostled him like a giant wrestler, throwing its terrible weight left, then right, then full centre, so that he bowed his head, fighting back with every nerve and muscle in his body, and because of his streaming eyes he fought blind.

Slowly, very slowly, he began to win, and threw up his head in a final effort so that his eyes drew level with the horizon but then a strange thing happened. The blue haze of the moor, and that point on the Dunes where, in lower temperatures he

434

could have seen the glint of the bay, began to advance like a long belt of cloud, and as it moved it absorbed all the colours of the Valley, the blue of Sorrel forget-me-nots, the yellow of the irises and buttercups, the bright crimson of a thousand and one foxglove bells and hedge poppies, the dozen shades of green from heather stalk to the near-white underside of cowparsley and beech leaf, a gloriously prolific cascade of colour a mile wide, crossing the width of the Valley and scaling the crest on which he was perched.

He watched it with the curiosity he had always had for every manifestation up here but as it rolled over the river and advanced up the slope his curiosity turned to wonder that such a kaleidoscopic miracle could be conjured out of a summer's afternoon. Then it touched him and he recognised the scent, a compound that he could separate, naming the tang of gorse, the resin of the pines, the smell of turned soil that would bring gulls flocking, and, behind all these, the sharp, healing whiff of the sea.

Each of them broke into a run when they saw the handkerchief trailing from his left hand and the backward tilt of his head where it rested on the arm of the truncated elm.

The handkerchief hung there like a drooping ensign on a windless day, its neatly creased folds as motionless as the fingers that gripped them. Simon, the first to reach him, did not need to make the routine tests. His face and hands were still warm so that he could not have been dead more than a few minutes, and at first the very narrowness of the margin filled him with a bitterness that brought tears to his eyes. And then he had second thoughts that helped to offset his feeling of guilt, for if Paul Craddock could have devised a death for himself it would have been death in these precise circumstances, high up, in the open, and looking across the Valley on a drowsy summer afternoon. They all had a private place in the Valley and this was his, had always been his, as far back as Simon could remember, and as he stood there, with John and Rumble bustling round him, it was this single memory that emerged from the turmoil of his emotions and gave him a measure of self-control.

The face was rigid but composed, the face of a dead man certainly, but with an expression of mute acceptance one might see on the face of an effigy on a tomb in an old church. It was that kind of face, all the way from hairline to jaw, resolute, patient, incapable for ever of registering anything but resignation, and the same could be said of the not ungainly posture of the long body held in the crutch of the two stumps jutting from the trunk of the improvised seat.

It was a pity, he thought, they could not bury him here, without fuss and without lamentation, private or public. There was nothing to lament about as there might have been had he died in his bed, with the sun shut out and a houseful of whispering relations below him. And then he noticed the handkerchief again and this time it registered in his mind as a flag of truce, a token of surrender but the conditional surrender of a man who had never stopped fighting from the moment he rode into this Valley and had, moreover, fought more cleanly than most, with self-forged weapons and a text-book full of good sense and kindliness. You could take your choice how you regarded him, and what he had done or tried to do in this backwater. You could call him a clown, a reactionary, a chaw-bacon, a fool; but you could never call him a knave, or poltroon.

Rumble, by far the least affected, said, "Are you thinking the same as me, Si?"

"That he almost willed it on himself? Yes, something like that, Rumble. I had a feeling this afternoon, when I went up to his bedroom. I didn't like the idea of him going."

"I'm glad you didn't stop him," Rumble said, and left it at that.

John, less shocked than Simon, took the handkerchief from the drooping fingers, folded it carefully and put it in his pocket. Rumble answered the question he was on the point of asking. "He didn't have much pain, not this time. You've only got to look at him." Then, unable to make the decision to move him, "He was a complete man, complete in every way. He was also the best friend I ever had."

They said nothing to this. Each was engaged in assessing the extent of their loss and their assessments were different from Rumble's and different from that of any one of them back at the house, or from Andy or Whiz, who would have to be told within the hour. To John he had always seemed an old man, someone who dispensed wisdom, enormous experience, and a kind of gruff joviality. Simon could remember much further back to a time when Paul had walked him through another wood more than forty years ago, and told him of his mother's death on the greasy French pavé, and then talked tolerantly of the men who had killed her. Tolerance, it seemed to him, had been this man's corner-stone, although there were those within and without the Valley who would have granted him many virtues but not this one. It was so, however, and he should know. He had sat with him in the forecastle of a Dutch collier the afternoon he had sailed to fight in Spain, and he had been met and driven home by him two years later, after his spell in Franco's gaol. He had always been ready with advice but if you rejected it, as Simon so often had, he didn't hold it against you, and he didn't show wisdom after the event. If that wasn't tolerance then what was? He said suddenly:

"Could you and John carry him back to the landrover, Rumble? I'd like to stay here a few minutes. You can wait or drive on home, whichever you please."

"We'll wait," Rumble said.

Between them they lifted him easily. He was tall but he did not weigh all that much. Simon moved to the very edge of the plateau, turning his back on them, not wanting to see his father carried away like a casualty at Teruel, or at the bridge over the Orne. Neither Rumble nor John had ever seen men in that condition.

He heard the door of the landrover clang but he did not move. He was watching a single gull coast down the valley from the Coombe and head across the narrow river in the direction of Four Winds. The gull, flapping lazily in the still air, lost height at the foot of the plateau and then, catching a cross-current, regained it and soared over at about three hundred feet. Simon, remembering Churchill's fly-past, saw it as a salute and somehow a fitting one. Below him the countryside was magically still and silent as some of the heat went from the day. Then, as the gull turned to a speck, everything began to stir again, the grain in the fields, the birds in the thickets, the insects on the wing. He looked down at his inheritance and then moved woodenly through the bracken towards the waiting trio.